STONE BY STONE
The Saga of Stoneygate

Winner of the 19th Annual
National Indie Excellence® Award

"Self-published, independent authors, and small to midsize publishers continue to impress with strong entries across every genre. Final decisions made by our jurors often come down to the narrowest of margins when selecting a single Winner per category. The Team at NIEA are proud to stand behind each awardee as representatives of Excellence in their craft and the enduring value of books in print today."
— Doug Fogelson, NIEA President

ALSO BY W.S. SIMONS

A Second Look

Losing August

Weeding Out the Lies

STONE BY STONE
The Saga of Stoneygate

By W. S. Simons

For information about permission to use or reproduce any part of this book in any manner, contact info@wssimonsbooks.com

Cover Design & Photography:
W Simons Illustration

ISBN: 979-8-9893594-4-8

FIRST PRINTING 2024

REVISED 2025

*This book is dedicated to my mother,
Betty Ann, my biggest fan.*

Stone by Stone was inspired by my years living in Chimney Rock and Flat Rock just outside Hendersonville, NC. In its pages lies a love of the land and the people. If you've never visited, settle in and let this story take you there. Then, once the devastation caused by Helene is repaired, visit. Walk the woods, seek out waterfalls, eat the best bar-que of your life and stay awhile.

- Wendy Simons

Many thanks to Phillip, the first reader
of the first draft, whose encouragement
so long ago gave me incentive
to continue the journey.

GEOMORPHOLOGY

The study of the origin and evolution
of landforms and the physical processes
which form them, based on the principle
that all landforms are related
to a specific geologic event.

CHAPTER 1

The boulder, as large as a Packard, had perched on the edge of the ravine since long before the first road was carved through the Saluda gorge. It had probably been there for hundreds or thousands of years, having at some point broken off from the granitic dome on the other side of the roadway, leaving behind the smooth vertical wall that rose from the laurel thicket. Perhaps the boulder had broken away during a great geologic uplift or over the course of decades as water seeped into a tiny vertical crack, froze, and expanded, prying the rock apart along the vertical joint However it came to be where it was, it had stood its ground even when the roadbed traveling southward out of the North Carolina foothills was widened.

Just as no one could say for certain how it had come to be there, no one could say with any authority how one day in the fall of 1927, it was dislodged, fractured, and came to rest at the bottom of the gorge, interrupting the flow of a stream, creating a small cascade between the two pieces. No one was traveling the gorge when it happened. No one heard. No one saw.

Baker Kenyon drove out of town at daybreak, heading south past the Hanford homestead, past the Baptist missionary compound with its handful of cottages that seemed to each be carved out of a hole in the woods. These were his landmarks. This was his territory, as it had been for three generations before him. He was driving the flatbed on his way to pick up a new saw blade for the mill. He could have sent nearly anyone else that day, but he needed to go, to be anywhere but where he should have been. He entered into the switchbacks of the gorge knowing every curve, every tree and rhododendron and laurel thicket and rock face along the way. When he came upon the site where the boulder should have been, seeing it was no longer there, he felt the impact of some deep seismic shift within, and he hit the brakes, skidding his truck to a halt on the narrow shoulder. He climbed out and slowly walked to the spot once occupied by the solid block of granite. Looking below, through the broken branches of thick brush, he saw the two pieces protruding from the streambed. "What device does nature engage," he wondered, "to undermine so impermeable a thing, rendering it to so much less that it was?"

In the spring of that same year, two men, each with their own sense of purpose, stood silently in the dark out by the giant rhododendrons of the Stoneygate guest cottage. Behind them, the main house, a six-gabled shingled Georgian Colonial, stood aglow in festivities, a house known as much for its welcoming nature as for the land on which it rested. The house, guest cottage, and stable were unassuming structures tucked into several hundred acres of hilly woods and pasture in the foothills of the North Carolina Blue Ridge. The faint melody of Rhapsody in Blue sifted out open windows, someone playing the piano.

Muffled laughter carried from the ten-stall stable where grooms bragged about the horses in their care, hashed over the past week's steeple chases, and laid odds on the final ones to take place the next day. Glassy Mountain, by no means a true mountain, yet the highest point in the county, stood sentry in the east. In all other directions, shadowy rolling foothills faded into the night sky. A crescent moon rose over pine tops, adrift on a river of mist. Damp air wafted down off Glassy through the adjacent woods, and across fresh cut grass to the two men alone in the dark.

The younger of them looked to his feet, pretending not to feel the chill setting in. The older one stood tall, chin high, rocking on the balls of his feet, his hands tucked deep in his pockets. His suit jacket hung open, an undone bow tie draped from the starched white collar open at his neck. "Marriage and love don't have a goddamn thing to do with each other, boy," he proclaimed. "It's tolerance and perseverance. So, you may as well make it count for something else." He was a pragmatic man of business and commerce, a stranger to the workings of the heart. If he could bestow anything of worth on his son, it would have to be the only thing he himself understood, that life was uncompromising. To survive, he would need to harden himself. "I think it's a whole lot easier if you don't fall in love with them," he explained, his eyes casting out over and beyond his son's face. "Keeps your expectations in line. This marriage of yours is important." He paused, expecting some sign of recognition. None came. "It means a great deal to both families," he continued, pausing yet again, growing impatient. "I know you understand, so buck up. This thing is a done deal. You are marrying the Stanton girl, and you damn well better start acting like it." He hadn't meant to be harsh, but he was unpracticed at kind conversations.

The young man was accustomed to his father's dictates. Their relationship was one of command and compliance. "You're right, father," he said straight out. "I know."

"You stick close to me, son, and I'll get you through this." There was a brief silence before he added one final directive. "And you be goddamn sure you keep your pickle in your pocket down here, you hear me, boy?" The son did not respond but to turn his face so far from his father as to almost turn his back on him.

"So, I can count on you," the father demanded.

The boy was left to wonder how it was that when all things true and important in his life had finally aligned, he was suddenly at his most vulnerable. "Yes," the son replied, looking back to his feet, and then to his father. "You can always count on me." It was a simple lie, told only to placate, yet it was believed. Especially by the one who overheard.

The next morning was the annual Steeple Chase at Stoneygate, an event Parson Kenyon had initiated twenty-seven years earlier to celebrate the turn of the century. It was such a success it was held every year until his death, leaving it up to his son, Baker, to carry on the tradition. What was initially a local race on a Sunday afternoon had grown into a weeklong event, the culmination of which was the festivities of this day. Every year, horses came by train to the North Carolina foothills from the East Coast and as far north as Chicago to run the various courses. Throughout the week, all over the county, races were held with as few as three horses and as many as a dozen. Racing the last day at Stoneygate was by invitation only having little to do with winning earlier contests. The three-mile course ran over rolling fields, through pine forests and deep woods blooming with mountain laurel, over natural obstacles and manmade alike. Streams, fences, hills, and uncertain terrain made for a grueling test of man and animal. Injuries were not uncommon. Some were serious. Though there was a silver cup and some money for the winner, unlike flat track racing, steeplechases were not run for the purse so much as a love of challenge. They were run for bragging rights.

While hundreds gathered along the length of the course, a few dozen guests wandered Stoneygate's grounds, gathered for the final day. The vast lawn was awash in blankets and picnic baskets. A dozen makeshift tables stood in the grass, draped in pressed white linen, set with polished silver, crystal, and exquisite china. Servants from multiple households, dressed in crisp black and white uniforms, busied themselves with meal preparations. Children ran about in their Sunday best. Women in white dresses meandered the wide expanse of close-cropped lawn sipping Champagne, their shoulders or hips splashed with colorful silk scarves signifying a particular horse and rider. Well-groomed men strutted about the south lawn, inspecting the new Packards, Fords, and Dodges parked in rows. Their white linen jackets provided high contrast to the bawdy silk ties, the colors of their rider's silks.

People began to stir as the announcement spread. "Riders, take your mount!" Eight stunning horses were led from the paddock, coats brushed to full sheen, muscles flexing, finely tuned athletes, agitated yet graceful, snorting, jittery, heads pulling up, fighting against restraint, riders doing their best to rein them in. They were led to the pasture and up the knoll to the old Baptist church, where the riders had to hold the anxious animals in a haphazard line. At the instant they became somewhat collected, the gunshot ripped the air, and they took off, thundering down the grade to the first jump, a pile of logs and brush, then on through pasture, woods, over fences, and through a meadow and beyond, eventually ending at the Presbyterian chapel. The crowd, some clinging tight to the fence, others scattered throughout the course, went into a frenzy, yelling and cheering. This was the first race of the day. The final two races of the week would be run after lunch.

Baker went looking for his daughter before the morning's race but couldn't find her.

"Baker," his wife whispered in his ear. "She's seventeen."

"What does that have to do with anything? Amanda should be here. She loves this."

"That was a whole year ago," her mother said with a little laugh, "when she was sixteen. Seventeen is oh so different. Maybe it just doesn't suit her this year." She gave him a kiss and drifted away to visit with their guests. "There's always next year."

"But," Baker insisted, "she was so looking forward to it this year."

"Seventeen, Dear," Suzanna said, her voice lilting over her shoulder to her husband.

Out beyond the bustling stables, beyond the crowds and the wooded pasture, beyond the field of grazing cows, in the woods up the hill past the cawing crows, a rope ladder slipped into the trap door of a tree house high in the branches of an old oak. A silk scarf slithered on the breeze, coming to rest in the leaf litter below.

CHAPTER 2

The old woman changed into her bedclothes, sat down at her desk, and began writing a letter to her grandniece, a woman named in her honor. March 14, 2000. My dearest Meg, I suppose I've finally died. Words came easily as she was certain of their purpose, and soon, she'd filled the page. Maggie Kenyon was a sensible woman. Certainty ruled her behavior in all she did. She had long ago honed pragmatism to perfection. As a woman of ninety, she knew her good health was bound to fail, leading her to accept her inevitable termination. She had, over the winter, been pondering her legacy and, having come to a conclusion, felt the imperative to formalize things. The papers were in order with her attorney, leaving only her personal notes to finish. Now, that task, too, was accomplished. Folding this note twice, putting it in an envelope, she wrote Meg Bishop on it, and sealed it closed. She put it with another envelope on the bookshelf, then rummaged in a drawer for a cigarette and a book of matches.

Stepping out onto the porch for a smoke, she slid her hand over a particular rock in the stonework of the cottage. It was smooth, round, and red, her husband's touchstone, the one he tapped upon entering and leaving, without fail, every day for as long as she'd known him.

She knew the stones in that wall well, and this night she marveled yet again at the perfect fit and artful distribution of color and shape, sending a quiet tribute to the mason who'd fitted each one with such loving care so long ago. Her home was what used to be the guesthouse, the only remaining structure left on Stoneygate.

The night air was balmy for March. A breeze drifting through the woods carried the scent of damp pine. She struck a match, lit up, and sat on the porch swing, the weight of her slender body setting it to a gentle sway. A plume of smoke rose and slid inside through the screen door.

An owl perched on a nearby branch hooted, then took flight across the yard into the wooded pasture. She watched him fly off as if he were an old friend wandering back to his house across the field. She bid him good evening with a slight wave of her hand. There was nothing in the lifting of her arm, in the hush of her smile, in the gentle beat of her heart to indicate death would visit soon. She was, in fact, planning the next day's tasks.

CHAPTER 3

"We're going to fight this with everything we've got!"

Monty hollered from the porch of Maggie's cottage as the Laurel County Sheriff escorted his survey crew off Stoneygate property. His smooth Charleston drawl had a sharp punch to it. A round-faced man in his thirties, Monty Adler was short and soft around the middle. His black hair wouldn't behave, and his beard suffered perpetual five o'clock shadow. With jerky little motions, he pointed inside to an old photograph hanging on the far wall. "You see that picture up there," he shouted. "That's Montgomery Kenyon. My great grandfather. Those are my people. Stoneygate estate is mine by blood."

"Your folks lost it once already, as I recall," Ford said from inside, his breath vaporizing through the screen door in the cold morning air. Ford stood head and shoulders above Monty, his mop of prematurely white hair belying his age.

"Oh, for Chrissake," Monty whined. "That's ancient history. That Northerner had no right to give it away. It wasn't hers. It's right in the Kenyon trust. Goes to the closest relative."

Ford studied the man's face, wondering how much of what he said was true.

"We have plans," Monty said. "Been in the works for a couple years now. We're ready to roll it out. Golf course. Homes."

"That's your plan, eh?"

"It's none of your business, now, is it?"

Ford returned the slight with a smile. The sheriff called out. When Monty turned to step off the porch, he got caught up in a wisteria tendril and yanked free. "This isn't over," he yelled, but Ford closed the door, muttering to himself.

"Just get your ass back to South Carolina and leave Stoneygate the hell alone."

"This isn't over!" Monty hollered again. "Not by a long shot!"

It was little more than a week since Maggie's funeral, and Ford was sick of the lot of them, all the Adlers, who were, by blood, as they liked to say, Kenyons. Within hours of Maggie's death, a dozen people from Stonemount LLC descended on the property's entrance with great enthusiasm, but Ford's truck blocked the bridge, and they left. Within days, the sales office opened in downtown Hendersonville. When the five cousins discovered Maggie tried to leave the estate to one of her own family, they found themselves trespassers on family land caught up in a fight to invoke their claim to the Kenyon trust. When Ford caught wind the survey crew was on Stoneygate, he called the sheriff and went out to see to it they were kicked off.

Ford watched from the window as Monty, the surveyors, and the sheriff drove off. He stood silently in the cottage, listening for echoes of the past. There was a snapshot on the table of the ninety-year-old Maggie in a party hat only a few weeks earlier. He picked it up. She was toasting the turn of a millennium with half the town at the Hickory Gorge Inn. When he drove her home after the party, she turned somewhat melancholy. "Beau should have lived to see it," she said. Ford suggested he'd have hated all the hoopla. "Just like you, I think," she said to him with a wise, gentle smile he now missed. She knew better than most that Ford was a loner. His circle of friends was small, yet even they would say they hardly knew him.

Ford lingered in Maggie's kitchen recalling better days, when everyone he loved was healthy and happy. He looked at everything as she'd left it. The stillness, holding such anticipation in life, felt stale in death.

She had called asking him to take her storms down, a brief exchange of little significance. He told her it was early for doing the windows and he'd make it over later in the week if that suited her, but she insisted it should be the next day.

He arrived in the morning expecting to find her with a cup of tea in hand, full of things to discuss with him. He remembered thinking he'd seen her in the window watching for him, yet walking in through the kitchen, he felt a disconnect, a vague emptiness to the place. Her cereal bowl and spoon were clean and dry in the dish rack, the fruit bowl was stacked with oranges. For reasons he still didn't understand, he didn't call out to her as he normally would.

He found Maggie in her chair, her head tipped unnaturally against the side wing, her shoulders in a deep slump, an open book in her lap. It looked to be a quick stroke.

Death was nothing new to Ford, yet each time it came, he'd not been ready.

Alone in her empty house, he wondered what his life would look like moving forward. With Maggie gone, he was clean out of family, a forty-two-year-old orphan. Though he wasn't related to Maggie or Beau, they were his surrogate family, drawn into connection by fate and fondness.

There had been two envelopes leaning against a stack of books on her reading table, one addressed to him, the other to Meg Bishop. Meg's had been sent to her, but his was still there.

Opening his letter, reading the date it was written, and realizing it was a goodbye, he wondered if she'd been hiding an illness. Why else would she have written them? The answer to this question and many more to come would just have to remain a mystery. He was used to the questions that tend to haunt after loss.

His letter said she'd left a stipend in a special account, asking that he continue looking after Stoneygate. It was a big property and took a lot of tending. A small manila envelope was inscribed with one last note from Maggie: Please believe I have only ever wanted to be true to Beau's wishes. Yet, I cannot carry this burden any longer. It contained Jarvis Payton's business card and a lock box key stamped Laurel County State Bank. Whatever was in that box, he felt certain it wasn't simple. He liked things simple.

Ford sat down in Maggie's chair, a diminutive wingback situated on a wall across from an east window. The cushions refused to conform to his body as if in protest of a body not Maggie. He studied the room from the chair's perspective. He could see east down the drive and north to to the pasture. He opened the drawer in the side table and casually rummaged around, already familiar with its contents: antacid tablets she took for their calcium, a nail file, cuticle stick, an assortment of pens and pencils, a pocket dictionary, a ragged book of crosswords, a deck of cards, and tucked far in the back, a half empty pack of

Marlboros and a book of matches from the Duck Inn. He took one out and lit up.

She'd told him one or two a day wasn't going to kill her as quick as all that lecturing everybody gave her.

He snuffed out the cigarette.

CHAPTER 4

Meg Bishop stumbled into her thirties disillusioned and emotionally adrift. She coped by carefully orchestrating her life into a tight routine. She did not welcome minor transitions, much less mandated changes of magnitude. When her great aunt Maggie passed, Meg was in the middle of illustrating the next in a string of children's books. A spring snowstorm through the Midwest had kept her from attending Maggie's funeral. If she'd been there, she'd have heard about her inheritance directly. As it was, the unexpected news arrived Monday morning via Fed Ex, complicating her small, quiet life. Along with Maggie's papers, including a copy of the will and deed of trust, Meg found a handwritten letter.

> *My dearest Meg, I suppose I've finally died. Some will say my will is proof I've gone senile, but I've given this a lot of thought. I'm leaving Stoneygate to you. Don't you take any guff from your dad, Uncle Larry, or your brothers. They wouldn't have the vaguest idea what to do with this place other than sell it off . . .*

Meg found it difficult to willingly accept responsibility borne of loss and began to exhibit the subtle symptoms of unease in a headache that wrenched her eyes into a deep squint and a barely noticeable twitch in her right cheek. Such telltale signs informed Meg she was further out of sync with the universe than normal, the recognition of which only served to make the angst more acute.

Refusing to let the contents of the parcel impede her day, she walked to her corner coffee shop, as was her ritual every Monday and Friday, hoping some sense of normalcy would settle her nerves. She'd always been fascinated with the architectural details of the brownstones down the block from her condo building and accepted that she was more familiar with them than with the people who lived within. The sun spilled down the buildings, setting the second-story windows ablaze in a golden glow, likely more resonant, details more striking, for the fact she would soon have to leave them.

The coffee guy hollered as she came through the door. "With or without?"

"Without," she called back.

"Single or double?"

"It's Monday, isn't it?"

The barista called out the order. "Double shot half-caf with soy."

Meg engaged in some innocuous banter with an old man, grabbed a copy of the Trib, traded a small wad of bills for her coffee, and headed back home. "So long gorgeous!" the old man called out. Meg shot him a skeptical glance.

Meg thought of herself as anything but gorgeous. Everything about her was ordinary. On good days, she felt moderately attractive. Most days, however, her mousy blond hair and droopy features let her comfortably disappear in a crowd. On bad days, she didn't leave the house.

There were moments when an accidental glimpse of her reflection in a window or mirror sent her soul to a dark, androgynous place. Her creative side could manage tolerably there, but her outward person suffered. It wasn't that her appearance was repugnant. It was something inside, like heavy water floating below the surface.

She used to be more vivacious, easily infatuated. Flirty. She recalled the period after the divorce when she swore off men entirely. One needs time to heal, she'd told herself, and opted for solitude that somehow morphed over time into isolation. There should have been a resurgence into the world. Yet, even when she started dating Vince, she was tentative. She hadn't found it at all problematic that his embrace felt slightly alienating, and his self-orbiting personality left her marginalized.

Meg came from reserved stock. Her people were of German and Anglo dissent, reserved on both sides, or repressed, depending on perspective. As a child, she was chided for being too much of anything – too sad, too happy, too mopey, too excited. She learned through trial and error how to push her feelings deep underground to conform and maintain composure. Her mother always told her: Don't burden others with your problems. It went deep, this culture of suppression.

She thought that maybe her physical transformation had begun to take hold after the six-week muscle spasm that wrung her body like a dishrag in one relentless twist. It came on just after the divorce as if her body took up revolt, physical pain overwriting grief over betrayal, loss of love made and obliterated, hate sex, indifferent sex, sex one has when there is nothing left to say. The assaults. The ugliness of its protracted end.

Then came Vince. While there were the rare occasions of feasting with a handful of friends, he encouraged her isolation, preferring to spend their time together at her place. Meg hadn't questioned his motives or challenged the arrangement. It was how she lived her life, or more to the point, how she avoided living it. Even when he wasn't around, her time was spent shuttered against the world. She spent days without ever leaving the condo, working on her children's books, writing stories of Emerson Bunny, distilling his dilemmas to the core of his angst. If she wasn't writing, she was working on the illustrations or watching movies over and over, finding comfort in their familiarity.

Occasionally, she spent the better part of a day at the Chicago Art Institute, something she felt compelled to do as an exercise in self-discipline. Walking the galleries, visiting Gauguin, Degas, Cassatt, Seurat, and van Gogh, she could reconnect, try to tap back into the artist she used to be before her skillset devolved into painting bunnies.

There were the times she sat quietly at home, in her old overstuffed armchair, exploring the progression of the mild self-loathing that periodically visited her. The most disconcerting aspect of this was the void of sensation, in opposition to the way such an observation should register, to at least some degree, on an emotional Richter scale. It, like any other aspect of her life – positive, negative, or otherwise – created no particular ripple in her mood save for a persistent angst, leaving her life a constant state of vacancy. She wondered if one day she might lighten up. Rejoin the world. Still, she was certain she would never return to flirting. Flirting presumes vulnerability, something she would never again allow.

Road trips can be, at best, exhilarating; at worst, an interminable torture. Meg was three hours into a solitary road trip with a good nine to go before she'd be in North Carolina, at Stoneygate Estate. On other drives down, going as far back as she could remember, Meg had hit this particular stretch of highway with a delicious anticipation of what lay ahead. Even as a child, she would pass the time taking imaginary walks along the rim of Stoneygate's crooked little streams, disappearing into the woods and sitting on the edge of the great pasture watching wild turkey and deer. The miles were friendly then, every hour carrying her closer to the lush, hazy ridges that would unfold their dark ravines to welcome her back. But this drive was different. The place she headed to had turned on her, had become something else, something foreign. It was now a responsibility. And she'd left Vince behind in Chicago because of it.

He said everything would be fine. She forced herself to believe, remembering how her great-aunt Maggie used to say things always happened for a reason. Meg found nothing in her own experience to bring her to the same conclusion. Her life was strewn with plenty of dark, unreasonable debris. Merging into traffic on the Indy bypass, her head swarmed with incongruent thoughts.

Crossing the Ohio River on the outskirts of Louisville, Meg was comforted by only one positive aspect of the previous week. She'd found a renter for her condo. Patrick was an instructor at the Art Institute.

"If anything my father ever said was true," Patrick told her when he heard she was moving, "the Carolina foothills are the most beautiful place on the planet. Never been there myself. He used to tell me stories about a childhood spent wandering endless forests laced with meandering streams …" Meg raised her eyebrows when his words took on a mimicking lilt. "… and paths leading to high hills and vistas reaching so far away you wanted to soar from your rocky perch and disappear into them."

"Your father was a romantic."

"That he was. Yet, for all the man's fondness of the place, he never took me there."

While the highway carried Meg farther away from Chicago, the emotional tether held fast. She thought about her last visit on the other side of Lake Michigan in a somewhat bohemian community of artists and writers. She'd attended a little gallery opening. Little gallery, little work, big party with people spilling out onto the street, champagne glasses in hand. Normally, Vince would have been along, but he bailed at the last minute, something he'd been doing more frequently.

At the party, a vague acquaintance waved to a tween-aged boy as he took Meg by the hand, drawing her close as if they were dear comrades. "Timothy!" he beckoned to the boy. "Come over here. I'd like to introduce our very own Caldecott winner, Meg Bishop." The boy rolled his eyes and walked off in the opposite direction. "She does Everson Bunny! You love those books!" The boy disappeared into another room.

"So awkward, that age," Meg said.

"His parents won't face it yet, but my nephew is gay," the man said. "I gave him all your books."

Emerson Bunny was more than a mere character in a children's book. He had become the poster child for the disenfranchised. Created out of Meg's own insecurities and self-deprecation, Emerson Bunny never seemed to fit in anywhere, even at home. The difference between the author and the character, however, was that Emerson always found a way out of his awkwardness to a place of well-being. His tidy little endings brought hope for readers, rarely for Meg.

Approaching Lexington, Kentucky, she maneuvered herself out of a pack of semi trucks. Echoes of the weekend's adulation failed to reassure her she was not a total screwup. Her life was defined by Emerson, and he had about played himself out. It was only a matter of time before her publisher would realize there was nothing else in her, that Emerson's creation was a fluke, and she was, at thirty-three, a talentless, divorced, dysfunctional mess. A mess with a deadline looming large. The next book was due soon. With that knowledge, she reassured herself she was not entirely without talent, yet the sense that she was so much less than people made her out to be was difficult to fend off.

Just inside Tennessee, she stopped for gas and lunch in Jellico, the mid-point if she was to drive straight through, something she had yet to decide. Six hours down, six to go. Back on the road, her car stayed true on course, but her mind was all over the map, and her heart was stuck in Chicago with Vince. He was a man already distant by nature, and now, entirely out of reach.

He'd shown up in the parking garage as Meg was cramming the last of her clothes in the car. He asked her about her route with an eagerness more suited to a vacation departure than the separation of lovers. He hadn't spent that last night with her. He said it would have been impossible, offering little explanation except to say she needed a good night's sleep for the drive. She remembered leaning on her car, eyes glued to his, reminding him that she hadn't planned the separation, that it wasn't her fault. His only response was to hold her tighter than he ever had before. He then kissed her cheek once, broke free, opened her car door for her, and stepped back. As she drove out of the garage into a cloudy morning, she looked in her rearview mirror for a last glimpse of him. He was gone.

Whether plagued by trepidation or fatigue, she hit Knoxville around five and stopped for the night. After dinner, she spent an hour in her room composing an email to Vince full of wanting and expectation and dread. She couldn't stop thinking about the one night they had together mid-week. He'd never made love to her with such intensity. There was desperation in his grip, even when he held her afterward as she fell asleep. His touch was still palpable. She clicked SEND, and her heart was on its way north.

She pulled out the Fed Ex pack with Maggie's papers. Sitting on the bed, Meg opened Maggie's letter, reading it for at least the tenth time.

My dearest Meg,

I suppose I've finally died. Some will say my will is proof I've gone senile, but I've given this a lot of thought. I'm leaving Stoneygate to you. Don't you take any guff from your dad, Uncle Larry, or your brothers. They wouldn't have the vaguest idea what to do with this place other than sell it off. I loved my Beau, and this land has been in his family for over two hundred years. It has been entrusted to me and I can't let anyone destroy it.

You have always held a special place in my heart. My sisters and I were for too long the only women in a sea of men and boys. We waited a long time for another girl to be born into the Morgenstern clan. You were it and are now the only one of us left.

I am giving you this land because of who you are, and what I have seen you do with your life. Through all of your wonderful accomplishments, you remain on the brink of life, never willing to go over the edge to see what joy there is in every day of living. You told me once it isn't in your nature to commit to anything.

Not in my nature to commit. That was Meg's chosen expression, an easy, though inaccurate explanation for her disastrous marriage to the painter, Marvin Stroop. There was no point in the family knowing what really happened. They weren't equipped. She was hardly equipped, and if they knew the truth, they'd never look at her the same again. No one would. To give them something to chew on, she'd fabricated a half-truth about his infidelities. Her former therapist knew the whole truth. And he, more than anyone, knew how close she'd come to going over a slightly different sort of edge.

I was thirty before my Beau found me and asked me to marry. So, you see, I know a thing or two about opening up to the possibility of love. All I ask is that you live at Stoneygate for a year. See if it doesn't win your heart and soul. See if it doesn't earn your respect and commitment. If, at the end of your year, you want to sell, do so with my blessing. My attorney has a short list of potential buyers, all good local people. Of course, the property is yours to do with what you want, despite my wishes. But I think you've always felt a kinship with these mountains. When you were little, I used to watch you out in my pasture spying on the groundhogs, meandering among the cows, and calling to the crows. You belonged here then. You belong here now. Live well, die happy. I did.

Love, Aunt Maggie

There was an inaccuracy in Maggie's letter made clear by the legal documents. The one-year occupancy was not an option. It was mandatory.

By midnight, Vince had still not responded to her email, or by one, or by two.

Exhausted from yet another in a long stretch of restless nights, she set out from Knoxville in the morning, facing three more hours on the road. Three hours further away from her life. The highway swept over the open lands of Tennessee foothills. From any given rise, she could see houses and small stands of forest dotting distant hillsides. Meg took a sip of coffee from her travel mug and glanced at her routing notes again. Her turnoff to North Carolina would be coming up soon.

It had been a few years since she'd traveled this road. She was not thinking of those journeys in planning this one. She focused only on the mechanics of what to pack, what highway to drive, and what needed to be done upon arrival. It was strictly a chore.

On other drives, hitting the continental divide outside Knoxville brought a shift, as if she were a river no longer flowing north but south. This time, the sign for Highway 40 inflicted only anxiety. Her grip tightened on what lay behind, refusing to allow possibility in what lay ahead.

As the road sank downward, forest rose up around her. Grass became rock. Rock became mountain. Mountain became cliff, blasted flat-walled. From one side of the gorge, she could see the road ahead, the cut of it a scar scraped through pristine wilderness. The highway rose up the face of the gorge to the next pass and down into the next, ever winding with the river.

She drove on with no sensation of fond memory or sentimental yearning. It was a gut-level sense of dread, of being carried from one gorge to the next and the next, deeper into the grip of the green-gray fog of the Blue Ridge Mountains.

CHAPTER 5

Ford fidgeted in a chair in the lobby of the bank waiting for Sally Callus, an old classmate, to finish up with a customer. Lost in thought, rubbing the key like a worry stone, he was startled when she stepped over to his chair.

"So, how's my favorite bachelor?"

He stood, and Sally gave him a big hug, her short arms drawing him in to her petite, round body.

"How're those boys of yours doing, Sal?"

"I'm glad to have this bank to come to every day, I can tell you that. At least one place in my life isn't chaotic. I swear they'll drive me insane if I let them "

He handed her the key. With her back to him, she pulled its corresponding signature card from a wooden box. She hesitated, then presented the yellowed card for Ford's signature without comment except to point to the proper line. There were no signatures on the card except the original, when the box was rented in 1936.

"Maggie, Maggie, Maggie. What's this all about?" he mumbled.

Sitting in a cubicle, Ford opened the box, curious and disinterested in equal measure. Whatever it was likely had something to do with the land, maybe original documents, Kenyon family stuff that could or should have been discarded ages ago. It held two items. He retrieved an old black and white photograph of two young women. One he recognized as his grandmother. He read the accompanying document from 1928, re-read it, then sat back, suddenly having to remind himself to breathe. Some secrets, he thought, are better off not unearthed. When he finally stepped out to the lobby again, Sally was waiting to return the box to the vault.

"Was nothin' much. Just a bunch of old papers," he said to defuse any interest she might have.

"No, now Ford. It's none of my business what you found in that old box." But her expression, somewhere between curiosity and concern, suggested she presumed it had been something significant.

Ford went out to Maggie's, wishing more than anything to see her, talk to her, ask her so many questions. He'd been concerned in recent years, wondering what would happen to Stoneygate after she died. He knew her response by heart: Don't worry. It's handled. Though he had to accept Stoneygate was Maggie's to do with as she wished, he was left to wonder what she had hoped to accomplish giving it to someone so alien to the Carolinas. So much was riding on her gamble.

He'd always considered Stoneygate home, though he'd never lived there. The land had been as integral to his life as Maggie and Beau. He couldn't bear to see Stoneygate broken up and sold off. Whether the niece from Chicago was a person liable to do that was yet to be seen. Meg Bishop was just a kid the last time he'd seen her, and he barely remembered her. He promised himself to hold judgment of her, to give her a chance. Still, his expectations were low.

He stood in the doorway between the bedroom and the living room, fully aware that packing up clothes for the resale shop would hardly carve out any room for a new person. It was a small cottage, crammed tight with a lifetime of accumulated memories. Originally built as quarters for staff and summer visitors, it had been added onto at some point. Though its meager rooms hardly sufficed, Maggie and Beau had lived there all their married life, and Maggie thirty-odd years after Beau's passing.

He looked at Beau's rifle on the wall and thought about the lockbox, wondering how many secrets had been kept from him over the years. Memories once vivid were obscured now with deceptions.

A faded black and white photo on the wall, the one Monty so adamantly referred to in his tirade over the surveyors, attested to the grand nature of the estate, back when the place was in its prime, back when any view of the little cottage was intentionally hidden by mountain laurel and rhododendron. A tiny brass nameplate on the photo's frame read: Stoneygate 1910.

It was a picture taken in the spring of two teenage boys, two men, and two women, one of whom held a baby, on the steps of the big house. The men wore English riding clothes with tall boots, long coattails, and riding crops. Both women wore long, white, gauzy dresses. The one holding the infant wore her hair in a tight bun on top of her head. The younger wore hers down about her shoulders. The house behind them was large and symmetrical, with two identical wings joined by a long central expanse. There were six dormers facing east to capture the morning light. The double front doors stood wide open, affording a view through to the matching back doors, and beyond to rolling wooded pasture. A single massive magnolia was in full bloom out front. Ford studied the photograph as though he was seeing it for the first time, even though it had hung in that very spot all his life. He admired the lines of the house and calculated in his head the layout and square footage. The photograph was all that was left. The house itself was long since gone.

He lifted the photo from the wall and turned it over. The lead pencil inscription was only slightly smudged. Thomas, Matthew, Baker, and Suzanna Kenyon with baby Amanda, Montgomery Kenyon, and Florence Blackburn.

Another photograph, much smaller, was corner-glued face down to the backing paper. Ford carefully pulled it off. The date was etched into the image. Oct. 1929. It was a picture taken from the same vantage point as the other, but only a solitary woman, middle-aged and matronly, stood on the front step. Behind her was a smoky pile of rubble.

Stepping outside, Ford wandered over to see what was left of the old stone foundation. Like a fragmented skeleton, it hinted at the original structure. There were remnants of two fireplaces. While he had always known it burned down, he'd never asked about it, and Beau never talked about it. After he died, it didn't seem important anymore, as though his family history died with him.

Jarvis Payton kept an office in downtown Hendersonville but practiced little law anymore. His son and another attorney did all the heavy lifting. An angular old man, he had a thatch of untamed white hair. A look of perpetual disdain etched his well-leathered face. He sat this day staring out his second-floor window through the branches of a potted Dogwood tree to the busy sidewalks below.

Main Street didn't used to be lined with trees and flower boxes and outdoor cafes with umbrella tables. It used to be functional with two-way traffic and plenty of parking in front of basic two-story brick buildings housing useful stores like Anderson's Hardware and Carrington's General Mercantile. A person could find nearly anything they needed between those two stores. Now, the street was a promenade of one-directional cars funneled through narrow passages to slow them down, giving gourmet shops and high-end boutiques a chance to grab their attention. And the buildings were dressed up in awnings and hand-painted signs. Now, the town was four blocks of pedestrian-ruled chaos. "Tourists," he muttered with contempt.

He heard someone walk into the office, work boots making a familiar thudding across old floorboards behind him. "So, what do you want?" Jarvis sniped, spinning his chair around to face the tall man standing in the middle of the room.

Ford did not speak, just stood there, calculating everything he used to know against all he did not.

"You're angry," Jarvis said.

"I don't know what I am." Ford looked around for an empty chair amid the piles and clutter of papers and folders. "Let's start simple. The fire. How'd it start?"

Jarvis resituated himself and rolled his shoulders, a might confused. "That's what you came to talk about? A fire? Well, now, there have been a lot of fires in my time. How am I supposed to know to which you refer?" He took pleasure in Ford's annoyance, studying him the way he used to study a witness. "You sure that's why you came to see me? With all the other questions swirling around in that head of yours, this is what you want to know."

"For now." Ford moved a box of papers from a chair and sat down. "Well, I'm comfortable," he said.

Still not able to get a read on the man, Jarvis answered the question. "I don't know about the fire out at Stoneygate. Ancient history." There was a finality to his words, something he was accustomed to people obeying.

"That's it?" Ford asked. "That's all you got?" Getting a straight answer out of Jarvis was never easy. "Let's have it."

"I told you. Nobody knows what started it. But I can't say it surprised too many people when it burned. Hell, I was only a kid. Fifteen, maybe sixteen. I can tell you what I heard from my father over the years. And I can tell you what I heard from my mother. Between them, I have a pretty good idea of what happened out there."

Words had been Jarvis's stock in trade for over sixty years. He'd used them to create and dissolve contracts, settle disputes, and keep dozens of people from going to jail. Having recently lost his courtroom rights over his inability to maintain any sense of decorum, resulting in one too many contempt of court charges, he found few willing to listen to him anymore, so took full advantage of any audience he found.

"That fire was the culmination of a lot of things that began some months before. It had become a favorite topic of discussion among the ladies of town that Suzanna was drunk the night she died." He paused, then appeared to regroup his thoughts. "I guess to get right to it, you'd have to go back farther than that, a year earlier, to the last chase at Stoneygate. Everything changed that summer. Amanda wouldn't have anything to do with us."

"Amanda." Ford stared at Jarvis. "The baby in the photo at the house?"

"Ah. So you do have questions."

"Amanda," Ford said with such lack of humor, it set Jarvis back.

"Baker and Suzanna were Beau Kenyon's parents."

"Maggie's Beau. I know this."

"Yes. You know this."

"But I never heard anything about an Amanda."

"She was Beau's sister." Jarvis's expression softened. "We used to be three peas in a pod, me, Beau, and Amanda. But she was unhappy that year, a year or so before the fire, in a manner I'd never seen before. Beau kept saying she was just being a girl, but it was more than that. She went away to school in August, and that's the last we saw of her." Jarvis glanced away, then directly at Ford. "This is painful territory, boy."

"I'm not a boy, old man."

"Anybody less than half my age is a boy." His demeanor shifted with a measure of irritation at the interruption. "So. Here we are all heading into the holidays. Beau and Amanda were due home from boarding school, and we're all planning our typical round of parties - the Kenyons, my folks, a couple other families in town. We'd all make the rounds. But Amanda didn't come home for Christmas, and the Kenyons stayed home, didn't entertain. And, of course, this had everybody talking. My father overheard Baker in the barbershop saying Amanda wouldn't be home because of a slight case of the flu. Well, you have to remember it had only been a decade since the big flu outbreak of 1918. People were dropping like flies back then. Did I ever tell you about that?"

"Another time," Ford sighed. He put his hands behind his head, elbows wide, and leaned back. "The fire."

"Well, so," Jarvis continued, accommodating the story at hand. "Word quickly spread to the women, who recalled it when later events came to pass. I overheard some of them at the funeral say it must have been that influenza she had at Christmas."

"Whose funeral?"

"Amanda's, of course. She died in February. Seventeen years old. A child, like the rest of us." His knuckles gripped tight to the chair, then relaxed, as if the worst of the memory had released its grip.

Ford leaned forward. "Amanda Kenyon. Beau's sister. Died."

"Glad you're keeping up," Jarvis said with a smirk. "I thought losing her would break my heart. She was the loveliest girl I have, or would ever, set eyes on." Jarvis slowly swiveled back to the window. "Everybody took it hard. My mother said everybody grieves their own way, but Beau and Amanda's mother Suzanna? She took all her sorrow and drowned it in a bottle of gin. And, as if Amanda's death, not altogether explained to anyone's satisfaction, was not enough to stir the curious, the events that followed at Stoneygate were also subject to speculation. Come April, Suzanna was killed in a riding accident. Some said it was the gin. Others felt the need to argue it was suicide. One and the same if you ask me."

Jarvis sat for a minute in silence before turning back to face Ford. "What was the question again?" he asked, feigning ignorance. He was tired. He wanted Ford to leave.

Ford shook his head. "I was asking about the fire but fuck it." He stood up.

"That is inelegant language."

"Well, none of this is really any of my business, now, is it?" Ford said on his way out the door.

"Well, that's not exactly true," the old man muttered, repeating it loudly as Ford's work boots faded down the hall. "That's not exactly true, and you know it!"

CHAPTER 6

Five weeks into 1928, on one snowy late afternoon, Baker and Suzanna Kenyon found themselves at the Hendersonville train station, bidden by the week's second telegram. They stood on the platform side-by-side, yet defiantly separate. The snow that had fallen all day padded the shuffle of the men working to unload the boxcar. Up the track, passengers stepped from the train, folding their collars up against the harsh chill. Baker paid them no attention. His focus was on the unloading. A sudden breeze stirred the snow into a veil of white through which Amanda's casket was lifted off the train and carried past them into the station. Suzanna lost her legs, and Baker caught her.

The first telegram, notifying them of Amanda's passing, had not revealed the entirety of the loss. At the funeral home, Baker and Suzanna awaited the viewing of their daughter. The tall, gaunt man dressed in a black suit worn shiny at the seams stood next to the casket. His expression delivered little in the way of condolence or dismay. As it was his profession to present loved ones with the remains of their departed, he had learned how to disappear into the background of the moment. With a slight nod from Baker, he lifted the lid. On a pillow of white satin, Amanda lay still, pale, flawless.

The extreme response that followed took even this hardened undertaker by surprise. The young woman in the casket was nothing out of the ordinary. In fact, he thought she looked lovely, peaceful. Hers was not the body of a young child plucked from life mercilessly too soon, or a soldier mutilated in battle. Her death was a tragic loss, of course, as all losses are, but not to the degree expressed by the woman now standing aghast before him.

"What is this!" Suzanna shouted. The words escaped as accusation aimed directly at the undertaker. In less than seconds, her sorrow transformed from rage and hysteria, to fear and panic. "I don't understand!" she cried. "Baker! Do something!"

The undertaker, having only recently moved to town, not having known Amanda in life, suddenly feared he had presented them with the wrong body. His eyes grew wide until he saw Baker's reassuring glance.

Like a summer wind devil whirling up from nowhere on a calm day, ripping leaves from their rest, carrying them up into the air, and then just as suddenly dissipating, the hysteria came upon Suzanna, then subsided. She turned and walked away silently on unsteady legs. Her body seemed to be held together with a delicate filament about to fray. Her husband followed close behind, ready to collect her should she unravel entirely.

"It will be a closed casket service," Suzanna dictated sternly as she walked out the door. The undertaker would think some weeks later, upon recalling the moment, he had witnessed a woman whose spirit had been broken to such a degree it could not be mended.

Townspeople began arriving at the house to offer condolences and share their grief. Amanda had touched the lives of most everyone in the area. They brought with them pies of every variety, which Suzanna arranged with care on the sideboard. For all the grief displayed by visitors through muffled sob and quiet sniffling, Suzanna's appearance was by all opinion unnatural. Her face wore a mask of indifference under which no one could have suspected the source of bitterness. As the mourners milled about in the living room, Baker was in his study, on the telephone to Hawthorn House.

"Mr. Kenyon," said Mrs. Nash, "you have our deepest sympathies."

"I'm calling to find out what became of . . . "

Though he could not say the word, she understood. "Why, gone, sir."

"Gone?" The word stuck in his throat. "The telegram stated," he could barely speak the words, "she died giving birth. It made no mention of the child."

"We thought it best, sir. We made arrangements. It has been well taken care of."

"I don't understand."

"These are difficult times, Mr. Kenyon."

"Please, Mrs. Nash!" he demanded, then softened. "If you please, was it a boy or girl?"

"But sir…"

"Madam, just answer the question." He forced the words through clenched teeth.

"A boy. God bless you and your wife, Mr. Kenyon. Good day." Mrs. Nash hung up.

Suzanna walked in as he put down the receiver. Her worst fear was revealed in the tears streaming from the eyes that would not rise to meet hers. "It was a boy," he said with a quivering sigh. "He's gone." His words left Suzanna consumed with an unrelenting dread. Not only had she lost her daughter, but a grandchild, a child she had chosen, had it lived, to give away to strangers to protect the reputation of the family.

"You will go get our grandson and lay him next to his mother," she said in a tone that would not acknowledge refusal. At the doorway, her back to Baker, she delivered another decree: "All care will be taken to see Beau knows nothing of this. Am I clear?" She paused. "I am clear on this," she demanded. Upon hearing a grunt, she returned to the ever-growing crowd of mourners occupying her house.

Later in the day, drawing on what little stamina he had left, Baker called Hawthorn house again. Mrs. Nash was not in. The young woman on the other end of the phone was most pleasant in delivering the prescribed line: "All files are sealed, sir."

"But what of the lost ones?"

"The lost ones, sir?"

He spit out the words to be rid of them. "Those infants who die at birth."

"They are buried in the Children's cemetery, sir."

"Where? I need to know."

"They are all together, sir. Unmarked. Unnamed. But the preacher does a nice little blessing on them. I've seen it. They're laid to rest with respect, sir. Most families prefer it that way."

He hung up the phone in slow motion. He felt his spine stiffen, his nerves and muscle turn to stone. It was up to him to keep this news within the sinew of his heart.

When all the mourners were gone, all the lights put out, Baker found Suzanna sitting in Amanda's room, shrouded in darkness. "Go get our grandson and bring him home," she directed in a thin, pained voice. "There is a tiny lost soul drifting untethered from his mother's embrace. You bring him home!"

"The infant was given a Christian burial," he said, knowing it would not be enough.

"Our grandson," she corrected him.

He knew his refusal, without further explanation, would bring a division between them of some permanence. Without giving voice to his refusal, Baker left his wife to grieve alone. Better to have her hate him, he thought, than know the infant lay cast off in an unmarked grave with fewer honors than those given a coonhound.

So caught up in their lies and guilt, neither Baker nor Suzanna had the capacity to face Beau. He had been summoned from school for his sister's funeral, yet from the moment of his arrival to his all too swift departure, he had been cast to the outer edges. He boarded the train alone with neither of them to see him off.

A few weeks later, Suzanna stumbled over the threshold to a stall, falling against Amanda's mare, grabbing onto the mane to steady her footing. "Best jumper in the world, isn't that what she said to you, my pretty?" The horse danced aside. Suzanna grabbed the bridle off its hook and struggled to push the bit past teeth to the soft of its mouth. The horse pulled away. After several awkward attempts, the bridle was fastened. Suzanna methodically laid the saddle pad in place. "You loved her too, didn't you, girl. I bet you miss her, too. And I haven't been giving you any sugar lately like she did, have I?" The words were sweet, but the anger of delivery set the animal on edge. "Well, these days, we're all learning to live without."

She lifted the saddle from the rack and slapped it onto the mare's back. It slid off the other side, leaving Suzanna to fumble around under the horse in the sawdust to retrieve it. "We have to get you ready for steeple chase." She began to sob. "We're all expected to carry on as if nothing has changed. We're supposed to tolerate all those happy people and put on our best face for them." She slapped the saddle into position. The horse shook and stepped away, but the saddle stayed put. "He says the chase must go on," Suzanna ranted. "The chase. The grand steeplechase, my ass. He can put on his bloody party, the dead-hearted bastard." She cinched the saddle tight with a quick, vicious jerk. "There," she said. "Now let's see what you're really made of."

Tugging the mare out of the stall by the reins, the horse jerked her head away.

Her hooves pawed the floorboards in agitation. "Now, come on, sweet girl," Suzanna sneered. "We can do this the easy way, or my way."

It was nearly dark when she rode out. The stable master saw her leave. He sent his young grandson running to the main house to alert Baker.

"Mrs. Kenyon, sir," the boy shouted. "She's gone riding. My father says she's been drinking, sir."

Baker headed out to the wooded pasture. He heard the unmistakable lope of a horse gaining speed to a jump, then the abrupt halting and snorts of refusal, followed by Suzanna's ranting. Baker picked up his pace, hollering out for her to get off the damn horse, to walk it back to the stable. Over his own footfalls, he could hear those of the horse galloping, a pause, and the thud of hooves hitting hard and galloping again.

The argument they had just endured pounded in his brain. "You blame me, don't you?" Suzanna had yelled at him. "You blame me, and now you punish me by holding the damn steeplechase as if nothing happened! I won't do it!" The vehemence in her eyes had seared his flesh. "I see you looking at me," she'd said, throwing her words at him, every one drenched in guilt and gin. He'd stood still and said nothing, rousing her anger even more. "You think you're so innocent in all this?" she'd screamed. "Well, you're not! She was your daughter and where were you? You let her go…"

Her words faded as he heard the horse snort against her rider's hand, approaching the stone wall that divided the pasture from the woods. Baker yelled as loud as he could. "Pull up, Suzanna, pull up!" then stopped cold when he heard a commotion of hooves, the horse screaming, cracks of branches, and silence. He took off at a dead run, yelling out his wife's name like an invocation to fend off the fear.

The stable master and a hired hand approached rapidly from the other direction, arriving just ahead of Kenyon. The stable master carried a rifle, his first thoughts with the horse, prepared to put her down if she was badly injured. Baker saw him collect the mount by the reins as the other man peered over the wall, grimaced, and started to climb over. Baker grabbed him by the arm and yanked him back.

"No, Mr. Kenyon," the man said, trying to hold Baker back. "You don't want to see her like that." Baker ripped free and quickly made his way over the stones.

Suzanna's body lay limp and contorted, draped over a fallen tree trunk. There was no movement of any kind, just an ever so slight breath sound. He knelt down and lifted her hand from the ground. "Suzanna," he whispered. Her eyes met his for only an instant before he watched them transform from life to the open stare of death. He touched her cheek and, in doing so, nudged her head off its precarious balance on the log. It nodded to the side, taking her eyes from his forever. "Don't do this! Suzanna!" he bellowed.

In the next instant, Baker was back over the fence, grabbing the gun from the stable master and pushing him out of the way, jerking the reins viciously on the bit. The mare's scream was cut short as Baker cocked a shell into the chamber and shot her. The once spirited thoroughbred collapsed to the ground, raising a cloud of dust billowing into the twilight. The men stood aghast, and one shouted, "Damn it, man! The animal wasn't hurt!" With an automatic jerk, Kenyon raised the gun to him and pulled the trigger on the second barrel. Only the body slam he took from the side kept the bullet from hitting its mark.

"You are plum out of your mind, man!" hollered the stable master as he wrestled the gun away. Baker was quick to his feet, fists clenched against them. An agony swelled within him so furiously he thought it would devour him. The men backed away. They watched Baker climb over the wall to collect his wife, lifting her body carefully, as if she were only sleeping. They watched him carry her to the house.

Before Suzanna's body was in the ground next to her daughter's, Baker sold all the horses, tack, saddles, and equipment to a trader heading north, out of the Carolinas. The stable crew was gone as quickly.

Beau was fifteen then, and for the second time that year, he was home from boarding school for a funeral. When no one showed to collect him, he caught a ride from the train station with a neighbor. On the way through town, there was little conversation other than the obligatory condolence and an understated word of warning. "Your father's having a rough time."

As they pulled into the drive, Beau wondered if the black wreaths on the stone pillars were the same ones hung out for his sister. It wasn't the kind of thing one asked about, and he kept the thought to himself.

The cold, gray day was no match for the dreariness within the household. Beau thought of the staff as family, the people who'd raised him, but none of them could look him in the eye, so unsure were they of what to do or say. The cook and maid were hesitant and distant, going about their duties without animation, methodically taking coats and hats of visiting mourners, refreshing the food on the buffet, serving coffee, tea, and the occasional highball. The discrete talk between them was that Beau was as good as an orphan, what with his sister and mother gone and his father out of his mind.

Beau went to the stable to prove to himself that everyone was lying, that his father had not sold his horse. When he opened the big double doors, the suction created a breeze through the central corridor, lifting bits of straw up and about. When it settled down, the ensuing silence was more than Beau could bear, and he collapsed to the floor and wept.

It was the week before steeplechase, a week normally devoted to preparing the stable and grounds for the onslaught of guests. He crawled into a stall and forced himself to imagine the sounds of the stable filled to capacity with the finest jumpers in from Charleston, Chicago, and Boston. Horses pawing the floor, sounding out with nervous whinnies and snorts. People would clutter the corridor, busy about their chores, bringing in tack and saddles, joking with each other, and getting reacquainted. It wasn't so much about all the races as it was the commotion surrounding the chase. Beau liked the excitement.

This was to be the year he would finally ride, but for the first time since the year the flu hit, the chase was canceled. Beau shouted to the emptiness. "I was going to dedicate this year's chase to you, Mandy! Instead, what am I here for? Another funeral! To bury Mother!"

He caught a glimpse of leather strapping under the straw and pulled at it. It was an old halter, either too worn to bother taking or just left behind by accident. He ran his fingers across every inch of it, closed his eyes, and tried to hear his favorite sound in the world, the muffled grinding of his horse chewing grain. It had always been a soothing sound capable of erasing any angst preoccupying his mind. But, as a mere memory, it held no consolation.

Baker ordered Beau back to school the day after his mother's funeral. Beau begged to talk to him about Amanda, but Baker would have no part of it. On the way out the door, Beau turned and shouted in his father's face.

"Why didn't you bring her home? Why did you and Mother leave her there all alone?" Baker's only response was to slap him down.

The sting of his father's hand was not so biting as the rejection it transferred.

CHAPTER 7

With two hours left to drive, Meg's mind wandered. Taking a person or place at face value makes life less complicated than it might otherwise be. This is how Meg approached most everything, especially Stoneygate. Having no knowledge of its history beyond her childhood memories, Meg refused to call it an estate. She demoted it to property, albeit property with a name. Estate was too elaborate a term for the woods, lawn, and pastures. She decided this as a child, listening to her mother flaunt the word easily when telling her friends of their summer plans. "We're going down to the estate again this year," her mother would say. A precocious seven-year-old Meg had contradicted this point with her mother during bridge club in front of four tables of ladies wearing earrings and pearls, stylish dresses, and pumps. "Estates have mansions," Meg said, like a teacher correcting a pupil. "Stoneygate has a cottage." Meg was sent to her room still having much more to say. "An estate also has a large garage with at least six cars . . ." she'd said as she walked away, her mother directly on her heels. ". . . and stables with lots of horses," she added as her mother closed the bedroom door on her. "Stoneygate has none of those things!" Meg yelled through the door, her words muffled though heard.

Stoneygate retained only three remnants of stateliness: the tennis court, a pool, and vast acreage. Still missing, to Meg's mind, was the primary element. There was no large mansion full of heirlooms and lavish fabrics, old bucolic paintings, and hundred-year-old portraits. Stoneygate was not a place visited by wealthy people attending dinner parties hosted by old money. It was, as it stood, just a large piece of land with a small stone cottage. Still, it was a spectacularly beautiful piece of land large enough to get lost on if one didn't know their way around its meandering paths through dense woods.

Maggie's cottage was cozy. It was one of the more delightful aspects Meg liked as a visitor. Close quarters, everyone all tucked in. The little bedroom in the back off the kitchen was just big enough for two twin beds, a dresser, and a tiny corner closet. Her parents slept there on family visits. The boys slept on the floor in the living room or out on the porch until mosquitoes forced them back in. Meg always slept on the other twin in Maggie's room, the best spot in the cottage, in spite of Maggie's snoring. There was never enough room in the kitchen for more than one person, but Meg's mother and Aunt Maggie seemed to manage it. As the kitchen table was barely big enough for two, all meals were taken outdoors at a big pine log picnic table.

The closer Meg got to Asheville, the more she began to wonder why she hadn't visited more in recent years. Had she really been too busy, or had she just presumed Maggie would always be around? Deadlines always seemed to put off her visit to next year, then the next, until all the nexts ran out. And she thought about the times she did make the trip, times when she needed healing or reassurance. Always needing something. Always drawn to Maggie, to the one person not likely to ask too many questions or make judgments. Her answer to every ailment: Go take a walk.

Meg escaped to Stoneygate not long after she married Marvin, about the time she was beginning to realize he was a mistake.

She'd driven straight through, all twelve hours, pulling up to the cottage around six in the evening to find Maggie on the porch swing, her toes to the deck, pushing to a gentle sway. Smiling and swaying.

"Dinner or a bath?" she asked when Meg emerged from the car, unfolding her limbs and reaching to the sky.

Pulling a suitcase from the back seat, Meg closed the car door, stood stock still, and took a long, deep inhale of piney woods.

"A bath it is," Maggie said, rising and going inside.

Maggie's claw foot tub took up half the bathroom. Six feet long, sloped on both ends, the spigot came from the wall to the middle of it. Two people could lounge comfortably in its embrace, though Meg could not imagine Maggie had ever done so.

As the tub filled, Maggie checked on a roasting chicken, its aroma filling the cottage. A three-meal bird, it would provide dinner this night, sandwiches the next day, and a potpie the evening after that. Meg dropped her things on a twin bed in the guest room, a room that had not changed in the twenty-odd years she'd known it. The white-painted, four-drawer dresser still had a doily on top next to a milk glass lamp. Even the chenille bedspreads with their pastel tulips were the same. The tiny closet was little more than a two-foot clothes rod anchored to a plank wall with a draw curtain. It was filled with Maggie's clothes, casual dresses, and a few blouses. It was Meg's favorite room. On the back wall, a bank of three windows faced the woods. Double windows on opposite walls allowed cross breeze. With windows open, it was like sleeping in the woods. She had always thought that if she ever lived there, it would be her bedroom.

Being August and hot was never reason enough to not take a hot bath. Meg slipped in and melted into its warmth. Residual vibrations from the day's drive diffused. She heard the oven door squeak open.

"Is it time to eat?" she called to Maggie.

"It'll keep," came the response, and Meg dunked her head under.

Cicadas serenaded an otherwise quiet dinner at the picnic table. Maggie did not ask about Meg's work or about Marvin. She did not ask about Meg's parents or her brothers. Meg presumed it wasn't out of disinterest so much as a privacy thing. If one wanted to talk, they could. If not? All the better. It was part of what made the cottage a safe zone of unconditional love.

"The fox is back again this year," Maggie said, spooning fresh applesauce to her plate. "Don't know where he went last year. Wherever it was, guess he decided he liked it here better."

"Out on the bridge, by the small stream?"

"Uh-huh."

They were both nearly finished eating before they spoke again. Meg said the boxwoods looked good this year.

"Had some snow last winter that I thought broke a couple down. Came back nicely."

Meg offered to do the dishes, but Maggie suggested she'd be better off taking a walk. "Go visit your stream. It's missed you."

This trip, Maggie would not be on the swing waiting. There was no one to draw a bath. No roast chicken in the oven.

Asheville came and went.

She used to think there was nothing that being around Maggie didn't help. Now, Maggie was the cause of the consternation.

Meg drove through Hendersonville, avoiding tourist-clogged Main Street like a local. She drove out beyond the tight-knit neighborhoods of well-kept houses and yards full of blooming azaleas and tulips. She stopped for groceries at the new food market two blocks from the old grocery that had serviced town for as long as she could remember. She passed a new strip mall with its six-theatre movie complex on one end and a pizza place on the other. She drove on until buildings thinned out altogether except for the bakery next to the tiny post office, and she finally came to the old stone church and turned onto a narrow gravel road.

Slowing to a crawl, her eyes searching the shrub row to her left, she saw the two stone pillars, half covered by honeysuckle bushes. Pulling in between them was a bit like creeping into a past life. Nothing seemed to have changed in the slightest. The laurel thicket seemed just as dense, the bridge over the stream just as ancient. The tidy boxwoods still bordered the gravel drive. The disheveled stone foundation of the old house was as undisturbed as a headstone. Across from it was a large patch of freshly turned soil.

Then she saw the cottage, and it took her breath for a moment.

It was far more handsome than she remembered. This thought bothered her. Was it because it was now hers that she took more stock in it, or had she simply grown more aware and appreciative of its beauty since she'd last seen it?

The stonework was exquisite both for the perfect fit of each stone and for the random shades of gray, tan, pink, and green. Its gray-shingled roof was mottled by moss. Four posts maintained the expanse of roof over the porch, which itself spanned the length of the cottage. As if divided in half, there were two doors in the middle. A window on each side split the distance between a door and the edge of the cottage. A porch swing hung on the right end. Three steps rose to the decking. No handrail. An ancient wisteria climbed two porch supports entwining great thick gnarls of woody vines, giving Meg the sense its tendrils would somehow embrace her once within their reach.

She turned to the tennis court and found it tidy, the lawn well-trimmed. She and the boys would play when they came to visit.

Walking toward the wooded pasture, she stepped onto the footbridge over the little stream, different from the big stream than ran at the entrance, and meandered the property. Some people might have named them to differentiate them, but Maggie had presumed big and little sufficed. The boards of the footbridge creaked with such familiarity she was instantly transported back to a time when her child self would sit beneath it on a smooth, flat rock, hiding from anyone seeking to make demands on her time. Looking underneath, her secret refuge was still there, though was more cramped than she remembered.

She turned back to the cottage and felt for an instant a tug in her gut, as if Aunt Maggie was watching, waiting. She took a deep breath, waiting on tears. When none arrived, she ventured in.

Meg half expected it to be empty, cleared of all things Maggie. Instead, it was a house still occupied by the belongings of its former resident. Even the smell, of old books and mildew, was familiar.

She stood as a guest, quiet, waiting to be welcomed by a host, eyes roaming about. The ten-by-fourteen-foot room that once felt cozy now felt claustrophobic, with no space for even a yoga warrior pose. She skirted Maggie's wingback and end table, next to which was the front bedroom door, and immediately, the door to the kitchen. The back wall was floor-to-ceiling bookshelves, even around and above the door to the bathroom. Each shelf was finely lettered in black as to the subject of the books it held. All manner of bookend, from rocks to antique irons, was employed to contain the collection. One was a rock of Meg's choosing, brought as a gift from the stream decades earlier. Space between collections allowed for a silver tea set, a china tea set, a few figurines, candleholders, a cut glass box, and other knickknacks, all antiques.

A couch not much longer than a loveseat sat only far enough away from the shelves to allow access. In front of the couch was a coffee table. Next to it, on the wall under two windows, stood Maggie's reading table and straight back chair. Too close to it, in the corner, stood a small woodstove, something that had entirely gone unnoticed on previous visits, all taking place in summer. "No way in hell," Meg said aloud.

She stepped for a moment into the bathroom, pleased to see her favorite tub in the world still there. Its rusty, clawed feet stood on faded, chipped linoleum. Above it, bolted to the ceiling, hung copper piping for the shower curtain, a brittle cloudy plastic that now hung behind the tub.

Stepping out and slightly to the left, she was in the kitchen, standing next to the refrigerator, a 1960 Kelvinator purchased from Sears and Roebuck. The framed catalog page hung next to it on the wall. Though the world had just entered a new millennium, this kitchen had all the modern conveniences any World War II housewife would employ. The porcelain sink and counter were open underneath with a shelf for a colander and mixing bowls. Opening the lone drawer, she found a rotary hand beater and a collection of mismatched utensils. Nearly every inch of wall space was utilized. Shallow racks of spices. A wire bin for produce. A well-used chopping board hung on a hook next to three knives magnetically affixed to a strip screwed to the wall. Hanging on hooks were three pans and a cast iron skillet. Clamped to the shelf next to the sink was a hand-crank coffee grinder. A stovetop percolator rested on the soapstone warmer Meg sent her aunt for Christmas one year. A small table between the kitchen door and the door to the back bedroom served as both prep area and dining table, and would soon become her art space. There she found four business cards, one from a man named Adler, one from a realtor, and two from lawyers. "Great. Complications," she muttered.

Glancing into both bedrooms, she quickly decided she did not need four beds. One would suffice. Unless her parents came to visit. Then she'd need the guest beds. The thought of visitors, any visitor, ramped her angst up a notch.

Go visit your stream. It's missed you. Maggie's words came to mind, and Meg headed out, seeking a familiar trail along the big stream, out to the open pasture, and back through the wooded pasture. It struck her how so little had changed. Over all the years, from her earliest explorations as a child, it hadn't really changed beyond the size of the rhododendron and laurel thickets. All this should have brought some calm to her restless soul, yet under the circumstances, being there not by choice but by edict, shifted her perspective.

After unloading everything from her car to the back bedroom, Meg took a shower, dislodging a rather large wolf spider from a fold of the curtain, startling it as much as herself. Placing a glass over it and sliding a piece of drawing board under it, she relocated the critter to the woods. After her shower, Meg was delighted to find Maggie's bottle of bourbon on a low shelf behind the couch. She poured a drink only to fall asleep on the couch soon after the first sip.

It was dark when she woke up, air chilled by the open front door. She thought she saw a wisp of smoke slide through the screen door and, with it, the smell of a cigarette. Slowly, she crept to the door, looked outside. Seeing no one, she stepped out into the moist night air. An owl hooted. She saw it, perched on a branch not twenty feet away. Its eyes flashed as they blinked, and it took off, swooping down out of the tree, then lifting gracefully, massive wings wafting, flying out over the yard, over the tennis court, up into a pine on the edge of the wooded pasture. Meg thought it was possibly the most stunningly beautiful thing she'd ever seen. As she opened the screen to go back inside, she heard the slight grinding of porch swing chains. A breeze had set the swing to a gentle sway.

With no space in the guest room for her to sleep, she slept in Maggie's room that first night, and the next.

Working on the illustrations at the kitchen table was impossible. She laid out the paints and pallet on a box perched on a chair next to her. The light was good for only a couple of hours a day, and her drafting light had to be plugged into an extension cord from the living room. At least the hard work was already done. The base drawings were finished. If they hadn't been, she might have drawn an entirely new aspect to old Emerson Bunny, one in which he was slightly deranged. At this point, it was only a matter of painting between the lines. The work wasn't exactly a no-brainer, but it didn't require congruent thought. Only when she was in the thick of a day's painting did the angst abate.

It took two days before the phone company finally activated her landline, connecting her to her world with dial-up internet. She made her obligatory calls to family, giving them the new phone number and every indication she was doing well; the cottage was fine; the weather was fine; work was fine. She called her publisher and left a voicemail for her editor that the book was still coming along and, in spite of the move, she would make deadline. She saved her call to Vince for the last so she could relax and savor their conversation. She was disappointed to get his voicemail. "I wanted to give you my phone number," she said, then he came on the line.

"So, you're getting organized, then. Good."

"Vince! Oh my God, I miss you already."

"Are you getting settled in? Internet and such?" He spoke as if he were just across town, able to stop in any time.

"Internet? A chisel and stone would work faster."

"Ah. Dial-up."

"Yup. It can keep a connection for almost a whole minute. So, how are you?"

"Good. Nothing changes here, you know. Do you have a workspace?"

"If you can call it that. Certainly not ideal. When are you coming down? I want you to see all this."

"Don't worry about me. Get settled in. I'll call next week."

"I miss Chicago." No response. "I miss you."

"Change is good, Megs. Give it a chance. I have to run now. Be good. Thanks for the number."

"Hey. I can finally make a good cup of coffee."

"I don't believe you," Vince replied with a vivacity that excited her.

"Yup. I use a stainless steel stovetop percolator. No filters. Well water. Good beans."

"You had to go seven hundred miles to learn how to make coffee. Go figure. Hey," he said, with a lingering pause potent enough to make Meg want to jump in her car and drive straight to him. "I have to get going. I have your number now." Then he went silent.

"OK." Meg paused, waiting for something more from his end. "We'll talk soon?" she asked.

"Of course." His goodbye was followed by a click in her ear. He was gone.

The disassociation Meg felt living at Maggie's was unsettling. Her mind raced with phantom questions of the night, the nature of which never mattered so much as their persistence. How will this work? Why am I here? When can I sell? Do I want to sell? Why did Maggie leave this all to me? Each day followed the next with quiet frustration. She called one of her friends in the city only to engage in a hollow conversation that left her feeling even more alone. "Call when you come back up" was the end of it, as if any time between was irrelevant.

Daily emails to Vince made him a repository for what should have been journal entries. His responses were brief. "Glad you're getting settled." "Sounds beautiful." "I understand it can be difficult." It hadn't dawned on her that he was doing with her was what she had done with him years earlier, at the agency, when he would complain about his marriage after his first child was born. Meg had listened impassively, volunteering nothing of herself. Now, it was Vince's turn to listen to her with the same apathy.

She timed her outings based on when she thought Vince was most likely to call. Each evening, the game became a little more perilous because he had, as yet, not called and was more and more likely to with each passing day. Afraid to miss the call, she was sure to be in at seven at night and only go out for a walk when she presumed he'd be at the gym, or at a late meeting, or out for his weekly card game. More than once, she'd begun her walk down the trail only to be overcome with the sense that he was calling her at that moment. She would, of course, run back to the cottage to check the machine and find nothing. The night he did call, she'd been sitting on the edge of the pasture, watching deer graze in the twilight. Tree peepers were chirping, something was whirring though she wasn't quite sure what, and the silence between and around these sounds left her feeling slightly vacant, like something was missing, as if the night was hiding from her, holding back.

Upon her return, she found his disappointing message on her machine. "Sorry I missed you. I'll try again later in the week. Bye." Meg immediately phoned him back. He didn't answer. She left a message to call again later. He didn't.

That night, and many more to follow, felt shallow, as if day had not quite relinquished domain to night. Sleep came fitfully. Meg awoke mornings yearning for the next night's sleep, hoping it would be better. She wanted to believe it was just the new place and peculiar circumstances, but she knew better. Even Chicago nights had felt thin and inadequate. It had been like that for so long, Meg figured maybe she should stop expecting it to ever be any better.

CHAPTER 8

Ford knocked on Maggie's screen door. When no one answered, he let himself in. He wasn't sure what he expected, but what he found wasn't as bad as it could have been. He took stock of all things out of place, not only those belonging to the new resident but the pushed-aside treasures of the previous one. "Get on with the task, man," he said out loud, and proceeded into the bathroom with a wrench and a small box.

His task accomplished, he was on his way out when the Winchester on the wall caught his eye. He took it down off the rack and ran his hand across the cold steel of the barrel. It had been Beau's.

He remembered what was to be their first deer hunt when he was ten. He and Beau had been out tracking for weeks in preparation. It was still dark when Ford got up that day and set out to Beau and Maggie's. He hadn't heard the phone ring as the door slammed shut behind him. The night's heavy frost made the grass crunch underfoot. He thought if they got out into the woods before the sun got to melting all of it, they'd have an easy time finding the night's deer trails. He pictured the glen where they'd seen all the tracks and pellets and gnawed off sumac, and tried to figure how long it would take the sun to inch over the trees, across its openness. He shifted the gun to his other shoulder and cut into the woods at the gristmill, heading around the pond and over past the post office.

He was anxious about his first kill. It didn't have to be the biggest buck of the season. It just had to be a clean kill. It had to be done right.

He made his way to Maggie and Beau's through the woods from the back and was annoyed to find his mother's car there next to a car he didn't recognize. They had no business interfering with his hunt day. He charged up on the porch, ready to speak his mind, and paused only enough to place the rifle carefully next to the door.

When he walked in the house, he stopped short, looking past his grandmother and Maggie huddled on the couch, to the doctor standing behind her. The man's expression was so dower it made Ford's heart roll over in his chest. His mother stepped from the kitchen, and all eyes fell to Ford. She walked slowly across the room, fixed on his confused expression. He watched her face twist up as her body met his and enveloped it. He stood rigid as her sobs reverberated through him. "He's had a heart attack, Honey. Beau's gone."

He looked hard to the bedroom door, thinking Beau was in there, in bed. His first instinct was to go in, to see him, wake him up. Yet Ford could not move from where he stood with his mother clenching to him, stroking his head. The truth seeped into his bones, and with it came an awful sinking feeling that whatever was coming next, he didn't want anyone to see. He pulled away from his mother and bolted out the door. He ran down the road and out toward the woods. Though his mind knew better, his heart knew he would find Beau standing in a thicket waiting for him when, in fact, had he looked past his mother, he would have seen him crumpled on the kitchen floor.

All those years later, as Ford stood in that very kitchen, the rifle in his hand, he chuckled to himself, half embarrassed for his childhood innocence. He remembered well-meaning people telling him he was lucky Beau died before they headed out that morning, or he'd have had to deal with him out in the woods, and what would he have done then, a boy out there alone with a dead man. Ford had seen it differently. There was no luck about it. He'd been denied the greatest adventure, and Beau was left to die surrounded by a bunch of women instead of out in the woods where he should have been.

He'd played the scene over and over in his head, a ritual his young heart demanded. In his vision, the two of them spied a huge buck, and Beau let Ford take the shot. He took aim, and just when the buck glanced up, a rustling behind Ford would make him turn. He'd find Beau leaning against a tree, then dropping to his knees, then down to the cold, wet leaves where Ford would kneel down next to him and hold him. In his last breath, Beau would say something meaningful about life, something meant only for Ford. Then, when the body went cold, he'd bury him where he lay just like they buried that coyote-killed deer they'd found a week earlier. Even if it took him all day and into the night to dig it deep enough, he'd have done it. And he'd have said all the right words over him and put stones there to mark the spot for everyone to find. Then everybody, especially Maggie, would have told stories of how brave he was. Instead, they were saying how lucky he was.

Meg arrived home from errands to find a dilapidated pickup parked in front of the cottage. It was red where it wasn't rusted out and was missing a back bumper and tailgate. A cacophony of old machine parts spilled out of a wooden crate onto a slab of plywood lining the bed. Still sitting in her car, she noticed the front door of the cottage was open. While such a thing might have made other women nervous, it enraged Meg. When she saw a man inside the screen door, she bolted out of her car and charged toward the porch, shouting all the way. "Who the hell are you, and what the hell do you think you're doing in there!" She stopped cold when she saw he held a rifle.

In that singular moment, she realized the isolation of her new situation. If she screamed, would anyone hear? There was a house somewhere through the woods, and no, they would not hear her. At home, she knew some of her neighbors, at least well enough to greet them on the street, exchange pleasantries from her stoop. But if she yelled for help, surely, they'd come running, or at least call 911. Or would they? She'd heard plenty of distressing things at one time or another, in the night, even during the day. She'd never called 911. She once believed in 911, thinking that making the call could save someone. But she learned the hard way there are times when things may sound like they're getting out of hand, but they aren't, not really; times when calling the police doesn't save a life, it ruins it.

"Hey," said the man with the rifle, his voice calm and quiet. "Are you always this pissed off? Take it down a notch, why don't ya." He saw her eyes were glued to the gun. He put it down and raised his empty hands. "Nothing to worry about. Just looking at it."

"It's a gun!" she shouted, her legs actually shaking.

"Beau's Winchester, actually," he said as casually as he could.

"And you're in my house." She didn't shout this, but there was a distinct edge to her voice. The anger was, however, defusing.

"Yeah." He opened the screen as if to welcome her in. She didn't budge.

"Why?" she asked to his confused gaze. "Why are you in my house?"

"Oh. I was leaving you a note," he said, holding up a key.

"You have a key," she said, stepping toward the porch. "You could have left it on the door. The note. That would have been the better move." Sizing him up, she saw he was tall and pleasant looking enough, but still, her eyes were drawn to the gun leaning against the door jam.

"Yeah," he said. "My being in here would upset you, I suppose. Would it help if I put the gun back up on the rack?"

"Tremendously." She took hold of the screen, and he picked up the rifle.

"Ford," he said, putting the gun back on the rack, his back to her. "I'm Ford Mercer. I look after the place. Maggie didn't tell you?"

"No. Must have slipped her mind."

When he turned around, the light through the side window hit him directly and he appeared altogether different from her first impression. His hair was not blond but perfectly white. And his face did not seem aged enough to match the hair. Thoroughly confused, she walked past him as if his presence had no impact on her, when in fact, it had caused a small quake along a previously unknown fault line.

"I didn't know if you were a gardener," he said with a slow, deliberate cadence. "I put one in like I always do," he said. "If you don't want to work it, I'll take care of it." He hadn't budged an inch except to turn toward her as she situated herself in the middle of the living room. He looked at her with the indifference of familiarity. She found it unnerving and couldn't help but think he looked more at home there than she did. "It's all in the note," he said. "If you need anything, call Jarvis. He'll find me."

"Thanks," Meg mumbled. She tried not to stare at his hair, but it was so perfectly white she couldn't help herself. She'd only seen hair like that on one other person, her friend Patrick, who'd taken over her condo. "I don't know about the garden. I don't know much about how to garden." This statement led into a full thirty seconds where neither of them spoke or moved. "So, you can do it. You can do the garden."

"Right." He stepped toward the door to leave. "I've got an old table in storage if you want something better to work on than the kitchen table. I can take a couple chairs out of here and bring it in. If you want to. Looks cramped in there."

"It is cramped. I don't know. Uh, I'll let you know about that." She didn't like that he'd been looking at her work or that he was free to come and go at will in her absence. "Do you, uh, come in here often when I'm not home? Because it's got me a little wigged out."

"Yeah. I see that. I replaced the bath faucets. Parts just came in. And I hung a new shower curtain."

"Oh," she said, trying hard to shift gears from annoyed to grateful. "Thanks." She smiled, a little embarrassed, though she didn't know why.

"Well, I'm gone then," he said on his way out the door. She watched him walk to his truck, subconsciously liking the way he carried himself. He seemed a man comfortable in his own skin, confident, strolling with the gate of an athlete.

"If you ever need to find me around dinner time," he said without enthusiasm, "I'm usually at the Silver Buck."

She had no reply but a simple shrug.

"I'm going there now. You could come if you wanted," he replied with a strong whiff of obligation.

Her next comment seemed to make them both more at ease. "That's OK. I'm fine here."

CHAPTER 9

The first batch of illustrations were on their way to New York. She was envious of them. There were three more to finish before she'd be done with the book, then it would be on to the next project, probably ""Bunnies on Podunk Mountain" if she couldn't manage an attitude adjustment.

Upon coming home from delivering the package to Fed Ex, Meg found a note on the door. "If you don't like it, I'll change it back - Ford." Taking a sack of groceries to the kitchen, she saw one twin bed had been taken from the guest room. Against the three windows overlooking the woods was a 3 X 4-foot pine table with an office chair, the swivel kind with lift control. Meg sat down, her gaze falling out to the woods. While she could have felt a sense of intrusion, she was instead grateful, until she went into the front bedroom. He'd taken one bed out and piled all her stuff from the back room there. He'd taken liberties. She wanted her key back. By the time she moved her art supplies to the new workspace, she had forgiven him, and decided to stay in Maggie's bedroom.

Meg poured a glass of Merlot and retired to the porch, lit up one of Maggie's cigarettes, took a long drag, and gazed out over the yard to the north pasture, enjoying the first honest sense of satisfaction since her arrival.

The late afternoon sun lit up the grass of the yard with an electrified brilliance. Forest hardwoods along the perimeter spread wide their shadow, painting the pasture purple as it crept across. A draw through the middle of the field created a hard, dark horizontal rift beyond which the meadow of glowing grasslands continued to a far tree line. A scattering of cows, black and white and large, ambled about. Meg stepped from the porch, lured into the scene like an artist climbing into a painting.

Approaching the wire fencing, she heard a sort of human barking coming from the far woods. It was a staccato succession of monosyllabic reports. Then, she saw the flash of black and white dart out from the trees, a dog running tight up behind a cow and her nursing calf, pestering them to move up the draw toward the others. Another quick shout sent the dog cutting around a small grouping of cattle, nipping at their heels, sending them up a hillock to the far fence line and a gate. It was a master at its craft, herding as naturally as breathing, returning upon one particular command to a man at the gate, lying immediately at his feet. Over the distance, through the trees, Meg saw the cattle sauntering one by one out of sight. She went in to fix her supper, still smiling at the sheer precision and beauty of it.

Meg stood in the museum that was now her home, wondering how she'd get along without all the equipment she had come to rely on: Her food processors, dishwasher, toaster oven, bread maker, electric mixer, smoothie blender, and electric coffee grinder. They were tools relegated to storage up north until she could build some cupboards or a pantry or an addition. Or, until she returned to her life in Chicago.

She took the cutting board from the wall and studied its many smooth indentions. Setting a red pepper on it, she took the largest of the knives down. It fit her hand perfectly. There was no telling how many meals had been prepared with these two items, but she assumed it to be considerable. She started about the task of chopping red peppers, apples, celery, and pecans for a salad. In doing so, as happened several times a day, her thoughts strayed to Vince.

He used to come to her condo once or twice a week for dinner, followed by a quiet evening before going to bed together. Cooking for him was a reason to shop, to research recipes, to buy good wines. She didn't realize how much his presence had influenced her culinary habits until she had no one to cook for, no one to impress. Her meals were now small, solitary affairs.

There had been a couple of dinner offers from the lawyer and his wife, one from a minister who was no doubt seeking another member for his flock, and the vague reference to a meal from Ford. All offers so far had been refused. After scarfing down her salad, she retired to the living room, deciding to get acquainted with her library.

Among Maggie's books, she found regional histories mixed in with stacks of biographies and a whole shelf dedicated to American warfare, from the French and Indian War, Cherokee War, American Revolution, Franco-American war, the War of 1812, Mexican-American War, Civil War, Spanish-American war, and both World Wars. By titles alone, she surmised Americans were an angry, land-hungry mob of greedy bastards.

Hoping for lighter fare, she pulled a book about Laurel County and leafed through it. First published in 1900, her copy was a 1978 commemorative reprint. Finding a section on Kenyons, she discovered her cottage was on a corner of the original parcel of land settled by the Kenyon family back in 1789.

The Kenyon family, Thomas (1765-1823) and Martha, arrived in 1789 from Virginia, after the 1785 Treaty of Hopewell had been well established and conducted. Their lands consisted of many hundred acres purchased with land grants offered in 1780. The only child born to them to survive, Montgomery Kenyon (1795-1860), followed his father's trade into stone masonry. The stone pillars at the entrance to the property were reported to be Montgomery's first lesson from his father. Thereafter, the property became known as Stoneygate. The stone cottage, built in 1813, served as his apprenticeship. Many grand homes in this county and as far as Asheville owe their fine stonework to Thomas Kenyon and son.

Montgomery Kenyon married twice, having lost his first wife and firstborn in childbirth. Born to his second wife, Agnes Claire, were Martha Agnes (1836-1857), Ruth Millicent (1837-1889), and Parson Rudyard (1850-). Neither daughter bore children. Martha, married for a mere month, passed away of complications of a broken leg. Ruth lived, unmarried, with her brother's family until her death.

The family's climb to prominence began when Parson Kenyon opened the Laurel County Feed & Seed in 1872. He invested its modest return into the Kenyon Brick Works in 1877, taking advantage of the abundance of clay in the county. As the commercial district in Hendersonville grew to welcome and accommodate the ever-growing tourist population, wood-frame buildings were torn down and replaced with block and brick.

The original house at Stoneygate was replaced in 1874 by the stately six-gabled Shingle Style house with aspects borrowed from the Georgian Colonial. The ten-stall stable with stable master living quarters was constructed in 1875.

The opening of the Spartanburg and Asheville Railroad in 1879 made transportation of goods out of Laurel County most efficient. Kenyon was among many who took advantage. He began logging his more remote parcels of land and founded the Blue Ridge Milling Company to mill the logs into lumber. The Kenyon Cooperage was erected soon after, in 1880. Kenyon business concerns prospered further, when in 1886, the rails opened access to Western North Carolina from the Atlantic coast through to the Ohio Valley and beyond.

A son, Baker Parson (1883-), was born to them, followed by Melissa Marie (1884), who passed soon after birth, Montgomery Sawyer (1885-), Rudyard Stewart (1886-1890), Thomas Edmond (1887-); and Matthew William (1892-).

In 1900, the first Steeple Chase at Stoneygate was held to commemorate the new millennium.

Meg found the passage mildly disconcerting, taking into account she was not related to any of these people. Rather than bring her into connection with the place, it served to alienate her further.

Though she considered herself somewhat well-read, Meg was not an avid reader. She was a very slow reader due to a mild case of dyslexia. She took in every word, speaking it in her head. Reading was a tough, tedious slog. Three different teachers tried to correct this habit with unsuccessful techniques. Ever the illustrator, words on the page generated intricate visuals in her imagination, slowing her down even more.

As if confronted by a challenge, she now found herself face to face with the most notable names in American literature: Samuel Clemens, Washington Irving, Emily Dickinson, Jack London, Faulkner, Frost, T.S. Eliot, Poe, and Longfellow. She randomly pulled a few and moved to the couch.

She leafed through them to see which one might draw her attention first. One was small and old, written in 1921. *Second April* by Edna St. Vincent Millay, inscribed "To Amanda, our family poet - Love, Beau." She thought, and could not recall, an Amanda in the family. The first poem was about the arrival of spring. Quite timely, she thought. The second, like the universe illustrating the dichotomy of her current life, gave her a chill.

City Trees
The trees along this city street
Save for the traffic and the trains,
Would make a sound as thin and sweet
As trees in country lanes.

And people standing in their shade
Out of a shower, undoubtedly
Would hear such music as is made
Upon a country tree.
Oh, little leaves that are so dumb
Against the shrieking city air,
I watch you when the wind has come,--
I know what sound is there.
- Edna St. Vincent Millay

She set the book aside to inspect the others. Reading the titles, one by one, an image of Maggie flashed through her mind. They appeared not to be random choices, but instead, each holding some relevance to her life, almost as if Maggie had directed her hand, an unlikely but entertaining notion.

Walden, by Thoreau, brought to mind a tool to help with her new isolation, a state she was momentarily indifferent to. *You Can't Go Home Again*, by Thomas Wolfe, was interesting in part because Wolfe was from Asheville, but more because she knew Maggie wanted her to make Stoneygate her home and not return to Chicago. *A Woman in the Nineteenth Century*, by Margaret Fuller, was perhaps important for its perspective on the freedoms Meg took for granted. *Last of the Mohicans*, by James Fennimore Cooper, she pulled because the movie had been filmed somewhere nearby, and she felt obliged to compare the book to the film. Then she remembered the words from Maggie's letter: "We waited a long time for another girl to be born into the Morgenstern clan. You were it and are now the only one of us left."

Overwhelmed by the coincidental nature of her selections, Meg carefully stacked them one on another, drawing her hands away slowly.

As dusk settled over the woods, she decided to go for a stroll about the property. Had she been home in Chicago, she'd have been coming in from her evening walk through her neighborhood by then. Part of her missed the sounds and clutter of the city. She missed watching all the people going about their lives, oblivious to her stares. In the woods, there was no one to watch, save two squirrels chasing each other around a tree trunk. When she returned to the cottage, she was again drawn to the wall of books, like a throng of voices she could not ignore.

Gardening comprised a large section with books on every aspect imaginable, from cross-pollination to organic pest control. One particularly thick book had a binding held together with silver duct tape, identified by black marker. Vegetable Gardening ©1898. As she gingerly pulled it off the shelf, a scrap of clean white paper fell out. On it was scrawled a note. Meg, this is the best book you will ever read on gardening. It is my bible on such matters and you would do well to study it in what little spare time you can find.

True to form, Meg thought. That was Maggie, succinct, direct, ever the teacher. Then, it dawned on her that Maggie had been planning for some time to leave the property to her. "No word or warning," she said aloud as if Maggie could hear. "What on earth were you thinking?"

In the bedroom, she saw a collection of identical books, nearly two dozen of them, all but one with well-worn bindings. They were set off on one end by a large chunk of quartz, and on the other by a massive geode. Each book had a small square of white paint near the top of its spine on which was written, very neatly, not titles, but dates. The first was labeled April 1946 - March 1947. The last book was marked November 1999 -.

She pulled one from the middle and opened it. In a woman's careful hand were notes on temperature and weather, rough sketches of various wildflowers, recipes, and page after page of commentary. Looking to the front leaf, she saw Maggie's claim to authorship. She had found Maggie's journals. Setting that one down, she carefully withdrew the last book with some curiosity about the final entry, to see when was it written, and if there was some sense of finality to it. Holding the closed book, its binding barely rumpled, a haze of melancholy washed over her. She returned it, unopened, to its place on the shelf and took the first book down. The opening words surprised her: June 11, 1946. What in God's name am I doing here?

The next day, she posted a note on the screen to Ford. Please take the twin bed in the back room wherever you put the other ones. Two days later, the extra bed was gone.

CHAPTER 10

June 11, 1946. What in God's name am I doing here? Beau is across the mountain in Spartanburg for three days. I am on my own out here. Alone. If it were fall and I had my teaching it would go better for me -- wouldn't have so much time to think of all the reasons I should not have come here. Yet the only reason that matters is the one that drew me here, the one I miss with every breath - Beau Kenyon. I miss my sisters up north. I'm quite certain they would have a field day with me -- mocking my worry -- if I shared my feelings with them right now, yet I'm sure it would be better than writing in this book. It is no substitute for them -- in any measure. I think Dorothy knew when she gave it to me I would need it. So I will keep this journal in their stead, assuming it incapable of judging me beyond the harshness with which I judge myself. I'm in the curious position of missing my husband even before he left. I miss the man who wrote such heartfelt letters to me over the months we were parted, before I came here to Laurel County. I awoke every day, filled with yearning for the morning mail. I re-read his letter from the previous afternoon, made my coffee, and prayed the post came before I had to head out to the school to spend my day trying to put my heart into teaching, all the while aching to hear word from my Beau. The only saving grace to missing morning mail was the surety of having a letter in the afternoon's post -- which I devoured immediately. Any doubt about his love I foolishly fabricated in the hours between was vaporized like so much steam. He held back nothing in his letters -- professed his admiration and love for me with the simplest of prose. I knew every action he took during any given day. He explained in great detail the home he was readying for my arrival, though what I found when I got here was all together different from what I was led to expect. So bare and empty. Suited to a man. Not nearly enough for a wife. He lived with only the barest necessities. And now, so do I. Be that as it may, what I see in the man I wake to each day is quite altered from the man who wrote such words -- so altered from those quick weeks when love swept us up -- or was it just the war? Finally over? He is a sullen man now, given to long stretches of deep melancholy. I am left to assume he is content with my participation in his life, for he doesn't put such things into words aloud. If I were to let my imagination run wild, I could conjure his dissatisfaction with me -- manufacture things he would say if only he weren't too afraid to hurt me. He would say he was mistaken to bring me to his mountain, that I am weak and uninteresting --

no skills in rural maintenance whatsoever. Yet by force of will, I keep the doubts at bay and take courage and sustenance from the slightest brush of his hand across my hip as he passes by me in the kitchen, and the gentleness of his gaze upon me in quiet moments. I find his love in the simplest spontaneous chuckle, and in the intensity with which he goes about the simple task of glazing a windowpane after I point out its need of repair. All these signs and more fill each hour of our lives together with assurance of love and devotion and I am better to set my mind to such imaginings as this than of the other. For, surely, what we think is what is likely to come to pass. I choose for the best of the situation. I miss my Beau and have two more days before I'll kiss him again and feel his strong arms around my body as I fall to sleep.

It hadn't even been a full year since she heard the first words Beau ever spoke to her. "Beautiful, isn't it? Bucolic." They met in the Chicago Art Institute. Maggie went that Monday to be where it was cool. July in 1945 was a hot one. Muggy. Getting lost in art was a lovely way to spend a day. He was the only other person in a small gallery, standing in front of a Bierstadt landscape. "Beautiful, isn't it? Bucolic," he said. She did not respond.

He spoke again. "It reminds me of home."

Though he had spoken twice, he had not turned toward her. She, however, took his measure: tall, sturdy, with thick auburn hair, dressed in a pair of dark trousers, a pale tan linen shirt tucked in, leather belt, a tan woven linen jacket draped over his arm, his brown leather shoes polished to a sheen.

He had noticed her two galleries earlier: Petite, in a cotton dress, straw hat tipped to one side, straw handbag on her arm, canvas shoes with just a slight rise to the heel, wavy blond hair, brown eyes, thin lips, coral lipstick. He saw she was going gallery to gallery, so he passed by one to gain foothold in the next.

"This Albert Bierstadt here," he said, this time glancing to her, pointing to a painting of a stream running through a clearing, a house or barn beyond some woods, misty rolling hills in the distance. "It reminds me of home."

When their eyes met, she flushed.

"Then you live in a very beautiful place," she said with a vague smile one allows strangers.

"Yes," he said. "I do." He pointed out a few features in the painting, making comparisons between it and his home. The stream was too wide, the distant hills suggestive but not quite the same. "I feel like I'm spying on these two people here, like we could just step out from behind a tree and join them, take a walk into those woods there."

His use of we struck her. Such a familiarity from anyone else would have been unwelcome. Hearing it from him gave her a tiny thrill.

"Where are you from?" she asked.

Now he stood facing her, eyes on hers until she glanced away, too embarrassed to linger in his gaze.

"Western North Carolina," he said. "The Blue Ridge foothills." He took a few steps away from her, looking about the room, pointing to another painting. "This Inness here. The way he captures the light through the trees on the water, the stream so constricted by the rock formation, spilling into a quiet pool. You can almost hear it."

"Do you know about art?" she asked.

"No. Just killing time."

"Do you like the impressionists?"

"No." He turned, perusing another wall.

She waited for something more, but he was silent. "I do," she finally said, hoping to revive the conversation. "I like the colors."

"I like this," he said, crossing the room to another Innes. "Feels like I could just step into it and walk for days. Feels . . ." He seemed to search for words. "Feels honest."

"Honest? Or do you mean accurate? Such accuracy was necessary," she argued, "before the advent of photography. Without such constraints, artists were free to see things differently. Interpret rather than record. It doesn't make their work dishonest."

"Point made."

Another silence followed.

"I'm a teacher," she said. "Sixth grade." He did not respond, leaving her to think she should walk out, but something about him made her want to stay, to engage. "Are you just visiting Chicago?"

Again, he said nothing.

"I'll leave you to it, then," she said walking away.

"I'm here for a couple of weeks," he said before she crossed the threshold to the hall. "On business."

Maggie stopped. She turned. "Have you seen Buckingham Fountain yet? Or the Lincoln Park Zoo? And the beach. You've certainly been to the beach."

"No. I've been occupied since I arrived." He lied.

They each walked the distance between them.

"Beau Kenyon," he said, holding out his hand to her.

She lifted hers to his, felt his callused palm in hers, his fingers wrapping around hers, gripping just enough to feel sincere. "Margaret Morgenstern," she said. "Maggie."

They left the gallery, walked the hall to the central staircase, descending to the lobby and out. As he held the door for her, his hand grazed the small of her back, stirring her to the core.

Hot air blasted them as they took the stairs out front, heat radiating from concrete. At Buckingham Fountain, they stood together, cooled by a breeze passing through its cascades.

Looking out on an empty Lake Michigan horizon where water meets sky, Beau said he couldn't see across. "I wasn't expecting that."

They did not speak of war, though it was hard to ignore the many sailors wandering about. They did not talk of VE Day celebrations or fears the war in the Pacific was about to escalate. After years of feeling like the world was on fire, something about this man-made Maggie believe all things were possible. It was safe to dream again, to want something in life, to expect good things.

He said he was in Chicago securing lumber contracts. He owned a sawmill. "There is going to be a lot of building soon. Guys coming home with one thing in mind. Getting back to work, to families. They'll need houses. I specialize in No. 1 grade lumber. Finish grade. Trim and fine woodwork."

"You seem too young to own a business like that."

Beau went silent. They walked nearly the length of a vast rose garden before he spoke again. "It's a family business. My father passed five years ago. I took it on. And I'm older than you think."

"How old?"

"Thirty-three."

"Hm. I'd have said thirty-one," she teased.

Beau became animated again, describing the streams and wooded pasture around his house. He told her about the steeplechase that used to be held every year. He was careful to leave out any inference to wealth that had over the years dissipated. He did not tell her about the big house he grew up in, as it was no longer there. He did not call the property by name or indicate how expansive its reach. Yet from what little he said, she gleaned a sense of grandeur.

She told him about a cottage in Wisconsin where she used to spend summer vacations. Woods all around a small lake, good for swimming. A dock with a small fishing boat. Raccoons and possums roaming at night. Crickets so loud they kept her awake. "Haven't been there since the war started," she said. "My father said he wasn't about to spend a week the only man with four women and four kids. This is the week we should be up there. Maybe next year."

"City girl like you?"

"I love it there. So peaceful. Doesn't feel like summer without going."

They talked all afternoon, sauntering the length of Grant Park, his slow, deliberate words lulling her. The day evaporated and he invited her to The Palmer hotel for a drink. Maggie said she couldn't possibly, as she wasn't dressed for The Palmer. He shrugged. "No one cares."

Walking the steps to the lobby, her hand slid along the golden banister. Stunned by its elegance, her eyes feasted on gold-winged Tiffany candelabras, a ceiling resplendent with murals, and ornate bas-relief moldings. It was like walking into a palace. "I've lived in Chicago all my life," Maggie said. "I've never been in here."

As they waited for their cocktails, Beau explained the history of the building as if he was giving a lecture. "The original was built in 1871 as a wedding gift from Potter Palmer to his wife Bertha. Two weeks after it opened, it burned down in the Chicago fire. He built it again. Fireproof. A rebuild in the '20s made it the first building with an elevator, light bulbs, and a telephone. Did you know Marshall Field introduced the couple? The Impressionist paintings you like so much? You can thank Bertha for them. She knew Claude Monet. Built quite the collection and donated it. This ceiling? Grecian murals by Louis Pierre Rigall."

Maggie sighed and sipped the last of her Gimlet. "You like history, I think."

"Majored in it at Chapel Hill."

"So, you could teach if you wanted to."

"I could never spend that much time indoors."

They said goodbye under the elevated train with people jostling to get past. "This is how you get home?"

"Yes. One transfer to a streetcar, and I'm two blocks from my house."

"How long does it take?"

"About twenty minutes. Usually. Depends on the time of day."

"I could never get used to that."

She took a step up. "I have to go, or I'll miss it."

"Will I see you tomorrow?"

"Yes," she said, running up the steps. "Meet me in front of your hotel at noon."

"OK. Noon!" Beau watched Maggie make it to the top, smiling when she turned back to catch one more look at him.

Over the course of the week that followed, he delivered mini-history lectures, something she found simultaneously interesting and annoying. On their way to the Museum of Science and Industry on Tuesday, he told her it used to be the Palace of Fine Arts, left over from the Columbian Exposition of 1893. "It was the home of the Field Museum of Natural History before it moved." She knew that but didn't let on. Wednesday was the Field Museum and a picnic dinner in Grant Park. When he started to explain how Ulysses S. Grant came to be associated with Chicago, she stopped him. "You do realize I've lived here all my life, right?"

It was a good fifteen minutes before he spoke again.

With a plan to meet on Friday, Thursday went unaccounted for, not because either of them had other plans, but because of a decision seemingly to have arrived independently to each, drawn from some ridiculous notion of propriety or decorum.

Leaving the house mid-morning Thursday, Maggie packed a fabric sling with a small blanket, a book, a biscuit from the night before, an apple, and a mason jar of sweetened cold coffee with milk. Wearing a dress prettier than she would normally have worn, she made her way to the lakefront. The day was not yet hot, the sky clear with clouds off to the west over the city. Walking past the fountain, she pretended not to be entirely preoccupied with finding Beau. She sat down under a shade tree within sight of the path, in case he passed, in case he might be looking for her.

Beau stepped out of the bookstore onto the street around noon, content in his purchase. He'd been in over the course of several days compiling an order to ship home. With a hard copy of *Bound for Glory* in hand, he headed to the lakefront and soon saw Maggie chomping into an apple, reading.

"Ayn Rand," he said. "Is this as bleak as her first two?"

Maggie looked up, startled. He'd approached from behind her. *The Fountainhead*, she said, showing him the cover. "Not bleak at all. Fascinating."

"Woody Guthrie," Beau said, holding up his book. "Mind some company?"

"It's a free country," Maggie said with a grin. She scooched over, allowing him a corner of the blanket.

Beau sat down against the tree trunk and opened his book, stretching the binding by opening it wide several times with little snaps and cracks.

"I do the same thing," Maggie said quietly. He did not respond as he flipped pages to the first text and began to read.

Engrossed in their books, neither appeared to notice or comment when the sun slipped behind a cloud. Only when thunder rumbled in the distance did they look at each other and close their books.

"Time to head to cover?" he asked.

"I believe so," Maggie answered. Another round of thunder rolled ever closer. She stood, Beau grabbed the blanket over his arm and they walked swiftly across the grass and across Michigan Avenue. He led her a couple blocks down and over, landing at the bookstore just as the skies opened up.

"Mr. Kenyon? Back again?" asked a store clerk.

"Seeking sanctuary, Bob. Just seeking sanctuary."

Whether Maggie fell in love when Beau cracked the binding of his book, or when an hour slipped by without interruption of conversation, or when he was known by name in her favorite bookstore after only a few days in town, she had indeed fallen for him.

Whether Beau fell in love when he saw Maggie reading under a tree, or when she said she cracked her bindings as he did, or when Harriet, another clerk in the bookstore, knew Maggie by name, he had fallen for her.

Friday, he led Maggie by the hand down a narrow alley downtown. When he saw the trepidation on her face, he assured her. "I have a friend," he said as he knocked on a metal door. It opened, and an old man greeted them with a wide smile.

"Mr. Waterman?" Beau asked as they shook hands.

"Yes. I hear you're interested in Chicago architecture."

Mr. Waterman walked them through a hallway to the backstage of a large theatre, rigging everywhere, ropes wrapped in long coils hanging from hooks, lights hanging from racks, scaffolds stretching high above their heads. Maggie followed along, impressed that Beau had connections allowing such private access. Standing center stage behind a thick curtain, she didn't notice Mr. Waterman in the wings, pulling on a rope, using his whole body, hand over hand, drawing the curtain, the parting of which, the mere movement of the thick velvet wall sliding open, sent a surge through her, an electric charge; a thrill of anticipation like an inhale before belting out a song; like living on the brink of something extraordinary; like the instant before flood waters of applause wash over the stage; all experiences foreign to her but made manifest in that one moment of curtain parting. It was like the moment before birth. Maggie gasped to find her breath. The expansive theatre opened to her, with its opulent red seats and ornate gold moldings.

"Welcome to the Oriental Theatre," said Mr. Waterman.

After giving her a moment to take it all in, Beau urged her to a doorway. She followed him to the mezzanine and lobby, one passage more intriguing than the next with an overabundance of decoration on every surface, vaulted ceiling sections with fastidious carvings, gold statues in intricate alcoves. The men discussed details. Maggie just drank it all in, feeling special, privileged. From there, the trio went to the Majestic Theatre, the Blackstone, and the Burnham Hotel, Mr. Waterman leading the way as their private guide. Beau invited him to join them for dinner at The Palmer. Again, Maggie felt underdressed for such an elegant restaurant. Again, Beau assured her it didn't matter. Aswarm of waiters, all wearing white gloves, poured water, took away the spare table setting, lit candles. One took their cocktail order. Another delivered appetizers. Yet another brought soup, then salad, then their main courses. Yet another brought an after-dinner liqueur. It was a new experience for Maggie. Dining out for her family was café fare.

Throughout dinner, the two men recited historical facts, speaking as if in competition. Maggie had little to offer.

It was dark when they said goodbye to Mr. Waterman. Beau insisted on taking Maggie home in a cab. "Too many sailors around," he said.

Maggie scoffed. "There have been sailors here for years. I've been fine so far."

Beau stepped into the street, waving down a cab. "Please," he said to a resistant Maggie.

"OK. But not because it's safer. Just to please you." Getting into the back seat, she laughed. "You just want to see where I live."

They drove north along the Lake Michigan shoreline for a few miles then cut in past a couple blocks of stores, through a neighborhood of lovely brick houses with tiny little grass patches out front, and sidewalks lined with trees and cars.

Beau kissed Maggie for the first time that night, upon delivering her to her parents' doorstep. It was a polite kiss. A single kiss. Followed by a hug. Arms entwined, snug, but not too snug. Maggie stepped inside and watched Beau from the front window as he got back into the cab and rode off. Her hands shook. Her heart pounded. Her whole body quaked. Beau was brilliant, handsome, and not afraid to spend money. He had connections. He dressed well. Most importantly, he seemed to think she was interesting.

She called both her sisters, her mood uncharacteristically giddy, telling them about a man she just met, a man she was beginning to think was special. True to form, Virginia was thrilled, and Dorothy cautioned.

The next night, Beau and Maggie planned to see a movie but instead spent the evening at the beach. Lake Michigan washed to shore in little rushes and retreats. Teenagers ran past, laughing in the night. Sailors strolled by, one after another, each with a woman on their arm.

"I still can't get over aircraft carriers in Lake Michigan," Beau said.

"Navy Pier," she said. "Trained a lot of pilots here. Did you know that a real carrier has an 800-foot surface, and . . ."

"And these are 500 feet."

"Of course, you know already. If you can land on this," she said, Beau joining in, "you can land on anything."

They laughed, and he kissed her.

"What was that for?"

"Felt like it."

"Me too."

He kissed her again, pulling her close, her arms reaching around him, sliding along his strong back. His hands slid around her, one on her hip, the other pressing the side of her breast. She did not pull away as she had with such attempts by other men. Now, she wanted more. She wanted him to hold her tighter, kiss her again and again. Everyone around them seemed to disappear. There was no one but the two of them. He laid her down and looked at her face, brushing a lock of hair from her forehead. He laid down beside her, pulling her next to him, her head on his chest, her arm draped over him.

A cadre of Navy pilots walked past, bemoaning the fact the war could be over before they had a chance to get in it.

Maggie asked what Beau did in the war.

He heaved a sigh. "Nearly every able-bodied man in the county enlisted, but I secured a military contract in December of 1940. So, the sawmill was deemed essential, and my guys became essential. Army wouldn't take them. Thirty men at the mill, ten over at the barrel factory. Rubbed some of my guys raw, the grade of lumber we produced. They wanted to keep making the good stuff. But we had to turn it out fast. Sub-par product fit the purpose.

"What wood wasn't any good for lumber went into making crates and barrels for the Army. Got a lot of bad trees in then. The Army did the purchasing. We just had to make do with what they sent us. Sapwood, small trees, loblolly, wood that was felled and left. But we made use of it all. A lot of equipment in that war was shipped over in our crates."

Maggie wasn't listening to his words so much as enjoying the feel of his voice against her cheek, the rise of his chest, the warmth of his body. The smell of him. Sweat and soap.

"Had a lot of women working over at the barrel factory. They were good at it, too. Good as any man. But the mill, different story. That's tough work. Took a strong back. Dangerous work. Experience. One slip-up can kill you.

"Our first contract was Camp Davis. The first antiaircraft base in the country. By '43, we sent everything we could mill to Oak Ridge. Eventually, sent some to Camp Hoffman out in Southern Pines but when that contract finished out, they were done with us. I shut us down and we finally got sent to the war. Barrel factory kept going full steam. I could have stayed to run it, but didn't feel right. Needed to be in the fight. I was sent to England. I didn't see any action, but I watched plenty of guys take off and not come back. But that was the extent of it."

"You contributed to the war effort every bit as much as they did."

"You're wrong. They put their lives on the line."

Waves lapped the shore. A car horn blared in the distance. The squeal of the elevated train sifted out between buildings. A woman's cackled laughter approached and passed.

"What did you do there?" Maggie asked. "In England."

"Airplane Woodworker. Worked on the Hadrian."

"A plane made of wood? No."

"A glider. Huge. Silent. It hauled men, a jeep, even a quarter-ton truck or a howitzer. Used thousands of them in the war. They were amazing. And those pilots? Flew them and landed them. At night. Having no engine gave them a better chance of landing unseen or heard. No way to dodge fire if you're seen. And no way to fly out of wherever they landed. They had to go straight into battle with the soldiers they'd just delivered."

"What happened to the planes?"

"They were just left there. Or destroyed. I wish you could have seen how the RAF towed them into the air, three at a time sometimes, behind their bombers. Cut them lose at altitude and they slipped in behind enemy lines without a sound. One after another. Delivered our troops, Canadians, Brits. That glider was an important part in Allies taking Normandy . . . I'm boring you."

"Never," she said, though she would have preferred if he'd stop talking occasionally. She sat up, stretched, and looked out over the water. Beau put his arms behind his head. "Your turn," he said.

"What?"

"What did you do in the war?"

"I did pretty much what I do now. I taught school. I used to have an apartment with two other teachers until Pearl Harbor. One went into the WAKS, and the other moved away. I moved back in with my folks. Been there ever since. Was a comfort being with them. Can't imagine living alone all that time. I volunteered at the USO until my dad said I had to stop."

"Why?'

"I think he thought there was more going on than there actually was. It was a lot of fun, but used to make me sad, too." Her face lit up. "Look. It looks like fireflies circling, coming down for landings." The carrier was doing night drills.

Beau watched her expression fall, a sort of melancholy setting in. "I'd dance with a guy, at the USO. We'd have a few laughs. I'd listen to them talk about home, joke with the other guys. And I never knew if they'd make it back home or not. I'd read about casualties and wondered if I'd danced with any of them. Dad thinks I stopped going because he said to."

"We sort of did the same thing, I think."

"Did a lot of dancing with sailors, did you?"

"Before I went overseas. We tried to maintain some kind of normal. Made sure it was all still here when they got back. That's not nothing."

"I kept a journal through all of it."

"Ah," he smiled. "So, I learn about history, and you record it."

"Nothing so eloquent," she laughed. "Just notes. Raw thoughts. The writing isn't polished."

"Life isn't polished. Every day we live is a first draft, isn't it? How many conversations would we rework if we had the opportunity?" He sighed. "But would it really make any difference? I'd like to see what you've written."

Maggie avoided his request and insisted he had to see a major league game at Wrigley Field. She told him the Cubs played the Cincinnati Reds on Sunday.

"Bring me one of your journals tomorrow. To the ballpark."

"No."

He recognized his own proclivity for abruptness in the brevity of her response.

"It's private," she said. "Journals aren't meant to be shared."

Beau had planned on being back home already, back to the mill, getting on with his life. Meeting Maggie changed all that. Something about her made him comfortable like no woman ever had. She wasn't particularly clever, but she was quick. Bright. Industrious. Not prone to extravagance. If he had to nail down one thing, it was that she seemed genuine. No airs or pretense. She was exactly who she was. And the way she looked at him, like she saw something special in him, made him feel like he'd finally found his way. A few more days, he thought. Just a few more days.

He moved out of The Palmer into a cheaper hotel, though he did not tell Maggie. So far as she knew, he was still there, still taking meetings.

Standing at the entrance of Wrigley Field, he wondered how in the hell he was expected to find her among the hordes of people streaming past him. Then, he saw her straw hat approach, followed by her entire family: parents, two sisters and their husbands, and four boys, five to ten. The introductions were delivered in a flurry as they pushed their way through the gate. "Dorothy and Walter Taylor, and little Gerald. That one is my older sister Virginia and her husband Larry Bishop and those are their boys, Dennis, Jack and Allen, five, nine and ten. And of course, my parents, Ernie and Emma. Dad, this is Beau."

Ernie brushed by Beau with a glance and urged everyone forward. "We're running late. Best get situated." In his next breath, he was hollering that the kids didn't need hot dogs, they'd just had lunch. Emma walked ahead of him, paying no attention.

Beau was out of his element. Entirely.

Sitting high in the bleachers, in the blazing sun, Beau was nothing short of miserable listening to Walter, Larry, and Ernie argue stats while Dorothy, Virginia, and Emma rattled on about the kids. The boys ran up and down the bleachers, arguing and pestering each other, all while a handful of men played a game on a field too far away to actually be seen. He wasn't used to sitting still. He liked to be productive. He believed sports were something you did as a kid. Not as a profession. He was ready to leave after the first inning, but stuck it out through the ninth, sitting silently throughout the afternoon. It was a concession for Maggie. He began to think again that it was time to go back to North Carolina. On the way out, he overheard Dorothy saying she was certain it was the last time Maggie would ever see Beau.

Beau sat in his hotel room that night, not in the plush Palmer, but in a sparse room, a rowdy sailor cavorting next door, a rhythmic banging against the wall in conjunction with a duet of excited exaltations. He found himself wrestling with the thought of taking a woman from a world so foreign to his own and depositing her on Stoneygate. He couldn't see her again until he'd made up his mind.

Monday and Tuesday came and went. Beau did not call. Maggie called The Palmer only to learn he'd checked out. She cried. Her father said he saw it coming a mile away. "Salesman," he said. "You fell for a salesman. You best put him right out of your mind, and I don't want to hear another word about it."

If her father was right, and she'd been played, there was no excusing Beau. She would never forgive him.

Wednesday. Beau called, inviting her to a play at the Blackstone. *Good Night, Ladies*, he said. "With Buddy Ebsen."

Maggie said no.

Beau said he didn't understand.

"My father won't allow it."

"My God, woman. You're old enough to make your own decisions."

"He says you're nothing but a salesman and I'm better off keeping clear of you."

"Is that what you think?"

"He knows better than I do."

"Is that how you feel?"

She could not speak.

"I'll be by at seven."

She was ready when he arrived, waiting on the stoop in her best dress. Ernie glared from the front window.

Whatever doubts filled the void during their two days apart slipped away immediately. The next day they stayed out of the rain in the Garfield Park Conservatory, and the next taking in an afternoon movie matinee. Saturday, they went to the zoo, and Sunday enjoyed a free band concert in the park. She did not question aloud how it was he had such free time. She only wanted more time with him. They did not talk about when he would leave, though they both knew it was inevitable.

Then, the bomb dropped on Hiroshima. He couldn't leave. The first person, the only person Beau wanted to be with, was Maggie. Though it was impossible to comprehend the power and destruction of the first atomic bomb, yet it left in its wake a palpable terror. Photos were slow to appear. The first one, taken two days afterward, showed land stripped of all buildings, a shredded tree in the foreground. Even without a body count, it was clear this was a weapon like no other in history. Every paper ran the same quote about harnessing the power of the sun. Mankind, Beau thought, should not be allowed such horrific capacity for death.

Maggie and Beau were inseparable now. He dropped her at home later and later, calling her first thing in the morning. Three days later, as they finished dinner in a restaurant downtown, the same one they'd eaten in several times over the previous two and a half weeks, a bus boy shouted that Nagasaki had been hit. "Another atom bomb! We dropped another atom bomb!" The communal gasp led to a moment of stunned silence. A woman in the corner shrieked and began to sob openly.

Maggie's eyes filled with tears as fear raced through her. "What does it mean?" she whispered. "What have we done?"

They took a cab to Maggie's, finding her whole family sitting on the front steps.

"There should be a law against this," Maggie said, hugging her mother. "Wiping out whole towns. Families."

"They were going to kill all the prisoners," her dad said. "All our men. Had to do something."

"But incinerating whole towns with one bomb?" Maggie argued. "All those innocent people?"

"It's war," her dad said. "And if that's what it takes to end this one, so be it. If it brings our boys home from the south pacific, I'm all for it. Teach those Japs a lesson."

"There is a law," Beau said.

"What?" Maggie asked.

Beau said it was Article 22 of The Hague Convention of 1907. "Concerning the Laws and Customs of War on Land states. The right of belligerents to adopt means of injuring the enemy is not unlimited."

Ernie glared at Beau. He wasn't used to being corrected.

"History major," Beau said, as if an excuse for speaking out. He could see the surprise on Ernie's face.

"University of North Carolina. Chapel Hill. I'm not arguing. Just stating facts. Honestly, I'm not sure where I stand on this right now. I don't think we know enough. We could end up paying dearly for this or it might work. Hell of a gamble no matter what."

"Drop another one on Tokyo," Walter said, finishing his beer. "That's what I say."

The two five-year-old boys chased each other up and down the sidewalk. The nine and ten-year-old brothers pestered each other until Larry intervened. "Allen, you touch Jack one more time and you're in big trouble."

"This waiting is torture," Dorothy said. "For all we know, we could be dropping another one on Tokyo right now like Walter says."

Larry said he was all for it.

"But when will it stop?" Dorothy asked.

"And what if we aren't the only ones with the bomb?" Virginia chimed in. "What if somebody else has one? They could hit New York or us any day. They could be flying right here right now."

Virginia said Japan could kill all the prisoners of war in retaliation. "Like Dad said. They said they'd do it. What's to stop them now?"

"Threat of another atomic bomb," Larry said feigning authority.

Ernie sighed. "Take it down a notch, everyone. Don't go getting yourself all worked up imagining things."

"She's my worst-case scenario daughter," Emma said of Virginia. "Always, from the time she was little, always looking at the worst possible outcome. The tiniest scratch was always life threatening."

Virginia rolled her eyes.

Emma looked at Beau, patting Maggie. "Not this one. Our Margaret is always finding solutions. She hits an obstacle and finds a way around it. Or through it. Not easy to rile her."

Maggie smiled.

"This was only two bombs," Walter said. "Look at what the Krauts did to London. Bombed the hell out of it for two months straight. Every damn day. I mean what's the difference?"

"Yeah," Larry agreed. "One bomb or a few thousand? One day or months on end?"

Beau responded, stating facts without inflection. He wasn't arguing, though Walter and Larry didn't see it that way. "In London, there are maybe 30,000 civilian dead, give or take, versus a whole Japanese city with a population over 200,000. Civilian dead. We don't even know all the numbers yet."

"What is he, an encyclopedia?" Larry moaned.

"You can't make me feel guilty about this." Walter sniped. "I guarantee we lost that many over the course of this war. Hell, we're still dying in the Pacific."

"Combatants," Beau corrected him. "Combatants are dying. These were civilians. It may end the war, but at what cost? It could, in time, be considered a war crime."

"Whose side are you on?" Larry asked.

Beau shook his head.

Walter's face turned red. "If this ends the war, I don't care what they call it. You didn't even fight. You didn't see it up close." Dorothy tugged his arm but he yanked it free. "You sat the whole thing out from what I heard. Not one day of combat. So, I don't see how in the hell you think you have one God damned thing to say about it."

Beau didn't argue the point. Walter wasn't wrong. Maggie told Walter to shut up, but Larry piled on.

"I bet all those boys over there waiting to hit the beaches of Japan are hoping pretty damn hard this gamble works."

Maggie's dad stood and walked inside without a word. Her mother followed muttering it was time they all found someplace else to be.

"What if this bomb could abolish war once and for all?" Dorothy asked with a peculiar optimism. "I mean if everybody has it, that's inevitable, isn't it? I mean, all out nuclear war would mean the end of civilization. So, how could there ever be another world war?"

"Now, please," her mother said through the screen. "I've had enough talk of war to last the rest of my life." She told Maggie not to stay out too late.

"In by midnight!" Ernie hollered from inside.

Walter walked off, leaving Dorothy to apologize to Beau before she carried their son down the street to their car.

Larry waited on the sidewalk for Virginia to say her goodbyes, knowing the woman could never execute a clean escape. "Allen," he said. "Get your brothers to the car."

"Beau," Virginia said, "it has been so lovely to spend some time with you and you mustn't take these guys too seriously. They're still getting used to being home and . . ."

"Come on!" Larry griped.

"Maggie," Virginia asked, "do you have plans this weekend? I thought maybe I'd have you two for dinner."

"Virginia!" Larry shouted, throwing his hands in the air.

"Yes, Dear," she said, rolling her eyes. "Maggie, I'll call you in the morning." She grabbed her handbag and took off walking beside her husband, calling back "Bye, Beau." The three boys were already a block away, waiting at the car.

"I need a walk," Beau said standing and stretching. It was a good six blocks before either of them spoke.

"I'm sorry about that. I told my sisters . . ."

"Don't worry about it."

"They were wrong."

"No, they weren't. Anyone not in it will never know."

Another three blocks.

"I worry about the future of the human race," Maggie said.

"We've survived this long. I suspect we have a few generations left in us."

A few days later, Maggie and Beau had just ordered dinner at their favorite restaurant when there was a sudden commotion outside. Yelling. Shouting. Sailors on the street started yipping and cavorting. The kitchen door flew open as somebody turned up a radio to catch the last of Truman's address to the nation.

Japan surrendered.

Maggie erupted in tears, an uncontrolled flood of emotion spilling forth in great shudders and sobs. The street outside filled with exuberant revelers shouting, hugging, dancing. The restaurant staff ran out into the street in their white aprons, some sobbing, others standing dumb struck with relief. Beau took Maggie's hand across the table. He did not try to sooth her. He let her cry. The restaurant owner came to the table, tossed the water from their glasses and poured them full of champagne, rushing off to do the same for other patrons. Beau held up his glass to Maggie. Maggie held hers to him. "Marry me," he said, but Maggie didn't hear him over the pandemonium.

Beau hollered. "Marry me!"

Maggie hollered through her tears, laughing and crying simultaneously. "Yes!"

The streets were soon pandemonium, full of drunks and revelers. It took an hour just to get a cab. Beau had Maggie home by midnight, kissed her in the cab and watched her go inside. He made it back to his hotel, stepping over drunks in the lobby and a couple making out in the hall.

Maggie rushed into the house, waking her parents. "I'm engaged!"

Emma rose to her elbow and told Maggie to stop shouting.

"Mother, Beau asked me to marry him!"

Ernie grumbled into his pillow. "Not if I have anything to say about it, you're not."

"Maggie, go to bed. We'll talk about it in the morning. Go on, Dear," Emma urged. "Get some sleep."

"Go to bed!" Ernie demanded.

"Sleep? I can't sleep," Maggie said, waltzing to her bedroom.

Ernie muttered something about not letting her marry some stranger and Emma reminded him Maggie was already thirty. "She's not likely to get another offer, Dear. Perhaps your standards are a bit too rigid."

Over coffee the next morning, Ernie told Maggie flat out: No. "The man's nothing but a traveling salesman."

Maggie shot back. "You're wrong. I'm going to marry him!"

Emma answered a knock at the front door to find Beau. The argument from the kitchen carried to the hall.

"Is that who I think it is?" Ernie hollered.

"Yes, Dear."

Ernie walked into the living room looking dower. "You!" he said to Beau. "In here."

Emma corralled Maggie in the kitchen trying to smooth it over explaining how she won't know anyone in North Carolina, and given time this will all blow over, and school will start again, and it will all be for the best.

"I can make my own decisions, Mother!"

"Margaret," Emma coaxed. "You don't know this man. We don't know his people." Maggie stormed into the living room in time to hear her father say he had no intention of letting his daughter leave her family for a life they knew nothing about. "It's for your own good," he told Maggie with the expectation it would settle the matter.

"Daddy!"

"He's right," Beau said, showing no sign of being flustered.

"What?" Maggie protested. "Beau!"

"You don't know anything but what I've told you. Your father has no way of knowing if I'm legitimate or not." He reached out to shake Ernie's hand.

Ernie took it with a tight grip. "Go home."

Beau walked out the door with a teary-eyed Maggie on his heels.

"I've been gone too long," he said. "I need to get back to work."

"You can't leave now."

"Need to. People counting on me."

"I'm counting on you. Stay here. You could find a job here and . . ."

These words shook him and his expression showed it. "If you think I could do that, then your father's right. We definitely don't have a future together."

"But, Beau …"

"He's right. You know it." She reached for him but he held her at arms' length. Ernie watched from the porch. "If it's supposed to be, it'll work out. But right now, I need to get home."

Beau walked away. He did not turn back to look at her. She did not call out or chase after him. Maggie felt certain it was the last she would ever see him.

Ernie was quick with his "I told you so".

Beau caught a southbound train that afternoon. On the way to the station, he waded through mounds of confetti, bottles, and newspapers, the debris of spent joy.

CHAPTER 11

Ford was in town when he ran into Jarvis heading into his office in the 505 Building.

"Taken that Bishop girl up to the Pisgah yet?" Jarvis asked.

"Didn't know I was supposed to," Ford replied.

"Well, you are. Where you headed?"

"Breakfast."

"Want some company?" he said, already having shifted course to walk with him.

Ford could smell the coffee, bacon, and pancakes two doors down from Sunny's Café, a shotgun cubbyhole with a handful of red Naugahyde booths and a counter with a dozen stationary stools, also red. Inside, a slim waitress in her fifties, wearing jeans and a T-shirt met them at the corner booth, coffee carafe in hand. "How would you like your eggs today, Ford?" she asked.

"Mornin' Gypsy," he answered as he slid into place. "I'm thinkin' over medium. How are the biscuits today?"

"Hockey pucks," she said, pouring. "Jerry's cookin'."

"Wheat toast."

"Got it. And, what are you in for Mr. Payton? Seconds?"

Jarvis shot her a sneer. "One stack of his pancakes is enough to stop me up me for a week. Coffee. Decaf."

"Thanks for that image," she said walking away. "I'll be right back with your decaf."

"You draw up those papers for me yet?" Ford asked.

"No. Yes. I did. But I'm not giving them to you."

Ford sighed, leaned back and glared at the man.

"You still want to hear about that fire?" Jarvis asked.

"I'm all ears." Ford grumbled.

"To really understand it," Jarvis began, "you have to go back a ways, to the previous generation."

Ford let go another long sigh. "Is that really necessary?"

"Yes. It is. I could go all the way back to the beginning. Would you like that?"

Ford groaned.

"Purchased the land with land grants in 1780," Jarvis began. "Thomas Kenyon and his wife Martha did that. But it was their grandson who made it what it became. Thomas was a stonemason and made a good living, but Parson's businesses built the estate.'"

"Parson?" Ford interrupted.

"Baker's daddy. Beau's granddaddy. Sometimes, I swear you're absolutely ignorant. Parson Kenyon. He gave his family a life of considerable comfort, and earned him a good deal of respect not only here, but out of the Blue Ridge, too. He had the brickworks, sawmill and the Feed & Seed. The Kenyon wealth, however, was mostly in land. Parson's love affair with these mountains made him greedy to own as much as he could. Now, for Baker, land was good business. He bought huge tracks of it, sat on it for a bit, then sold it to speculators, who sold it to the tourists who overran us even then. It was never land adjacent to Stoneygate, mind you. It was twenty acres over off Asheville Road, or ten acres out of someone's fallow field. The last of his acquisitions was that tract up there in the Pisgah. By the time Adler began his sell-off, the boom was over. Everything he sold, he sold at a loss. But it wasn't his loss, now was it? It was just easy money. Then came the Great Depression and . . ."

Ford heaved a sigh. "And who the hell is Adler?"

"What? Well, I'll get to him if you let me," Jarvis chided. "Everything that Stoneygate was died that year."

"What year?"

"For Chrissake let me tell the story."

"So, what year?"

"1928," Jarvis said with great exasperation. "First Amanda died. Then Suzanna. The stable was empty. The chase was canceled. Forever, as it turned out. And Baker lost his mind. He closed the businesses without telling anybody. Just locked the doors. My father opened them back up long enough to fill outstanding orders then had to send everyone home again. That was a hundred men out of work. Maybe even more. I remember the night the old groundskeeper came by our house."

"Groundskeeper where?"

"Stoneygate, of course. Keep up. Beau and I turned sixteen that year. Campbell comes to the back door and says straight out that Baker's gone mad, took the ax to the rose arbor and started chopping it like it was so much kindling. He said that he'd pulled Suzanna's roses out of the ground, with his bare hands by the look of it, his hands were bloody."

"The fire," Ford interrupted.

Gypsy delivered breakfast and refreshed both their coffees.

"I'm decaf!" Jarvis sniped.

"Is decaf," Gypsy said. "See the orange lid on this pot? Means decaf. Next cup will be real," she said to Ford walking away. "It's brewing."

Jarvis continued, falling easily into the rhythm of his tale. "Now, Harry had a thing for …"

"Who's Harry?"

"Campbell. Harry Campbell. If you'd just stop with the interruptions, it's a much better story."

"Not if I don't know who the hell you're talking about, it isn't"

"I don't think a man should live alone like you do. Makes him out and out discourteous."

"Then what's your excuse?"

"If I may continue. Harry Campbell had a special place in his heart for Suzanna's hybrid tea roses. He couldn't keep up with all the rest of the yard work on his own, but he made sure those roses were fed and pruned and watered. 'There is no better tribute to God's wisdom,' Mrs. Kenyon used to say, 'than the beauty He chose to bestow the rose.'"

Ford spread strawberry jam on his toast and gave Jarvis an exasperated look.

"Yeah, I know. The fire," Jarvis moaned. "Baker built that arbor as his wedding gift to Suzanna. Each spring he had it painted with a fresh coat of white. You could set your calendar by it. The trellises got painted, bright white, and within a week, the azaleas and laurel bloomed.

"It's safe to say it wasn't the destruction of the roses that sent Campbell packing, though I swear it broke his heart, so much as the way Kenyon went about it. Harry said there was a constant indecipherable muttering coming from Kenyon. And his hands, all bloody, smearing that pristine white lattice work with a bloody crimson reminiscent of the roses it supported mid-summer."

Ford raised his eyebrows. "A bloody crimson? Reminiscent? I'm not in a jury box, old man. You can pass on the theatrics." Ford wiped the last yolk with a crust of toast.

"You want to hear this or not!" Jarvis took a long sip of coffee, set the cup down, wiped the corners of his mouth with his napkin.

Ford accepted a warm-up on his coffee, the real stuff this time. Jarvis asked Gypsy for a fresh cup as his had gone cold. "This is leaded," she said.

"So be it," he replied. She obliged, filling an empty cup from another table and taking his cold one.

Ford pulled out his wallet. "Are you ever going to get around to the fire?"

Jarvis sat motionless except for a loosening of his shoulders, a slight slump overtaking his posture. "Baker had lost everything he ever held dear except for Beau. His parents and all his siblings? Dead. Wife? Dead. Daughter? Dead. And suddenly, he's got his brother's two boys."

"Boys? Who?"

"Enter the Adlers." Jarvis's eyes grew wide and he straightened up. "Baker's widowed sister-in-law, wretched woman. She and her spawn arrived. Took over the place. And Baker let them. He knew those boys, his nephews, had as much right to the land as Beau. The Kenyon trust guaranteed it. Well. Adler went right to work. All in the name of the boys of course, and over the course of a year he damn near decimated the whole estate and . . ."

"Jarvis?" said Ford.

"Yes?"

"The fire."

"Electrical." Jarvis took one sip from his fresh coffee and slid out of the booth. "Adler had the place wired up for electricity. It burned to the ground. I've got work to do. I'm sure you have something of your own you should do. Somewhere to be. Doing whatever it is you do.

CHAPTER 12

When Suzanna died, the house was once again open to mourners. Baker stayed clear of everyone. Like an injured wild animal, he wandered the woods. So long as the intruders lingered, he slept in the stable master's quarters, there being no stable master left. The silence from the stalls was a self-imposed torture. He desperately wanted his life, in every aspect, back the way it was. The fact it would never be was only beginning to take its toll.

The morning after the funeral, Cook found a note on the kitchen door. "To everyone but Campbell: Your services are no longer required." From the hayloft, Baker watched them all leave, taking their things from the house and cottage, pulling away and out of his life. Only then did he enter the house, through the back doors, the ones that faced out over the wooded pasture. The house had, to that point, been as beloved as any family member. It watched them in their sleep, welcomed them home from journeys, held in its walls all the cherished memories of three generations. Upon his entering, however, the structure seemed reluctant to evoke any recognition of him. He felt no welcome, no sense of belonging. He ambled through the rooms, careful not to touch anything, as if doing so would somehow make it all disappear like the stuff of dreams.

In the middle of Amanda's room he saw her trunk, still unpacked. He retreated swiftly to the hallway and then forced himself into Suzanna's dressing room, where, on a shelf, glistening in the morning's sun, like faint taunting laughter, lay her beaded dress, the one she looked so brilliant in at the steeple chase party the year before.

Pushing himself beyond what he believed he could stand, he stepped into their bedroom to face the bed upon which both Amanda and Beau had been conceived and birthed, upon which Baker and Suzanna whispered their devotion, and shared dreams of a future ripe with possibilities. He'd tried to sleep on it the first night, after she was gone, only to find himself retreating to the chair in the corner of the room like a schoolboy frightened of the monster under his bed. He wanted back all the nights he pretended to sleep, turning his back against her quiet sobs; all the nights spent walking the property in solitude, longing only to hold her, but instead waiting to go in until the gin had put her to sleep; all the moments he let slip away when the slightest touch of his hand on hers might have brought them together. He wanted back all the wasted opportunities to be more than he was.

Whether he dozed off in the chair that night or had been wide awake, he felt Suzanna's gentle hand on his knee the way she would touch him so often when she sat on the floor leaning against his legs and he'd stroke her hair and they talked about the day or the children or little things, the insignificant details of life that slip away so easily. He felt her hand on his knee and bolted from the chair, from the house, retreating to the stable, to sanctuary.

In the days that followed, things that should have brought comfort by the very nature of their familiarity, taunted him instead. The ornate French dining suite Amanda adored, the exquisite silver tea set Suzanna used every day, the cutlery that arrived from England with the original Kenyons, the rugs and armoires, the chairs and paintings, and all the clutter of common things, the cup and saucer his mother used to take her tea, the doilies his aunt tatted during her visits, the family bible, all these tangible elements of his life possessed some cruel ability to generate ethereal yet vivid memories of more perfect days, leading him seductively to delusions of normalcy.

Such were the moments he believed it possible Suzanna would appear through the door, a bouquet of roses in her hand, rattling on about getting them into water before they wilted in the day's heat. These brief rushes of anticipation, passing in the space of a heartbeat, were quickly followed by images of Suzanna's twisted body, her head cocked impossibly to the rear, her jaw slipped to the side, her eyes wide in lifeless retreat.

It was one of those moments that led him to the rose arbor, where the canes were beginning to shoot new stalks with supple green nubs. If they were left to grow, he would have to tell them of the winter's tragedies, and in their grief, they would surely turn into something hideous, something of an abomination of nature. Baker knew this could not be allowed and he set about the task of eliminating them, the desecration Campbell witnessed.

Baker closed the sawmill as well as the Feed & Seed. It didn't matter that it put people out of work. Nothing mattered. He moved into the stone cottage, allowing himself only what he needed, and nothing more. He entered the main house only to eat what little food he could scrounge from the cellar, whatever was left of what had been put op the summer before. He would wash his dish, wipe it dry, and return again to the barren confines of the cottage. This austere existence seemed a matter of survival, as he was convinced the house bore some vindictive stance against him and would no longer permit his presence. It was something in the chill he felt within its walls, its silence.

The only one permitted on the property beside Campbell was Merle Payton. The two men had known each other since birth. Like leaving food for a feral animal, Merle would arrive by the back road delivering groceries and the occasional meal prepared by his wife. The only sign of Baker's existence was the clean pie plate or casserole dish left sitting on the cottage porch.

Anyone else seeking Baker was likely to be greeted by a single shotgun blast over their head.

Gossip, being what it is, travels from place to place with the ease of a breeze. Bad news, however, travels like a storm. Word of Stoneygate's decline made its way to Charleston in the form of a visitor on Florence Blackburn Kenyon Adler's doorstep. Florence had been married to Montgomery Kenyon, Baker's brother. She'd moved back home to Charleston when Monty died.

"It's such a pity," the visitor had said. "Someone ought to do something," she'd said. "Florence," she'd said, "you are the only one up to the task."

Having written to Baker twice in a month's time without reply, Florence arrived at Stoneygate late summer with her husband Jason, thirteen-year-old twin sons, and her housekeeper. Pulling onto the winding road leading to Stoneygate, Florence was anticipating a battle of wills with Baker. She had passed the long hours of the journey, composing in her mind all necessary arguments to make her way onto the estate. *You need help until you are fully over your grief and on your feet again*, she would say. If that failed, she would use her boys as leverage, her right to protect and ensure their inheritance, no, heritage. Much better word, she thought. Their *heritage*. That was the tricky part. She had never actually gotten around to telling Baker she was pregnant when she left Stoneygate after Monty died. Her twins were raised as Monty's boys. She was afraid if she'd told Baker about them, he would have made her return to North Carolina with them, or maybe even take them from her. It was a delicate matter that would require a steady head and careful tongue.

Her rehearsal stopped abruptly when Jason brought their Auburn to a jolting halt at the entrance to Stoneygate. The stately fieldstone pillars flanking the drive were nearly obstructed from view by the huge jack pine lodged securely between them. It seemed for the most part to have lain as it had fallen, probably some weeks earlier. Even the woods, it seemed, were determined to keep Baker isolated.

Unable to go any further, he parked the car on what little shoulder the road afforded. While the boys occupied themselves exploring the woods, the other three walked the drive to the house.

Florence took the lead, her stout form marching bosom first, her chin pointing the way. Her lackluster husband, tall and gaunt, sauntered behind. The housekeeper, taking three steps to every one of Florence's, picked up the many errant pine boughs in her path and tossed them aside. "Must have been some storm," she said flippantly.

They rounded a bend out of the laurel thicket into view of the front lawn. The grass was knee high where it wasn't matted and chewed by the cattle grazing freely at the tree line. A downed limb of white oak rested neatly in a large round of boxwood. "Would you look at that," said the housekeeper. "Looks like a knife in one of my plum puddings."

Rarely hesitant to share her caustic observations, Florence had no words for what she saw up ahead. Never in her life had she imagined a property could fall into such a deplorable condition in so quick a time.

A cawing from the roofline of the house drew her attention. First one crow flew off, followed close by another and another, and three more exiting a broken window. The lot of them flew off into the woods, cawing their irritation at the intruders.

The tree responsible for the damage leaned uprooted against the house, one branch having charged its way through the roof of the living room, another taking out the corner of the verandah. Its root mass, torn perpendicular from the ground, stood nearly twice as tall as Florence.

Silent to that point, Jason said he wanted no part of fixing the place up. "I'll sell it for salvage and raze it before I lift one finger to help the bastard." Florence, however, had her ways of working a man.

"Let's not forget whose money you're talking about, Dearest," she said with nonchalant ease. While it had been her money when they married, the fortune he'd made through his investments he considered to be his, something she failed to comprehend. She insisted it was all a matter of the boys and their interest in the property. With Baker's brothers killed in the war without having had any children, Monty's boys had just as much claim on the family estate as did Baker's boy, Beau.

Unaware of visitors, Baker walked the wooded pasture, his mind chewing on scattered bits of thought and spitting them out. He caught a glimpse of a boy darting along the far fence line, sunlight illuminating curly red hair. Just as suddenly as he appeared, he slipped away like an angel at play. Baker stopped cold, straining to see the ethereal vision again, and again it appeared, rosy cheeked and red haired running the same path, looking every inch to be his brother Monty as a child, so many years dead and buried. "Baker, my boy," he said out loud to himself, "you have finally lost your mind."

Florence's screeching skewered the woods as two boys ran together over the footbridge. "Mother, there are no horses," yelled one of them. "We can't be expected to live here!" hollered the other. "It's dreadful!"

Even in his addled state, Baker saw Florence and the boys and put it together. The boys, carbon copies of his brother, had to be Monty's sons. For the first time in months, he had a sensation of hope, as if their arrival was a gift. They would be his salvation.

"Baker!" came Florence's infamous shriek. "Would you mind coming over here? I can't be expected to walk out there. I'll ruin my shoes!"

Some people never change, Baker thought, striding up to her.

She stood her ground until he did not seem to be slowing his pace and she backed up in retreat, stumbling a bit. The boys hooted and pointed and laughed out loud at her.

"You should have told us about the boys," Baker said to her, standing within striking distance. Over her shoulder, he caught sight of her husband. "Who's that?"

"You need my help here, Baker," she stated with stern intent. "Look at you. Look at this place! It's a disgrace, so don't you go telling me what I should or should not do."

"Who is that?"

"Jason. My husband. Jason Adler. And we've come up here to put this place back together. It's my responsibility to make sure the boys' heritage is intact for them, and, well, from what I see, you're letting this place fall to ruin. So, what we've decided is …"

Baker watched her spew her diatribe.

"You give me control of the trust," she said with a tone of condescension, "in the name of the boys, of course, yours and mine, and I'll raise these two here. It'll be like having Monty back, I mean, just look at them. They are his spitting image." She contrived a smile that was anything but warm. "You do this thing, and you'll have family back. Don't do it, and I'll take you to court." Her smile decayed. "Either way, I'll have control. But it's up to you. Fight me, and you'll never see them again."

Baker stood silent, watching her await his response, watching one corner of her mouth twitch. He took a deep breath, lifting her anticipation, exhaled, turned and walked away.

"Baker?" she scoffed. "This offer won't last forever. You have to make up your mind. Baker!" she yelled after him. "What will it be?"

He did not turn back. He was heading up to Glassy, cutting through dense woods to the steep and rocky back trail to high ground, where everything breaking his heart lay behind him, and he could get a clear view of his foothills rolling into the future, where he could breathe without feeling like his lungs were caving in, like his heart was breaking. How easy it was, for that instant, to see his little brother young again, to believe time would do that for him, give him back his past, let him do it all again, better this time. He would pay attention. He would listen. He would never let his children out of his sight. He would hold his wife and console her and be the man she needed him to be. The arrival of Monty's boys gave him that second chance. Maybe if they could love him, if he could find Monty in their eyes, he could be redeemed.

In return for the opportunity to know his nephews, Baker surrendered control of the trust save the fifty-acre core that held the house, the stone cottage, some woods, and the pasture, the unassailable heart of Stoneygate. In Baker's mind, the transaction was a simple trade of land for blood. Merle Payton, however, had pleaded with him to reconsider.

"I am clear of mind on this," was the response. "Do it." And so it was done. Not three days later, the carnage began. Because it was not in Baker's nature to destroy a thing, it had not come to mind that Florence's husband would dismantle the property. The first sale, of Monty's old house on the other side of the pasture, cut to the quick, yet Baker accepted the injury as penance for all his failings.

It did not take long to come to the realization the boys were only Kenyon skin deep. Inside, they had their mother's temperament. They were unruly whiners accustomed to getting whatever they wanted whenever they wanted it. He caught them fighting one day, both with bloodied noses, and pulled them apart, one of them landing a blow to his chin that knocked him off balance. His stumbling was met with great delight by the boys.

Baker had become accustomed to walking the woods, sometimes from sun up to sun down. On one such walk, he was taken by a peculiar smell. The acrid stench of rotting meat seeped in through his nose and settled on his tongue. There was something else in it, something sooty. He followed it and came upon a raccoon carcass, one leg tied to a tree with bailing twine. Its fur was half burned off and its torso stuck through with a stripped and whittled sapling. Only the twins were capable of such cruelty. As he sorted out whether he should beat the living shit out of them or let them be, he heard faint chopping sounds.

He would have heard it sooner if it weren't for the wind rustling the trees. Walking to higher ground, pushing laurel branches aside, he looked to the old-growth forest in time to see first one, then another, then a third massive tree fall in slow motion into the tall grasses of the meadow, branches cracking and splitting, not unlike his heart. Baker stood silent, living in such a state of inertia as to be unable to retaliate. He cut free the raccoon, grabbed it by the string, and carried it back to the main house.

Adler was barking complaints to the workmen on the roof when Baker threw the oozing dead animal at his feet and walked away. Adler hollered and yanked his bloody boot in disgust. "What's the meaning of this?" he yelled.

"Your boys. That's what they do for fun."

"Get rid of it!"

"How 'bout you just get rid of them," Baker said. "One more thing. You call off the logging. Now."

"Under contract. None of your concern anymore."

Baker stopped and turned. "Call it off," he demanded. A rage was brewing within every muscle, every vein. He fought it back as best he could.

When the chopping commenced again at daybreak, a shotgun blast rang through the air, and all the men stopped what they were doing, listened, and started again. Another blast. More chopping. Another blast. And so it went throughout the morning, until the gunfire stopped, and the afternoon's work continued without interruption. It was an experienced crew, and they worked fast, already leveling half an acre, not along the edge of the pasture, but from the edge inward, like slicing open an artery to the heart of the woods.

The logging crew arrived the next day to find a note tacked to a tree. "Today, I'm going to aim." Adler, no stranger to legal fights, put a stop to Baker's attempts to thwart the logging. When it was all over, ten acres of old-growth timber was clear-cut.

Baker stood on the hill staring at the scar, taking in every stump, every pile of scrap, every splintered sapling. He memorized the sight, burned it into his brain as evidence of his weakness. He had no more fight within, just a bone-deep ache that would not relent.

Adler sold off Stoneygate piece by piece. He built a clay tennis court next to the main house, as was the fashion of the day, though he didn't play and the boys weren't interested. Like Adler himself, it was for show. The boys pestered him to repair the swimming pool, but it was too badly damaged to warrant his attention. What proceeds weren't spent on the house and grounds went into an ever-increasing stock portfolio. He sold the stable and open pastureland, and took loans out against timber futures on another fifty acres. Within the year, land holdings in trust were whittled down to its untouchable core: the house and fifty acres. The bank had paper on the rest of what hadn't been sold off.

CHAPTER 13

While Adler was busy liquidating Kenyon holdings, Baker began a task of his own. From the time his grandfather had built it, the stone cottage was meant only as guest quarters. As it stood, it had no kitchen, just a sitting room, bathroom, and two bedrooms. Anyone staying there took meals at the main house. Baker began turning the inconvenient shell of a cottage into a serviceable house. A bedroom became a kitchen. Not a man accustomed to doing a thing halfway, he ordered the newest and the best appliances through his shuttered Feed & Seed: a Holyoke kerosene hot water heater, an electric refrigerator, a Hotpoint electric range, and an oil-fired steam boiler from American Radiator Company. He plumbed for radiators, and installed an oil tank outside.

He shored up supporting timbers and spent long days alone at his milling company, making finish grade floorboards for the whole cottage out of old oak planks. He took great pains to plane each plank to a uniform thickness, clean and flat. Then he cut them all parallel in width, then milled each and every one for a tight tongue-and-groove fit. Arriving home from the mill one day, he found a crew had removed a vast section of lawn. Adler was building his tennis court.

What had been a root cellar in the basement was transformed by modern mechanicals. The stone walls and flagstone floor were well suited to this new purpose. He paneled the back wall with 2 X 10 cedar planks, securing hooks to it for garden and carpentry tools. He constructed shelving and filled them with spare parts and boxes of nails and shingles and anything he could find, careful to conceal the hinges and latch to a door behind the shelves.

With that task accomplished, he took the flatbed out to the far pasture, land he no longer owned, and collected fieldstones from the piles along the tree line. The foundation for a new room would soon be accomplished.

He went back to the sawmill and loaded up a truck with lumber, nails and cedar shingles. Soon after, the pounding of hammer to nail echoed through the woods well into the night, and the next, and the next.

There was neither joy nor contentment to be found in his labors. Each day was dedicated to the next task that led to the next, and the next. It was something to do; something to keep his mind occupied; a physical endeavor capable of wearing his body out to such a degree he could not help but sleep soundly. He worked with complete indifference to the people in the main house, having given up on the boys. From the first light of day to long after sundown, the pounding continued from the cottage.

What began in December was accomplished by mid-October. Baker had more comfortable living quarters but was at a loss as to how to spend the first hour of that day, much less the whole of it.

The night of the fire, Baker was alone on the estate. The Adlers and their housekeeper were off visiting Florence's sister in Charleston. Baker stood at the pool, looking into a shallow algae-thick soup settled into the deep end. A frog sung out, a desperate whirring. A kingfisher stuttered from a limb above it.

He'd had the pool built for Suzanna in 1922, the year the country club in Asheville installed theirs. Baker hired the crew to do one more pool before leaving the area. It was to be a surprise for his family when they arrived home from spending nearly three weeks on the Outer Banks taking in the sea air. Suzanna, however, had cut the visit short and arrived home to find not only a huge pile of dirt and clay blocking the drive, but an entire row of azaleas torn out, sitting in unruly mounds of dirt. Before even saying hello, she accosted Baker, and he let her go on just long enough to be good and embarrassed before showing her the cement hole in the ground. "It's still curing," he told her. "If you'd come back when you were supposed to, you'd be swimming in it." She was as giddy as the children about the prospect of a swimming pool.

Had Baker been in his right mind, standing alone in the night by the pool, this might have been a pleasant memory. He was, however, not right in his mind about much, and he pushed hard to get the thought of Suzanna out of his head. As if to torture himself, he went into the main house. Adlers had rearranged things. Nothing was where it should be. He didn't recognize his home.

Wandering the wooded pasture later, he stumbled over a branch sticking out of a pile of brush that once served as a steeplechase jump. Baker fought back the memory of the last chase, but it swept over him relentlessly. He imagined people gathering at the fence behind him, beginning to stir as the announcement spread: "Riders make the line!" Dozens of races mingled together in his head, all the same, all unique.

It was the first race of the last chase that Baker remembered most clearly. It was when he sensed something was wrong. He'd tried to find Amanda that morning. The first race of every chase was something they'd shared together since she was a baby. Suzanna had insisted there was nothing to worry about. He recalled her tone as mildly condescending. She gave him a kiss and drifted away to visit with their guests, but not before delivering the words that now haunted him: "There's always next year." He had all too often thought back to that conversation, wishing he had followed his gut.

Kicking apart what little remained of the old jump, a subtle glow in a window of the main house caught his eye. It grew brighter, infecting the next room and the next. He stood motionless, watching flames dart out of the bedroom window, giving the curtains wings upon which to fly like tethered birds. The house quickly exploded into a blazing spectacle. Sparks, like a flood of angry tears, flowed up to the sky.

Baker observed with detached fascination as the intricate stained glass images on the sunroom windows buckled, their leading melting like so much icing on a fritter, compositions loosing form as colorful fragments fell away, snapping and shattering on stone below.

The Baptist minister, whose church property lay adjacent to the estate, rang the church bell in alarm. Even if the fire crew had arrived in time to save the structure, there was no getting past Baker. From the fence line came three warning shots over their heads. No one argued with the man in the shadows with the gun. The sheriff tried to call him out, but in the end, could only accept his duty to restrain and protect the fire fighters.

The ferocity of the blaze, like an entity without mercy or compassion, gave Baker the first release he'd known since burying his wife and daughter. He believed it to be his grief and rage made manifest. As the flames devoured the house with insatiable appetite, a sensation swelled within him, a feeling of such overwhelming love he fell to his knees and wept. The fire freed him of every tactile aspect of their memory. He was free to face a day on new terms.

Vehicles lined the road as word traveled through town. A cluster of onlookers stood on the lawn and watched into the night with the reverent silence of those sitting vigil over a dying loved one. As the flames diminished, so too did the crowd. By three in the morning, the flames no longer threatened the woods, and the fire chief and the sheriff directed everyone to leave. Baker was once again alone on the property and spent the night propped against a sweet gum tree, feeling what he would later remember as peace.

Clear into the next evening, a few timbers still burned. Hand-hewn from old-growth hickory and oak, they burned hot and long as all good hardwoods will. Their embers still smoldered through the next day when the Adlers returned.

As Jason and Florence had been traveling the previous two days, they were uninformed of the disaster recently befallen Stoneygate. When the car pulled up to the smoking ash heap, Florence's shriek was loud enough to be heard in the parsonage of the church. Once again, the minister was drawn through the woods to survey a situation at his neighbor's.

One of the twins jumped out of the car and began searching through the rubble. Florence slowly climbed out and fell to her knees, sobbing. The other boy rummaged through the car for his camera and instructed his mother to pose on the steps. Jason Adler sat in the car, paralyzed at the sight of the charred remains.

He had been exceedingly anxious to return to Stoneygate that day. It represented to him their only refuge from impending poverty, an existence for which he held nothing but contempt. All his well-chosen investments and securities were suddenly worth no more than the ashes before him. Wall Street had just crashed, leaving him with little else but the land he'd mortgaged and a worthless timber contract. Seeing that even the house was lost, he could not divine a way out. He was broke in both matters of finance and spirit. He watched as faint smoke trails lifted up from the debris and dissipated, carrying with them all hope.

It was the sound of the gunshot, its echo cracking through the woods, that drew Baker's attention from the cottage. He ran to the drive to find the boys and Florence standing like statues, looking out over the lawn to the old balsam fir. The minister, approaching the tree on the run, slowed his pace as he drew closer. Jason Adler's body lay crumpled in a heap at the base of the great tree, his head awash in blood, the gun still in his hand.

Florence and the boys spent the night at the Wheeler Inn. In the morning, Merle Payton paid a visit with a packet full of quitclaim deeds. It was a gamble on Baker's part. Florence could either sign on the boys' behalf, extinguishing any right to the property forever along with responsibility for its debt, or forfeit the boys to Baker's keeping. Baker didn't want any part of them, yet the only way to insure their extraction from his life was to threaten to dislodge them from hers. As this had been the tactic she'd employed in acquiring control, it seemed only fitting. She signed without hesitation, leaving with her boys the next day.

As the country faced financial calamity, Baker felt better than he had in a very long time.

CHAPTER 14

Something lurked on the fringes of Meg's awareness. She'd noticed it more than once lately, in the middle of the night. The sleeper awakens to something, hears it again but falls back to sleep, aware only that whatever it is is far away, not a threat yet. Her physical tasks – the move and her deadline – were nearly accomplished, both with requisite intent and control. She awoke to daylight with an awareness she was approaching a void without task, away from home, in a strange town.

Coffee in hand, she sat on the porch step staring out across the tennis court to the wooded pasture and felt a pang in her chest, just a small passing twinge. A leaf caught her eye, dangling at just such an angle as to catch the sun more than any other, and as if to acknowledge her glance, it began fluttering wildly, the only thing in motion within sight. Just as suddenly, it stopped. Her eyes welled. A tear fell. Whether it fell from stress or sadness or simply the beauty of that singular leaf, her first foray back into the emotional world was brief, passing as quickly as sun on that leaf.

Meg went to bed early that night, exhausted for reasons she couldn't identify. Somewhere in a thick sleep, she woke from a dream she could not remember, haunted by a feeling that she was missing something. What, she didn't know, but she missed it with all her heart. The sadness wrapped itself around her like a blanket and she fell back to sleep strangely comforted by it.

Two days later, Ford arrived to take Meg to the Pisgah, to the tract of woods Maggie left to her free and clear. He was dismayed to see she'd trimmed back the wisteria so severely it would take years for it to recover.

"It was overgrown," Meg said, noticing his displeasure.

He started to tell her she'd cut off what would be the year's blooms but stopped himself. What would be the point?

The trip was a favor to Jarvis, something that needed to be done. Ford drove the scenic route along the river, peripherally observing Meg's expression. She was a very large question mark to all concerned. She hadn't yet given anyone a clue as to her intentions.

Meg sat in the beat-up truck hoping it would make it to where they were going and back again without breaking down. It was filthy and cluttered with scrunched fast food bags.

They drove for fifteen minutes without a word. She watched the landscape flow past her, each bend in the river more inviting than the next. She saw a dozen places she'd like to put a house and live contentedly ever after. "Are we still in Laurel County?" she asked. Ford replied with a simple nod. He gave no indication he was going to elaborate. She was about to say something innocuous about the garden, about how she'd noticed the peas needed trellising, and the chard was leafing out, and the beets and carrots were growing, but suddenly they cleared the woods and came upon a great sloping valley of vibrant green grassland. Late morning sun set it aglow, sweeping away every thought.

Pastures bordered by trees and fences were sparsely populated with cows and horses. The houses, modest and old, with all their outbuildings, looked like little towns unto themselves. Some were right along the road. Her favorites were deep in the middle of a field at the end of long unpaved driveways. There were flowers and gardens everywhere. The plague of development had yet to discover this place. It made her sad to think it was only a matter of time before the condos would creep in and mini-mansions of the all too wealthy would devour the family homesteads. The road went straight through the middle of it all and up the other side, into the woods again, and up through a series of gentle switchbacks.

Ford pulled off along the side of the road and parked. "We'll walk in from here."

Meg followed him through a thicket at the edge into tall timber with very little undergrowth.

"Is this it?" she asked.

"Yeah," he said flatly. "This is the southwest corner. I'll walk you over to the eastern edge."

"Is there any development up here yet?" she asked, hoping it was somehow illegal to destroy even a single tree in the Pisgah.

Wanting to discourage any plans she might be making to subdivide and sell off, he told her it was too difficult to get utilities that far out. He lied.

"Good," she said.

It was the first indication he had of her mindset. When he casually pointed out some trillium and lady slippers, he unintentionally unlocked a conversation.

"Did you know Maggie well?" Meg asked.

"Yeah."

"Have you worked for her long?"

He took a long time to respond because nothing he came up with was appropriate. Meg knew nothing about his life, and for the most part, she didn't know much about Maggie. "Yeah," he finally said with a distinct tone of dismissal. Meg stopped talking.

For maybe twenty minutes, they hiked until they came to another thicket, beyond which was a clearing. Ford held back some branches so she could make her way through. Before her was a ten-acre meadow surrounded by trees. On the far edge stood a huge house. The tin roof of the gables glittered like diamonds in the sunshine. A stone path led to wide stairs to a porch that ran the length of the house. Beyond the house sprawled the Blue Ridge Mountains. Meg was instantly drawn to it.

"That's not mine, is it?" she joked.

"No." He turned, walking back the way they'd come.

In the little burg of Brevard, he dropped Meg at Maxine's, an artsy coffee shop, its walls lined with paintings for sale. "Double shot half-caf with soy," she said to the woman behind the counter. The simple act of speaking those words, and having them understood, made her feel better than she had since her arrival in North Carolina.

She sat at a window table munching a cheese Danish, savoring her coffee, her mind drifting to the final illustration of the book. One more day's work and it would be finished. Suddenly, a dash of white jumped up from the street and shot up the tree, across a branch to another tree ,and on down the street. "Oh my god," she said aloud. "I just saw an albino squirrel!"

Patrons at other tables chuckled. One of them dropped a pamphlet on her table on his way out the door, *An Unusual Story About An Unusual Squirrel*. "They're all over town," he said. She was about to read the story when Ford came knocking on the window. When he drove her home via a different, quicker route, she joked that he was trying to make sure she would never find the Pisgah property on her own. He did not respond.

She was happy to be dropped back at the cottage with most of the afternoon left to work. She went to sleep that night only to be awakened at four in the morning by the lamp falling onto the bed from the nightstand, followed immediately by something clunking on the dresser and a small thud on the floor by the bed. She recoiled, turned on the light, and saw something jump from the couch to the bookshelf and fly to the table like a furry kite. She'd never seen a flying squirrel before. She stood in the doorway, very still, watching its nose twitch, its huge black eyes trained on her. Sliding along the wall, she opened the door and propped the screen to let it out, but it startled and soared back to the couch and to the floor, scampering into the back bedroom and up to her drawing table, sending pencils to the floor, knocking over a jar of brushes. Following it, she closed the door and opened a window only to realize the screen had to come down from the outside. Shooing it out into the hall again, it finally went for the door, jumping with such grace to the back of the rocker and up into the wisteria and into the tree. Unable to sleep, she made a sketch of the creature flying through the air with a wicked little grin.

Meg had a very specific routine after all her book deadlines. The initial phase was exhaustion and momentary despondency, followed by euphoria, followed by hunger.

Despondency was easily treated with a stack of movie rentals of obscure origin. The euphoria, hitting two or three days later, brought with it the urge to be social, to host a dinner party. This required serious shopping to restock the larder, with mandatory visits to Chicago's Italian and Greek markets, farmer's markets, and the specialty gourmet grocery down the block. The hours spent cooking and baking somehow brought her back to the real world, away from the carefully crafted stories she wrote, the minutely detailed characters and surroundings she illustrated. It was nothing unusual to spend peaceful, languid days making handmade pastas, braided breads, and Viennese tortes. A handful of lucky people looked forward to her deadlines, relishing the feast that ensued.

Vince had been in the picture for two such deadlines. The first time, he was fresh on the scene, merely a guest. The second, he was right in the thick of it with her, going to market, helping roll pasta, choosing wines. He'd made it all about her. She reveled in his attention.

This deadline was altogether different. Instead of the organized single package she normally sent off, it had been a piecemeal affair, the culmination of which did not hold the same celebratory inspiration. She checked her e-mail a dozen times the next day, waiting for the one that said the last of the book packages had arrived safely and was accepted for publishing without revision. Mostly, she was looking for something from Vince. His notes were growing fewer and ever more brief. *Been busy at work . . . Glad the book is going well . . . We've had a cold spring here.* He never mentioned missing her. She took this as a good thing. No point expressing what you can't do anything about.

"Great work!" came her editor's e-mail. "Take a break and we'll talk at proofs." There it was. Within the month, she would go to New York to look at the printing proofs. It was a day's work she always turned into a week's outing. The proof trip had always been a time to bask in the perks, get stroked for past accomplishments and primed for the next one. It was a trip she looked forward to after each book, and especially so after this one. It was her ticket back to civilization. More than that, when Vince joined her there, they would make up for lost time. Optimism bloomed.

In the meantime, she was officially off task, but at a loss as to how to spend her time, stuck in the middle of nowhere, with nothing to do. Sitting on the couch, her foot bouncing, eyes darting, a shoebox high on a bookshelf caught her eye. Taking it down, she found letters. Lots of letters. Two on top were wrapped in white ribbon.

> August 15, 1946. My dearest Maggie, I was so disheartened when I left you this morning. It's making for a terrible train trip home. I'm only an hour into the ride now. Wish I could turn around. But I have a lot to tend to if I'm going to convince your father to let me marry you. And I want that more than I can say. Write to me so I can know you still want the same outcome. I love you so very dearly. Yours, Beau. P.S. Please send a photo of you.

> August 17 - My dearest Beau. You can't know how much I needed your letter. My heart broke when you left, thinking I would never see you again. How could I have doubted you? Yes! We want the same future. I miss you so terribly. I have retraced all our steps, imagining you by my side,

remembering our conversations. I didn't know love could hurt this much. Please write every day. And I'll do the same. Here is a picture of me from last spring. My sister Dorothy took it. The postman will be here any minute so I'll close now. I hope you know my love was on that train with you and I can't wait to be with you again. My heart aches so. All my love, Maggie

CHAPTER 15

Ten days after Beau left Chicago, Maggie and her parents were invited to lunch at a posh restaurant downtown. Their host, a distinguished gentleman in his sixties, introduced himself as a close friend of the Kenyon family. He told them he'd known Beau since birth, that his parents had been dear friends. He explained how Beau carried on with the family businesses after his father passed away, how he'd prospered, how he'd been responsible for keeping many men out of harm's way for most of the war. When the lunch dishes were cleared, Ernie finally spoke.

"Sir, I don't know you from a hill of beans. If this is your way of ingratiating Beau Kenyon into our lives, I'm afraid you've come up short."

Maggie's mouth fell open. "Daddy!"

The man smiled and invited them across the street, up several floors to his office, where they were met by a lovely woman in a suit carrying a tray with coffee and creampuffs. When she left, she closed the door behind her.

"I have been asked by Mr. Payton, Mr. Kenyon's family attorney, to present these documents to you, Mr. and Mrs. Bishop. Here is the deed to his sawmill as well as the accounting for the last two years prior to closing during the war." He pointed to some figures on a page, and laid it in front of Ernie. "Here is the deed to the cooperage, and statements as to its solvency." He laid it on top of the first papers. "Here is the deed to Stoneygate estate, including its acreage and the most recent appraisal, acquired last week. The appraisal was ordered entirely for your benefit. Here is some literature about Hendersonville, Flat Rock, and Asheville, North Carolina, including tax revenues and business development. You'll see the area fared better during the Great Depression than many areas in the country, which is not to say it wouldn't do worse in some future calamity, but the history speaks for itself."

Maggie and Emma grinned, both of them looking to Ernie with expectation of approval. It was not forthcoming.

"No." Ernie said flatly.

"Daddy!" Maggie hollered.

"No," Ernie said again. "I'm not sending my girl seven hundred miles away to a strange place based on facts and figures. He has no people. No church."

"Daddy?"

"I talked to the man, Margaret. He doesn't go to church. Said you could go if you wanted but he has no interest in religion. You'd be on your own and I don't know enough about this man to leave you in his care. You've never been alone in your life. You're not a woman likely to enjoy a life away from your family. No. That's the end of it."

Ernie stood, leaving the documents on the table. Emma rose with her husband. Maggie could not muster the energy, and tried not to cry.

"Mr. Bishop, I assure you he has people who care about him. She won't be alone."

"Family," said Ernie. "Family. He's an orphan. No one to count on. Not really."

Ernie put his hand to Emma's back escorting her out of the office. He barked at Maggie to follow. She obeyed, believing she would never see Beau again, much less marry him.

August 27 - Dear Beau, I can't stop crying. Father still says no. You went to such effort and still he won't allow it. I don't want to go against his wishes but I can't let him stand between us. I will leave my family if I have to. I will leave them and come to you. I ache so for you. Please tell me you still want this. Please tell me things will turn out well. I've never been so unhappy. All my love, Maggie.

August 29 - My dearest, Maggie, please do not worry. It will all work out. Do not under any circumstances argue with your father over this. He only wants what's best for you. Anything you say could jeopardize our family in the future. Be patient with me. And be patient with your father. Our love will survive this. I promise. Yours truly, Beau

One week later, on a Saturday morning, a red-haired woman in her late thirties arrived on the Bishop doorstep. "I'm Sara Mercer," she told Emma. "I've come to meet Maggie. I've come to see if she is the right fit for my friend Beau."

Emma, caught entirely off guard, invited her in and called out for Maggie.

Once inside, Sara took one look at Maggie and winked. "Put some clothes on, girl. I'd like to take a tour of Chicago." In short order, the two women were hustling onto the streetcar to go downtown.

"Is he here?" Maggie asked, giddy with hope.

"Yes," Sara said. "He'll be by for you tonight. This is our time. We have a lot to talk about." They were a good fit, neither demonstrative of emotion, both speaking directly. Sara assured Maggie that Beau's house was manageable, as was his temper. Maggie assured Sara leaving her family behind would not be a hardship. By mid-afternoon, Sara was ready for the inquisition. Ernie was waiting.

Sara told Maggie to leave her alone with Ernie. Sara and Emma sat out back with lemonade. Waiting.

"I own a store," Sara told Ernie. "The local Feed & Seed."

"How did you come by it?" he asked, skeptical.

"My husband and I owned it. He died. I took it over." Hopefully he would not detect the slight falsehood. She began her pitch, knowing it was Beau and Maggie's last best chance. "I am not a southerner. From Indiana originally. She will be like having one of my own there. It can be a challenge to acclimate to a new place, but I've spoken with your daughter. I believe she will be very happy there. I have taken the liberty of speaking with the principal of our elementary school. Presuming all her credentials are in order, I have secured Maggie a teaching position. So, you see, Beau and I are committed to making her happy. Keeping her busy. I have found it a most agreeable environment to raise my son."

"How old is your son?"

"Jeffrey is 18."

"And how is it you know Mr. Kenyon?"

"My husband and his father were in business together some years ago. Before we owned the Feed & Seed."

"What business was that?"

Finding a euphemism for bootlegging, she called it warehousing and transportation. "They had two facilities. One in North Carolina and a second in Kentucky." By the expression of Ernie's face, she wasn't sure he'd let it pass.

"Why did he give that up?"

"It was a family decision." Another slight falsehood, but one excusable under the circumstances.

"How'd he die? Your husband."

"Automobile accident." She did not elaborate. "Mr. Bishop, Ernie," she said before he had a chance to inquire further, "I believe your daughter will be very happy with us. She will not want for companionship and Beau is a very good man. My family are all gone. He is like family - he *is* my family. Like an uncle to my son. Who is to say that isn't as strong a bond as blood? I have never seen Beau in love until now, and I have to tell you, it brings me great joy to see him so happy."

Ernie called out to Maggie. "Go tell that fiancé of yours, you say yes."

Maggie ran through the house, hollering thank you, thank you, and bolted out the front door. Within the hour, she returned with Beau, and plans were formulated for a June wedding.

Emma invited Sara to move her things to their house for the duration of her visit, and offered to show her the sights. Sara declined, but only because she had to catch the early train home. "The Feed & Seed won't run itself." Ernie appreciated her commitment and insisted she stay for dinner while Beau and Maggie went to the restaurant where he'd proposed.

When Beau planted a small diamond ring on Maggie's finger, the proprietor poured them champagne.

Beau and Sara were on the morning train out, having enjoyed a successful visit.

> September 9 - My Sweet Beau, You've just left and my heart is still hopping in my chest. I can't stop looking at my beautiful ring. Virginia and Dorothy are envious. I can't believe we are really getting married. How will I wait so long? How will I focus on my students tomorrow when all I want to do is be with you? Oh how do I tell you how much joy you bring me. You won over my father. No small feat. But you did it. 14 weeks and 4 days before I see you again. Christmas will be so wonderful this year. I can't bear to stop writing this. If I'm writing, it's like I'm with you. Please call me soon. I can't wait to hear your voice.
> All my love, Maggie.

> September 9 - Dearest Maggie, Sara is laughing at me. She says I'm love sick. I suppose I am. Putting that ring on your finger was maybe the most wonderful thing I've ever done. It is real now. A thing with a future. If I finish this quickly I can drop it at the next station. I love you and look forward to our life together. Love always, Beau

Snow kept Beau away from Chicago over Christmas. He made the trip north for a weekend in early February. If not for Maggie's teaching, they might have moved the wedding up. As it was, they married in a quiet affair with family and a hand full of friends as soon as school let out for the summer. Sara and Jeffrey rode the train up with Beau, and were tasked with managing the transportation of Maggie's belongings on their way home.

Beau arranged a brief honeymoon in Gatlinburg, Tennessee. Their train would leave Chicago at seven in the morning, arriving at nine at night if there were no delays. In the meantime, he reserved a room in the Palmer House for their wedding night.

Maggie was assured by her sisters she had nothing to worry about concerning her first night with Beau. When she changed out of her wedding dress into her traveling suit, they explained the night would take care of itself. "If you love him as much as you seem to, it will all be fine. Nature has a way of …" the women giggled "… taking over."

"But I don't know what to do," Maggie whined.

"You'll be fine. Just let him show you what he wants," Dorothy said.

"What does that mean?" Maggie asked.

"You go into the bathroom," Virginia said. "Put on your pretty new nightgown and robe, and then you come out and present yourself."

"What do you mean present yourself," Dorothy argued.

"Well, what do you call it?"

"I never had the chance to put my nightgown on," Dorothy laughed. "We were ripping each other's clothes off before we even got in the room!"

A knock on the door meant it was time for Maggie to leave with Beau. It hadn't hit her until that moment what it meant to be leaving home. Being caught up in anticipation had been magical. Doing the actual leaving was entirely different. She began to cry for reasons she didn't understand. Her sisters hugged her and laughed out loud. "You waited long enough for this. Go to your husband! You're married!"

Beau hired a driver and a fancy car to take them to the hotel. Maggie felt like a queen waving goodbye to everyone on the curb. She had her king, and her life was beginning. After a light supper in the dining room, Beau ordered a bottle of Champagne to be sent up to their room. He took Maggie by the hand and led her to the elevator. "You're shaking," he said.

"Aren't you nervous? I'm nervous. I want tonight to be perfect, that's all," she said.

"Just relax. Nothing to worry about."

Maggie's first night as a bride turned into her first night as a wife, replete with disappointments and doubts. Their lovemaking was awkward and rushed. He didn't caress her face as lovers did in the movies. He cupped her privates before she was comfortable with it and didn't expect him to maneuver her legs apart and put his whole body between them. His kisses weren't tender any more. They felt desperate. What came next stung a bit and she pulled away, but he kept promising it would all be alright, and he pushed in deeper, and began going in and out, his full body weight pressing against her until he stopped suddenly with a shudder, groaned, and then slid out and rolled off of her, managing to kiss her once before he told her he loved her and fell asleep.

Nothing was as she'd expected. She didn't expect to sleep on a wet sheet. She didn't care for the smell. And he snored. Given a little more gumption, she might have gotten dressed and taken a cab home. Instead, she stayed and told herself she was a wife now and wives have to keep their husbands happy, no matter how uncomfortable it might be.

She'd hardly fallen asleep when it was time to get up and make their way to Union Station. Onboard the train, they had a fine breakfast and Beau regaled her with what she could expect in Gatlinburg. "It's a lovely little hotel on the river," he said. "We can go hiking, shop, take our time. And sleep."

"Sleep," Maggie laughed. "Yes! Sleep!" The night's trepidation slipped away with the passing terrain.

Over their three nights in Tennessee, Maggie and Beau began to find their way to each other, their bodies finding a rhythm, his arms bringing her comfort. By the fourth night, she let him watch her brush her teeth and wash her face. By the fifth night, she let him see her naked, and even let him wash her back as she bathed. On the seventh day, Maggie and Beau set out for home.

Once planted in North Carolina, there were no more fancy dinners or theatre plays or linen jackets. Beau was up and out of the house at dawn and home at six for dinner. He said as soon as she was ready to learn to drive, he'd buy her a car. Until then, she was stuck alone. All day. Every day. In the cottage. In the woods. The journal Dorothy gave her as a wedding present became her confidant. Her only confidant. At some point in every day, she feared her father had been right. At some point in every day, she cried

CHAPTER 16

June 29, 1946. I am awash in questions and almost afraid to ask them. Beau will be back here tomorrow but I want to ask him now. Right this minute! I can't believe what I've found in the cellar. He must know it is all there but why is it there is what I don't understand. Boxes and boxes of the most beautiful things I've ever seen. I live here, but I feel as if I've ventured where I was not supposed to. Why would anyone hide such fine things? Such a mystery it is and here I sit in the cellar, surrounded by all of it, like a child discovering a pirate's loot. All I wanted to do down there was re-arrange things - move one of the shelves closer to the stairs for my pantry. It was just a matter of convenience. But when I took down all the boxes and tools I saw it - a handle in the wall. Stupid me I didn't even think twice. I just moved the shelf and pulled it and the wall opened with a stubborn drag of old hinges. And there it was - crates of all sizes stacked floor to ceiling, trunks, a brass ash hod, china urns, and a hand carved pair of chairs in very bad condition, chewed by mice I suspect. I haven't opened every crate yet. But I have made my way through two cedar trunks and found several elegant beaded dresses, silk scarves, and a fur wrap. It's all very musty, but in amazingly good shape. I have an urge to record it all but see no real purpose to it. I don't know if Beau will be angry or just as surprised as I am. Oh I wish he'd get home! One crate has a full set of china painted with the most intricate pattern I've ever seen. And in one of the trunks was a simple English tea set with four matching cups and saucers. How could anyone pack this away?

When Beau returned home from Greenville, Maggie took her time approaching the subject of her discoveries in the cellar. First, she asked him why he lived such a spare lifestyle. He shrugged. She gathered her nerve to delve deeper, asking if his father hadn't kept anything from the main house. His answer was abrupt and meant one of two things: he was lying to her or he didn't know about the secret room.

"It all burned. Nothing but a pile of ashes left."

"Beau, dear," she said softly, "I need to show you something." She recognized the possibility that if he had no idea of their existence, seeing all those things, if indeed they were from his childhood, could overwhelm him. She took him by the hand and led him outside to the storm cellar steps. She started to open the door when he lifted it for her and latched it to the post. With an expression of puzzlement, he asked what she was up to.

"I found something yesterday, Dear. Something puzzling." At a loss for further explanation, she urged him down the steps, reached around him and switched on the light.

Tears welled in his eyes venturing into the cluttered cubby. He turned and reached out for Maggie, pulling her tight to his chest. "I don't understand," he said. "That's Amanda's trunk. And that one is my mother's. That's Grandmother's tea set. My god! The old ash hod from my bedroom. It came from Holland. You see that handle? The hand-painted tulips on its handle." He knelt to the floor and touched everything within reach.

"Here," he said with some urgency. "Help me get this upstairs." With those words, their unpacking began. Over several days, each crate was carefully opened, contents unwrapped and set out on display. The once stark cottage was soon cluttered with more things than it could comfortably hold. "I'll need to build some shelves up here," he said.

It was as if the presence of the recovered artifacts brought with them permission to remember things Beau had tried to forget. It was through his protracted explanations of nearly every item, that Maggie met her husband again. And, through his explanations, fell in love with him even more deeply.

While Beau was carefully polishing silver in the kitchen with a toothbrush, Maggie rummaged about in one of the cedar chests. She pulled something bundled in black velvet. Its thin black leather cover was worn at the binding and dog-eared at the corners. She opened it and leafed through the tissue thin pages until landing on one filled with handwriting. It was the Kenyon family bible.

"Beau Harrison Kenyon, July 29, 1911, born at 9:12 in the morning," she said gleefully.

Beau stopped wiping the teapot and set it down. He made his way around boxes to Maggie's side. He asked for the bible, which she graciously surrendered. He ran his middle finger slowly down the page, passing over each entry in the list with such concentration, Maggie thought maybe all their souls would materialize right there before them. Reaching the end of the list, two-thirds down the second page, Maggie posed a simple question: "Why does it stop there?"

Beau seemed almost not to have heard her, until finally he responded. "Because that's when everything disappeared."

Maggie didn't know what to make of the comment. "You should keep it up," she said as she stood to go to bed. "It's left to you now to keep up the list."

"Not much more to put there. My father passed in 1940. We married in '45. That's the end of it then, isn't it?" It was a finality that didn't set well with either of them. For Maggie, it was a reminder she desperately wanted children. For Beau, it was a quip derived of deeper wounds having nothing to do with his wife.

Maggie readied herself for bed. As she slipped under the covers, she heard the front door open and Beau's footsteps across the porch. It was some time before he returned. When he got into bed, he took his wife's hand and kissed it, knowing she was still awake waiting on him. "I'll tell you all about it in the morning," he sighed. "Let's just sleep now." His words and touch together concocted the tonic she needed to chase away her anxieties. She soon fell to sleep.

In the morning, no words passed between them beyond the typical. Maggie did not ask about the bible and Beau did nothing to indicate he would broach the subject.

Maggie took the buckwheat starter from the shelf and began making griddlecakes. As she ladled the first thick, well-bubbled batter onto the griddle, Beau came in from the living room, bible in hand. "Looks like a good batch," he said, admiring the height to which the cakes were rising. "Nearly an inch today, I'd say." He retrieved molasses from the cupboard,

"Not quite," she responded with quiet pride.

Beau said most of family history in the bible was recorded before he was born. "It was a gift to my grandfather on his wedding day. Let's see here, Thomas and Matthew. I was so young when they went off to war, don't remember much about them. Except..." He paused, the thought only just that instant coming to him. "Matthew used to take me riding. I remember him hoisting me onto the saddle and climbing up behind me. I think I was probably jumping with him before I was five. Then one day, he was gone, along with Thomas, and neither of them ever came back. They enlisted just after the steeplechase, and died in the Great War. The war to end all wars. Well, I guess that didn't work, did it?

"Let's see, says here Matthew was the first to die, in October, but he went missing in the spring. Somewhere on the Western front as I recall hearing later. The chase went on as usual, no grieving allowed. Says here he died in Holland. Since the body was never returned to us, everyone held out hope that he was still out there somewhere and it was all just some horrible mistake. And I remember Christmas that year. We didn't have one. News came that Thomas was dead, and again, no body to bury. My father declared enough was enough, and held a funeral for both of them at the same time two days before Christmas. I remember seeing my father out in the wooded pasture, all alone, crying. I sat down right where I was and cried, too, for him. Can you imagine? He was the eldest of six children, and outlived all of them and his parents by the time he was thirty.

"It's right here. His baby sister died days after birth when he wasn't much more than a baby himself. Then, when he was seven, his little brother died." Reading down the list, he said little Rudyard was only four years, three months and sixteen days old. "I don't know how he died, what happened to him. Then, he loses his mother when he's around nineteen. And over the course of four years, he loses all three brothers and his father. Somewhere in there, he married my mother and they were all that was left, along with me and my sister."

"You have a sister?"

A darkness slid over Beau. Maggie watched him power his way out of it without answering her question. "Then, there was the flu epidemic of 1918. Ah!" He said, his voice peculiarly chipper for such a dreadful topic. "Mandy and I must have been around seven and eight. The flu hit our mountains in September."

"Mandy?"

"What? My sister. Amanda. I remember one of our stable hands, a Negro man living over on Seventh Street, by the tracks, died within two days of getting sick. When my father heard, he closed our gate. If you wanted to leave, you could go, but there was no coming back in.

"I remember he went into town one last time to stock up on staples - grain for the horses, flour, sugar and a clutch of chickens. He slept out in a tent for a week to be sure he hadn't brought the flu back with him.

"That fall and winter, all of us, staff and family, joined together. We ate together, and worked the tail end of the garden and canned as much as we could possibly can. In that pile of stuff in the other room somewhere are photos of all of us. First thing you'll see right off is a Negro sitting at the main table, right next to my father. Never happened before then, never happened again after.

"Mr. Robinson. Our stable master and trainer. Had one hell of a way with horses and a reputation that brought him offers to go somewhere else every year, come chase week. But he liked it here and stayed. He lived in the rooms in the stable. He had a wife and son somewhere, but I never met them. Well, actually I did meet the son once, the day he dropped off his own son. Left him with Mr. Robinson and never came back. That was a couple years later, after the flu trouble. What was his name? I remember he was only about eight or nine later on, when my mother died, and everyone left." Again, the darkness tried to work its way over Beau, and again, he pushed it away.

"Any way, we all had lots of chores because we were short the stable hand, and the maid lived in town with her family, so she couldn't come out here. My mother helped Ruth with the cooking and cleaning. Ruth was our cook. Wonderful woman. Amanda and I took turns milking the goat and cow every day. I churned butter. Ruth made cheese. My father slaughtered one of that year's calves around Christmas. That was a chore in itself because of all the sausage making and smoking and drying and brining. I never knew there were so many ways you could preserve meat. Ruth was German and made amazing sauerbraten. I don't think there was a crock in the house that wasn't full of meat or pickles. But my parents were determined not to let anything go to waste.

"And there was Harry, the groundskeeper. Lazy as I recall. A bit of a problem but my father straightened him out. I think he'd have left if he had anywhere to go. I remember the first meal we all took together, at the same table, my mother and father, Amanda and me, Mr. Robinson, Ruth and Harry. Harry pitched a fit about eating with a Negro, but decided it was better than no meal at all. That was the deal."

Beau took a sip of cold coffee and Maggie poured some fresh.

"My father. Now, he made it fun. I was so young, and there was no going to school for us, and no going to work for him. He drove into town to the mill and brought out lots of wood. We built a fort in the woods and kept adding to it. He taught me how to build a chair and a table. This table. I built it with him."

Maggie ran her hand across the beautifully grained surface.

"The local paper published once a week. Mr. Carter and his wife wrote and printed it and drove it around to everyone. My father left a note in the box out at the road about opening the Feed store on Tuesdays. No one could come inside, but he'd get them what they needed so long as the stock held out. I wrote a note about our fort. Mr. Carter printed both notes in the paper and soon everyone was leaving news and suddenly we knew all kinds of things, more in some cases than we knew before, about people in town. There was a big headline when the war ended. Then, another wave of flu hit and my father was not going to let us leave until he was certain it was safe. We didn't care. I loved being home.

"We passed eight months together before it was declared safe to leave. School didn't open 'til the next fall. Businesses opened again but people still wore masks all summer in town. It may have been a dark time for most folks, but for our family, it was my favorite year ever.

"We took in a young woman from town that spring. Maripat Buttons. The flu took her folks along with her older sister. I think it was Ruth who arranged it after reading about it in the paper. She'd been alone for two weeks, so Father figured she wasn't a risk and he put her in the room over the kitchen. Ruth moved out to the stone cottage. Out here, but of course it wasn't much more than a place to sleep back then.

"We didn't hold a chase that year. That year, and the hurricane of '22. Only times the chase was canceled." The darkness pushed hard this time, and Beau was hard pressed to fight it back. "Until we stopped having it at all."

"Dear," Maggie interrupted, "What's a chase?"

"What? What's a chase? Ha! It's a horse race all over hell's half acre. It was tradition. Used to hold it here every spring." His animation soon dissipated and he paused. "Just a horse race. They hold something like it over in Tryon now. Nothing like ours, but I hear it draws a lot of people to the area. I've never been to it." He took a sip of coffee, cold again, and Maggie poured the last of the pot for him as he continued talking.

The pancakes and sausage had gone stone cold. On any other day, Maggie would have scolded him. She let it be this time. She sat in stillness, taking care not to sever the tenuous thread between Beau and his past. He talked slowly and generally without animation.

"Maripat was maybe seventeen and tried her best to keep me and Amanda in line. And Ruth taught her to cook. A few years later, Ruth turned sixty and decided to leave us. She moved in with her sister over in Black Mountain. Maripat fell in love with Harry. I thought he was way too old for her but what did I know? They moved in together out here for a while then moved into town. When Maripat started having babies, we had another housekeeper move into the room over the kitchen, but she kept pretty much to herself. Harry stayed on as groundskeeper.

"Somewhere in all that time, Amanda and I grew up. They started sending me away to school when I was fifteen. I spent summers and holidays at home, but the rest of the time I was away, and hated it." He continued with the abbreviated version of the rest of it to get through it as cleanly as possible. "Amanda passed when I was seventeen, then Mother. And I think that was just too much death for my father. Something broke in him. He closed himself off for a very long time. The house burned down. The Depression hit. I don't know how any man survives what my father did."

Beau stopped talking. Maggie could see he was in some distant place.

He didn't tell her that all those people he'd grown so close to were summarily extracted from his life after his mother died. He sanitized it, spared Maggie the truth.

When he finished, Maggie could see there were volumes left unsaid. Yet it was over this uneaten meal that Maggie learned not only about her husband's past, but also about the true meaning of hardship. She quietly stood up to clear the table, but Beau stopped her and ate every bite of his cold breakfast.

The bible was wrapped again in its velvet and placed in a drawer.

Kenyon Family Bible

Thomas Parson Kenyon 1765 - 1823 born in Virginia

1789 Arrives North Carolina with wife
 Martha Pentwater Kenyon
Montgomery Edmond 1795-1860
Weds Temperance Lydia Wood 1820-1821
 mother and child lost to miscarriage
Weds Agnes Claire Shaw 1835 - 1880
Martha Agnes 1836 born Died 1886
Ruth Milicent 1837 born died 1889
Narcissa Patience 1838 dies 2 days old
Parson Rudyard 1850 born - died 1916
Parson Rudyard Kenyon 1880 weds Marie Louise
 Sawyer July 9
Agnes Claire 1880 September 14 - dies 65 yrs
Baker Parson Kenyon August 21, 1883 born Midnight
Melissa Marie Kenyon October 2, 1884 born
 dies 4 days later
Montgomery Sawyer Kenyon February 27, 1885
Rudyard Stewart Kenyon June 14, 1886 born
Rudyard Stewart Kenyon September 30, 1890
 died 4yrs,3 mos,16dys
Thomas Edmond Kenyon January 2, 1882 born
Matthew William Kenyon May 8,1880 born
Marie Louise Kenyon August 10, 1902
 Loving Wife and Mother died 41yrs,3mos,3dys
Monty Kenyon December 28,1908 weds Florence Anne
 Blackburn
Baker Kenyon July 5,1909 weds Suzanna Morgan Swift
Amanda Kenyon November 4,1910 born to Baker and
 Suzanna 11:28 P.M.
Beau Harrison Kenyon July 29,1911 born to Baker and
 Suzanna 9:12 A.M.
Monty Kenyon September 1,1915 died in sawmill
 accident at 30 yrs,10mos,1dy

Parson Kenyon January 28, 1916 died at 65 yrs.
April 6,1917 We are at war.
U.S. declared war on Germany
Thomas and Matthew May 11, 1917 Enlisted
Matthew Kenyon October 1917 our beloved son became a casualty of war in Holland. 24 yrs We have no bones to bury

Thomas Kenyon On a cold December Day 1917 our beloved son became a casualty of war having died of pneumonia in England. 25yrs We have no bones to bury

Sept-March 1918 Spanish Flu - We survived!

July 14, 1946. I don't know how long it will take me to get used to such a huge vegetable garden. Seems like so much work when we can get nearly all we need from the local farmers. I'm still trying to find a place for everything we took up from the cellar. I can't get a good read on him. These things have stirred him in ways I don't understand. I feel I never will. He works the garden. Turning the soil over and over. I think it is not so much for the sake of the vegetables as it is hard labor for his mind and body.

July 19, 1946. The sawmill is hard at work filling contracts. The timber is coming up from South Carolina. I asked why he wasn't cutting any of his own -- he walked me over the stone wall into the big trees, the old-growth where the floor of the woods is just a mat of leaf litter. Then we started into waist high weeds, grasses, and brambles to an area where the trees were much smaller. Then I saw the stumps. For every three young trees, there was a huge stump, some of them three and four feet across. Something about that place made me feel like we were standing in a gaping wound. I will never ask him about cutting Stoneygate trees again.

July 22, 1946. Beau took me up Glassy Mountain and we met a man on the way up. He didn't say much but that there was clear viewing today. He looked very familiar to me but for the life of me, I couldn't place him. Beau said it was a piece of luck running into him -- teased me for not recognizing another Chicago transplant like I would know everyone in the city. He laughed at me good for not recognizing Carl Sandburg. He was right. I'm a teacher. I've taught his poetry in my class!

July 25, 1946. I have made it a rule to walk Glassy each week. I enjoy walking past the Sandburg's goat barn on my way. I am always tempted to introduce myself when I see someone, but the fact that no one ever waves at me – well I just leave them to what they're doing. Alone with the mountain I find myself entirely enthralled by it. I am beginning to know certain bends and stones and roots so I anticipate their appearance so many steps ahead. I have seen fox, and birds, and rabbits. And all this on the way to the top, which some might surmise is the purpose or destination of the trek. It isn't, although the air and clear view from there does give one's mind room to stretch. I see more than ever why Beau won't harvest this forest. This place becomes a part of you. Cutting into it would be like cutting into your own flesh.

CHAPTER 17

A few days after getting confirmation the book package arrived in New York, Meg received two unexpected e-mails. "Just saw the promotion slicks," one read. "Why didn't you tell me this was the last we'd see of Emerson? I had no idea. Call me when you come up and we'll drink ourselves stupid - Elaine."

Meg read it again, and again, hit reply, and began typing. Her throat tightened as she punched at the keyboard. "What are you talking about? This isn't the end of any…" It hit her hard that something was very wrong and everyone knew but her. She called her editor. Voice mail. She called her agent. Voice mail. She called Elaine. Voice mail. Then her agent's e-mail arrived.

"I have some news," it read. "Bit of a casualty to report," it continued. Harry was British and Meg couldn't read his email without hearing his accent. Yet even a charming accent couldn't soften this blow. "Emerson has seen his last little adventure. So sorry, deary. I fought for him, but these new people have their minds set. Nothing to be done." Harry explained very graciously that the book just finished was not to be the next in the series, but the last. It was delicately justified as a marketing strategy by the conglomerate that just purchased the publishing house that printed all her books. Unbeknownst to her, they'd canceled her contract. They were planning to introduce a boxed set at the Booksellers trade show in San Francisco on Memorial Day weekend.

"You'll be there, won't you? Need you to smile brightly and sign a few hundred posters for the book buyers. Please don't kill me, deary. I'm just the messenger."

She sent a cryptic reply. "I guess I have no more need of Monet."

The third email was more bad news. "Can't make it to New York. Too much going on here. -Vince."

Meg felt a sharp jab in her chest and gripped her breastbone. It hurt to breathe. She slowly got up from her chair and made her way to the porch, her chest wincing, the pain growing with every inhalation. She sat for a minute, hoping it would pass. It didn't. The pain spread to her neck and jaw. "Shit," she said aloud. "Just breathe, Megs, just breathe." She looked out over the pasture and tried to focus on something peaceful. A breeze stirred some leaves out at the footbridge and swept them away. She imagined herself being carried away with them. She watched a particular leaf fly up and around out of sight. The breeze dissipated, and all was still again. The pain also diminished, and finally stopped. It had been a year or more since her last panic attack.

"What the hell am I doing here?" she yelled so loud it hurt her throat. Nothing stirred. The trees didn't rustle. The crazy woman on the porch made no impact on them.

She stormed inside, pulled her duffel out from under the bed, and began to pull clothes out of drawers. She was about to flee, until it hit her she had nowhere to go. Her place in Chicago was sublet, and if she left, she'd lose the inheritance. Stoneygate had become her prison.

She pulled a cigarette from Maggie's old pack and went back to the porch, lit up with shaky hands, and took a long deep drag. She wanted to feel the hot smoke penetrate and burn every air sack to the bottom of her lungs. She needed to feel a pain she could identify, any pain that could overwrite the anger. Her fists formed themselves, tight and fast, the cigarette broke between white knuckles. She smashed it on the floorboards with her shoe.

She yanked a jacket from a hook and headed out to the pasture with long urgent strides. Her hamstrings began to sting, but it wasn't enough. She picked up the pace and began to run across the uneven ground, dodging rocks and ruts, and cow pies. She leapt over a log, lost footing, and went down, smashing her forearm on a stone. In an instant, she was back on her feet, running. Her arm throbbed.

By the time she reached the road, a fog bank was rolling in, offering a strange sense of refuge. Hidden in its shroud, Meg slowed her pace, rubbed her arm, and caught her breath, yet the anger persisted with every step.

She thought about New York, how it would be like going back into work after being fired. "They can send the fucking proofs to me," she muttered.

Walking the dirt road, her mind wandered. With the abrupt end of the series came an end to her day-to-day structure. What others perceived as lack of organization in Meg's life was actually a lack of understanding for the way she worked. She had a free-formed system in which every day held some form of work, though not always recognizable as such. Even a trip to the Art Institute was work related. After painting the same rabbits more than a hundred times over the course of a dozen books, she often looked to the masters to recharge her batteries. Her favorite was Monet's series of haystacks. Filling an entire wall in the impressionist gallery, the paintings were of the same haystack painted at different times of day, different seasons, each the same composition, eliciting very different esthetics. She could sit for the better part of an afternoon studying them.

Meg arrived at the end of the road, landing at a two-lane she'd never seen before. She looked across to the woods, seeking an opening to Glassy Mountain, muttering to herself about the unlikelihood of the old path still being there. She crossed and wandered a bit eastward until she found a narrow service drive. No more than twenty yards in, she came across a path marked with a small National Historic Site plaque: Carl Sandburg's Home. Connemara Farm Goat Dairy.

As she walked along the trail, past the fenced pastures and goat barns, the synchronicity of her commonalities with Sandburg put her in an even deeper daze. She and Sandburg had both lived in Chicago. They were both writers. She had a friend on the other side of Lake Michigan who lived four houses from Sandburg's old Michigan home, and now she lived next to his North Carolina home. There had to be some purpose behind the coincidence, something she was supposed to glean from it.

Engrossed in these thoughts, she strode by a trio of hikers emerging from the mist. She noticed them all look at her queerly and it occurred to her that perhaps her preoccupations had become a way of life. She had become one of those peculiar people so absorbed in conversation with themselves that other people can't help but stare.

People often gave her a hard time about her attention span, or lack of one. She sometimes lost her train of thought mid-sentence ,and missed half of what was said to her. They were correct in that it was an attention issue, but not for lack of it. It was that she was entirely preoccupied with her work. The creative process of developing story lines and elements of composition didn't stop on command. In the beginning, she tried to push the work to the back of her mind and really try to live in the moment out of common courtesy for friends. Eventually, she realigned her priorities and gave the creative flow free reign.

The trail grew steep and she slowed her pace to accommodate. She wondered what her life would look like without Emerson. To that point, she was stepping from one project into the next. For months at a time, she would rise at six, work intensely for five or six hours and cruise the rest of the day. She went to matinees, took walks and visited bookstores to scope out the competition. It was a system that worked for her for the eight years since the inception of the Emerson series. One book followed another with a guarantee of publication and income. With that security gone, there were suddenly too many questions as to what she was going to do in Laurel County without a plan. Without her work. Without her life.

Suddenly, she found herself at the summit and her angst vaporized like the fog. The air was crisp, drenched in sunshine. For as far as Meg could see, there were hills rolling out of misty valleys under a pale blue sky. Once again, seduced by the mountain's sweet narcotic, Meg felt instinctively that her world was most certainly fine. There was nothing to worry about. She drank in the clarity with deep cleansing breaths before descending again into fog and her malaise.

When she returned to the cottage, she looked on the shelves for anything by Carl Sandburg. Finding one, she read a quote scrawled on the inside front cover.

"It is necessary now and then for a man to go away by himself and experience loneliness; to sit on a rock in the forest and to ask of himself, 'Who am I, and where have I been, and where am I going?' … If one is not careful, one allows diversions to take up one's time - the stuff of life. - Carl Sandburg from a letter to Ralph McGill."

Meg put the book back, and went to the fridge. She spent the rest of the evening with a roll of cookie dough and a bottle of chardonnay, neither of which was a curative for her loneliness, but it helped kill the time.

Her third glass of wine brought her life into rather cruel perspective. She missed Emerson. He'd been her constant companion, always on her mind, living out his little life, finding trouble and wriggling his way out of it. His moods, his friends, his calamities, occupied most of her waking hours, and often followed her into dreams. Everything she imagined for Emerson came true, over and over again, every time someone read his books. Publishing made him real. It was then she realized that thinking about him, thinking about his next adventure, was pointless. It was almost as if her dear pal had died, and she was left behind, able only to imagine what the rest of his life would have been. It was a goodbye that came too quickly. She wasn't ready. She downed another glass of wine.

She picked up the phone at midnight to call Vince, but the line was dead. If Maggie was right, and things always happen for a reason, it was no accident she couldn't call out.

She turned out the light and sprawled on the bed. The full moon through the trees illuminated the room and cast dancing shadows on the bookcase. The delicate fingers of one particular branch bounced in such a way it looked as if it was trying to reach for something on the top shelf, a photograph set off like a cameo on black velvet ribbon. Meg took notice of a large flat book under the photograph. Climbing on a chair to reach it, she pulled it down and took it to bed.

She ran her fingers slowly over the thick tooling of the leather cover. In the moonlight she could easily make out the subtle pattern of horse heads and saddles. She opened it and found pages filled with photographs, some held in place with corner tabs, others just tucked in the binding. They were pictures of the old house and stable, horses, and posed group shots. She was about to turn the light on but decided instead to save further visitation for another time. She was wine weary. As she closed the book and lifted it over to the chair, a dog-eared photo fell to the quilt. It was of two women in riding clothes, one quite young and the other possibly her mother. Both were beautiful, with fine features and radiant smiles. Meg liked the 1920's feel of the photo and propped it on her nightstand where it would stay all summer. She heard the owl whoot somewhere off in the woods as she drifted off to sleep.

CHAPTER 18

Meg first noticed the sign for Stonemount when it was just a printout taped to an office window downtown. Now, it was a three-foot wide shingle hung from an ornate iron support ten feet above the sidewalk. It was carefully crafted with Albrecht Dürer style drawings of small woodland animals. The primary text was an elegant black lacquer with gold bevels: Stonemount. Below it, in a much smaller nondescript font with letter spacing too wide to make sense to anyone but the graphic artist who designed it, were the words "Golf Club and Home Sites". Meg went in.

The walls were covered with aerial views of Stoneygate overlaid with plans for a golf course. She calculated that her cottage sat midway on the third fairway. The wooded pasture was mostly cleared for two other fairways. She walked to the detailed diorama of the project. Current hills were leveled. Flat land was sculpted into various elevations to accommodate not only the design of the golf course, but to allow views of it from every home site – all one hundred of them. On easels throughout the room were architectural renderings of six house designs. The smallest house - a two-bedroom, two-and-a-half bath with granite counters and marble entry – started at

$250,000. There were only three of those. The rest ranged from $450,000 up to $700,000.

As she leafed through a sales package, a woman in her early fifties approached. Her hair was cut in a flat angular style, her make-up was perfect right down to the deep salmon colored lipstick. She was on the plump side, with a deep tan. Tawny Gale introduced herself and began to explain the project.

"The lots that are available now are over here." She pointed to a singular row of bright pink lots adjacent to Stoneygate land.

"You do realize who I am, don't you," asked Meg.

"Of course," Tawny replied with the disingenuous congeniality. "I'd love to show you around the area. Ever been to Lake Lure?"

Meg accepted the offer out of blatant curiosity. They climbed into Tawny's bright red Range Rover and headed out of town. Tawny never once stopped smiling as she cheerily bubbled on with colorful tidbits of useless information. It was a beauty queen talent, Meg thought, to be able to use one's facial muscles in such a manner. Meg found herself smiling in some weird automatic response until her cheeks began to ache.

They drove over hills covered in blooming apple orchards, their well-ordered rows delineating the rise and fall of the terrain. Nothing Tawny rattled on about interested Meg. The landscape, on the other hand, captivated her until Tawny reached behind her, the car swerving with the effort, and retrieved a Stonemount packet and handed it to her. Meg leafed through the pages, estimating in her head the cost of the printing. The paper was lustrous, heavy and dull, photos highlighted with spot varnishes. "Somebody seems to have spent a lot of money on something that's only speculation."

Tawny's response was unexpected. "Really, Meg," she said. "Friend to friend? It's a done deal. The lawyers have it sewn up."

"And how is that?" Meg asked.

Tawny did not flinch. "The trust is ironclad. Your Maggie was only allowed the land until her passing. Then, it reverts to the original trustees. Hasn't anyone explained that to you?"

Meg stared out the window. No one had put it to her in such definitive terms.

"Our investors are highly motivated."

Tawny turned into a narrow ravine of hairpin turns and steep cliffs. Occasionally, a glimpse of small coves could be seen, water glinting in the sun. Eventually they pulled in front of a rather largish English Tudor cottage. It was surrounded by old-growth trees through which could be seen a bit of water below. Tawny handed Meg a key. "Go take a look," she cooed.

The house was stunning with a view through to the full length of Lake Lure. It was a huge, long lake, notched with coves, lined with boathouses, docks and stairs leading up through dense woods to homes hidden deep within the trees. Meg followed Tawny around the house and down a flagstone stairway to a boathouse nestled into a small cove.

"There are three acres with this property," Tawny said. "Prime lake property. It's yours," she added as innocuously as possible. "Free and clear. All you have to do is relinquish your claim and let the Adler's take possession."

"This is worth two million dollars?" Meg said doubtfully.

"Two million? Whoever told you Stoneygate was worth all that? This land here, acreage on Lake Lure, with this view, even without the house, it's worth at least two mil."

Meg looked without expression at Tawny, who was careful not to make eye contact, her gaze resting admiringly to the far reaches of the lake.

"So, there you have it!" Tawny said as she bounced around and headed back up the steps to the house. "You'll get used to all the stairs. We all do. My own place has fifty-seven . . ."

"I don't understand. I don't yet have full legal right to Stoneygate yet, so, if . . ."

"We'll take care of all that." Tawny's flat delivery of those six words carried a definitive certainty. "Every day we can't build is a day we lose money." She turned and looked at Meg without a hint of a smile.

"And if I don't agree?" Meg asked.

Tawney turned and continued her climb. "Oh, I think you will. One way or another, you'll come to the right decision."

Getting back into the car, Tawny added one more salvo. "Wait too long, and you'll end up with nothing."

The offer suddenly resonated as a threat.

"What were you doing with the vulture yesterday?" Ford's edgy question met Meg as she stepped out to her porch with her morning coffee.

"Well, good morning to you, too," she grumbled. "Want some coffee?" He threw out his gas station coffee and walked past her inside to get fresh. Half way through the living room, he stopped and smiled. "Sorry," he said to a clearly annoyed Meg. "Old habits. I'm used to coming and going, and, well . . ."

"Go ahead," she said. "You know where everything is." As he disappeared into the kitchen, she asked what vulture he was referring to. Tossing his paper cup, he took a mug off the shelf, poured his coffee, and scoped out the kitchen. Nothing was out of place. It was either a good sign or a bad one. He couldn't tell yet. "You know who I'm talking about," he hollered out. "Tawny Gale. I saw you in Big Red."

He returned to the porch and found Meg curled up in the wicker chair, looking very at home. "Tawny's Range Rover," he said, taking a sip of steaming coffee.

"Yeah. So? What's the problem?" Her tone was dismissive.

"What did she say to you?" His tone was assertive.

"What do you mean? Aside from a thinly veiled threat?" Meg looked up at him under arched brows. "They want this land. Badly."

"They've been after Maggie to sell for the past four years," Ford explained. "You should know who you're dealing with."

"Who says I'm dealing with anybody?" Meg grumbled.

"When she wouldn't sell, they did a little digging, found the old trust, and went after Adlers. You're not up against Adlers. They're pawns. You're up against some big money. People who don't take no for an answer. They have a reputation."

"So, this was all in place before Maggie ever died."

"Yeah," he said with a tilt of his head, eyes looking squarely at hers. "You know," he informed her, his gaze shifting out to the pasture, "she's not even supposed to be approaching you."

"I guess I sort of approached her."

Ford winced.

"Ya know," she continued, mimicking him, "you seem to know an awful lot about all this. Why is that?" The edge in her voice grew sharper. "She made me an offer. I bail out of this fight, relinquish my interest to the Adlers, and I get a house on Lake Lure."

Ford heaved a heavy sigh, his view taking in all that lay before him: Wooded pasture, cows, forest, Glassy Mountain. "Big house? Tudor? A couple acres?"

"Three acres."

"It's a foreclosure. Boathouse is about to cave in. Footings are rotted. Pipes broke two years ago. Black mold. Wiring needs to be replaced. Has termite damage. And they're presuming the trust is still in effect, that Adlers have rightful ownership. That, my friend, is still up in the air. It isn't yours to do anything with but enjoy until the court decides."

Meg sunk a little deeper into the chair.

"If all this does become yours, remember they have to get past me first. First right of refusal."

"You?" Meg laughed. "You get first dibs?" She looked at his beat-up truck and shook her head.

Ford's face took on a hard, cold countenance.

His arrogance ticked her off. "Hey," Meg said. "I didn't ask for this land, the responsibility of it. Do I want to see it turned into a housing development? Of course not. But it isn't my fight."

"Yes, it is. Now, it is."

"I don't want it to be my fight." She glared at him as if it was somehow his fault. "My life is in Chicago. My home, my friends. My life. This place is a fond childhood memory to me. Do you have any idea what it's like trying to preserve a memory? It can't be done."

"Then why did she leave it to you?" He glared at her as if it was all her fault.

"Well. That's the question now, isn't it? I don't know."

Ford looked again to the pasture and took a draw of coffee, rolling it around in his mouth.

"Careful with that cup," Meg said. "It's chipped. I should toss it out." Ford just grunted. He remembered the day he broke it, knocking it off the fence post at the tennis court after Maggie told him not to put it there. It landed mostly in the grass but was chipped none the less and Maggie let out a big 'I told you so!' from the porch.

"Your coffee's better than Maggie's," he said.

"Don't do that," she snapped.

"Do what?"

"Don't be nice to me." She shifted in the wicker chair and drew her legs up underneath her.

He turned and shot her a glance of incredulity. "It's just a comment. Why? Are there rules?"

"Of course there are," she sighed, exasperated. "You can't barge over here first thing in the morning accusing me of some shit and then suddenly be decent. I don't know how to do that, the going back and forth crap." She got up and went into the house.

He stood in the doorway and hollered to her. "That's some mouth you got on you. And what is it I am supposedly accusing you of?"

"I don't know. What *are* you accusing me of?" she sniped as she returned, pouring him more coffee. "And what *is* your problem with whatever I did yesterday that you had no business bothering with anyway?" She was almost waving the percolator at him.

He took a fresh sip and let her stew for a minute. "Are you always this cranky in the morning?"

Her jaw dropped. "When I'm faced with the likes of you before my first cup of coffee, yeah, I guess I am." She forced a demure little smile. "Normally, I'm as tame as a buttercup."

"Right," he said in a tone that did not convey any particular intent. "Well, here it is. *IF* the will is binding," he lectured, "and *IF* you decide to sell, I get first right of refusal. That's my interest in your activities."

"O.K. Yeah. Like you could get your hands on that kind of money. I mean, two million dollars is a hell of a lot of yard work." There was something ever so slight in her expression that indicated her words had regrettably slipped past the filter between her brain and her mouth.

He took a deep breath in search of self-restraint. "What would you do with that kind of money?"

She mumbled that he wouldn't understand money like that and he grinned.

"What's so funny?" she snapped.

"Meg, you are an award-winning author. You need more money? Go make it. Get back to work on another book. It will mean a hell of a lot more to you than any money you make off this land."

"So, again," she said with eyebrows lifted. "Why is it that you seem to know so much about my business, Ford?"

That was it. Anything more would be a waste of breath. "I have first right of refusal," he reminded her, stepping off the porch. "I'd hate to see what happens to you the day you drive by here and see the bulldozers tearing it all apart." He drank his last swallow and put the empty cup on the floorboards. "And you shouldn't take any less than four."

She called out as he walked away. "It isn't going to matter much if the Adler cousins win out anyway, now will it? I'll have no choice. Tawny made it perfectly clear about that."

He stopped without turning around, said nothing, and left.

Over Memorial Day, Meg headed out to San Francisco for the American Book Sellers Association's Book Expo to promote the upcoming book. From her fourth floor balcony, San Francisco looked like a beautiful sea creature, lights undulating in and out of hills and valleys, reaching out to the sea's edge. She imagined it about to slip back into the water and disappear.

She felt askew. Someone was supposed to be waiting for her phone call to hear she'd arrived safely and tell her about things at home; the call where someone said they missed her. She left a voice mail for Vince without expectation of response. There was such a distance between them, emotional and physical, she felt very much like a single entity, the emptiness of which reminded her of the hollow tree trunk by the stream near the cottage. She wondered how it came to be that way. Was it a gradual process of decay for the tree or something catastrophic? The certainty was that it would never again be whole.

A stack of invitations awaited her review; obligatory hospitality suites demanding her attendance; one for small booksellers, two for big boxes, and one for the honchos at the new house that just canned her. Her anticipation of a difficult few days was nothing compared to the reality. Nearly every exchange was excruciating. At one point, she had to explain who she was to the CEO of the new publishing house. Later, she found herself wiping the tears of an emotional owner of a little bookstore in Monterey, distraught over the end of Emerson. "It's just like he died!" the woman sobbed. The condolences from industry insiders for her getting dumped were intolerable. There were empty promises from publishers feigning interest in picking up her contract. One book buyer in particular stood face to face with Meg, somehow compelled to tell her Emerson had run his course, citing lagging sales. The man moved on, hands folded behind him, nose high as if sniffing out his next victim. His assistant stumbled after him, schlepping totes of free books, gismos, and posters.

After three days in hell, Meg found herself dozing in her seat somewhere over the Plain States. In a dream, she struggled to get her bearings. She couldn't get the picture of home right in her head. Something told her it wasn't her kitchen in Chicago but she couldn't see deep enough into the fog to make out an image of anything else. A jolt of turbulence woke her. Relief settled in as the cottage and grounds came into focus in her mind. It's home for now, she thought, and was deeply comforted by the anticipation of crawling under the sheets that night with the door open so the morning bird songs could wake her to a quiet day alone. Her thoughts lingered on the photograph by her bedside, the image of the two women, wondering who they were.

CHAPTER 19

In February of 1928, Beau sat on his bed at boarding school studying for a history examination. His roommate came in and tossed a letter on his papers. It was from Amanda.

> Dear Beau, I need to see you. Please come right away. It's the big yellow house across from the grocery on Hawthorn. I'll explain when you get here. I've made such a mistake and I'm terribly afraid. All my love, Amanda

It took Beau two days to get on a train to Raleigh. Even though her letter sounded urgent, he knew his sister had a way of making a thing more dramatic than it was. She had been too ill over the holidays to come home but she'd written since that she was fine.

From the train station, he asked directions to the school and made his way there. It was a bright February day and somewhat warmer than normal. He walked with easy strides, his coat open. Finding the school, he looked for Hawthorn Street and finally asked directions. Several people later, he found someone who knew. "You're a long way from there, kid," said the man. "You need to go clear cross town, a good twenty blocks from here. You stay on Third till you hit Townline, cut east a few blocks, then head north again. You'll run smack into it."

For reasons Beau didn't quite understand, he started to run without even thanking the man. He darted his way through crowds of pedestrians on the sidewalk and dodged cars at intersections. Beau wondered why Amanda was in a boarding house so far from classes. The crowds thinned and the buildings grew less commercial and more industrial. Out of breath, he slowed to a jog through a neighborhood of small ramshackle houses. A few blocks further, the houses grew larger and were better maintained. Eventually, he came to a small market and went in. Trying to catch his breath, he asked the woman at the counter if she knew where 125 Hawthorn was.

"And what would you be wanting with that place?" she said sternly.

"It's a long way from the school," he said, "so I'm thinking I'm really lost."

The woman's bewildered expression begged for further explanation.

"My sister lives there," he quickly added.

"Ah, I see," she said sadly. "You'll find it across the street, then. That big yellow house over there. With the big yard."

As the boy shot out of the door, her chubby-cheeked husband stepped to her side. "There's a story behind those eyes," he said.

The shingle at the gate didn't mean much to Beau. HAWTHORN HOUSE. HOME FOR WOMEN. He entered through the front door and asked for Amanda Kenyon. Mistaken by the housemaid for someone else, he was deposited in the parlor to wait. From there, he saw an office where a couple sat with their back to him, listening to a man behind a large desk speaking in hushed tones. As the matron of the house approached, she closed the office door and took a good look at Beau. "You're not here from Sheffield's, are you, son?"

"No, ma'am. Never said I was." The house matron glared at the maid and told her to leave the room with a simple shift of her eyes.

"I'm looking for Amanda Kenyon," Beau said.

"And why would you be doing that?" said the matron, direct but not stern.

"She's my sister. She wrote to me to come. Here I am."

The house matron puzzled over her next words. "I'm sorry son, she passed this morning."

"What do you mean? She passed." He didn't understand at all.

"Mr. Kenyon, your sister passed away this morning. She's gone."

"I don't believe you. Why? How?" The denial would not let the truth reach his heart. "I want to see her. I came here to see her!"

"I'm sorry, but that would not be a good idea."

"That's it? Not a good idea?"

"Yes. It is not a good idea."

Tears welled in his eyes. "Please," he begged quietly.

With great reluctance, the matron walked Beau down a back hallway into an altogether different area with tile floors and white walls. It looked to him more like a hospital than a house, sterile, except for the dark red, almost black drops on the floor. The matron's footsteps snapped against the tile. There were four rooms on either side, each with a bed and a table. As they approached, a man in a white coat closed the door to one of the rooms.

Arriving at the end of the hall, they stopped at a door. The house matron stood erect, chin high, jaw set, and knocked with a firm fist. A middle-aged black woman emerged, her white apron stained with blood, some old, some fresh. She had a rung-out rag in her hand. "We're coming through," the matron said curtly.

"Kinda young for an undertaker, ain't he?" asked the woman.

"I'm not . . ." Beau stuttered.

"That will be enough, Anna May," the matron scolded as she ushered Beau through.

The heavy metallic smell of blood coated his nostrils, seeping into his mouth and lungs. He saw the high metal table, and red stained sheets, the tray of bloody surgical instruments, and wads of blood-soaked cotton. The house matron unlatched a door on the other side of the room. "In here," she directed him.

Beau hesitated.

"You're sure?" asked the woman.

"Yes." He stepped through the half-open door into a storeroom of sorts with shelves of boxes, a couple wheelchairs, and a gurney with a body draped with a large white sheet, a body too big to be Amanda, and for a moment, he believed there had been a mistake.

The door latched shut behind him.

He turned quickly.

The woman went to the gurney and drew the sheet slowly from Amanda's face.

A sound surged within Beau from far in the distance, growing louder and louder until it filled his head with the deafening pounding of a single drum. He stared, transfixed, at her face, the colorless hue of death. He could not process what was happening. What lay on that table was a counterfeit sister, her body like the shell of a cicada clinging to the bark of a tree. His breathing became strained, his lungs cramped. He found her hand and touched it hoping for something familiar, but instead, felt the cold reality of cadaver. A door slammed shut in his mind and his stomach rolled over. He bolted out the side door, through the yard, pushed through the fence gate, and ended up in the alley, vomiting and sobbing. He glanced beyond the row of garages and saw a couple walking down the sidewalk. They seemed very happy. He hated them.

Beau took a room in a boarding house by the train station. He showed up at the loading dock before sunrise, waiting on one particular westbound train, the one he would know by its cargo, and spent the day there until the last train pulled away. The weather turned cold and his coat was too thin to offer much warmth.

One of the workers, a lanky man with a quick smile, asked him what he was waiting for. Without explanation, Beau said he was waiting for his sister. The man asked if he was hungry and offered him a sandwich. Beau tried to refuse the kindness, but the man gave it to him anyway, then left him alone. Beau wolfed it down.

The next day, the man saw Beau sitting in the cold on the bench again and called out to him. "I told my wife about this kid hanging around the docks, and she decided to take pity on you. Here," he said holding up a sack. "It's pot roast sandwich. We had it last night. She makes a real mean pot roast."

Beau's stomach got the better of him, and he climbed up onto the loading dock.

"What's your name, kid?"

"Beau Kenyon" He took a huge bite and thanked the man with his mouth full. "I mean, thank your wife. This is good."

"Enjoy, kid." A bell rang from street side and the man said he had to get back to work. "Hey," he said. "My name is Max, in case you care." He chuckled and made his way up front for a delivery.

Max inspected the bill of lading he was handed by his boss. "Sheffield's Funeral Parlor," he said out loud. "Oh, man. I hate these. Sending a body home to rest and all those people waitin' and sobbin'." Both men looked at the casket. "I know they're in there dead and all," said Max, "but don't it just strike you as a lonesome trip? On that train in that box all cold and alone?" He read the rest of the paperwork and sighed, his jovial nature evaporating. He went to the dock and rested his hand on Beau's shoulder.

"Son, I believe your sister has arrived."

CHAPTER 20

Beau sat alone on a half empty train, his head lobbing slightly with the rhythm of the tracks, his hands resting limp in his lap. His sister, his best friend, was dead for reasons beyond his understanding. He tortured himself for not having asked how she died. There was an assumption of surgery, but why? What was wrong with her? How sick had she been when he ignored her plea to come to her. His unanswered questions felt like they'd eat him alive.

Thoughts of Amanda washed over him until she flooded his mind and spilled out through his eyes as thick tears. He struggled to erase the last visage of her on the table and to remember instead her smile and how beautiful it was. He marveled to himself how her laugh always had that giggle that trailed off at the end. He tried so hard to hear it in his head, but like a silent movie, he couldn't, making her absence vividly real.

Beau and Amanda, born barely a year apart, had features so similar people mistook them for twins. The first time their mother cut Amanda's hair, Beau cried so long that Amanda promised him she'd never let anyone cut it again. Her mane, as he referred to it, had grown half way to her waist. She was lean and athletic. She looked regal on horseback and could ride any jumper in the stable. Of all the memories he could conjure, he was stuck on one particular day: the day before she left for school.

They were about to go off to separate boarding schools and they'd spent the afternoon horsing around like eight-year-olds in the pool, just the two of them. The pool was out by the rose garden on the edge of the big lawn, protected on one side by boxwood bushes, on the other by woods. The stream rattled thru a furrow a few yards away. There had been rain that week, and the water was running high and fast around the bend right there. He remembered lying on warm concrete, listening to it, and watching Amanda on her back, eyes closed. There was a breeze up high in the oaks and it made the leaf shadows dance across her face and body. A smile curled her mouth. She told him to stop staring at her.

A jerk brought him back to the train, and he pulled his knapsack up closer to fend off the chill. He stared out the window, thinking about a fragment of an argument he'd overheard between their parents. Amanda had never gone away to school before, and their father fought the decision, but Mother insisted she go. Either by plan or bad timing, Baker went on an errand to Saluda and didn't get back in time to go the station to see Amanda off. Beau and Mother put her on the train. Amanda smiled at them through the window, but the forced nature of it bothered Beau for weeks afterward.

Snow flurries began to obscure the view out his train window. They were still on the flatlands of the Piedmont, an hour or more away from the foothills of the Blue Ridge. A few rows up, a woman held a tiny infant that had been crying from the first jolt out of the station. Nothing the woman did could quiet it. She checked its diaper. She tried to give it a bottle. The baby exercised newborn lungs, needing something she didn't seem capable of offering. Someone called out to "Feed the tike!" and the mother, too, began to cry. A matronly woman strode down the aisle and offered her assistance. The baby's father told her to mind her own business. On her way back to her seat Beau heard the woman muttering "There ought to be a law..." The father lit a cigarette and stepped out of the cabin.

The young mother tried walking the aisle with the infant, bouncing it not altogether gently in her arms, tears flowing down her face. The jostling of the train made her steps tentative, and she sat down across from Beau. The baby continued to wail.

Beau couldn't take his eyes off the woman and the infant, both of them suffering similar estrangement.

She saw this teenage boy, his stare so intent on her, looking so despondent. "Are you alright?" she asked him. "You look so sad."

"You should see yourself," he quipped. It brought a slight smile to her face.

"I don't know what I'm doing," she confessed in quiet desperation.

"I can see that," Beau said. He reached out and opened the blanket enough to see the baby's face, squished with a refreshed wave of sobs. "Would you look at that hair," he teased. "Could it be any redder?"

"Like mother, like son," said the young woman smiling, her strawberry red hair tied up in a bun.

He reached out, then thought better of it and withdrew. "Please," she said. "I don't mind," and she put the baby tenderly in his arms. Beau's hands cradled every inch of its body in sanctuary. As he murmured something in low gentle tones, the staccato sobs lessened to little puffs and whimpers, and soon stopped. He'd fallen asleep.

When a tear welled in Beau's eyes, he handed the sleeping baby back. He wiped his face with his sleeve.

"His name is Jeffrey. Jeffrey Mercer," she said quietly. "I'm Sara."

"You're not from the Carolinas," Beau whispered. "Your accent. Northern. Where are you headed?" Sara looked over her shoulder to the back, maybe to see if her husband was watching. There was no one there. "We're heading over to the foothills, a small town on the Green River. My husband knows people there. Came from Indiana originally."

"I'm from Flat Rock. It's the most beautiful place on earth. It's a ways from the Green, over a couple of ridges. If you're ever over that way, you be sure to look me up. My name is Beau Kenyon."

"Nice to meet you, Beau. My name is Sara. Well, you know that now, don't you, and my husband is Errol." About then, Errol returned, visibly relieved to find the baby sleeping.

"Who are you, boy?" Errol sniped. Sara made introductions and excused herself. She went back to their seat to settle in with the baby. Errol pulled a shiny silver flask from his pocket, took a long draw, and offered it to Beau, who refused it. "Ever had good whiskey, boy?" It was the height of prohibition. Beau was cautious.

"Can't say as I have, no sir," he lied.

"So here," Errol insisted. "Plenty more where this came from." Beau took a polite sip. It was harsh and hot, not at all like the smooth, warm bourbon from his father's liquor cabinet.

Over the next hour, in spite of the more than fifteen-year difference in their ages, Errol engaged Beau in conversation, asking all about school and his friends and the people back home. Beau gave him straight answers without embellishments. He didn't know what to make of the false familiarity of the man, but found him a good diversion.

"So, who is it you know over in Saluda?" Beau asked. "We may know some of the same folks." Errol explained he was going to connect with some "friends of an acquaintance" but didn't offer any names. "I've been working up in Indianapolis, but my associates and I sort of had a bit of a falling out," Errol said with a sneer. "Nothing serious," he explained vaguely, "but it was time to move on to new territory." He boasted about being well-connected and was looking for just the right people to get set up with in the South.

"How long have you been married to Sara?" Beau asked.

"Well now, I was in business with her daddy up in Indiana. Her daddy and his brother was all she had, and now I'm all she has." Errol's face changed demeanor for an instant into something grim, then seemed to pretend sympathy. "Poor thing. Her daddy and uncle died." He shook his head. "Tough times we live in, son. Some tough times."

Errol was careful not to betray the truth about the day the men died, when he had them pull off the road every twenty minutes so he could shit in the woods thanks to some bad sausage he had for breakfast. That's where he was when a truck pulled up and three men got out. Errol hid when those men shot Sara's daddy and uncle with a spray of bullets and left them in the middle of the road, puddling in blood. Errol went home and told Sara men would find her and kill her, too. She took all her father's money, sold the house to a neighbor for a fraction what it was worth, packed up what she could carry, and hit the road with Errol. She married him first day out, believing he would keep her safe. All he wanted was the money and an air of legitimacy made all the better with an infant in tow.

The train started to slow as they approached the station. Beau said it was his stop. "Maybe we could do each other some good," Errol suggested. "Never know, son," he said with a cockeyed grin. "You can always do with a bit of cash from time to time, eh? Maybe we could come to some mutually beneficial arrangement. Maybe you could introduce me around some time, over in your neck of the woods." He slapped Beau's back as they parted company.

Beau made his way to the back of the passenger cars where the porters were exiting and walked off among them. He worked his way around to the side of the station, waiting silently in a recess of the brickwork, out of sight, watching the loading dock. There was a bite to the air, and he turned his collar up against it. He watched the boxcar door slide open with a grinding thunk.

A couple stood together on the freight dock, stoop-shouldered, looking somehow impervious to the cold. Beau watched them in their long black coats, waiting. The man watched the workers in the boxcar. The woman bowed her head, her face momentarily nestled in the deep fur of her collar. When she looked up, her knees gave way and the man caught her by the shoulders before she collapsed entirely. Beau's chest caved when he saw his sister's casket pulled from the boxcar. He watched the man, his father, help his mother to a bench, then sign for the shipment. Beau felt little pity for either of them. They'd forced Amanda to school knowing she was ill. His anger was only matched by his grief.

As he watched his parents walk away, he slid down the wall to his knees. He waited until the High Point train arrived later that afternoon, the one he would have been on had he been coming from school, had he received a telegram they certainly must have sent.

Beau's mother shut herself off in Amanda's room, refusing to see anyone. His father stewed in a solitary hell of his own making. Beau stayed only long enough to see Amanda put in the ground. He was sent back to school, left to grieve on his own. It was only a few weeks later when he found himself home yet again, for another funeral. This time, for his mother. And, yet again, he was sent away, discarded, to grieve alone.

Both times, Harry Campbell dropped Beau at the station to catch a train back to school. "Well," Harry told Beau, "you get on back to school and live your life as best you can. It's going to take some time before your father gets right again, I suspect. It's nothing you need to get wrapped up in." When Beau didn't respond, Harry decided it best to leave the boy to his thoughts. Like father, like son. He left the station fighting the urge to take Beau to his house, to put him up for a few days, to let Maripat mother him. Had he acted on his impulse, their lives, and possibly those of the whole town, would have all taken a different path. But he didn't, and that's when Errol sauntered up in a sharp new suit with shiny new spats.

"So, I guess it looks like I'm doing a whole lot better than you are, my friend. Are you always this hang-dog, Boy?" Beau's blank expression prompted Errol to reacquaint himself.

"Yeah, Errol," Beau muttered, "I know who you are." Looking around with piqued interest, he asked if Sara and the baby were with him.

"Not this trip. They are tucked away at home. Ya know, that baby still cries like a damn fool. It's enough to drive a man to drink!" He pulled out his flask with a wide grin. "Why, you're not heading back up to Raleigh, are you cause I'm heading over to High Point, on the next train."

"What? Raleigh? No. I'm heading to High Point. That's where my school is."

"But we met coming out of Raleigh and I thought… aw, never you mind. Doesn't much matter now, does it? I guess it's just our luck that we're traveling companions again." Errol elbowed Beau, nudging him onto the train.

By the end of the trip, Beau had agreed to work for Errol's new company, Mountain Made Novelties, doing pick-ups and deliveries. Sometimes, he'd sign for a few boxes at the train station and deliver them around town. He knew full well the boxes were loaded with Kentucky Sour Mash or rum, but he never let on.

Summer came, but Beau stayed on in High Point. Still angry. Still grieving. He didn't want to see his father any more than Baker wanted to see him. When he heard some cousins he'd never met moved in, took over the house, there was no reason to go home. It wasn't home anymore.

Beau stayed occupied. He was the perfect runner for Errol, the last one anyone would suspect. He had a sweetness about him and a gentility people naturally mistook for innocence. So much so that customers thought he was too green to think on his feet should the need arise, until one afternoon, he proved himself up to the task.

Beau got caught up in a conversation with the local constabulary down on the loading docks. "So, tell me, son," asked the cop, nosing around at the addresses on the bills of lading. "What's a place like Hadley's Machine Works doing with a dozen boxes of Mountain Made Novelties?"

"Well, you know," Beau said with exasperation, "it's not for the business, it's for Hadley's wife. Seems women are getting the idea they want their own money. I'll be darned if they don't sell a whole lot of this junk right out of their houses."

"No!" exclaimed the cop. "Next thing you know, they'll be wantin' their own bank accounts!"

Before long, Beau was doing more than deliveries. He was taking orders and gaining a reputation. And visibility. As if by providence, a telegram arrived at the residence hall. BEAU KENYON STOP STONEYGATE HAS BURNED TO THE GROUND STOP COME HOME STOP FATHER.

The cop he'd spoken with weeks earlier was leaning on a post, watching Beau board the train home. "Get while the getting's good, boy," he muttered as he tipped his head and waved him off.

CHAPTER 21

The train ride through the foothills rejuvenated Beau. He'd been down in the Piedmont too long and missed his mountains. The smoky haze that rested in the valleys all the rest of the year disappeared in the fall. The air was almost electric. He was on his way home, and fire or no fire, home was still home and he'd been away too long.

There was an apprehension about seeing his father again. He was still angry at him for selling the horses, for Amanda's death, for abandoning him. Yet, when he saw Baker on the platform, waiting for the train, his eyes welled up.

Beau hesitated on the step down until the conductor nudged him off. He walked slowly toward his father, dodging eye contact, yet the silence between them didn't seem to matter. They were together. That was the simple goodness of it and it was enough for Beau.

"Let's go get your trunk," Baker said, and they walked toward the dock. Baker stopped, and when Beau turned to him, his father reached out and pulled him to his chest. It was an awkward embrace of unpracticed arms. Beau was so taken by surprise that one arm got caught up between them, leaving the other protruding with the satchel. It was a brief connection, lasting only long enough for Beau to feel the flex of large arms about him.

It was a silent drive from the station. Nothing his father could have said would have prepared Beau for what he would see. Baker drove slowly past the charred remains of the house to the cottage, which had changed considerably since Beau had been home last. Beau felt a twinge looking at the ashes, but it didn't bother him as much as he feared it would. When the car stopped, he got out and wandered about. The swimming pool, something the Adlers had no interest in repairing, was less than half full, and green as swamp water. A kingfisher kept watch over it from the oak. The paddock was full of tractors, cars and engine parts. "A mechanic," said his father. "Hawkins bought it off Adler last summer."

"It's OK," Beau said. It was just one more disappointment in a mountain of disappointments to get used to. He enrolled in the local high school for his senior year.

A month later, Beau walked into Deller's Drug in Hendersonville when someone slapped him on the back, spun him around and hollered in his face. "Well, if you ain't the luckiest son-of-a-bitch ever to walk the face of the earth!" It was Errol.

Beau was surprised to see him and not all that comfortable to be seen with him. "What's that supposed to mean?"

"What's that supposed to mean? Well, let me tell you. Not an hour after you put your sorry ass on that train home we were busted. Feds took down my whole warehouse. Just so happens I was cross county lines at the time, so I escaped the net. But it put a dent in my livelihood as you might imagine. A big dent."

"Sounds to me like you were the lucky one," Beau replied.

"You know for a minute I entertained the thought that you had something to do with it. Then, I said to myself no, no, Beau Kenyon isn't the sort to stab a man in the back like that. Not my Beau." He slapped him on the back again. "Yeah. Well, I'm just going to have to improvise."

"At least you'll be able to spend a little time with Sara and the baby."

Errol shrugged. "I got my little family all tucked away in the woods down Saluda way. They're just fine."

A week later, Errol came by Stoneygate. Beau told him to leave.

"You and I both know I need what your father can bring to the game," Errol argued.

Beau didn't want his father to know what he'd been doing in High Point. He'd been brought up to be honest and law abiding. But since Beau came home, he'd noticed something different about his father, something akin to the same disillusionment he felt, a rebelliousness borne of having lost so much.

"Just let me talk to him, kid." Errol insisted. "It won't hurt nothin'. Hell, he doesn't have to know you ever had anything to do with my business."

Baker sat at his desk in the living room watching Errol Mercer make himself comfortable on the couch, legs spread wide, twiddling his thumbs, spouting off about his business prowess. Beau stood at the door, stillness masking anxiety. When Errol started complimenting Beau on his quick thinking, Baker stood up fast, knocking the chair over behind him, shouting. "My boy is off limits to this illegal mess of yours!" At his best, Baker was not a patient man. He hadn't been at his best for some time.

"But father," interrupted Beau.

"You shut your trap, boy. You, Mr. Mercer, are an arrogant man without foundation. If I go in on this venture, that is what you're here for isn't it?" His glare was too much for even Errol to confront. "I will run it." This is not a negotiation.

Errol shifted his jaw then smiled. "No. It's my show."

"Then run it. Leave me - and my boy - out of it." Baker stood up.

"But what an opportunity, father! And Errol, you don't have the connections here. He does. And I saw how you run things. You can use his help."

Errol slowly turned his head towards Beau. "I don't need some snot nosed kid telling me how to run things either."

"Well, just hear him out, Errol. That won't hurt."

"Listen, jackass," Baker said to Errol, "You have nothing to lose here. I have everything."

"Seems to me you already lost it all." Errol's chuckle was unwelcome.

Baker walked to the door, turned and looked Errol dead in the eye. "A man has to know what's of value before he can lose it. My name is all I have at the moment. That and my reputation will open doors. Errol Mercer, you are one lousy business man. And I'm not sure I like you as a human being. But I've never let that get in the way of a sound business deal. You're moving an illegal commodity across state lines in boxes for a product that doesn't exist. I know why you left High Point." This revelation came as a shock to Errol. "We're close around here," Baker warned.

"I know about you. You got sloppy and they ran you out of town. The authorities will look the other way for a price, but they don't like personal risk. You became a risk." He watched Errol stew for a moment before delivering his final offer. "We'll do this my way or I see to it you're run out of this county and the next. And the next. Take it or leave it."

Errol stood and mustered everything he had to be nonchalant. "You can't do that."

"Try me." Baker insinuated Beau out of the doorway and held the door open, a clear signal it was time Errol left.

Errol turned his collar to the chill and headed to his car. He stopped half way and kicked the dirt. He watched Baker saunter out to the pasture. "Alright. Partners," he hollered, caving in to Baker's demands. Baker stopped without turning round and waited for Errol to come to him. The two men shook on it and the directives began to pour out of Baker's mouth.

"There's a barrel factory downtown that's going under. Wasn't doing well before the crash, won't last long now. I'm going to buy it. We're going to keep those people working and put a few women in town on the payroll."

"What the hell does that have to do with running liquor?"

"Your Mountain Made Novelties. We're going into the knick-knack business, Errol. And we're going to ship your bottles not in boxes but in barrels. And we're going to get lots of sea shells from Florida to pack on top of that good Cuban rum you'll be bringing up here. Then we'll take those shells and have the nice ladies of Laurel County turn them into all kinds of interesting things like ashtrays and dolls and souvenirs. And we'll send them right back to Florida. We'll make salt and pepper shakers out of piney wood, and dolls out of acorns and pinecones. And we'll pack all those barrels of rum heading north out of here with all those trinkets and when the local police have to check, they'll have every good reason to just let our loads through." He looked at Errol as if he were a child. "We're going to share the wealth, Errol. This little venture is going to put a lot of people to work."

"Sounds like a lot of overhead to me," Errol grumbled. "You want to pay half the town for nothin'? I don't want any part of it."

"Don't worry. You won't have anything to do with that aspect. You'll take a straight percentage off the top."

"Wait one minute!" Errol shouted.

"It's the deal you want," Baker insisted, quietly. "Believe me. You'll be happy with it."

Errol looked doubtful.

"Don't worry," Baker assured him. "You'll be a rich man."

Errol left and Baker went for a long walk in the woods. He'd been expecting Errol to come knocking on his door. Baker knew all along Beau was working for him. He'd made regular payouts to keep the boy safe. The beat cop at the High Point rail station was one of Baker's poker buddies and the chief of police over that way was married to Suzanna's second cousin. Once he heard Beau was getting in too deep, he pulled the plug. It was Baker who ordered the High Point raid.

CHAPTER 22

Errol repeatedly proved himself a necessary evil, taking the physical risks Baker was unwilling to take. Errol ran the trucks, made the connections, found the buyers. Between the feds and competition, every haul was a potential suicide mission.

The rum running venture proved lucrative, allowing Baker to revive the lumber company and begin reacquiring lost land. Baker struck deals and got it back piece by piece for next to nothing. All of Adler's mortgages had been bought and sold for pennies on the dollar as one bank after another failed. Hawkins sold the stable back and Baker let him use part of it to keep working on cars. Upon retrieving the last parcel of land, Baker repaired the swimming pool and set about building a new arbor. *Gin taketh,* he said to himself as he planted a rose bush, and *rum giveth back.*

The tennis court he left in place. No one he knew played the game, yet it served as a reminder of financial folly.

Four years into the partnership, Baker wanted out. More and more shipments were getting hijacked. The employment of so many people was all that kept local law enforcement complicit in his crimes. But Baker's protections only reached so far. He had no pull outside the county anymore. The Carolinas were fighting hard to make sure the twenty-first amendment repealing prohibition never got ratified. And, desperate for one last big bust, the Feds were coming down hard. It was only a matter of time. The risks were too high.

Beau's first day home after graduating from University, he came across Sara and Jeffrey in town. "Who's this?" he asked the boy. "Can't be Jeffrey! You're too tall! When I saw you last you were puny."

"Was not puny!" Jeffrey argued.

Beau laughed and raked the boy's head.

Sara uncharacteristically tried to avoid Beau's glance. Meaning to tease her, he tugged at her scarf only to find it was hiding a badly bruised cheek and jaw. "I stumbled over Jeff's toys, off the porch," she quickly explained. Beau didn't buy it.

"Yeah," he said softly. "Woman, I know when you're lying."

"We're fine, Beau. Don't worry about us." They were quiet lies spoken to console. "You promise me. You'll leave it be."

He didn't say a word but looked at Jeffrey whose eyes said it all. He looked afraid. "It has to stop," he said to Sara. "You know that."

Her response left no room for argument. "Stay out of it, Beau."

Wasn't but a few days later, when the bruises had faded enough to be unnoticeable, Sara stopped over at the stone cottage looking for Beau. She needed a chore tended to and Errol was away. Jeffrey climbed up on the porch swing as his mother knocked on the screen door. She'd never been there before. Baker hollered out from the kitchen to make herself at home and Sara stepped inside. She glanced about the room, taken by a photograph on the bookcase. She gasped a shallow breath and reached out slowly, her fingers tracing the curve of a young woman's face. A tear welled up. Baker stepped into the room, startling her.

"That's Amanda," he said taking the photograph from the shelf. His thumb worked the heavy silver braiding of the frame. He wiped some dust with his shirtsleeve. "That was our Amanda. We lost her to the flu a few years back." He startled himself at the ease with which the lie was told. He heard a scratching on the screen and saw Jeffrey standing against it, looking in, sunlight catching the red in his hair. The boy looked so familiar Baker gasped.

Sara spoke, barely holding her composure. "Honey, now you stop that scratching. I'll be out in a minute." She told Baker it was her boy, Jeffrey.

"Yes, ma'am. He's grown since I last saw him. You doing all right down there in Saluda?"

Sara smiled enough to assure him she was managing, but not enough to encourage further engagement.

Baker put Amanda's photograph back on the shelf.

"She was beautiful," Sara said, "and so nice . . ." Her eyes went wide and she stuttered. "I mean, I mean I'm sure she was a wonderful person, and, well, I, I really need to be on my way. So would you please send Beau down to see me when you see him?" She was out the door as quickly as she'd come in. Baker watched her grab Jeffrey's hand.

"I suppose all little kids look alike at that age," he said with a smile through the screen door. "It's amazing how much he reminds me of Beau." It was Sara's panicked glance back that sent something akin to an electric surge thru his body.

Turning back to Amanda's picture, he felt his legs shudder and he sat down hard in the chair. He could barely fathom the possible likelihood of what he was imagining.

As Sara drove away, she was so preoccupied with Amanda's photo and Baker's comments, she nearly ran off the road.

When Beau came home hours later, a quiet voice spoke to him from the chair in the dark. "Tell me again how you met Sara and Errol."

Eager to finally tell the truth, Beau confessed to being on the train with Amanda's casket. He told his father about Amanda's letter and the boarding house and how he was told she'd died in surgery. He said it was on the train back that he met Errol and Sara. "We were all on Amanda's train."

"Ah. Well then." Baker's words were quiet and distant. "Go to bed now," he said.

For what little response there'd been, Beau wondered if Baker had heard a word he'd said.

Not long after that night, Baker went looking for Errol and found him on the loading dock at the barrel factory. "It's over," Baker said with unquestionable finality. "I'm out. You're out. It's done with."

Errol was livid and started cussing. A couple of men overheard, then a couple more, and soon half a dozen stood behind Errol.

"You can't shut this down now!" Errol spewed. "No way in hell I'm letting you do that!"

Baker, watching the man fume, spoke with an honesty no one would have reason to doubt. "I'm giving you half interest in the Feed & Seed," he said. "You can move that pretty young wife of yours and your son into town. Give them a good life here."

"Ain't no way I'm a shop keeper," Errol griped. "I need something bigger, more exciting, more like me." He swaggered in front of the men. "He thinks he's shutting us down. Ain't no way. I think we need to show him different, what do ya say, boys?"

The men looked at each other, arriving at a silent consensus. They moved on Errol, picked him up and threw him off the dock into the dirt. "How's that for somethin' more excitin'?" one of them hollered.

Baker walked through the factory for the first time in nearly a year. Up on the third floor he found himself amid the clatter of two-dozen large wooden looms, tended by women busily turning out cotton rugs made from colorful scraps of material. The looms stopped rattling. All eyes fell to him.

"Tom, we need to talk," he said to the manager.

"I already heard. Small place. Women. Word travels fast."

"What the hell is this?" Baker asked about the looms.

"Aw, this? I picked them up real cheap a few months ago. And the material was in huge scrap piles at the mill over in Forest City. They almost paid me to take it! There's a real market for these rugs, believe it or not. A real market for 'em."

"Really. And just how is it that you know that, Tom?"

"Well, I've been selling them."

"You've been selling them. Well, just how am I supposed to shut this place down if you're investing in equipment and selling wares? You think this is some kind of business or something?" One corner of Baker's mouth turned ever so slightly upward to a degree hardly noticeable to anyone but those who knew him.

"You know me, Mr. Kenyon. I'm a natural salesman."

"So, what are you trying to sell me, Tom?"

Tom motioned for the women to get back to work and looms resumed their clatter. "Well, sir, I don't know if you've been paying any attention to what we actually do in your factory. Now, don't you go getting upset with me, but you told me I could dispose of the product any way I wanted. Well, most of it's sitting in a tobacco barn outside Lexington, Kentucky. You see, my sister, you remember Fiona don't you? Well, she married a no count fella from up there and he had this big old empty barn because he couldn't grow bacca to save his life. No kind of farmer at all." Baker's gaze slid away. "Any way," Tom continued, "I've been storing everything we made. Up there. In that barn."

Baker perked up and gave Tom a sly piercing look. "Up there. In that barn. Everything that you made to pack the barrels of rum and bourbon. It's all in that barn. Well I'll be a… That storage barn wouldn't be what saved our asses last spring would it?"

"The very same, sir. That would be our Kentucky facility. Even says so on our bills of lading. I wish I could have seen their faces when two dozen Feds used those axes of theirs and broke into all those barrels, one after another, and found nothing but trinkets. Fiona thought the big guy was going to have a cow! Said he turned all red and his veins were burstin' out of his neck alright!"

"Well, I'll be damned. I thought that was just something Errol cooked up."

"No sir. Errol's not that smart."

"You're right. He's an idiot."

"I've already sold most of it," Tom said, getting more animated. "The novelties. The seashell dolls are real popular with those northern cities. They're buying them like crazy in Cleveland if you can believe that. And these rugs, I have an order from a big department store downtown Chicago. Marshall Fields. And I bet I can sell these little chairs, too," he said holding up a toddler sized rocking chair. "So you see, as long as I can sell it, we can keep makin' it, and I can keep the place open. Everyone can keep on working."

"You willing to take the risk on it?" asked Baker.

"Yes, sir."

"Alright. But I own the building and I'm not one to give up real estate. You sign over that empty house you own up on Fourth Street and I'll sign over this business. Pay me enough rent to cover taxes and I'll be happy."

"My own business? Yes, sir! You have a deal, sir."

"Well done, Tom. Well done." Baker climbed up to the platform that oversaw the second floor wood workers. He rang a big brass bell that hung from the ceiling. "I'd like your attention!" he called out. Everyone looked up to him, expecting the worst, to be told the plant was closing.

"First, I want to thank you," Baker said loudly. "Each and every one of you." He saw heads looking away and realized what they were thinking. "So, you there, Elliot Mason. What are you so down in the mouth about?" The man looked up and shouted out "Well, we're all out of a job, ain't we?"

"Well, all I can tell you, Elliot, is that you don't work for me anymore. I just sold the whole kit and caboodle to Tom here and he has orders to fill, so I suggest you all get back to work!"

What happened from there on out didn't matter so much as what came before. What restored Baker's reputation was not reacquiring estate lands, it was giving people a paycheck in hard times.

CHAPTER 23

Beau heard about the scuffle at the factory. Afraid Errol might take it out on Sara, he set out to confront him. He hoped just talking to the man would keep him from hitting her again. If not, he'd threaten him first and back it up with the .22 Rimfire rifle. He'd just take it out of the car and hold it, making clear his intention. Up to that point, Beau had been a gentle person of quiet ways. The anger lurking within him was unfamiliar in its volatility.

A storm was threatening as he drove over the ridge that afternoon. The drizzle turned into light rain. The forest began to steam. Another half a mile, another switchback and he'd be face to face with Errol.

The more he thought about what he would say, and how Errol might not take to another man interfering with private matters, thinking how Errol might retaliate, his foot got heavy on the gas and the car sped up throwing him into a tight hairpin turn too fast. The tires climbed the wall and bounced back down to the road. The steering wheel snapped out of his grasp almost breaking his thumbs. He grabbed the wheel and tried to regain control on the wet gravel. That's when he saw a car coming right at him, Errol's head bobbing behind the wheel. Beau laid on the horn and he saw Errol's head snap up. Their cars swerved to avoid colliding.

Beau cut sharp coming to a halt in the middle of the road while Errol veered the other way, passing right in front of him, and flying full bore off the edge disappearing into the haze. A quiet crunch followed from the bottom of the ravine.

Beau's motor sputtered itself off. He got out and, in no particular rush, stepped to the edge. A shrouded glow flared up from deep in the ravine. He didn't attempt to climb down to help. Didn't even consider it. There was, in simple fact, some satisfaction in the moment. The light rain turned heavier and the glow dissipated. Beau waited, listening for a door latch or any sound at all. All he heard was a tire scraping against something and slowly spinning down to silence.

Just up the road, Sara sat on the floor of her house rocking back and forth, holding Jeffrey, both of them inconsolable. The boy reached up and touched his mother's face. Like finger paint, his hand left three bloody stripes on her cheek. She frantically wiped his hand clean with her dress, murmuring assurances that it would never happen again. She would kill the son of a bitch before it ever happened again. Then she heard the tires slipping on gravel at the drive.

"You go into the kitchen and wait!" she told him, jumping up and pulling the shotgun from the rack. Snapping it open, she rummaged in the drawer for the box of shells. "I mean it, son. You go into the kitchen and if I tell you to run, you run for all you're worth. Don't look back." In an instant she had both barrels loaded.

She ran onto the porch as the vehicle came to a stop down at the road. She couldn't see through the haze and trees. She could only hear. A car door opened. Her voice carried through the woods like a screech owl. "You set one foot out of that car and I'll shoot you dead, you bastard!" She discharged one barrel into the air.

"Don't shoot!" came the voice from the car. "It's Beau! Put the gun away, woman!"

Realizing she'd nearly shot her only friend, her knees gave out. She crumbled to the floorboards, pushing the shotgun out of reach.

Beau ran toward the house, stopping at the steps, dumbstruck watching Sara wipe her face with her apron as if the blood was nothing more than rain. She did not invite him further. Her words, quietly spoken, were vacant. "Oh, now don't you worry about this. It's nothing."

Beau yelled. "What the hell did he do to you this time?" His voice cracked. He climbed the steps and reached out to touch her. She slapped away his hand and stood up.

"What are you doing here, Beau?" She asked. The man staring at her in the rain didn't answer. "What?" she demanded. His glance went beyond her to the window, to Jeffrey's frightened face staring back at him.

"What is it, Beau?" Sara insisted, more quietly.

"It's Errol."

"What about him?"

"On the road," he said. An almost imperceptible grin crept over his lips. "He went over."

"Over?" Sara asked, not understanding his meaning.

"Over," Beau repeated. "Off the road. Into the ravine."

"Take me there," she said dispassionately. She motioned to the boy to come along and he followed to the car. "I want you to stay here in the car when I get out," she told him as Beau drove up the road. "You stay right here and lay down on the seat." Jeffrey did as he was told, shaking, not so much from cold, as fear. Tears streamed down his face, but he made no sound.

Beau and Sara soon stood on the shoulder of the road watching the rain erode Errol's tire tracks until all indication of a stray vehicle was erased. They were getting drenched, but neither seemed to notice.

"Do you think he's dead?" she asked.

"Do you want me to go down there and check?"

"No," she said. "Let the man rot in his own piss." Thunder rolled over them. "I'm never setting foot in a church again," she said.

"What do you mean?"

"If I believe in a god then I have to believe in the devil." She turned from the ravine straight to Beau. "If I believe in the devil, then he owns my soul."

Beau's face twisted up. "If he's got anybody's soul," he said, "it's mine. I saw it was Errol. I came up here to confront him, to kill him if I had to. I as good as ran him off the road." He fought against the tears working their way out of him. "Sara, I wanted him to go over that edge! I wanted him to ..." Sara took hold of his shoulders.

"You could no more kill a man than I could! Look at me! Beau, you look at me!" He settled down and looked at her face. The rain had washed the blood clean away, and in the half-light, there was no sign she had just been beaten. The swollen cheek and eye were hidden in shadow.

"Maybe we both had a hand in it and if that's the case, I set the thing in motion. When he left the house tonight, I asked God to never let him come back. But in my heart, I was begging the devil to take his sorry ass. And if there is a God, he knows the difference between what we say and what we mean." A crack of thunder opened the skies and the rain nearly drowned out her words. Yelling to be heard, she tried to explain to Beau so she could understand herself. "I can't believe in any of it because if I'm a believer I have to face the fact that I made it happen and I can't live with that. The man was just plain drunk and ran himself off the road. That's all that happened here tonight. That's all! And he's not worth one single tear, you hear me?"

A bolt of lightning lit up the gorge. The subsequent crack of thunder nearly knocked them to their feet. They heard the crunch of breaking wood and then the snapping branches. "Run!" Beau hollered. "Get behind the car!" As they ran, lightning illuminated the boy's face framed by both his hands against the glass, looking wide-eyed into the woods. They all watched as a massive tree, struck in half by the first bolt, fell twisted thru the sky, its preponderance of branches tearing apart everything in its path.

The next lightning was high and away. The storm moved quickly over them to the south. In a moment, the rain let up to a light patter and the dark clouds gave way to patches of clear sky. The full moon crept up from behind the ridge.

Sara shook her hair and pulled it back away from her face, wringing it out, when something caught her eye. "Well, boy. Looks like the devil just took up residence." She slowly lifted her hand to point to the end of the fallen tree trunk, its top half horizontally lodged in the crook of another. Its mangled end was configured in such a way that, from their perspective, when the moonlight hit it just as it did at that moment, it resembled the face of the devil. It was grinning.

Beau took Sara and Jeffrey back home.

"I ought to go down and check on him," he said.

"Don't you dare," was her response, delivered with a decisive glare.

Had the big granite boulder still been there, Errol's car would have hit it and bounced back onto the roadway instead of careening into the ravine, flipping upside down, and landing half on the bank, half in the stream. If the boulder had still been there, he'd have survived to drink again; to beat Sara again; to threaten Jeffrey's tender life.

Beau pulled out of Sara's drive headed for home, fighting hard against the urge to climb down to see if Errol was alive or dead. He pulled onto the shoulder just past the place where Errol had gone over. He got out of the truck and listened as he looked into the ravine below. He didn't hear Errol, pinned inside the car, the stream running over his chest, unable to move, begging for his life. It was too dark and the rising mist too dense to see Errol's overturned car let alone the man in the rain-soaked slicker standing in the mud next to it with the pistol in his hand. Beau got into his truck and drove away before the man in the woods put the gun back in his pocket and walked away without having said a word.

Beau was so preoccupied with the events of the evening he didn't notice the sawmill's flatbed parked in a cut along the side of the road.

Beau arrived home, hung his wet coat on a hook on the porch and left his muddy boots beneath it. His father arrived home somewhat later, leaving his muddy boots and slicker on the porch, next to Beau's. Neither asked where the other had been.

When Sara went back into the house that night, something was different about it. From the moment they'd moved in, it had offered little sanctuary. Aside from her devotion to her son, the place was devoid of love. Yet, that night, the house in the woods took on a new aspect of darkness. It had become her captor. It was important she pretend nothing had happened, that her husband had gone off like he always did, that she was merely awaiting his return. Life had to appear normal to anyone who might notice such a thing. Not that there was anyone who'd ever taken notice of her life save Beau.

As her husband's car rested deep in the gorge, she lay awake that night next to her son, watching him twitch through difficult dreams. She touched the tender swollen cut over her eye. A fox screeched in the woods. Fat drops of water fell flat on the roof. She thought she should feel some peace, some reassurance of having been saved from further abuse, but her heart would not rest. Her muscles clenched so tight she lay more above the bed than on it, and wondered how many nights it would take before it would be otherwise.

Sleep came fitfully as it had most nights of her married life as it was Errol's custom to arrive home very late, very drunk, and very hostile. She woke with a start. Looking at the faint green numbers on her watch she saw it was one in the morning. She remembered eleven-twenty, and twelve-ten, and twelve-thirty. Habit left her to wonder in the fog of semi-wakefulness if Errol was home or not, and if he was, how drunk he might be. Then the events of the night came to her and she worried about what might have startled her awake. The boy, curled up into a tight ball next to her, was sound asleep. What, she thought, if Errol hadn't died down there in the gorge? What if he was downstairs tending his wounds? She listened hard, holding perfectly still. A sensation of rage crept into her bones, bringing with it clarity of thought and strength of will. If Errol had not died down there, he would die in this house by her hand. Tonight. She padded through the darkness, past her son's empty room, downstairs, to the living room. All was still. She stood listening for any other presence in the room and heard nothing. She stepped out onto the porch to listen. She did not turn on a light for fear it might seem an invitation should Errol be walking the road.   Hearing only the undisturbed sounds of the night woods, she stepped back inside and sat in a chair facing the door. She woke the next morning with Jeffrey on her lap.

Three days passed. Sara told herself Errol was dead and gone, yet every flux of the floorboard, every hickory nut or twig on the roof could have been him. She thought about going down into the gorge to find him, to assure herself he was dead. Only the thought of finding him still alive stopped her. How long does it take to die, she wondered. As she was thinking that thought, the last breath escaped unheard from a very sober drunk pinned under a car in the bottom of a gorge.

Two weeks passed. Her house grew colder. She wanted to leave everything in it behind, set a torch to it and walk away. But it was all she had. And Jeffrey had to be considered. Where would they go and how would they live?

As had often been the case, a neighbor stopped by to see if Sara wanted a lift to town for groceries. She accepted the kindness pretending nothing had changed.

Three weeks passed. The last anyone could recall seeing Errol Mercer, he'd been drunk leaving Malcolm's Tavern. The fact that his wife hadn't reported him missing was nothing unusual, accustomed as she was to his disappearing on her for days and weeks at a time.

A month passed when his truck, with him in it, was discovered upside down at the bottom of a gorge. No one questioned how he got there. The story of his death varied little no matter who was doing the telling. He was drunk. He drove off into the ravine and died there. His death, however, left Sara Mercer alone with a young child to tend and no money to speak of.

"I deeded Errol half-interest in the Feed & Seed before he disappeared," Baker told the barber.

"Seems she's set up pretty good," the barber told the grocer.

"Baker's giving the widow the Feed & Seed," the grocer told the postmaster.

"Errol was his partner after all," the postmaster told the pastor.

"It's the least I can do," Baker told Sara when he signed the Feed & Seed over to her.

Packing up the house was a dispassionate, methodical task for Sara. If Errol's money bought it, it was left behind.

Under Jeffrey's watchful eye, Sara packed her family dishes and glasses, pushing decorative bowls and candlesticks aside. He watched her drop her sheets on the floor and walk on them as if they were no better than rags. Things fell to the floor and broke. She didn't sweep them up. Either by mimicry or intent, given a crate of his own to pack, Jeffrey chose only a box of dominoes, a stuffed dog and his slingshot. When they walked out of the house for the last time, they left behind a mess. The dining room chairs and table remained, the bed remained, the rugs and sofa and easy chair remained. It appeared as if someone had left in such a hurry, they hadn't time to take it all. But it was not a rushed affair. It was accomplished very carefully. What was left was left for a reason. They were of Errol. And Errol was dead.

CHAPTER 24

Being without a husband suited Sara. This was a state of mind borne of a deep sense of self. Sara was only eight when her mother died, leaving her upbringing to her father. He was a man of solitary ways. Dinner was a fried pork chop or boiled chicken and two potatoes. A neighbor woman started going to market for them and taught Sara how to cook and keep house. After that, he came home from work, ate whatever Sara pulled together for a meal, tended to chickens, then retreated to his chair where he read the paper, then a book. Sara sat across the room reading or drawing. Sometimes she wondered if he even knew she was there for as little as he spoke to her, but when he did, it was with respect and kindness. "You make a good shortbread," he said the third time she tried making it, without mention of the previous failures. "You keep a clean house," he said out of the blue one evening. "Got those beans just right tonight," he said the first time she put a rash of bacon in the beans she picked that day. Saturday mornings they went to the library for the week's books for each of them and the market for the week's food. The little chair in the back of the library was her second favorite place. The chair at the table across from her father was her first. Her mother used to say about him *He's a good man of quiet ways. We could do a lot worse.*

Sara was about seventeen when her father lost his job. She brought in a little money cleaning houses. Still, it was a long hungry year before Errol insinuated himself into their lives. He was a loud, verbal man who never said anything worth hearing, and he had a physical presence that crowded a room even if he was the only one in it. Her father and uncle went into business with him, though she hadn't known what it was they did. All she knew was that her father would come home with wads of cash and made sure she knew where he hid it. "Protect this, girl. It may be all you have to get by on." Sara had no idea what he meant until her father and uncle were murdered and left to die like road-kill possums.

Errol Mercer moved into the house with Sara. He hadn't asked. He just moved into her father's room. Six months later, when Sara turned nineteen, he married her.

Years later, after Errol took the header into the ravine, Sara came to a good many conclusions about her life, about how it had occurred so far without her own intentions. It always seemed to be one thing or another coming at her and she just tried to make do as best as she was able. That changed the instant she heard somebody discovered Errol's body. She was finally free to find a place in the world. Her place, not one chosen for her or dictated to her. While the Feed & Seed was more or less thrust on her, she interpreted it as an opportunity.

The day Baker and Beau opened the door to the Feed & Seed and handed the keys to her, something shifted within her soul and she became a new person to such a degree she felt certain that if she were to look in a mirror, she would not recognize herself. She liked this new person, her confidence and daring. She anticipated, which was no small sensation. She had lived her whole life anticipating nothing but disappointment. Suddenly, she found herself expecting something better, a luxury never before bestowed on her.

While Baker showed her around the office, Jeffrey ran wild in the isles hollering and clanging on whatever he felt like. Beau kept a sharp eye over him, surprising him from around a corner causing raucous squeals. Baker and Sara watched them, the moment bringing such contentment to Sara it would for years be recalled as one of her life's perfections.

"Every life has them," she would later tell Jeffrey. "If you're lucky, you recognize them at that moment they occur. Still, the nice thing about them is that you can look back on them later and even then, from that distance, no matter how far, still know it for what it is and hold it dear. Perfections," she said, "are few and far between. Just one may be all you get, so pay attention and whatever you do, don't let it go unnoticed."

The Laurel County Feed & Seed was one of those sacred places in town. There wasn't a man in the county who didn't know exactly what shelf the lag bolts were on, or where the saw blades were or the drill bits or udder salve. It was an unchanging thing and that was in itself a comfort. As a young man, Baker had taken it over from his father when Parson died and kept old Jacob Whiles on as manager. Even then, Wiley was getting on in years, and had, over time become somewhat over-ripe. Retiring the man was Baker's last task before deeding it to Sara removing her from all possible blame. "It isn't mine any more, woman. It's yours,

" he told her. "And, my sending Wiley home was my doing, but your problem to contend with. Good luck," he added with a wide grin.

When news spread that a Yankee woman had taken over the Feed & Seed, conversations throughout town centered around sizing up this stranger, Sara Mercer. What could she possibly know about hardware, or feed, or animals, or fishing, or trapping? Where would men go to get out of the house now that a woman hovered around their communal wood stove. Many felt they'd lost a dear friend, not Wiley, the store. God knew he couldn't remember how to buckle his overalls anymore and had taken to tying them together.

Baker's faith in her, however, hardly offset all that worked against her. She was not of the mountains and worse yet, came from the north. And, though Errol's foul reputation had made its way through the county, few knew anything at all about his wife. Her visits to town had been brief and she hadn't tried to fit in which led some to presume she thought herself too good for them. It was what even good people think when they don't know what else to think. Her other obstacle, perhaps the greatest, was that she was a woman in a man's position. Running, much less owning, the male dominated store in town was difficult to accept, not only for the men, but their wives.

Sara shuttered the store for a week while she studied its inventory and consulted with Beau and Baker on the basics of being a merchant. As it turned out, she had a penchant for numbers and organizing. It would take her a month to put the office the way she wanted it, but when she was finished, Baker was quite pleased with himself.

"The world is righted," he told her.

In the beginning, when she re-opened the doors, few entered. After four days of the town's abstinence, Sara painted a big sign and put it near the road. "I don't bite. But the catfish are and I have bait." So it was that the Feed & Seed reopened. The first customers were accompanied by their wives, something that before that time was unheard of. When word spread that nothing had changed, "Hell, she hasn't even dusted!" things began returning to normal. Things were going to change, but it would be gradual and by the end of her first year, there was hardly a person in town who didn't think they'd had a hand in the improvements.

She asked Mrs. Markham if she thought the store ought to carry some dry goods. She told Mr. Jones she was thinking about bringing in a line of boilers, asking if he thought it a good idea. "Hey there," she said to the men sitting around the wood stove smoking. "What would you think if I put in hoppers for the grain and seed you all buy the most?" They chewed on that one for a while, and came up with all manner of suggestion until, in the end, things stayed as they had been, as was her original intention.

Women noticed that Sara was an agreeable woman who spoke to them in the same manner she spoke to men, with a familiarity that kept its distance. While some would boast to knowing her well, they did not. A conversation with Sara was one-directional. She fished information out of every soul walking through her doors. The best anyone could say was that Sara knew them well, but none knew her at all.

The next few years passed with care and comfort. Sara did not seek another husband. She found contentment in the near daily company of one man too old for her, Baker, one too young, Beau, and her son, Jeffrey. The Feed & Seed, once considered the domain of men, a private club for passing spare hours and discussing world affairs, became a general store of sorts. Sara was careful about this delicate transition keeping in place the Holy Grail, the potbelly stove and its seven rickety chairs. New merchandise, everything from building supplies to household goods, was positioned in such a way as to protect the original inner sanctum of the Feed & Seed. As it prospered, so too did Baker in his ventures. In the process, hearts mended and temperaments mellowed.

As was often a late afternoon habit, Baker took a walk out in the pasture. It was mid-winter. Quiet. Even the cattle were still. He inspected the streambed where the bank had eroded. He planned on laying down some logs to protect it. There was a lot of dead wood to be cleaned up and he thought he'd get Beau and Jeffrey on it the next day. He came to his favorite old tree, a spot he knew well for providing many delicious naps over the years. It was the spot from which he'd watched the house burn down. As he knelt down, wincing against sore joints, his mind filled with Suzanna. For years he'd tried to forgive her for quitting on him, and some days he thought he had. Other days he felt he never could. On this night, he struggled.

She had, of late, been heavy on his mind. It happened that way. She'd be absent from his thoughts for weeks at a time and then, all of a sudden, show up to infiltrate his every waking minute. He felt a peculiar shifting of time and with it a sense of being adrift. Though it was especially warm for February, his mind was drawn to a snowy February many years earlier, when they'd received the news about Amanda's passing. Suzanna's anguish devoured her.

She was the one who sent Amanda away. His girls had decided it all without him. "Really, Daddy," his daughter coaxed. "I'll be fine. You'll see." It was a decision he fought, but not hard enough. He should have demanded she identify the father as soon as she told them she was pregnant. He should have stood up to the situation. When it was all said and done, it was a decision neither of the girls could hold up to, and guilt was what killed Suzanna. Not grief. From the moment the telegram arrived to tell them Amanda died, life as they knew it died, too.

The memories of these events were as specific in their detail as if they had only just occurred. Sitting against his tree, he felt anew the cold separation of his once loving wife. He thought, as he too often did, about the night she took the fall. He regretted the argument earlier that evening, and he regretted all the nights he didn't go to her, didn't attempt to comfort her. Yet into all these dark thoughts, drifted a beautiful smile gazing at him. Just through the trees, he saw her, an armload of roses, eyes calm and sweet, without a care. She laughed but he could not hear it. Her gentle auburn hair gleamed in a dying shaft of sunlight, her beaded dress swayed with her hips as she ever so slowly approached. Baker sat at that tree drifting in and out of time as the sun set beyond Glassy Mountain. He didn't make it to Jeff's eleventh birthday dinner.

Baker was known to get caught up in things, making him late, but he'd never missed a meal as entirely as he had Jeffrey's birthday dinner. Unwilling to cut the cake without him, Jeffrey, Beau and Sara drove to Stoneygate looking for him. They found him, sitting peacefully, propped against that old tree. He didn't stir at their approach. Sara was the first to realize, and she grabbed Beau's arm.

"Hey, you old coot," Jeff hollered. "You missed my birthday party." He knelt down and touched Baker's hand only to snatch it back fast, embarrassed by the reflex. "He's dead," he said with what little breath was left to him.

"Yes, dear," Sara said.

Beau knelt down to steady himself. He looked at the soft shadows of his father's face, peaceful in the dusky light. "This is a good ending," he sighed. "A good ending."

The damp woods muffled Jeffrey's soft sobs.

"What happens now?" Beau asked.

"It's all yours now, Beau," Sara said. "You're good Kenyon stock, and you've got a good education. Just think what your father would do and follow your gut. If that doesn't work, just think of what Errol would have done and do the opposite." They both half chuckled.

"C'mon, Jeff. We'll come back out to fetch him with the truck."

"I'll stay with him," Sara said. She took Jeff by the shoulders and he shrugged her off. "Go on now, son. You go help Beau with the truck. I'll stay with him." Jeffrey turned away to hide his tears. As they walked off, Sara sat down next to Baker and took his hand in hers. It was callused and cool. "You saved our lives, I think. And I don't know that I ever properly thanked you." She began to sob. "You were a good man, and I love you."

CHAPTER 25

The fox knew Maggie, her smell, her habits, her noises. When he was young, he'd crouched very still in the laurel watching her, smelling her on the breeze, listening to her humming. She came very close to him once, when he was careless. He'd been on the scent of a rabbit and not quite caught up to it when he found himself on the open path, the old woman not two jumps away. They both stopped fast, startled with the presence of the other. The old woman's eyes soon quieted and he, presuming she posed no threat, sauntered into the bushes and headed up into taller grasses. He often sat on the bridge over the stream and watched her on her porch, having come to accept her as easily as he accepted the groundhog and the cows. But, she was gone now, the old woman. She was gone and this new one smelled different.

He encountered Meg much as he had Maggie, by her smell along the path. He watched from a far thicket, just as he'd watched the old woman. In time, he drew closer. He saw her eyes were not as quiet as the old one's so he kept his distance, but still, he was curious about her. Knowing he could leap to safety, he went to his favorite spot, on the bridge over the stream and watched her. He sat for the longest time over several days, watching her, wondering if she was something to fear.

On the wall of the cottage porch hung a small branch, like a work of art, barkless, silky pale gray fingers spanning from the end of a two-foot shaft. It or one like it had hung there for as long as Meg could remember. It was a Maggie quirk. She'd never paid it much attention. Coming home with groceries one afternoon Meg found a note dangling from it. It read: *Nice day for a swim.*

It was hot day, felt like summer, but it was only June. Swimming hadn't crossed Meg's mind presuming it too early in the season, but maybe it was just too early had she still been in Chicago. She took a walk up the drive, around the garden, admiring the vigorous growth. Caged tomato plants were in flower, knee high bushes held clumps of tiny green and yellow beans, feathery carrot greens crowded two rows, ruffled kale and potato plants with purple flowers ran the length of tidy rows. She heard a drone emanating from the pool shed and took the path between four fat boxwoods stepping onto clean white concrete. In front of her, the crystal clear water, ablaze in sunlit sparkles, beckoned. Beyond it, a backdrop of woods provided a chorus of birdsong. She raked her hand across an Adirondack chair sitting in the sun, its smooth white surface warm to the touch. She knelt to water's edge, dipped her hand and swished it, the crisp splash reminding her of childhood, of summers spent doing cannonballs off the edge, her dad teaching her to swim, sunbathing as a teenager, Maggie's fresh lemonade in sweating aluminum tumblers.

When the water felt warm a full hand's length in, Meg looked around for any sign of Ford's truck and saw nothing. She looked over the bushes and into the woods in all directions and saw nothing but the church hundreds of yards away up the hill through the trees. She pulled her T-shirt off over her head, pulled off her jeans, stripped out of her underwear, took a deep breath, stepped to the edge and cannonballed in.

The water was like ice. Her lungs convulsed and for an instant she imagined herself deeply inhaling water, drowning, and wondering how long it would take before her naked body was discovered on the bottom of the pool. Erupting back to the surface she flooded her lungs with fresh warm air and swam furiously to the ladder at the far end. The goose bumps were too enthusiastic to be subdued even by the heat radiating off the cement. She dried off with her shirt and ran buck-naked to the cottage. "Nice day for a swim, my ass," she yelled.

Days of unseasonably hot weather followed one after another. It seemed more like deep July except for the quiet as there were no whirring cicadas or chirping tree frogs yet. The first high humidity always took some getting used to. The wisteria she'd trimmed so severely leafed out but there were no flower buds, something Meg regretted. As Ford arrived to finish trimming the boxwoods, she headed out on errands.

The boxwoods lined the drive from the front woods, along the wide sloping lawn, to the old foundation. The job would be finished when each of the twenty-plus bushes once again resembled giant bonbons.

He was working on the last one, his tee shirt drenched in sweat, when he heard a car turn off the road onto the gravel of the drive. A black BMW crept very slowly toward him. "City dweller," he muttered. The car stopped and the tinted window whined down. The man inside looked cool and dry.

"Haven't you guys ever herd of asphalt down here?" he grumbled. "I'm looking for Margaret Bishop. Do you know where I could find her?"

Ford just stood there, wiping his brow with his arm, appearing almost not to have heard him. Finally, he said in his slowest Carolina drawl "She's not here."

"Is that her house? That's all I'm asking," the man said.

Ford replied slowly. "Yeah, that's her house."

The window slid up as the car pulled forward to the cottage.

Ford watched the man emerge from his car and saunter up to Meg's porch. He looked to be about 5'10", medium build, blond hair far too quaffed. He wore a white polo shirt and khakis. When there was no reply to his knock, he tried the door, a move Ford found irritating.

Ford feigned work long after his task was accomplished, keeping his eye on the man lurking about the cottage and grounds. He watched him lean on a net post at the tennis court with the posture of impatience, rolling his head back on his neck. Ford packed up his truck and drove the old service road out behind the cottage and parked out of sight but still able to watch.

Meg didn't see him when she drove in. All she saw was Vince Santos's black BMW. Ford saw Meg get out of her car, run over to the man and melt into his arms. That's when he left. Unnoticed.

Feeling Vince's arms around her body was like finally coming home from a long uncomfortable journey. "Oh my god," she moaned in his ear. "I've missed you so much!" She took his face in her hands and kissed him. His response was docile.

“I brought you some wine,” he said pleasantly, carefully stepping away from her. “As a housewarming gift.”

She led him inside, forgetting about her groceries, and began babbling on about San Francisco, and losing her contract, and living in the south. All the time she was talking she had visions of making love with him, his hands traveling her body like familiar back roads. She anticipated driving him around her mountains, taking him to restaurants she had not had the nerve to go to alone. She didn’t notice he wasn’t really listening, that he was waiting for her to wind down. To finish. It wasn’t until he said he needed to tell her something that the quietness of his demeanor hit her. Then came his words.

“I’ve gone back to my family,” he said, his eyes looking directly into hers.

Meg’s brain slammed to a full stop.

“My absence from them,” he continued, “was a mistake, and we’ve decided to work it out. We’ve purchased a townhouse in a good neighborhood close to Michael’s school and there is a beautiful park for Tina to take Shelly to play.” What began with an apologetic tone turned into eager enthusiasm as if Meg was supposed to be happy for him; as if she cared that Tina had a park for Shelly; as if she was happy they bought a house together. The rage shot through Meg like lightning.

“When did all this happen?” she shouted.

Back in apologetic mode, he said they’d been talking about it since February.

“February? While you were still sleeping with me?” she shouted. “Were you sleeping with her?”

He said nothing.

“Have you been sleeping with her?” Meg demanded.

"Of course," he said.

"You don't love her!" There was more to the thought, volumes in fact, but the words didn't find her voice. Her hysterics embarrassed them both. "I don't believe this shit!"

"You knew, Meg. If you really look at it, you knew." He was quiet and somewhat consoling in a disconnected sort of way. She watched him perched on the arm of the couch, slouching. He looked exhausted.

"You made a choice," he said calmly. "To be with me even when I wasn't there for you."

His hands didn't move. His arms did not raise up to invite her over. His eyes were lifeless. He had said what he came to say. "I need to be leaving."

"What?" Meg shouted. "You show up, drop your bomb, and run?"

"What's left to say? I've gone back to my marriage and …"

"You're divorced!"

He was silent.

"You. Are. Divorced."

His one-word response was delivered with a distinct admission of guilt. "No."

Meg slapped him crisp across the face so hard her wrist hurt. She instantly recoiled, breathless, watching his revulsion register as his cheek reddened.

"They're waiting for me," he said rising.

"They're here?"

Vince walked out.

"This is my town now. You get the hell out!"

He went to his car, climbed in and drove away. He never looked back.

Meg could not get a grip on the moment. Her whole body buzzed. Her wrist stung from the slap. Both hands white-knuckled into tight fists. Her legs gave out and down she went. Tears flowed forth in inconceivable volumes, followed soon after by involuntary wailing, and a strange convulsing as the sobbing swept through her. When it did not stop, and she could not regain any semblance of composure, she stepped outside herself and observed the puddle she had become. Perhaps, she thought, I am having a nervous breakdown. And, well, I don't know how to do that.

From her detached perspective, she could not accept that grief could incapacitate her so completely and she tried to pull herself off the floor. The mere effort of trying and failing only served to feed the maelstrom of misery. Eventually, she could only submit to whatever was taking over her body and soul and she lay flat on the rug, arms limp at her side. The bawling was unrelenting.

The experience was all the more confusing because she knew she was not in love with Vince. She knew there were fatal flaws in her need of him. Nothing he'd said or done was bad enough to deserve a response so gut-wrenching, yet there she was, crying maniacally over him, until old grief began to rise up like magma from a deeper reservoir, from a place his insults were too fractional to register. Long buried pains awakened from their repose and exploded to consciousness.

She cried for Maggie's passing, and for missing her funeral, for bad weather denying her that last vestige of connection. She cried for Emerson's passing, as if he was a dear friend whose funeral she'd also missed. Other injuries, other heartbreaks, every failure and disappointment for as far back as she could remember found escape in this tsunami of despair. She cried for loveless years and for a life without children. She grieved over things she never knew mattered until that day and over things unidentifiable. She grieved over denied grief as her therapist had warned she eventually would. *Repression is dangerous,* she'd been told. *You've got to face pain head on and feel it.* But her people were not made like that and she stored it all away, every shred of disgrace and humiliation. And as the grief spewed forth, so too did the anger. Anger at her family for not pushing for answers when her marriage fell apart, for not noticing there was something so much more going on than a divorce, for not bothering to ask anything that might challenge their strangled view of propriety.

Her chest tightened. Her breathing grew shallow. The clenching pain hit. She pounded her breastbone to make it stop but the pain would not relent. And there it was, in the thick of the panic attack, the pit of the problem: Marvin. The man who'd exposed everything vile and abhorrent in her rose up from her past to remind her the darkness still dwelled within, not deeply hidden but just below the surface. Slapping Vince was proof.

The old rage toward Marvin renewed itself to full potency: The assault, the police, the restraining order. She was angry with herself for failings not just that night in his studio but for what came before and after, for the lies and retaliations. She never felt the possibility of exoneration for her part in it all, a time when maybe she would not hold herself at fault; a time when she could separate her behavior from circumstances and lay the blame somewhere other than at her own feet.

Sitting on the floor of the cottage, tears spilling forth, she was angry at her therapist for making her rehash it over and over without getting her past it, and because even after years of therapy, the mere thought of Marvin still brought irrational pain even though it was all so long ago, another life. She could hardly believe the pain still rendered her so helpless. Crawling onto the bed, exhaustion brought sleep, delivering dreams of disjointed places and events. She awoke to again be overwhelmed by tears. She pulled the comforter up over her, griping its edges as though it might try to escape. A sharp chill filled the room from the open window but she could not muster her limbs to close it. A wind washed through the tall pines, then the patter of rain, a few drops at first, then a steady quiet rain, a soaking rain, the kind of rain that encourages new life, new beginnings. Meg fell back to sleep.

It was nearly noon before she woke again. With the coffee on to perk, she signed into her email account. Nothing. Her life was imploding yet no one sensed even a ripple in the universe. She turned off the computer and unplugged it. She unplugged the phone. She took the coffee pot and a mug to the bedroom and crawled back under the covers listening to fat plops on the roof from overhead branches, patterings to flat magnolia leaves, splashing of roof water falling to puddles.

A stiff breeze rose sending rain to the sill, turning into little puddles, spilling to the floor. Meg made no attempt to close the window. Another storm swept through, wind shifting, high branches swaying, dodging. Thunder pounded above, one after another, reverberations felt as much as heard. A sudden, vibrant gust of wind lifted the curtain like arms reaching toward the bed. A spray of rain reached Meg's face, spattered the comforter. Lightning flashed. More thunder. Rain buffeted the cottage. Magnolia swept the siding. A battle raged, engulfing her. Then, as if a surrender, the curtain came to rest. The rain stopped.

Had the day been sunny it would have felt like a betrayal, a mocking of her mourning. Instead, the day recognized her pain and acknowledged it. Tears came again, and like the storm, visited in waves throughout the day.

The sun appeared through the clouds in time to sink below the tree line that evening. Meg was exhausted. Emotion had wrung itself out. She slept soundly. The next morning, a squirrel woke her, chuttering in the tree by her window, insistent and agitated. He looked right at her, making her smile and as she did, it stopped scolding, rubbed its face, and jumped to the ground.

Meg lay there, quietly, waiting to see how she felt, to see if the smile, the feeling of calm was only an aberration. It wasn't. As she ground the morning's coffee beans, she realized she had allowed her marriage to Marvin and its aftermath to define who she was, not to others, but to herself. She had let it make her unworthy. Vince was proof. No more.

As her coffee perked, a thought quietly crept up on her. It hung softly in the shadows before slipping into the light: Perhaps it did not have to be that way for the rest of her life; perhaps, she could move past her self-loathing and guilt to exoneration. Where it had previously been impossible to imagine a life without the darkness, she suddenly realized she was already there. All remnants of pain had dissipated. There had been a cleansing. Though she could identify the origins of the pain, she was finally released from feeling the emotion of it.

She'd slept for fifteen hours straight awakening on the other side of her life. It was unfamiliar territory, but she was ready to make something of it. There was, however, a strange new hollowness to the hours, something she would not be able to identify right away. There would be no more emails from Vince, from her editor, from her publisher. There were no drawings to begin, no story to fine tune, no

Emerson to mentally cavort with. There was no place she needed to be, and nothing was expected of her. Hers had become a life without anticipation. More salient, was the feeling of having no one to celebrate her emergence with. The isolation, so necessary for the trodden soul, was suddenly unsatisfying. While she reveled in this great uplifting, there was still a measure of the weight to which the tether held strong. Perhaps some trauma holds fast no matter how one tries to move past it.

CHAPTER 26

Within weeks of graduation from the Art Institute of Chicago, Meg landed a job at a national advertising agency. Marvin found a studio space and sold a few paintings. Life was exciting. Meg and Marvin married. But something changed in Marvin the instant he said I do, as if the ceremony transformed him.

His wedding kiss was a dispassionate peck. He refused to dance with her at the reception, choosing instead to sulk in a corner. He refused to consummate the marriage on their wedding night proclaiming it would have been *pedestrian*. He withdrew from her touch.

He withdrew from everyone.

As weeks passed, he continued to avoid her. He was no longer the man she'd spent the last two years with; the man she stayed up with all night talking, drawing, exploring the city; the man who loved to cook exotic food and seek out new restaurants; the man who loved having people over; the man who thought making love was good for the soul, but rousing down-and-dirty sex was good for his art. He became isolated and angry.

Meg believed if she were kinder, stronger, more resilient, he would be happier. They would be happier. Whatever his failings, they were hers to bear. It was what she thought wives did. Especially wives of talented men. Believing his unhappiness was as much her fault as his, she tried to put up with his moods and be supportive, no matter the cost to her won sanity.

Even though Meg's paycheck supported them between sales of his art, Marvin thrived on belittling her. At gallery openings, his favorite jab was introducing her as an art pimp, holding firm to the belief that commercial artists prostituted themselves for the capitalist society. Since she hawked their services, she was a pimp. He never disputed that it was the same capitalist society that bought his paintings. "But I paint what I feel!" he pronounced. "My soul is on the line! They sell their souls."

A year into the marriage, Meg had morphed into someone she hardly recognized. She'd become submissive, powerless to stand up to Marvin's irrational behavior when he'd explode at her with little provocation. What little sex they had was aggressive, without a shred of compassion. He stopped looking her in the eyes and she turned away from kisses that felt like assaults. His grip grew tighter, his movements rougher, more convulsive. She was sometimes left with bruises. He got so rough one night she pushed him off to the floor. He left the apartment, reappearing three days later without apology or comment, something he did more and more often. It wasn't the kind of thing she could tell anyone about. It was the kind of thing that happens behind closed doors. It was the kind of thing that happens in a marriage, yet the shame of his behavior and her response to it, whether submitting to it or defending against it, had her waking every morning with clenched fists.

He'd stay at his studio for days at a time, not bothering to call home. "I'm an artist. You can't tie me down!" When he did come home, he drank himself into his hateful place, assaulting Meg verbally as the sole cause of his inadequacies in the studio.

Two years into the marriage, Marvin had his first one-man show. It was small but impressive. Warren Woshaw, a famed Chicago designer, purchased several of his pieces, landing one on the cover of *architectural digest.*

As Marvin's career took off, Meg's did as well. When her team was up for an award at a Chicago Area Advertising Awards banquet, Marvin was a no-show. Everyone at the table but Meg seemed to know why he wasn't there.

"What's the matter, honey?" asked a co-worker. "Lose your husband to Warren tonight?"

She left.

Marvin's studio was in an old factory. Walking the stairs to the third floor, Meg tried to move past her own sense of betrayal. If Marvin was with Warren, if he was really gay, it was time he came clean with her. She even imagined he might appreciate having it all out in the open.

She walked the long hall past an open door. Glancing in, she made eye contact with a woman smoking a cigarette standing next to a large block of stone.

She continued on, passing the communal bathroom and arrived at Marvin's studio.

She knocked on the locked door, then pounded. Marvin finally opened it, agitated. Naked, he fumbled with a cotton kimono, her kimono, the one he said he'd thrown out. Her sanity began unraveling. She was shocked by the squalor of his studio, the smell, a thick salty-crotch-sweat-stench tinged with turpentine and linseed oil. Marvin stood at an inebriated tilt, glazed eyes trying to focus. One dim lamp barely lit the space behind him.

He started yelling at her before she could even speak. "You have no right to demand my time for anything. I wasn't about to go to that fuck fest of whoring dilatants pretending to be creatives collecting their little awards celebrating their own incompetence."

This time, she did not fight the adrenaline surging through her body. This time, it boiled to full froth and she pushed her way in and slammed the door behind her.

"This is my studio!" he shouted. "My space! You can't barge in here!" He mocked her life as meaningless, pathetic, and small, declaring she would never know what accomplishment was because she was a whore. "A pimp and a whore! The ugliest of all possible human things!"

Without an instant of hesitation, Meg slapped him. Hard. So hard, he lost his balance and fell. He came up swinging, his fist grazing the side of her head. She stood her ground, braced herself and gave him a hard shove, sending him careening into an easel, sending the canvas, paints, brushes and linseed oil flying. He was down, flat on his back and she dared him to get up, hoping he would, wanting with every fiber of her being to hit him again, not just a slap, but a solid fist-clenched punch. Her hands shook, her head throbbed. This was new. Her people did not have rage. They did not give in to uncontrollable urges. They were not violent. This was depraved.

He stood up, his face awash in blood from a gash on his nose. He spewed another vicious diatribe at her, each word drizzled with thick red spit. She yelled something vile back at him. He took a step toward her but lost his balance and fell. As he lay there, at a loss as to how to right himself, she heard a click from the corner of the room. It was a Zippo lighter snapping open.

She saw the flame illuminate the features of a man's face as he lit a cigarette. It was Warren Woshaw, sprawled naked on the couch.

"Children, children," he taunted.

Meg began to wretch and made it down the hall to a toilet just as her dinner came back up. She sat for a minute, on the filthy floor, splatters of puke on her new dress, wondering how her life had become such a shit hole.

Her hands shook. Her breath came in fits and starts. Her head pounded. Trying to stand, she crumpled back to the floor. She had no sense of how long it took to get her body to calm enough to stand, get to a sink, rinse her mouth out.

She was splashing her face when a uniformed police officer barged in on her. He grabbed her by the arm, his fingers squeezing so hard her hand tingled. He let her go when she didn't resist. She leaned against the wall answering the officer's questions as calmly as she could. "Yes, it was an argument that got out of hand. Yes, I hit him. Yes, I pushed him. I found him with a man for Chrissake!"

The cop escorted her back to the studio where another officer was looking around. Marvin was holding a rag to his eye, fresh drops of blood falling in streaks down his shirt. Warren was gone.

"Did you do this?" one of them asked Meg. She said she couldn't remember, that it was all a horrible blur. The same cop noticed a bruise on Marvin's jaw and another on his arm, older bruises, not fresh.

"She do this to you, too," he asked and Marvin's eyes darted around the room.

"Yes," he spurted. "All out spouse abuse. She does it all the time. I'm just her punching bag. And I'm sick of it! Sick of it, you whore!"

Meg stood silent, deadened by a situation she could no longer comprehend. She was handcuffed and taken from the building. The woman from the studio down the hall watched from her doorway.

Down in the street she hid her eyes from the strobes on the police car. The officer asked to see her hands before he put her in the car. She held them out and he squeezed her knuckles. When she didn't flinch, his demeanor softened. Riding away, Meg saw her parked car and wondered if it would be there when she came back, if she ever got to come back.

Meg spent the night in a holding cell with a dozen other women. Making her way around a huddle of them she stepped in a slick of puke and some of it got onto her open toed shoe, between her toes. She closed her eyes and fought back the urge to throw up. Somebody bumped into her and she turned expecting to be confronted with some street-wise punk wanting to make a point, but the woman had meant no harm, and wandered to a corner on her own. A small section of bench was still open and Meg claimed it, sitting there all night, without sleeping, without speaking, accepting her punishment for having lost her temper, for assaulting Marvin, for giving in to her basest instincts.

At some point, a woman who had been staring at her began taunting her about her dress.

"Think you're hot shit, don't ya, bitch?"

Realizing it wouldn't take much incentive to beat the living crap out of anyone at that point, Meg glared at the woman, almost taunting her to open her mouth again. The woman turned away.

Meg was released in the morning. The arresting officer told her Marvin changed his statement too many times to be credible. And he couldn't come up with lies good enough to counter what the woman in the hallway said. She was the one who called the police before Meg even appeared at her door. She told them about other fights in Marvin's studio and she was tired of it. "I guess some people like it rough," the sculptor told them, "but that poor boy gets the shit kicked out of him by Woshaw at least once a week."

The officer explained it all as he drove Meg to her car on his way home. He was a man in his fifties, someone who'd seen it all. "I sure as hell know my wife would beat the crap out of me if I pulled that shit on her," he said, trying to make Meg feel a little better, but she wasn't listening.

"But how'd you know I didn't ..." Meg asked.

"Your hands. If you'd landed those punches your knuckles would have hurt like hell. Punching someone in the face hurts. Believe me." When she got out of his car, she stood in the street too dazed to know what to do next. He got out, found her keys in her purse and opened the car door for her. "Want me to follow you home?" he asked. "Yeah, why don't I do that?"

"No. I'm fine," she said, and she got into her car, put the key in the ignition and started it. The officer went back to his car and waited. After a few minutes, he opened his door and started to get out to check on her. Before he took a step, she drove off. He tailed her, a few cars back, to make sure she made it home.

When she got inside, she stripped down, stepped into the shower, and sobbed uncontrollably, hoping the steam would somehow cleanse her of the night's events. It was a week before she went back to work and no one knew what had transpired.

She divorced Marvin. What followed was an ugly year and a half before he moved back to his family in Florida.

The experience with Marvin had ignited something obscene in Meg. It was rage. It was foul. It was a poison that tainted everything she thought about herself. A psychologist would eventually give her labels for the anger, even justifications for it. But still, it did not go away. It found a place to live within her and would not be dislodged.

CHAPTER 27

July. Steamy. Lush. Green. Two weeks since Vince came and went and five days since she'd gone anywhere. She hadn't even been out to the post office, though her curiosity about what awaited tucked into its tiny metal sleeve was beginning to get the better of her. She planned to go to the Fresh Market on Saturday for corn and muskmelon, country ham, eggs, cheese and fresh butter. In the meantime, Stoneygate was all the company she needed. She kept up on world events via websites, visiting the New York Times, Washington Post and the BBC until she realized none of it related to her and the overload of useless information, stories about pain and violence she could do nothing about, was too much. She unplugged. She weeded the garden as it seemed Ford had abandoned it. She read. She took walks and watched the cattle meander through trees in the wooded pasture.

In the obscurity of the new moon night, she walked the length of the drive to the road. Darkness still fascinated her. The city never afforded such luxury with its halogen streetlights and neon signs. And sound. Chicago was never quiet. Not like this.

Her feet knew their way in the dark, where the pea gravel blended into grass and where it fell off slightly at the cut of the tile-lined gutter. She knew that when the drive began sloping downward, she was at the end of the boxwoods. She knew precisely where the delicate fringe of the balsam limb would brush her forehead. She knew that when it leveled off again it jogged left by the massive rhododendrons, then straightened out for a bit before veering right, next to the bearberry patch between two cedars. The trickle of water meant she was coming up on the stand of bamboo, beyond which the driveway bridged the stream at the bog filled with brilliant yellow swamp marigolds rendered invisible by the night. Another straight stretch up a slight grade and she'd be through the crumbling stone entry pillars at the the road, the warmth of its pavement still radiating from the day's heat. Standing in the middle of the road, she turned slowly about, seeking out any light through the woods from a neighbor, a car, any sign of another human being, and found none. The thought occurred to her this was as it should be. Her solitary mood would not have welcomed intrusion. She ambled back to the cottage and went to bed, yet her soul felt too large to be contained in a room. Opening the door from her bedroom to the porch, the moist warm air filtered in as her spirit slipped out, taking flight with her resident owl over the pasture, through the pines up to Glassy.

The next morning, she picked up the fresh sketch journal lying on the dresser and rummaged in her tackle box for her drawing pen. STONEYGATE-2000 she wrote on the first page. She went to the porch to look about, to figure out what would make the best first drawing. Opting for what was right in front of her, she began drawing the wood slat swing hanging by two rusty chains from the ceiling. She studied its shape and broke it down into lines and angles taking into account all the elements at play behind it and to the sides until it was all aligned in her head and she put pen to paper. The first lines went down with confidence. The rest followed as easily. As she drew, a shadow crept across the slats. When it reached mid swing, the sketch was complete. She felt empowered.

The rest of the morning was spent in the garden. The vegetable plot had been patient with its inexperienced attendant. In late spring, even when Meg still saw the tending of it only as a chore, it offered strawberries, then raspberries. By the time the first wax beans were ready, the garden had won her over. At present it offered tomatoes, basil, oregano and thyme, and green beans, all of which were collected in a basket beside her.

The flower garden appeared indifferent to her abandonment. Tending one garden was enough for a novice. The perennials, so long established, couldn't help but produce an abundance of color, fragrance and texture. Even as Meg cut multitudes of flowers for arrangements, they flourished, suffering her mutilations with further growth and more flowers.

Clipping a haphazard handful of flowers, she stuck the stems in a mason jar perched on a stone of the old foundation. The simplicity and serendipity of her random selections gave the arrangement a certain perfection. Suddenly, clear-sky rain had her grabbing the jar and the basket, running for cover, rescuing her journal on her way indoors. The clouds moved in and with it more rain, a steady drink for thirsty plants.

With the aroma of first picked tomatoes simmering on the stove, Meg curled up on the couch and picked up the journal again. As was her habit when journaling, she put drawings in the front and comments in the back until the words met the pictures and it was full. She turned to the last page to begin.

She was surprised to find an entry from earlier in the spring. She read the words as if written by a stranger.

May something, 2000. Stoneygate. I'm hoping that if I put it all in order, thoughts into words, into sentences, into logical rationalization, I'll be healed. I'll have some epiphany of enlightenment. I will have order in my life. hmmmm........ Even I can't fool myself into believing that. Believing. There's always a "lie" buried in the middle of that word, the one you choose not to see, or choose not to accept. And here I sit, pouring my guts out to a piece of paper, alone, lonely as hell.

What was it Maggie wrote in the beginning - something like I can't wait until the journal is about the garden and children and observations on day to day life instead of emotion and whining. I feel that way. I'd like to be writing some bucolic entry about the new calves chasing around in the pasture yesterday, or the spectacular display of azaleas, or the way the light this afternoon is perfect beyond any day I can recall in recent history. But all that comes to mind is the ache in my gut. The yearning. The absolute disillusionment. I guess that's what this is all about. A journal isn't a book of essays, all written to a point of conclusion, edited and reduced to coherent thought. Not much about my life lately is coherent.

She wondered how she could forget writing it and vaguely recalled a bottle of wine possibly having been involved. Determined to move forward, she began a new entry.

> *July 2000. I picked tomatoes in the rain today. I'm making sauce before the ones I picked earlier in the week go bad. Only three romas and a beefsteak today. The rest are green. I think maybe I garden for reasons more than aesthetics and consumption. Weeding seems to keep the darkness at bay - I still sense it on the far reaches. I feel the vacancy that comes from not giving everything to something. I live my life like I'm painting a canvas, or building a set - a backdrop for some fascinating story that has yet to take place.*

She re-read her scrawlings and found herself, yet again, wondering who'd written it. She felt too good to be expressing darkness. *New rule,* she wrote. *No more words in the journal. Just drawings.* Then she wondered if maybe she was still repressing her emotions and decided probably so, but chose not to think about it. With that, Meg closed the book and went in to stir tomatoes. The next morning, she took her coffee and went for a walk.

Crouching in the soft sand along the stream bank, Meg watched a bug scurry across a small pool of water behind a downed branch. Its body weight only dented the surface as if it was cellophane. Below it, there was movement, tiny bits traveling on currents, green feathers swaying. In Chicago, she had been that bug, her life merely skimming the surface.

The syncopation of the city created such a tension it didn't allow for anything to break through. Even in the quiet stillness before sleeping, there were all those other people through the next wall, across the street, down the block, and the hundreds of blocks after that. She didn't realize until she left how much the static of their energies interfered with her perception of the world, of her life. There was no such clutter in her new surroundings, only the clarity of an awakening as the natural world began to resonate within her. She wondered how much time she'd lost on the periphery of her life, how much she'd missed from sheer inattention.

A warm river of air wafted over her. Closing her eyes, she slipped into its current, drifting over the trails through the woods, over the cool dank earth of the garden, between tomato leaves, around the sleek surface of bulging eggplants, expanding further, in through the living room window, reaching through the bedroom, spilling out over the porch, rolling on the heat waves off the tennis court, and on out over the pasture. This spreading outward did not thin her, but made her more than she was, and less, at the same time. She began to see herself as an integral part of the whole, of no more importance than the waterbug.

That night, Meg crawled into bed and pulled the soft clean sheet up over her tightly curled body, the fabric clenched in her fingers. She breathed out and in, out and in, then slowly out, and slowly in, then even slower. She unclenched her grip, released her shoulders and rolled over onto her back, stretching her legs out straight, relaxing them. She concentrated on the muscles in her feet until they let go of themselves, then her calves, knees, thighs and lower back. She placed her hands on her belly, feeling it softly rise and fall with each breath. Something was missing about the moment, something she couldn't identify. Then the thing slipped into her consciousness. The inner vibration she had lived with for as long as she could remember was fading. In its stead was a comfortable, gentle, physical peace. She dozed off soon after, waking only once in the night to the sound of the owl in the woods near the house. Recalling it in the morning, she remembered smiling and thinking *thank you* before she slipped off again. She wrote a line of text in her journal next to the day's drawing. *The night was deep. I slept.*

Throughout the week, sunlight moved across the property with what seemed to her a deliberate intricacy. One day it highlighted a log in the pasture, turning it into a shaft of polished gold. Another day, an array of flickering white triangles sifted through the woods as the late day sun illuminated the wings of doves. For the first time in her life, she found herself living in the moment, drenched in the satisfaction of it.

Living each day became an art in and of itself. Meg made a concerted effort to observe everything that surrounded her, to sense their presence in her life and her presence in the world. She was creating a pattern to her days, not habit as some might think of it, but a pattern of specific design. She enjoyed beginning her day at the coffee grinder, pushing the hand crank, feeling the rigid beans give way against the iron grinding surfaces. The aroma became morning. She drank her first cup on the porch, feeling the last of the night's pungent dampness on her skin. Once that week, as it would several times over the summer, the fox appeared on the bridge over the stream out toward the pasture. As it sat there grooming itself, she quietly watched, wondering if it was at all mindful of her presence.

She made a point of swimming laps several days a week. It didn't matter how many she swam so long as she made the effort. On days she didn't get in the pool for whatever reason, she found she missed the activity. Soon an afternoon swim became standard practice. Some days she lounged like a lizard afterwards in the sunshine resulting in the kind of a tan she hadn't had since childhood. She was living a life of small luxuries, the value of which was not wasted on her. It was becoming a life of synchronicity.

Wandering the stream, she found newts and salamanders and palm-sized wolf spiders. The paths offered tracks and scat for Meg to identify. In her efforts to identify such treasures, she became somewhat of an expert discerning raccoon scat from fox, and found great pleasure knowing the fox was a frequent visitor.

One day she found an owl pellet, which occupied her for the whole of an afternoon dissecting its contents of fragmented bones, teeth and claws, drawing them in her journal.

Often, she encountered irritating strands of sticky spider silk across the path on her morning walks. Sometimes she picked up sticks to wave in front of her, and then tossed them aside. On this day, she found the perfect branch with a fan of fine twigs at its end. It was lightweight and fit her hand perfectly. Held out in front of her, it caught its first strand, and the strand in turn caught the sun like infinitesimal diamonds.

She brought it back to the cottage and leaned it against the chair as she went in. Later in the day, returning from the garden, she looked onto the porch and laughed. Her web catcher was strikingly similar to the lovely bare wood branch hanging on the peg. She had done exactly as Maggie had. "A purpose for everything," she said aloud.

She awoke that night to a still, clear sky filling her window. A crescent moon rested softly atop the woods. What a wonder, she thought, that she had mysteriously stumbled onto the tune that put her in such fine harmony with her surroundings, and that this connection somehow directed her days, allowing her to spend her time sketching, thinking. She took walks, worked in the garden, and prepared meals from the day's harvest. It was a satisfying life. It occurred to her she was living a perfection, one she appreciated for its uniqueness, and cherished for its likelihood of brevity. The thing she tried to ignore, but sometimes could not, was the ever-present question of ownership. It was an unbearable impossibility to imagine that all she had come to love could be taken away.

For no reason she could manage to understand, no shift in ambient air, no fever, no embarrassing thought to cause a blush, a warmth grew from her chest outward until she felt as though her entire being was aglow. The warmth carried with it a sensation of absolute love and comfort. It was gone as fast as it came, but the sensation of complete well-being lingered. Whatever it was, it was good and true and something she could draw on for strength. Like so many other experiences of that summer, she would not share it with anyone, ever. It was a sacred gift belonging only to her.

CHAPTER 28

June 16, 1962. Heaven steady my nerves. It's almost July. Time for the invasion. On the subject of July visitors, I have written the same words over and over each year. I used to phrase it more politely but have of late lost that urge. They are a simple fact of life. I love them all, but three days is plenty with three days in between. Most come for a week and I'm lucky to have 24 hours to myself in between. They come - I feed them- they get in my way - I send them out on expeditions. I have learned not to accompany, as I have no need to see the same things every year again and again as they seem to. I have instituted only a few rules, the most important being: THE PHRASE "I AM BORED" IS NOT ALLOWED. Over the years I have learned that some people make good houseguests and some do not. A good houseguest asks how to make a pot of coffee. That means I can wake relaxed knowing they are taking care of themselves. A good guest will go exploring on their own. They will have a plan for each day without my having to muddle through their indecisions. A good guest will offer to take me to dinner and not insist on cooking for me in my own kitchen. A good guest understands that just because I have my summers off does not mean I have nothing to do with my time. And the most important element to being a good guest: conversation is not mandatory. After nine in the evening, it is not even appreciated. From here on, each year, I shall make reference each July to this entry, as all Julys are the same.

Maggie's journal entry soon rang true for Meg. Her peace was about to be interrupted. Her parents called suggesting they visit in September with a dozen reasons why it would not be the best time for them to be away. "July really would work better for your father," her mother whined. "But we feel bad coming on such short notice." In the next breath she said they'd be there by the weekend, leaving little time to reconstitute the guestroom.

Meg hadn't seen Ford in weeks. She called Jarvis to find him and have him bring two twin beds back. Someone she'd never met delivered them a day later and took the drawing table and chair to the cellar, out of the way. Her parents were the first to arrive.

It was all too much: The suitcases pouring into the cottage, the extra towels on the line, someone crowding her kitchen and her living room, her mother's constant chatter, the smell of burnt matches whenever her father walked out of the bathroom, followed by the unnatural smell of a rose-scented candle her mother lit. Her parents could not possibly understand how much Meg did not want them there.

"When you kids were little," her mother said, "it was all we could do to keep you all corralled. Between the endless trails and the pool and the cows and the stream, you were a mess whenever you came in the house. And you slept all over the place. Remember that?" As she rambled on, Meg tuned her out, recalling her own memories of visiting Aunt Maggie.

Then as now, the pasture was rented out to the neighbor who kept a small herd of cattle. He used to grow alfalfa in the back field and used the stable to store hay and equipment. She hadn't thought about the stable being gone, presuming it either fell down or was sold off for barn wood. As a kid, she preferred to skip the family day trips. She didn't want to go to Linville Caverns again, or the falls, or Boone. She recalled a particularly wicked tantrum she'd thrown because of wanting to stay behind.

The cottage suddenly felt claustrophobic and Meg went for a walk.

Her dad sat on the big rock at the edge of the wooded pasture, behind a bush, out of eye line of the cottage. When he was a younger man, he used to escape there for a smoke. Though he'd quit years earlier, he still had the urge to light one up. He greeted his daughter with a gentle smile when she walked across the grass and sat down beside him.

"I miss her," he said quietly.

"I know, Dad."

There was a long silence in which a great deal was not said.

"I can't see a golf course out here," he told her.

"Either can I."

"I didn't think so." He patted her knee. Meg kissed him on the cheek and left him to his solitude. She wanted to ask him if he remembered Ford, but that would have led to conversation and she could see he wasn't in the mood.

"Enjoy," she said with a warm smile. Walking back to the cottage she saw her mother looking around and calling out.

"Is your father out there, Dear?"

"I think he went for a walk," Meg called back.

Jack chuckled from his perch on the rock, hiding from anyone demanding his time, his attention, bathing in memories they were no part of. He could feel his boyhood in his bones, a time when he was set free to wade streams, search for salamanders under an outcropping, find wolf spiders sunning on moss. He yearned for a time when he held no expectations of himself except to spend all the hours of a warm summer day away, breathing piney woods, soaring with crows, traversing deer trails, tramping rocky paths, padding through fern forests; no one waiting for him to show up, make a decision, act the chauffeur, pay the bill. Closing his eyes he listened to memories carried by cool waters, certain he heard a boy, long since gone, footfalls on moss, the boy he was when Beau woke him at dawn with a gentle hand on his shoulder. He remembered seeing the rucksack and canteen, and grinning, knowing they were going off on adventure. A quick trip to the bathroom - without flushing so as not to wake anyone - and then tiptoeing past his brothers and out the door to the porch where Beau waited with clothes he'd picked up off the floor. They were his jeans and shoes, but his brother's shirt. He didn't fret. It fit just fine.

If Beau knew where they were headed, he pretended not to. They followed a deer trail into the brush up one hill after another. They ate sandwiches on a rock high on a ridge. They drank from a spring. They ate their apples down in a gorge wading in a stream. When they didn't make it back in time for dinner, they ate chocolate bars. Beau regaled Jack with Civil War stories and geological facts about the terrain, about the Blue Ridge Mountains being older than the Sierra Nevada or Rockies. They identified animal tracks and scat. Even found dried bear droppings. Weeks old. No need to worry. For as much as he talked, Beau was often stone silent. Sometimes they just sat on a rock or against a tree and listened to the woods, waiting for whatever might come along. That day their patience paid off. An eight-point buck wandered by.

Fifty years later, Jack sat on that rock, hiding from his wife, looking about at what had changed so little since his childhood, thinking about his summers with Beau, about that one particular day. Probably the best day of his life. Ever. How does a person peak at ten, he wondered.

A couple days later and a full three days before expected, Meg's brother Sam and his wife Ella showed up. Sam was the middle child, two years older than Meg. Having driven all day, it was nearly nine when they arrived, irritated they had to pay for a motel until the guest room was vacated. Meg greeted them at the door, said goodnight, and retreated to her room. On the other side of the door, Sam and Ella argued about how to spend the next day. Their tone of voice didn't strike Meg as being much more than civil and she entertained thoughts of a pending dissolution of their marriage.

Climbing into bed with one of Maggie's journals, she came across an entry of interest.

> *July 18, 1975. SEE JULY 1962. I should have*
> *intervened today. Jack had no business dragging*
> *that girl all over the countryside with those boys.*
> *They treat her no better than a pesky dog. I*
> *suppose you can't reward that behavior by giving*

in to it but she clearly did not want to leave and what harm would it have done to leave her behind here? She tends to herself well enough. I don't trust those boys out of my sight, but Margaret, well, she's different. It was fun watching . . .

The screen door slapped shut. "Be quiet, you two!" hollered her mother not two feet from Meg's door. "Meg's trying to sleep!"

"She is not," Sam griped. "Her light's still on."

Car doors opened and closed and Sam and Ella were off to their motel. An ease set in and Meg turned off her light. The knock on her door was followed immediately by its opening. "Honey, are you asleep yet?" her mother asked as she stepped in. "So, dear," her mother said, making herself comfortable on the foot of the bed. "Have you decided what to do with this property? It's so far from town."

Her mother knew the rule: No conversation after nine o'clock.

"And you are so alone out here," she continued. "Are you sure it's safe?" Allowing no opportunity for Meg to respond, her mother kept talking. "Well, that's silly, I suppose. Aunt Maggie lived alone out here for years and years. Poor dear. It would be a shame to sell it to some developer, but just think of the opportunity that would give you to get something you really want. And your retirement would be well funded. You need to think about these things. But I'm sure you'll do the right thing. Just don't let Sam get to you. He's been so adamant about you developing this on your own and that's all he talks about when he comes for dinner."

"Mom?" Meg faked a yawn. "It's late. Maybe we can talk tomorrow?"

"Now, Dear, you don't worry about it. You have plenty of time and I don't want to interfere in your business. You sleep now and we'll all be up bright and early tomorrow to enjoy another day! Maybe we can all hike up Glassy." She tucked the covers in around Meg as if she were wrapping leftover meatloaf. "It's a shame Tim and Izzy don't want to bring the kids down. They'd love it."

"Tim hated it here. Too much silence. Can you imagine Izzy here? In these woods? With those little kids? She'd never let them outside. One brother these days is plenty, thank you."

Her mother kissed her on the forehead and drifted out of the room. "Good night, Sweetie," she whispered as she closed the door.

Meg sighed hard and un-cocooned herself. She turned the light back on and picked up the journal again.

> *. . . what harm would it have done to leave her behind here? She tends to herself well enough. I don't trust those boys out of my sight, but Margaret, well, she's different. It was fun watching Ford defend her yesterday.*

Meg lay stunned and reread the words. It was fun watching Ford defend her yesterday.

She tried to remember him back then but couldn't. Had he been there often? And how had he defended her? A crashing came from the kitchen followed by her door opening again. "Sorry dear. I was just thinking I'd do a little cleaning for you. I'm usually watching TV at this time of night and I can't sleep yet. Go back to sleep. I'm fine, dear."

"Mom," Meg asked, "do you remember another kid who used to hang out here when we came to visit?"

"Another kid? No. The three of you were plenty."

As the week passed, her mother ran out of things to say and things to bake. There were more cakes, cookies and cobblers than Meg could ever eat. Unlike Maggie, Meg felt obligated to go sightseeing with her family. She took them all to a Bar-B-Que hut in Saluda and hiking in Chimney Rock. She took them over the mountain on the old road with all the switchbacks, up to Asheville to see the Biltmore House. They had to pull over so Ella could throw up. Carsick.

Her parents left a day early to beat Sunday traffic, opening the guest room to her brother and his wife. They left the next day. Apparently, little about the visit was reminiscent of previous sojourns and Ella was bored. Their departures had the feeling of a page turning. Old traditions were falling away, new ones yet to be created.

August. Meg stood in the librarian's office looking at a poster of the Blue Ridge Mountains. There was a pale haze resting in the valleys between softly serrated rows of ever fading hues of deep blue. It was a photo she'd seen many times on the wall at her dentist's office augmented with some unmemorable motivational phrase printed in widely spaced letters. How many times had the fates placed that image in front of her, offering subtle hints of what lay in her future?

"We're ready for you, Miss Bishop."

Meg turned, smiled, and followed Mrs. Martin, the head librarian, upstairs toward the children's reading corner. Meg had done readings all over the country, from Santa Cruz to Portland, Maine. The audiences were universal, only the numbers varied. She thought of her readings as little performances and dressed accordingly in a fashion she presumed the children assumed an author would dress. This day, she wore an Indian print cotton skirt with a sleeveless black top. The effect of the August humidity on her hair was impossible to contend with so she chose one of her beaded headbands to hold it back off her face. Leaving home that day, an impulse drew her out of her car and back in the house, in search of a scarf to wear around her neck and shoulders. It was an exercise in contrast, for none of her many scarves were at all similar to the skirt, but the color of one in particular was perky. She grabbed it, draped it about her neck and caught only a quick glimpse of it on the way out the door. The final ensemble was more than a bit eccentric, and an effort probably wasted on the children. They only wanted to meet the person who painted the pictures of Emerson.

From the stairwell she heard the cackling and giggles of children. Emerging into the midst of them, one of them spoke out. "You look just like your picture!"

"Thank you," Meg said with a teasing grin. "Good thing, don't you think?"

The library had done a wonderful job of getting the word out and the day's event brought kids from throughout the area. Meg figured there had to have been more than fifty ranging in age from toddlers to young teenagers. She settled into the wing back chair as directed, and the children moved in close. Mrs. Martin told them to quiet down and get ready. Even as the squirming continued, little butts finding just the right position, the chatter subsided and all eyes were on Meg. She opened the book, read the title, and the author.

"That would be me," she said raising her eyebrows and making eye contact with a glance through the group. Then she began to read the story.

"Emerson found himself in a pickle. He had worked for two days on a birthday present for Harry. And, here it was, the day of Harry's birthday party, and Emerson had not yet received his invitation . . . "

The reading went well, Meg thought, as she stepped back into the heat of summer. She enjoyed being around so many little southern voices, their accents so soft and comforting. Their fondness for her books translated into instant fondness for her, an illusion she enjoyed and did her best not to dampen, which meant escaping the library before any of the mothers could invite her to dinner. If they got to know her, their impression would certainly sour.

Meg never learned the fine skill of social small talk. She found it impossible to appear to be interested in things that bored her, and talk of inconsequential things bored her. It took a sunnier disposition than hers to get along with perfect strangers, even admirers. In fact, particularly admirers, for they expected more from her - more cleverness, more insight, more awareness of all things literary. But she was none of those things. She was, by her own estimation, uninteresting.

An involuntary smile stretched across her face when she looked across the parking lot to her car. Ford was leaning on it, watching her. "Nice reading," he said with a straight face upon her approach.

"You were in there?"

"Yeah. I'm the one who told them you were available."

"You?" She took a breath to speak but nothing came to mind.

"You need to get out more," he said.

She hadn't seen him for weeks. One day some kid showed up to mow and that was it. No more Ford. It was after their argument about the Stonemount vulture. At the time, she hadn't thought too much about it. But seeing him again made her think maybe she missed him. "You sort of disappeared, don't you think?"

"Yeah. Stuff to do." He opened the car door for her. "You need help with all those tomatoes?"

"Tomatoes? YES! And beans and zucchini and basil and eggplant and, and and."

"OK. I'll come by tomorrow and we'll figure it out."

"OK." She got in her car. He shut the door. She pulled out. He walked away. Smiling.

CHAPTER 29

Seven-thirty the next morning Ford arrived at Stoneygate. He parked the truck at the vegetable garden and walked toward the house. Meg was there, sitting on the porch swing with a mug in her hand. The sunlight delineated edges in a hard yellow glow. She stood up and suddenly he couldn't move. The light beamed off her, turning her cotton robe translucent about her form, making graceful shining angles of her hips and legs.

"You want a cup of coffee?" she hollered out to him, and she disappeared into the house. When she returned, she wore a T-shirt and shorts, but the vision lingered in his imagination throughout the morning. They wandered the garden drinking coffee, surveying the situation.

"Lots of produce out here," he said.

"I don't know what the hell to do with it all," Meg sighed. "I don't can stuff. Jars, lids, preserving – food poisoning."

"How 'bout we pick it. Then we take it to the co-op for processing. If you join and volunteer to work in the kitchen or on the dock, you can build credits good toward stuff from the general supply." Meg looked a bit dazed.

"I'm from the city."

"What, they don't have food in the city? Let's say you like okra."

"Who in their right mind likes okra?"

"Oh, those are fightin' words down here, girl."

"Oops."

"If you wanted okra but didn't grow any, and you brought in 10 credits worth of tomatoes, you can walk out with 10 credits worth of okra. Gives us all a good variety. Some of our gardeners really get into the oddball stuff." Ford set his cup on the bumper and started pulling half-bushel baskets out of the truck. "If you don't want to join, they'll process your produce and give you credits on half of it. They will process and sell the rest. Up to you. It's a deal no matter what." He watched her eyes glaze over. "Yeah. How 'bout we pick and let them process this time. How's that sound?"

"Great. It sounds great."

They each wandered a row and began to pick in silence. Though they were in close proximity to each other, Meg sensed no obligation of conversation. It was a comfortable feeling. For weeks she had been reveling in her solitude, believing it was becoming her preferred lifestyle. But this activity, this quiet presence in the garden with her, was changing her perception, ever so slightly, but ever so compellingly.

"The garden looks great," Ford said, breaking into her thoughts. "You've been busy out here."

His compliment gave her great satisfaction. She hadn't done the work to impress anyone, but the fact that it impressed him made her happy. He had, after all, begun the garden in her stead, and then left it to her tending. It had been a labor of love for Meg, and looking at the results, so many baskets of produce, generated a deep feeling of accomplishment. Ford noticed her grinning at the load in the truck.

"Kind of primal, isn't it?" he said.

Primal, she thought. Yes. That was it. Instinctive. Growing food and stocking up to feed oneself. "This is really something," she said. "Really something."

They drove to the old train depot. It sported an elaborately painted sign: Laurel County Food Cooperative. The loading dock was a hive of activity with other gardeners dropping their produce, and volunteers sorting through it. A black haired wisp of a man named Bevo greeted them with a clipboard. Ford unloaded as Meg answered questions.

"Any petro-based pesticides?"

"No. Actually I didn't use anything. What survived, survived."

"Soil amendments?"

"No idea."

"Horse and cow shit," Ford said.

"This is Maggie's patch?" Bevo asked.

"Yep," Meg and Ford answered together.

"Ah. You're good then. We try to keep the organic crops separate. Are you joining or dropping off."

Meg hesitated.

"Show her the kitchen," Ford said.

The front of the building, what had been the passenger lounge of the depot, was full of bins of fresh produce, grains, nuts, and fresh and dried herbs. The shelves along the wall were stocked with mason jars of tomatoes, peaches, beans, corn, okra, cherries and more. Meg couldn't help but compose the painting of it in her head, trying to decide which view would be most interesting. She was led into the back where a dozen people, mostly retirees but a few in their twenties, worked in close quarters at two long counters and three stoves. Their movements were well choreographed.

"Hey there, Ford?" said one of the older ladies at a stove.

"What's it this morning?" he asked, peering into the pot she stirred.

"Tomato jelly here, pepper jelly there, basil and thyme tomato sauce over there."

One of the workers called out for another load of tomatoes and it seemed a good time to leave. Ford told Bevo they'd be processing as a non-member this time.

"That's fine, that's fine," he responded. "We'd be happy to have you join up ma'm when you can. In the meantime, thanks for the contribution," he said to Meg. "Come on back in a few days and you can pick up your share. And remember. You get the organic stuff."

She smiled and climbed back in the truck. "How much do I get in the end?"

"Equal to half of what you brought in."

"And they know how much that is?"

"They do." Ford sat behind the wheel. "Back home?"

"Yeah. Back home."

Ford's presence was more frequent over the next few weeks, reclaiming chores he had delegated to others. Meg found herself anticipating his visits and enjoying their time together. He was safe company. That Maggie knew him and trusted him created a commonality between them, and may also have had a lot to do with her distance from him. She did not perceive him as a free range male, but instead, relegated him to a cousin figure. He was the groundskeeper cousin who drove a beat-up truck. For a woman with her history of failure with men, Ford was perfect. No threat. No risk. No involvement. In fact, she knew nothing about him and chose not to ask. She liked his anonymity. It was easy.

Their conversations were about the mountains, and the town, and the needs of the property, and sometimes about very generalized, loosely formed philosophies on life. They both seemed to agree that money was a problem for most people. Either they didn't have enough or they had too much. And both extremes were trouble. Ford latched onto the subject and really had a go with it until he realized he was saying more than he should and shut up. "The expectation of a lot of money," he explained, "can make a person suddenly think what they have isn't good enough when it was just fine before. Just the anticipation of it upsets the balance. Actually getting it can really squirrel things up. Make you change a life that maybe didn't need changing."

Meg agreed and figured he was a fine one to talk since he seemed to live hand to mouth.

One morning in September, she awoke to the whine of a chain saw off in her woods. She prepared a thermos of coffee and wandered out to find Ford dismantling a fallen tree. He looked up at her ambling through the woods. "Got a couple of eggs and some potatoes to go with that coffee?" he shouted to her over the sputtering of the idling saw. She found his easy Carolina drawl a pleasant voice first thing in the morning. She enjoyed watching him rev the machine to a high whine and cut off the trunk into usable cordwood.

"This is next year's wood," he said, cutting off the saw and taking the coffee. "I'll stack it and let it sit here to cure. That stack over there is for this year. I'll move it next week." He pointed to a small wall of cordwood about ten feet off the path. A chipmunk sat atop it chattering. "Ever use a wood stove?"

"How hard could it be?"

"I'll show you. When the weather turns." His tone carried an unspoken directive: Don't even touch it till then.

"So," Meg asked, "how do you like your eggs?"

"Nah, don't worry about it. I have to get to a job."

"A job?"

"Yeah. I do some carpentry now and then."

He gathered up his things and looked at the clouds moving in. "I was going to finish this later, but looks like I won't be able to. Rain's moving in. What are you doing with this dreary day?"

"Read. Or write. Maybe work on a new book? Not that I have an idea yet, but never know when I will."

"Never know."

The air changed. Cooled. The smell of rain crept in. They walked along the garden's edge on the way back to the cottage.

"I wonder why Maggie never put a garden shed out here," Meg muttered. "Something to do all the potting in, start seedlings, store gear. Seems kind of inconvenient schlepping all the stuff back and forth from the cellar." Meg stopped and stood facing on an angle to the flower garden and the vegetables. She put her arms out wide. "I'd put it right here. With a nice overhang and sitting area, and ledge, and large doors, and a plexi panel in the roof to let the light in. Maybe even a little greenhouse area off the southern side."

"Maggie wasn't into conveniences much," Ford muttered. "Gotta go."

The drizzle began and Meg watched Ford drive away. Unlike other days, this one had a defined aspect to it. There would be no more visits from him until the rain stopped, and it was supposed to be a slow moving system. An uneasiness settled in her stomach. What would she do with all those hours? She faced something she never thought she'd suffer again: boredom.

She sat in the big wicker chair on the porch holding a lit cigarette as the rain started to fall in earnest. It was the last of the pack she found in Maggie's drawer. Like Maggie, Meg wasn't a real smoker. She used to light up when she painted in school, stepping back to look at the canvas, taking a few draws, then snuffing it out. She took a long drag and watched the smoke slide away on a thin current of air, then tossed it to the wet grass.

It suddenly occurred to her she was lonely living in someone else's surroundings. It wasn't hers yet because she hadn't decided yet. More importantly, the courts hadn't decided yet. For the time being, she was not at all certain where she belonged. So much for being a contented recluse.

She went in to retrieve one of Maggie's journals. The first year's journal had been a hard slog. Maggie was very lonely and put nearly every thought down on paper. Tucked into the back of second one were letters from Maggie to her family. Somehow, they'd made their way back to her.

Setting the letters aside for the moment, Meg settled into the couch with an afghan, a fresh cup of coffee and the next journal. She skimmed through some entries, others she read word for word. Prowling around someone else's life was, if nothing else, a way to pass time.

CHAPTER 30

October 21, 1947. It is a beautiful fall day. I seem to over use that word in here. But so much here is so strikingly picturesque. I am not used to it. By now, at home, the trees would be past their prime colors and into the brown, dead tones . . . here, the beauty lingers. I am on our porch swing, looking over the tennis court to the pasture. Beau is gone for the morning . . . Tomorrow I will be back in class, busy with fifteen hungry minds. Today is mine.

October 23, 1947. Last night, Jeff and Lizzie announced their engagement. I seem to be the only one worried that they're too young. I wish I felt I could talk to Sara about it. But we aren't close. Beau seems to think it was a given that she and I would be fast friends since both of us are from up north. But women are less predictable than that. She seems a part of all this here, just at home as the locals. She even talks more like them than me, that's for sure. Everything I say seems to offend her. She's so stern all the time. I know the wedding should be news that brings happiness,

but now, more than ever, it makes me feel like
even more of an outsider.

Maggie sat by the stove at the Feed & Seed after all the men had left, waiting for Sara to come down. They were heading over to a dinner at the Baptist church. It was warm, sitting on the hard wood chairs, the heat softly radiating out from the potbelly stove. Steam drifted up from a pan of water sitting on top. Women should have a place like this, she thought. Why does everything always have to be so formal with the women, pillows and lace and food on plates with doilies.

"I like it here, too" Sara said from the steps. "I'd sit with them if it wouldn't upset them so. Men're so damn fragile."

Maggie had never thought of men as fragile. Not yet. It would come to her later, a few years on. One would think she might see it sooner, the seed of it planted at this very moment. But in her heart, Beau was still her pillar, the source of her strength.

"I heard today your Errol was a bastard." Maggie said it without warning. It had, in fact, just slipped out. She hadn't meant to say it, realizing it was not polite and the friendship with Sara was not so close as sisters where one can get away with being so direct. In the instant it took to say it she wanted to take back. She apologized with her eyes so wide open Sara almost laughed.

"You have to stop that, Maggie," Sara said quietly.

"What exactly?"

"Your directness. People around here don't like it. Only someone from up north would do that. We're used to it, you and I, but they aren't. They think it's rude. I've been real careful to play by their rules so they accept me. But I'll never be one of them. We'll never be one of them. You understand?" She watched Maggie's face turn red from embarrassment. "My livelihood depends on fitting in here," Sara continued. "You remind them of where I'm from. So, you aren't doing either of us any favors."

"They do accept you," Maggie tried to comfort. "And I try to be careful what I say, what I do. But I'm always going to make a fool of myself. I feel like they're all just watching and waiting for it."

"You have to get over that." Sara enjoyed exercising her Yankee will for the moment, knowing she would have to put it away soon after. "Actually, that apologizing smooth-it-all-over makes you more like them. Always so damn polite and sugar-coated. Some days, I feel like slapping one of them just to wipe that smile off her face." Before the words were out of her mouth, she had a flash of the flat of Errol's hand flying through the air to her eye. Some aspect of his violence lingered within her, like a dormant infection.

Even though Maggie was only eight years younger than Sara, Maggie felt like an adolescent just learning her way in the world. Sara was a good teacher, but could be cold.

"And, yes," Sara confirmed. "My dead husband was a bastard." She grabbed her coat and Maggie's off the hooks. "Shall we go then?" she said with a sweet smile gracing her fair cheeks. Maggie couldn't help but smile back. It was an automatic response, not particularly genuine.

October 30, 1947. What fun we had at school today. The children all in costume and our dessert-only lunch! How fun! The women down here are fabulous cooks. And I think I found my way in with them. When the mothers showed up for our little program, I made a point of learning who went with what dessert and I asked for the recipes. Women I knew back home would no more share their best recipes - like it was a competition or something. One woman - Bonnie Harper - even asked me over to show me how to make her sweet potato soufflé pie.

October 31, 1947. Just arrived home from Bonnie's. I've decided to give a bridal shower for Lizzie. Bonnie said she'll help me.

November 12, 1947

Dear sister, How do I even begin tonight? Such a magical day! 75 degrees in November! We decided to have Lizzie's shower at Sara's on her porch. As I've told you they live upstairs over the Feed & Seed. It is wonderful quarters. Not at all what you would expect. Much more spacious than our whole house. She has two bedrooms, an office, a reading room, huge kitchen, walk-in pantry, and a massive living room. But her covered porch is wonderful. It runs across the entire second floor length of the building. And in the middle, it extends out even farther, like a big room. It overlooks the back yard, which is half inventory for the store and half garden. We hung streamers and paper bells from the rafters. Very festive!

Lizzie seemed very excited to be the center of attention. I'm sure at nineteen it must be like a dream come true. She is very much at ease around her mother-in-law to be. (that would be Sara) Lizzie and Jeff have been best friends all their lives. Everyone at the shower got up and told a story about Lizzie. Sara had the best one. She said Jeff asked Lizzie to marry him in second grade. She said no then, and it took him this long to get up the nerve to ask her again! And this time she said yes! I was so afraid I'd have nothing interesting to say when it was my turn. And it came to me what Beau said when they announced their engagement. "Two peas in a pod, those two. Two peas in a pod." So that's what I said and I sat down. All in all it went very well. Am enclosing our menu and all the recipes. All my love to you and Mama and Papa and everyone else. Maggie

November 18 - The more I get to know Sara, the more I see a gentleness in her. She is so strong and confident and good at managing the store and everything on her own. I don't think I could do what she does. I am not made of stuff so tough. I hope we can become close friends.

Dec 20, 1947.   Maybe it is just the holidays, but I feel more and more like part of a family. It isn't the traditional arrangement, but one of extension to friends. Sara, Jeffrey and Lizzie, Beau and me, Jarvis Payton and his family. We are spending Christmas day together. I miss snow. They all say we could get some any day. Some years they get it, some years they don't. School is fine, the children are all anxious for their winter break....

Jan. 15, 1948. I see now the pleasures inherent in putting up one's own produce. I feel like Midas sometimes when I go down to the cellar. I can't help but count the jars, and reorganize them by size and content. The colors are so pretty and the jelly jars look like gems. Current red, apple gold, marmalade orange. Even the shapes fascinate me - long and slender green beans, yellow wax beans cut short . . . corn, and tomatoes. I sometimes just stand there and stare at the abundance brought by our labors last fall. I find that I eat less than I used to, being somewhat of a hoarder now. And I waste nothing!

March 1, 1948. Sara has purchased a car for the newlyweds. And Beau and I are giving them the little house in town he's been renting out. Two young people never had it as good. So much love. So much love.

April 22, 1948. The wedding was sweet and quiet. Reminded me of mine. The weather held for the picnic out on the lawn here. Beau spent the weekend trimming the boxwoods . . . I don't know what I got so worked up about. Things seem to be easier down here, not as much fuss as I'm used to up north. I suppose I should write more, but the garden is taking a lot of time these days, and school keeps me very busy. I guess a few notes now and then are enough.

April 30, 1948. Housewarming. Now that was a party! Jeff and Lizzie will be cleaning up for a week after that hullabaloo. No doubt that house is well warmed! Lizzie and Jeff are both working at the Feed & Seed with Sara now. They have it running slick as can be. I can't think of a thing I need that they don't have. Like the sign says, "If we don't have it, you don't need it!" By her own admission, Sara has turned it into a general store basically because she likes to order things . . . if she likes it someone else is bound to want to buy it. She buys housewares and notions, hand salve and lotions just as fast as block and tackle, harnesses and hardware. Somebody actually came in last week and bought six sets of sterling silver corn cob holders! But the ceramic clown cookie jars I think will be there for a very long time.

July 26, 1948. How is it that bad news sometimes travels hand in hand with the best news? Scratch that. There is no bad news, only an abundance of self-pity. Lizzie is three months pregnant and everyone is thrilled. She's bringing a new life to our world. And all I could do was spend my afternoon crying. I want so badly to have children of my own. A baby to bathe and nurse and love. Every day I teach someone else's children and wonder what makes them so lucky and me so ill-

fated. My arms ache to hold an infant, one that Beau and I made. It is an emptiness nothing can fill. I see the sadness in his eyes as well. I grieve for what may never be.

Sept 8, 1948. Saw Lizzie today. She is beaming! It's twins! That explains why she is so big for 5 months. So here I am, journaling from the garden, about to pick our dinner of eggplant, corn, tomatoes, and beans. I am surrounded by the fruits of my endeavors. We have had good rains this past couple of weeks and the abundance of vegetables surpasses my wildest imaginings. It will be long hours in the kitchen this weekend putting up beans, tomatoes, pickled zucchini, beets, spiced carrots, and then the first of the peaches are in and they need to be jammed and buttered. It is a frantic time of year, but one I am growing to enjoy for its productivity.

Sept 12, 1948. I doubt that writing now will improve my state of mind or make it worse. The day's events are like a bad dream - so awful. I think I'm alright for the moment and then I break down into tears again. Beau is at the hospital with Sara and Jeff and I am here trying to find something to do to be useful when I know there is nothing any one can really do except stay out of the way. Lizzie lost the babies.

Sept 13, 1948. I'm surrounded by jars and lids and bushels of vegetables and peaches. Lizzie and

Sara and I were to spend the day canning. Now I don't much care if it all rots. Jeffrey's with Lizzie at the hospital. She's awake, though God knows she'd probably rather not be. We don't really have the whole picture yet, but from what Lizzie has been able to tell us, it was an accident. Jeff was down to Spartanburg for a couple days so Lizzie stayed with Sara. She couldn't sleep and went out to the porch. She didn't see Nestor asleep on the chase and he startled when he heard her. One way or another, she took a tumble down the stairs and Sara found her in the morning. They're keeping her in the hospital - I can't imagine what she feels. Those babies have died but she has to wait for them to be "expelled". What a horror - I don't think I know how I'd survive such a thing. So many dreams were spun around those babies. The twins. They were the beginning and end of every conversation. They were the future. And now it feels as if there is no future. Only an interminable stretching on of this one event. They are gone, but only in spirit. The doctor says it could be days or weeks before their bodies are delivered.

Sept 18, 1948. God has finally granted us our prayers. The twins have been delivered. A girl and a boy. How do you say goodbye to someone you never met?

Sept 23, 1948. My rock, my Beau. Seeing him cry broke what was left of my heart to a thousand pieces. I heard him last night in the living room and saw him put his sister's photograph back on the shelf. I don't suppose I'll ever understand the deep friendship between Sara and Beau. I know she's older than he is, and it isn't jealousy that I feel. I've never had a friend that close. My family always got in the way. I wanted so to hold him last night, to comfort him, but he wouldn't let me. He said he needed some air and was out the rest of the night. I know because I didn't sleep a wink.

Sept 26, 1948. One would wonder how could things get worse, but they have. Now the doctor says Lizzie may never have children. Just when you think you've taken all you can bear. This is one pain, one I regret to be so familiar with, I wouldn't wish on my worst enemy.

Oct. 5, 1948. Oh, dear Lord, how much more are we to take? I suppose we should have seen it coming. Jeff is a good boy but he is young, and heartbroken. Not to say he did it, but if he did, it was an act of passion, not brutality. Jeff is in jail. They say he murdered Nestor. I don't believe it. Beau's getting Merle and Jarvis Payton on the case. They'll fix this. They have to.

.

CHAPTER 31

Wiping tears from her eyes, Meg closed the journal. It was a horrible thing to admit that she, too, cried more than once at the news of someone's pregnancy. It was harder when it was friends because the disappointment was two-fold. Not only did it mean one less friend to hang out with, but it was one more reminder that she did not have a family. It had become more and more difficult over the years to deliver the obligatory congratulations with sincerity.

The worst were friends who miscarried. There was never anything appropriate to say. There are no condolence cards that quite cover it. There isn't even a ritual to give it the significance it deserves. A miscarriage, at any point in the pregnancy, is a misery kept within the marriage. Friends can only get so close to it. Aside from not being able to conceive, Meg thought miscarriage was the worst and most un-mourned aspect of womanhood.

It was all too sad and she didn't feel like digging any deeper. She dozed off thinking how everything Maggie wrote about made her own life look simple in comparison.

A rumble rolling down from the mountain gently woke Meg from her sleep on the couch. It was dark and felt like very early morning. She glanced at the clock. 4:50. The journal fell from her lap to the floor. She left it and pulled the afghan up snuggly around her. Another roll of thunder resonated, bringing with it a steady easy rain. She lay there, not quite awake, but not likely to sleep, her thoughts roving about with little cohesive nature.

As if living in some strange shifting of time, she thought she heard Maggie in the kitchen. It did not occur to her to question it, as it seemed perfectly natural. Even when Maggie stepped into the room with a cup of tea it didn't cross Meg's mind to question it, or when Maggie reached down and picked up the journal, placing it on the table. "It's nice you're reading these, dear," she said as she nestled into her chair. The click of teacup to saucer woke Meg.

As sunrise filtered through overcast skies, it seemed time hadn't decided yet who lived at Stoneygate. Meg felt she was living within an echo of the past, wondering if she was its future. In all her weeks of exploring parameters of contentment, she was beginning to encounter the significance of living entirely among Maggie's belongings. Perhaps whoever she was before moving there was beginning to seep back to the surface. This thought brought with it some sadness. What if all these days were only a flicker of a candle, and the candle was burning out? Would she return to the busy preoccupied person she was, unable to take notice of how her thread fit into the fabric of something greater?

She leaned up to adjust the pillows. A twinge shot up her spine. Her own couch would never have done that to her. She missed it. She missed her bed and dresser and chairs and dishes. The bulk of her belongings were packed away. Patrick had filled her space with his stuff now, leaving her feeling fragmented as though one of her limbs was in storage, another lay on his coffee table, and the rest of her was in Laurel County caught within the wake of Maggie's life, drifting toward whatever was to become of her own. She picked up the journal from the table and put it back on the shelf.

With a fresh cup of coffee in hand, Meg withdrew another journal and chose a page at random.

I understand now. And I could be upset but I'm not. I've given my word to keep what he's told me safe. And I'm almost glad he didn't tell me before now. To know something so important and have to stay silent - giving it no acknowledgement - is harder than anything I've ever done. He is my husband. As much as it pains me, I will oblige him with my silence.

Meg read the entry again, scanning backward, wondering what the secret was but found no indication, no reference, no further explanation. She tore a strip of paper from a magazine and tucked it tight into the binding of the page. Certainly, at some point, Maggie would be compelled to write about it again, elaborate, reveal. But the only other reference she found was written the year Beau passed away. And it, too, was cryptic.

Now it is mine alone to carry and I am no more used to it than I was when he told me. And in his death, I am empowered to do what I think best, but I still hear him and see his face, those eyes glaring at me, warning me to not be foolish. So, I will continue to do as he asked though it doesn't seem fair to me. And what good could come of it in any case.

By mid-morning, clouds broke up. Sun broke through. Errant drops of water plopped from the trees to the roof.

Meg took a shower and was soon on a mission. She was going to find the Laurel County Feed & Seed.

She knew it was across from a school so drove and found the two elementary schools. No Feed & Seed in sight. She asked at a gas station but the East Indian attendant behind the counter had never heard of it. She went to the library to ask the young woman at the desk but she didn't know. "Wait a minute," she said to Meg. "Follow me." She led Meg to the basement.

They walked past broken bookshelves and old desks stacked one on another to a room in the back. The woman knocked politely and entered.

"Uh, excuse me, Mr. George," she said to the back of a bald man hunched over a long oak table surrounded by curator boxes and stacks of photos and papers. "Can you help Miss Bishop? She's looking for the old Laurel Feed & Seed." Without another word, she left and Meg standing in the middle of the dim room in an awkward moment of silence.

"Interesting room," Meg eventually said.

"Uh huh," came the man's first utterance.

"Is there an old town map that I could maybe use to find the . . ."

"Yes. Lots of maps. Lots of artifacts." He enunciated artifact with great care as he did all his words. "You don't need any map. Head out 25 just outside of town. There's an abandoned Landmark school," he said, placing a great deal of disdain on landmark. "The store is across from it a block down."

"Thanks."

"Certainly, Miss."

"If you don't mind my asking, what do you do down here?"

"I'm nosey," he said in a dismissive manner. She was nearly through the doorway when he added, with a tease in his voice. "Interesting history there. That Feed & Seed."

Meg stopped. "I've gathered that," she said. "I've been reading Maggie Kenyon's journals. They're quite a read."

Mr. George turned, facing her with desire in his eyes. "I would love to get my hands on those journals." He was a rotund man in his seventies, wearing a plaid shirt and baggy jeans.

"Yes," Meg said. "I imagine you would."

"So, if you don't mind my asking, what are you reading about now. Maybe I can fill in some gaps for you."

"Right now, Lizzie Mercer has just lost her babies and Jeffrey is on his way to jail, I think, for killing somebody."

"Sad tales. Sad. Would you care to read some newspaper articles of the time?" Mr. George asked, "because I would be happy to pull some for you. It was such a tragedy. All the way around. Here. You have a seat right here and I'll get them."

"That would be fascinating. If it isn't any trouble," Meg said.

"Trouble? I live for this. Flip on those lights behind you," he said, rising to his feet. He arched his back and rolled his head. His neck cracked repeatedly. "It's hard these days to find anyone who wants to talk about history." His voice muffled by three rows of shelves, he said Jeffrey and Lizzie were classmates of his. "Here it is. 1948." He reappeared with a wide, flat curator's box. He opened a drawer in the desk and pulled out two pair of white cotton gloves, handing a set to Meg.

"Nobody knows any of it for fact, how any of it really happened." He spoke as he tediously leafed through issues of the Forest City Monitor. "Lizzie insisted it was an accident that Nestor knocked her down the stairs. Now, Nestor. He was a real piece of work. The worthless son of a local politician. A drunk, but harmless - used to do odd jobs for Sara at the store. He was always good to her, never a bother. I used to spend a lot of time over there at the Feed & Seed myself. Jeff was just about the best friend I had."

"What was Jeff like? Maggie sort of had a biased perspective. He could do no wrong."

"She's not too off base. He was a good kid. Real quiet though. Didn't have a lot of friends. Either did I." His voice was low and reflective. "He got screwed six ways over."

He stopped leafing the pages and called Meg to the table. "Here."

FOREST CITY MONITOR, November 4, 1948. Jeffrey Mercer of Flat Rock was tried and convicted of second degree murder of Nestor Tyler, son of Congressman Abraham Tyler of Forest City. Mercer's wife, Elizabeth, recently suffered the stillbirth of twins as a result of a fall down a flight of stairs. The incident report stated Tyler was under the influence of alcohol and trespassing the night of Mrs. Mercer's accident and may have caused it. Congressman Tyler testified his son was in Saluda with him at the time working on his re-election campaign. The Congressman gave a public statement outside the courthouse. "This is a clear cut and sad case of mistaken identity. My heart goes out to Mrs. Mercer for her loss. But my son had nothing to do with it. And now, through a vicious act of revenge, I too, have lost a child. A life wasted. A tragedy all round."

Mercer will be sentenced on November 10.

"They gave him fifteen years," said Mr. George. The prosecution had half a dozen witnesses who heard Jeff say he'd sooner like to see Nester dead. Hell, even I heard it. It's the kind of thing people say when they're in pain but they don't mean for it to happen. Not really. I watched what I said after that, you can be sure of that."

"What really happened?" asked Meg.

"Like I said. No one knew and it didn't much matter. The congressman wanted something and he got it. Jeff told me he ran into Nester on the outskirts of town and Nester took a swing at him and stumbled off the road into the ravine and hit his head. I believed him then. Still do. He was devastated and so ashamed. One minute life was grand and the next his life is destroyed and he's carted off to prison.

"Didn't matter what Jeffrey did, how good he was, he still wore the stain of his father's sins and sometimes people just get caught up in the worst of a thing. Everyone from the barber to the postmaster was saying things like the apple didn't fall far from that tree, that he was his father's son after all because Errol was one mean son of a bitch." Mr. George's expression said more than his words could. He hadn't forgiven anyone for their hand in convicting Jeffrey.

"Errol?"

"His no-account, bootlegging father. No getting away from bad blood. It was like a virus, the notion that Jeffrey was bad by blood. It infected even the well intentioned. The jury was not immune, leading them to their guilty verdict.

"Lizzie moved in over the store with Mrs. Mercer. She didn't want to be alone in the house in town and her folks wanted her to get a divorce so she could get on with her life."

"That's pretty low."

"You sit back down. I've got some letters in here you might find interesting."

Mr. George again disappeared and returned with a smaller box with a hinged lid.

"Christmas that first year was tough, I remember. I stopped over to the Feed & Seed to pick up something, I don't know what. And there they were, Mrs. Mercer, Lizzie and Mrs. Kenyon, all crying themselves silly, stringing garlands and red bows all over the front of the store. They told me to just go in and get what I needed and I suppose I did, but what I remember is helping them with those greens. People stopped in all day long. Sometimes those ladies would burst out laughing, other times just cry. Mr. Thompson helped me hang the wreath from the roof. Mrs. Carlson came by looking for a new coffee pot and helped string Christmas lights around the windows. And then I sold her three new strings of lights for her own house. As the day went on, I don't think there was anyone who came by that didn't help out and didn't shed a tear or two. I think it was kind of a cleansing, maybe for the whole town. I was still there when Beau Kenyon showed up to find the whole place all lit up.

"Of course, by then we were all drinking the last of a bottle of warm muscadine wine they had mulling on the Franklin." He began rummaging through the box of letters. "These were collected for the tuberculosis project. Some of Jeff's letters home are in here. Ah," he said, pulling envelopes from the box. "Here's a couple."

Meg read one aloud, then another.

April 10, 1951, Received April 25   Dear loved ones, I have mentioned my persistent cough, though I didn't want to worry you, so until now I thought it best not to tell you all of the news. I have been moved to the isolation wing of the prison hospital. You must address me at the HOSPITAL SEC.ISO while I am here, or I won't get my mail. I will be in the company of a dozen others with the same condition. They are not ready to call it consumption, but I fear it is. I am strong, as you know, and will fight it off. I expect to be back in general population soon. I love you and miss you more than you can ever imagine. Love, Jeffrey

April 22, 1951, Received May 10   Dear loved ones, I am writing to report on my circumstances. I am happy to say the conditions, though as Spartan as my old cell, are superior to it. Our linens are changed every other day. Our food is fresh, though I miss eating what they laughingly call meat. (I'm sure it was goat or horse.) We get no meat, eggs, cheese or milk. We suffer through a cold shower each morning. For the life of me I can see no possible good in that other than to torture us but they call it treatment. The rest of the time we are to lay flat on our backs in bed. Next week, they'll take the healthiest of us for a walk outside. They weigh us every 4 or 5 days and take our temperature twice a day. One of the guys had a hemorrhage last night. The staff was quite considerate and tended to his fears as well as his ailment. They are not as harsh as they could be, though I long for the loving touch of my sweet Lizzie and dear mother. With the both of you I know I would mend with more immediacy. I have been doing well so far and you are not to worry about me. Have not received any mail - The post just arrived. What a wonderful thing! There must be two dozen letters tied in a bundle for me. I shall ration them out to last a few days. All love and deepest longing, I am as always, Jeffrey.

Meg rummaged in the box. "Here's one with a Morganton postmark," she said. "He must be out of jail?"

"Yes. Congressman Tyler finally died. He was the only thing blocking Jeff's appeals and they finally let him out of prison. But he was still too sick to come home." He searched in the back again for more newspapers, talking as he went. "Even when he did come home, he wasn't ever really well again."

Jan 19, 1952, Morganton Sanatorium   Dear loved ones, a year ago, I had so little hope. I can tell you that now, because I am so full of it and expectation too. I am settling into life at the Sanatorium in Morganton. Someday I may need to tell you of the horrors of the prison hospital ward. I survived my many months there, while most were not as fortunate. But I think it best now to spend the rest of my life rejoicing. Each day is a day I sometimes doubted I would ever see.

I think I am so used to the near vegetarian diet now that a thick red steak would turn my stomach. We eat chicken once a week and eat most everything else from the gardens here. There is a large bowl of olives on the table each evening and we are encouraged to eat our fill of them. I have eaten enough collards and turnip greens to turn into a leaf myself. I may never eat them again! Three times a week, we are given a full body massage. They tell us it boosts our immune system. I am on a regimen of streptomycin, and a tincture of herbs - Echinacea and golden seal. It may take weeks or months, but they say I will be able to go home as good as new. And, in the short term, if I continue to show strength, I'll be able to help in the garden this summer. It is especially nice to be here in Morganton for all the pleasant memories I have hiking the mountains here with Beau and Mother. Some days I can close my eyes and breathe the air and almost believe I am up on Glassy. Love to everyone, Jeff

"Here's the last article about it," Mr. George said, handing it to Meg.

FOREST CITY MONITOR. JANUARY 10, 1952 The appeal brought by Payton and Payton, attorneys at law out of Hendersonville, on behalf of Jeffrey Mercer, resulted in his release late yesterday. Charges against Mercer in the 1948 death of Nester Tyler were reduced to involuntary manslaughter. His sentence was reduced to time served. Mercer, who has spent nine months in the isolation ward for tuberculosis, will be released and admitted into the Morganton Sanatorium.

Meg read the paragraph and took off the gloves. "Well, we've got him out of jail and on his way home. Let's leave it at that today, shall we?"

Mr. George agreed. "I've enjoyed this. Come back any time. And if you ever decide to donate those journals, I guarantee they will be handled with great care."

"We'll see."

Meg decided that finding the Feed & Seed would wait for another day. Focusing on more light-hearted things, she hung about town, prowling antique shops for discarded books. She walked out of one shop with three books in hand, the complete works of William Faulkner, thinking they would be a fine addition to the library in the cottage.

After a trip to the market, she went home. Though it was little more than mid-afternoon, she made dinner of sautéed vegetables and scallops with angel hair pasta in a light white wine sauce. She dined on the porch, dismayed to think it was too delicious to be eating it alone.

CHAPTER 32

Late fall of 1948, Beau was at the sawmill early to do some bookwork when the call came from Sara. Her voice never wavered. She could have been placing an order for shingles. "Beau, they've got our Jeffrey in jail. They say he killed the Tyler boy. Would you mind coming over please."

His response was equally matter of fact. "That's preposterous. We'll get it straightened out." After calling Merle Payton to start untangling the legal mess, he called the sheriff to get specifics. He instead was told to call back later. The sheriff was at the scene. Beau went to fetch Sara.

She was waiting on the loading dock in a cotton housedress. Beau's quiet sureness should have sustained them both. But the darkness shrouding Sara's presence unnerved him entirely and there was little he could do to comfort himself, let alone her. He opened the car door for her. With the pace of one heading to the gallows, she approached the car and got in. "I need to see for myself," she said with an unnatural calm in her voice. "You take me there. To where it happened. Then you take me to the jail to see my boy."

"I don't know where it …"

She cut him off cold. "You know where." She glared right into him so hard he shivered. Without another word, she sat with her hands limp in her lap as they drove over the ridge toward Saluda.

The narrow winding passage through the gorge felt strangled by laurel and rhododendron thickets. Rounding one bend after another, branches of conifer and hickory reached over them like a tunnel.

Beau took the switchbacks more slowly than usual expecting to see police cars at any point. The further he went without sight of them, the more anxious he became.

The sun was just breaking over the ridge as he pulled out of a curve down a section of road he knew all too well. His heart skipped a beat when he saw where the police cars were parked. Beau rolled slowly to a stop and turned off the engine. Sara's gaze was drawn to the woods and fixed on a mangled old tree trunk. She did not budge as Beau stepped out, walked to the edge, and looked down into the ravine. Time slipped out from under him and he faltered. The sheriff grabbed him by the arm. "Hold steady, there, Beau." His voice carried no comfort.

"He didn't do this, John," Beau stated quietly.

"That's up to the courts now, Beau. I'm just gathering facts. Why don't you go down to the office. They'll let you and Miss Sara see Jeff. I think the boy could use her right about now."

Beau climbed back into his car and slowly drove around the vehicles. Sara was fixed on that old tree until it was out of sight. "He's still there," she stated with the certainty of a threat.

"Who?" asked Beau.

"The devil."

A short ways up the road, she told him to stop the car. "Now, come on, Sara," he moaned. "You don't need to do this."

"You don't know what I need. Pull in."

With a heavy sigh, he turned into a gap in the brush, into an overgrown cutaway. Back in the woods were the remains of her house, its roof caved in, windows broken. Sara stepped out. She waded through the tall grass and stepped over fallen trees and branches. Beau got out, stood against the car, and watched her climb over broken steps onto the porch. It had been a lot of years since he stood where he stood now, dodging buckshot from the porch.

She looked back down the drive as she had countless times before in another life. She remembered nights waiting for Errol to show up. She looked through the doorway at the rotted floorboards, at a few dishes, some broken chairs. The decay suited the memories. She thought about how every day of their lives since leaving there had been a gift. Until this day's events unfolded, she thought maybe Errol's death had indeed been just an accident; that nothing she said or prayed had anything to do with it. Yet always a thought lingered, like the cobwebs she ignored in the high corners of the Feed & Seed. She feared one day, sooner or later, that devil in the woods would come to collect his due. And collect, he had. Neither she nor Beau spoke as they drove over the ridge and back to town.

Jeffrey was the only one who knew the truth about Nestor's death and as the only suspect, his testimony didn't count for much.

He'd been on his way up from Saluda when he came across Nester on the grade, stumbling drunk. While he entertained the thought of hitting the gas and running him down, he pulled onto the shoulder instead and offered him a ride.

"Who is it?" Nestor called out. "What do you want?"

"It's Jeff Mercer."

"You leave me be, you hear me? You just get away."

Jeff walked toward him.

"You stay back! Leave me be!" Nestor yelled. "I didn't mean your wife harm. It was an accident! A goddamned accident!"

"Get in the car," Jeff told him. "I'll take you into town." But, when he got close enough, Nestor took a wild swing that caught Jeff square in the jaw, knocking both of them off balance. Nester staggered and took a header off the side of the road and slid down about twenty feet. Jeff kicked up a scattering of gravel and let out with a long chain of profanity. "I ought to just leave you there you drunken son of a bitch! Like you left Lizzie." He kept hollering on his way down the edge to retrieve him. "I ought to just leave you to die down there!"

When he rolled Nestor over, faint words slipped out of the man. "I didn't mean any harm. I would never hurt our Lizzie or those babies."

Jeff couldn't see the blood so much as feel it warm and sticky on his hands. "I know that, Nestor," he said with a shaky voice. "I know it."

"I'm hurt pretty bad," Nestor mumbled. Jeff tried to get his arm under his neck to lift when Nestor cried out in pain. Jeff released him and leaned back against a rock. Nestor's strained words rose up through the darkness. "You can't save me. Don't know why you'd even try."

"I'm going to get help," Jeff said. "You just stay put. Can you do that? Just don't move."

"Couldn't if I wanted to."

Covered in blood, Jeff worked his way back up to the car and drove into town to get the sheriff, never thinking for a second he'd be charged with assault.

When they got back, Nester was dead. The sheriff took off his hat and rubbed his neck. "The Congressman's not going to like this. Not one little bit," he said. The deputies brought Nestor's body up to the road. "I need you to come back into town with me, Jeffrey."

"Why?" Jeff protested. "I already told you what happened." The sheriff took him by the elbow and Jeff pulled away. "If I was going to kill the man why would I come in to town to get you?"

"Well now that's an interesting question, isn't it? Maybe you changed your mind about it. Pushed him down there and thought better of it. Maybe you got scared. I don't know. But now you have to come with me."

Jeffrey's trial was swift. The congressman saw to it.

Three years into Jeffrey's fifteen-year sentence, Sara and Lizzie were summoned to a meeting with Judge Bender over at the county courthouse. When they got there, they were surprised to see Merle Payton, Beau and the widow Tyler. The five of them were directed into the judge's chambers and the door was closed behind them. The judge slowly situated himself behind his desk. The room was still.

"My sincere condolences to your family, Mrs. Tyler," he finally said.

No one else in the room concurred.

The widow sat straight as a board in her chair, resolute in her intent. "Judge," Mrs. Tyler began, "I need to trust that you will never ask me to say in public what I am about to say in here. Because, I won't do it. Do we have an understanding?"

The judge hesitated, looked to Merle for a nod, and agreed.

"My husband was a pig's ass," she announced.

"Don't you mean a horse's ass. Ma'am," asked the judge.

"No, Harold. I respect horses too much to associate them with my late husband. As I was saying," she continued, her speech seeming to be something she'd planned for a very long time and was trying to deliver perfectly. She turned and spoke to Sara. "Sara Mercer, you are one of the best people I know. My son was very fond of you. And I knew if he was anywhere near your Feed & Seed, he was safe. If you must know the truth of it, I sometimes suggested he go to you, when I knew his father was due home. I sent everyone I knew to your Feed & Seed to make sure your business thrived as best it could. So you'd be able to be there for my boy.

"And another thing." She glanced over her shoulder to the judge. "My son had no more interest in working on Abraham's campaign than he had in sobering up. I'm quite certain he was on Miss Sara's porch that night, and I'm quite certain what happened was an awful and heartbreaking accident." She looked down at her lap. Her gloved hands worked the beads of her purse as if they were fidgety children she could not will to hold still.

"I know what happened that night, Sara. He told me. He was drunk and he was scared. Laying that blanket over her was the decent side of him breaking through the fear."

Sara gasped. No one knew about the blanket. It wasn't in the newspapers.

"Nestor came home that night, I think to get me to help," Mrs. Tyler continued, "risking a beating from his father. Abe couldn't tolerate the drinking. No son of his could be allowed to have such weakness. It must have been two in the morning when I heard the ruckus and went downstairs to find Abraham slapping the boy around, yelling at him to shape up. I intervened, but Nestor ran out the door. It was days later when he told me what happened. Yes, he ran from Lizzie, but he was scared. He thought she was dead. I'd have done something if I'd only known. I'd have called you and the doctor. I swear I would have."

She broke down into tears, apologizing for doing so. "I am so sorry for all of it. And I am sorry that I was not strong enough to stand up to my husband. He knew what happened. Every last bit of it. And he lied to protect his precious reputation." She dabbed at her eyes and stiffened up again. "I have no doubt in the world that Jeffrey didn't push my boy off that road. And I am as certain as I am sitting here today that he was only trying to help Nestor. Why else would he have gone to town all bloody, for God's sake?"

Turning to the judge, she demanded he take action. "I don't know how you're going to do this, but you are going to get that boy out of jail immediately. My only regret is that my husband didn't die any sooner!"

On her way to the door, she turned, pointing a stern finger at each of them. "I will not have my husband's name soiled. You understand that." And she left.

Jeffrey was released to the sanatorium within the week.

July 6, 1952. We all traipsed over to Morganton for the 4th. Jeff is doing so much better. Liz is growing weary of the weekly drive to visit him and anxious to have him home. It is frustrating to see him looking so well, good color, but see him still so weak. I was not prepared to see him so thin.

August 2, 1953. Life resumes. Jeffrey is home and in reasonably good health although none of us can get over his hair turning gray so young. Such an ordeal he has endured. He and Liz will move back into the house as soon as the renters find another place. Sara is going to be alone over the store and will surely miss having Liz with her. I see a relief in Beau, as if some dark shadow has finally lifted.

October 7, 1953. We are concerned for Jeff as he doesn't seem to be well enough to do much. His color is not always what it should be and he has difficulty digesting his food. Sara says he complains of aches and pains. He had cross words for us all yesterday. Says we hover. He's right. We do.

New Year's Day, 1954. Jeffrey is resting comfortably. His surgery went well but they haven't told us what it was they found. They did some work on his lower intestine and gave him a temporary colostomy bag. His spirits are awfully low. Lizzie is propping him up with her sunshine smile, but even she is wearing thin. We would all be happier if we knew what was wrong with him.

January 15, 1954. Several of my seed catalogs arrived today. Sometimes I think the post office collects them and chooses to deliver them all at once. This is one of my favorite times of year - sitting by the fire, my Beau reading his books on the couch, and me on the floor with all my catalogs, planning next year's garden. I could spend a fortune right now sending off for some of everything - but of course I get all our seed from Sara. I'm thinking of sectioning off a new space for only dried beans. Parks has a dozen varieties that look colorful and delicious. I'll show Sara so she can order some. If I could grow them all, imagine the colorful soups I could make, and the interesting bean salads. If I ordered everything I fancy tonight, I would need a ten acre parcel to grow it all. Feels good planning the garden while it's snowing outside.

Jeff's surgery brought the diagnosis: Beock's Sarcoid had attacked his intestines, lining them with lesions. Whether the disease came from the TB or the TB came from disease made no real difference. Even the arrival at a diagnosis affected no significant change. After the removal of the bad gut section, Jeff was still tired, still had bouts of horrific nausea and ached all over. At the moment, he was feeling relatively well. He couldn't put on any weight, but he felt more normal than he had in years, which wasn't saying much.

February 20, 1954. Jeffrey is in for a follow up surgery to remove the colostomy bag. Perhaps now he'll be in better spirits. He hasn't let any of us near him in weeks, says he's afraid he smells.

July 4, 1955. Only a year ago we were in Morganton visiting Jeff and this year we were all on a boat on Lake Lure watching fireworks. Beau rented a cottage for the month in a lovely little cove. Sara and Liz are alternating days at the store and come out in the evenings. I think if I had to give up Stoneygate for another home, this could be it. Beau and I have been canoeing each evening, wandering the shoreline as it curves in and out of coveys. The lake fills a basin at the end of the Hickory Nut Gorge. I suppose the road ran straight through before they damned it. Looking up the gorge, there are massive stone cliffs that change color in such a profusion of hues as the sun sets. These are peaceful days, rich and luxurious. I have never been as tan as I will be this summer. Us girls have taken to our afternoon float. We take the canoe out to the raft in the middle of the cove, take a thermos of iced tea, our magazines, and we swim and sun bathe. We are absolutely spoiled rotten! The inn down in town has entertainment each weekend and Beau has made it a practice to take me dancing Saturday nights. He told us that officers were sent here for R&R during the war. How could they return to war after visiting here? Men. Only men could do that. But that would be too complicated an entry for today, or even this summer. I am too happy and carefree to ponder such things. We are only twenty miles from home, but it feels like a lifetime away.

Jeff sat in the Adirondack chair up on the hill in the shade watching his wife, mother, and Maggie lounging on the raft. Their brightly colored bathing suits dotted the little white square floating on the glittering water of the cove. They had five hours of sun there before the shade of the high woods overtook their lair.

Being Sunday, it was the only day all three women could be together as the Feed & Seed was closed. Beau was in town leaving Jeff to his own thoughts, not necessarily a good thing. Too often Jeff found himself lingering in the dank corners of his life. The harder he tried not to focus on his time in prison, the more it seemed to infiltrate his every thought. He chastised himself for wallowing in his own hardships when his dear Lizzie had gone through so much pain of her own. Who was he to let life's travails weigh him down when she seemed to move through each day with such grace?

Lizzie waved up to him. He raised his arm high and waved it back and forth. No need to force a smile. She couldn't have seen it any way. There was so much he hadn't told her. He thought about the day Milo started hemorrhaging in the shower. Every morning, they were mustered out of bed, handed a stiff gray towel and taken down the long cold hall to the shower room. There were twenty shower heads and thirty-two men. If you were lucky, you waited your turn. You were naked, but dry. If you went first, you waited for the others while you were naked and wet to the bone. The towels were too thin to do much good.

In some manual on tuberculosis, the prison doc read that cold showers were part of an earnest treatment regime.

In practice, however, it was nothing short of torture. There were days when the chill never left Jeff's body, when the cold water felt like daggers on tender skin. Pains he already suffered were aggravated to where he could barely walk or eat for days. The morning Milo died was the worst day of Jeff's incarceration. It was in that death that he envisioned his own. They all did.

The coughing spell had come upon the already frail man only seconds into his shower. It took hold of him with such violence everyone cowered away. As his body convulsed, the blood in his sputum hit the gray-green tiles and ran in little rivulets along the dingy grout to the drain. Unable to stand, he went down to all fours, desperate for breath, his eyes singed with panic. The blood came spewing in chunks and drizzles. It was as though the man's lungs were disintegrating. Two of the guards corralled the men into a corner, turning off the water. One tossed a towel that fell short. Milo was too weak to reach for it and lay naked and shaking on the wet tiles. Blood covered his hands, his face, and drained from both sides of his mouth. The prisoners were escorted back to their beds. Jeff was among the lucky ones that day. No shower. Milo died.

"Jeffrey," Lizzie's voice startled him. She was right beside him. "You were day dreaming again, Honey. Would you like some lunch? We're thinking about cracking into that watermelon. Would you like some?" She hurried away into the cottage before he had the wits to answer her.

Sara stood unnoticed at the steps watching this peculiar exchange. She sauntered by her son, paused briefly to rest her hand on his shoulder, then made her way into the cottage. She found Lizzie with a knife stuck in the watermelon, tears streaming down her face.

"It's stuck," she said. "The knife is stuck."

Sara took the girl in her arms and held her tight.

"I don't think he's ever really coming back to me," Lizzie sobbed.

Sara and Maggie decided it was time they packed up to leave as soon as Beau returned. They were gone within the hour. "They need some space," Sara said.

"Did I scare them off?" Jeffrey asked.

She handed him a tall glass of sweet tea with lots of ice. "No," she said. "I think maybe I did."

She nestled into his lap and took a sip from his tea. "Can I ask you something?" Her voice was hesitant.

"Sure. What is it, Sweetie?" His voice was soft and a little distant.

"Remember how it used to be?" she said. "In the beginning. When we were first married?" She put her hand to his face and drew his gaze from the lake to her eyes.

"Of course I do," he said with a sad grin. "It was beautiful."

"Do you think it can ever be that way again? I mean, well, I miss you." She quickly followed up with a disclaimer. "I'm alright the way things are, we'll be fine. It's just that, if your illness made you too weak, or," she tried not to cry, "well I was thinking maybe you don't want me now that I can't have children. Or is it that you think you can make me sick? Because I asked the doctor and he said you aren't contagious."

"Geez, you talked to the doctor about us?" Jeffrey looked at her eyes welling up. They hadn't made love since his return home. Not since before she lost the twins. He wasn't sure until that moment exactly why and then the confession slipped out. "I don't know. I don't feel much of a man these days." He looked away and again she drew him back.

"You are my husband. I love you. Don't ever lose track of that."

"Well, I think maybe I've been afraid you didn't want me to after you lost the babies. I don't know."

"And I've been afraid," she said carefully, "you were too sick or maybe it left you, you know, so we couldn't any more. So I didn't say anything." They looked at each other in quiet amazement. "Well, if we aren't a ridiculous pair," Lizzie said, tears now steaming down her sunburned cheeks. "Do you suppose we can pretend for just one afternoon that the last few years never happened and we're just a couple of lovestruck kids again?" She stood up and reached for his hand. He took it and together they walked into the cottage, through the living room and upstairs to the bedroom. "You're wrong about something," he said to her. "We are still just a couple of lovestruck kids."

Christmas 1955. Joy - too small a word for the enormity of my feelings - The sheer improbability - the IMPOSSIBILITY - of the news makes it all the more miraculous. In spite of all we know has happened and all we know can happen, the human spirit has the capacity to spring up and cry out a gigantic YES! to the universe. YES! and thank you, God, for this joyous gift. Liz and Jeff are expecting a baby in May. Lizzie's pregnant!

CHAPTER 33

Meg set out to find the Feed & Seed based on Mr. George's instructions. She had no difficulty finding the landmark school he mentioned. It was an unremarkable brick box of no great architectural significance. The windows were boarded up, and there were chunks missing from the concrete cornerstones. Four pillars held a portico that even Meg could tell was not part of the original design, but added later. The building was an eyesore in its dilapidated state, and probably hadn't been much better in its prime. On the front lawn, now a weed patch, stood a large plywood sign. "Save this important piece of history. Contribute today to the Save High Country School Landmark Fund." Even the sign was old and beat-up. Apparently, the fund drive hadn't succeeded.

She turned her attention up the road and saw another brick building, possibly the Feed & Seed. She pulled into a weedy parking lot next to the loading dock of the two-story building. The windows on the second floor were dark and empty. The doors on the dock were badly in need of paint. She walked around the corner and saw a storefront window filled with tattered boxes, old machine parts, abandoned kitchen utensils, various stones and rocks, and faded old magazines in sloppy stacks. A curtain behind it obscured any view inside. A very faded OPEN sign hung crooked on a string in the door's window. She tried the doorknob but it didn't budge, rusted in place.

There was a high wooden fence at the back of the building. It looked newer, but the weeds were tall and gave it the sense of having been abandoned long ago. There was a door in the fence and when she pushed, it swung open wide. Peering in, she called out. Hearing no response, and assuming the property to be abandoned, she ventured in. What first seemed to be a junkyard soon realigned itself in her eyes as a well-arranged collection of cast offs. A lean-to covered a variety of lumber scraps, some 2X4s, 2X12s and a few as large as 12" X 12". Old doors leaned one against another. Windows of every style and size were tucked away neatly in an open-ended crate. Three huge millstones rested in a corner. Old glass milk bottles in metal crates were stacked next to empty Green River soda bottles by the case. There were terra cotta drain tiles, pipes, sheet metal scraps, wheelbarrows, tires and hubcaps. And then, she looked up.

There above her, was the porch Maggie described in her journals. She touched the hand railing on the steps leading up to the deck, and suddenly realized she was standing where Lizzie must have fallen. Curiosity pushed her up the stairs, though cautiously, for fear the wood may have rotted. At the top, she stood still, drinking in the history of the place. A dozen wooden chairs sat about like people, each different, all worn down, some facing in conversation, others looking away. Meg imagined them as the ladies at Lizzie's bridal shower.

She peered into the windows but they were too hazy to reveal much. She knocked on the door and in doing so, it slipped open. "Hello?" She hesitated. "Anybody there?"

She stepped inside to the kitchen, a large room, half of which was stacked with boxes carefully taped shut.

The boxes and dirt aside, it was not all that difficult to imagine Maggie, and Lizzie and Sara wandering in and out, industrious in their preparation of lunch or dinner. The checkerboard lattice on the linoleum floor, its edges lined with roses, drew her in. She ran her hand along the edge of the huge white porcelain sink. As old as it was it didn't even have a chip in it. "Hello?" she hollered. Still no response.

The counter extended long and wide on either side of the sink, its linoleum surface cracked at the edges. It was cluttered with boxes of what looked like yard sale scraps, seemingly insignificant junk. The cupboards filled the wall to the ceiling.

Feeling empowered by her knowledge of the intimate history of the place, she ventured down the hall to other rooms. The first three bedrooms had no doors and were stacked with old junk furniture and boxes. Then there was a bathroom with a claw foot tub, a rusty piped sink and a toilet, seat up, clean water. The door to the next room, perhaps a fourth bedroom, was closed. Before opening it, she summoned the spirits of Sara and Lizzie for permission. She turned the knob and pushed it open. The hinge was quiet, and she realized none of the hinges had squeaked, so someone was tending the place. A white painted wrought iron bed sat squarely in the middle of the west wall upon which lay a clean quilt and a blue wool blanket folded neatly at the foot. The bureau had a small bowl, an empty vase, and some old books laying atop a white lace doily. A braided chair mat on the rocking chair in the corner caught her attention. As she reached out to touch it, she was startled by a thump behind her and she turned around, her breath caught in her throat.

A small calico cat, disturbed from its perch on a high boy dresser behind the door cozied up to her leg, then sprawled languid on a sunny patch of floorboards. Meg took a deep breath to calm her nerves and proceeded back down the hall to what must have been the living room, but now was filled with shelves of machine parts. There were gears of every imaginable variety, giant bolts, pulleys, leather bands, and hand cranks. She opened a door more substantial than the others and found herself faced with a wide set of open stairs leading down to a dim room. She took the steps slowly and stopped on the landing overlooking the entire room below her. The huge faded sign hung from the center of the ceiling. Laurel County Feed & Seed.

Like walking into a museum, Meg was lured with ever growing intrigue into the dusty nooks and crannies of the place. She walked the maze of shelves stocked with dust-laden goods from as far back as the thirties. She found assortments of household fuses, mousetraps, nails, and lamp wicks. There were birdbaths and lawn ornaments, candlesticks and wine glasses. She pulled out an oilskin picnic cloth that crumbled in her hands. In one isle she found dozens of cans of house paint and brushes and thinners.

"They just shut the door on this place," she sighed. She walked isle after isle, inspecting the saw blades, ax handles, oil lamps and aprons. "Sara," she said looking up with a smile, "this place really needs you back." She laughed out loud when she saw two clown-faced cookie jars on a top shelf.

Making her way deeper, she found a small hallway leading to what she guessed was the loading dock area. The door was stubborn but having lost all inhibition, Meg pushed hard and opened it expecting more disarray and clutter.

Instead, she stepped into a well-ordered workshop. A drill press, lathe, and table saw glistened in the sun spilling in through the large side window. A variety of antique tools hung next to new power tools on a wall of hooks. A large workbench held center stage. At one end of it a vice grip held tight several pieces of wood sandwiched together. In the middle was an intriguing piece of manual machinery without purpose that Meg could tell. The woodwork was elegantly finished, the assemblage of gears was ingenious. She turned the hand crank and watched the various gears turn at their different speeds. It didn't accomplish anything, except to entertain. There were countless such items around the work shop, some small and one that stood floor to ceiling, over twelve feet tall. It had what she guessed to be a huge gear from an old elevator, a couple of pulleys with large leather straps and a massive plumb bob on a chain.

Until then, she had believed she had the right to snoop around and was prepared to present her case if confronted. But in the workshop, she realized she was a trespasser, and had no excuse if the resident artisan should find her there. She found a side door and went back around to her car, quickly got in, and drove home.

T Mercer - A Retro-Spectacle. Reception 7 PM. The 505 Center. September 15, 2000. When Meg read the invitation, she assumed her anonymity was shattered. She was on the list now. Everyone would be inviting her to openings, readings, showings, and parties. It happened in Chicago after she won the Caldecott award for Children's literature. It was only a matter of time before it would happen in her new home. To go, or not to go, was the big question. There was no photo with the invitation so she didn't even know what to think of the work, whether it was worth her time or if it was just going to be a 'see and be seen' occasion. She dropped the card on the desk with her other mail.

Some days later, Ford stopped by to check the tarps on a long stack of firewood. Meg went out to see if he wanted to come back later for dinner. His expression suggested it was a ridiculous idea. "I'm a good cook, I promise," she said.

"I'm sure you are, but I have things to do," he said securing the tarp that had blown off. "You're going to the 505 tonight, right? You got your invitation?"

"Oh. So that was your doing?"

"Well, yeah. I thought you might enjoy it."

"Maybe."

Again, he looked confused, shook his head and left.

The crowd gathering at the 505 Center was eclectic beyond Meg's wildest preconceived notions. There were college kids from Asheville in goth and grunge, well-heeled retirees in stylish city wear, middle aged mountain hippies, craftspeople in their natural fibers, business people in suits, carpenters still in work boots and dusty jeans. Jarvis Payton welcomed her to the art Mecca of the mountains. His dashing white hair and deeply creviced face made him look the part of an ancient world-renowned artist, not the mostly-retired attorney he was.

She'd only met him once, when she'd first arrived to North Carolina. It had been a brief encounter where he told her what she already knew, that she had to live at Stoneygate for the year to fulfill her obligations, that ownership was in dispute, and not to look for any of it to be reconciled any time soon. He'd also asked her to his home for dinner, which she declined.

"Well, my dear," he said, tipping his head back to look down his nose at her. "I am so happy to see you out and about. Ford managed that, did he?" Before she could answer he was drawn away by a flamboyant woman with wild black hair and flowing skirt.

Meg milled along with the crowd from the reception area into the gallery, reading the handout on the way. "…serendipitous semi-functional sculptures of found objects, wood, and machine leftovers." Once inside, Meg stood in amazement. In the center of the room was the elevator gear and plumb bob from the Feed & Seed workshop. On a podium in front of her was the concoction of gears from the worktable. It was then she realized it was Mercer's studio she'd infiltrated. And then it finally registered with her that he was related to the Mercers in the journals, maybe even Sara and Jeffrey's son. She almost giggled.

She thought the work had a sense of humor, each piece an explosion of imagination, combining hand-rubbed wax-finished wood with mechanicals made of anything from rusty nails to well-oiled cogs and polished steel.

"Hey, you clean up pretty good."

She was relieved to hear Ford's familiar voice. She took a look at him and returned the compliment. Even though he was still wearing jeans and a T-shirt, they were clean. She'd never seen him in clean clothes. But something else about him that evening was different, it was an attitude shift so remarkable it was like meeting him for the first time. He actually seemed joyful. He walked her to a group of people at the drink table.

"Meg, this is Rosco, Leroy, Helen and Jules. Guys, this is Meg Bishop, the children's book author I told you about." They were gracious in acknowledging her then turned their attention back to the show.

"Great work," Leroy said. "Some of the best so far, don't you think?"

Ford agreed and Meg added that it was amazing stuff and she'd never seen anything like it.

"And you never will," said Jules, planting a casual kiss on Ford's cheek.

The hair stood up on Meg's neck.

Ford suggested Meg mingle. "Pretend you're not a hermit. It will be good for you." He disappeared into the crowd. Feeling every bit unsteady in public, Meg decided to leave. She could visit the gallery on a quiet day to get a better look at each piece without having to deal with people. But before she left, she needed to know which one was the artist. She wanted to meet a Mercer. "Where are you, old man," she muttered to herself. Without making eye contact with either Rosco, Leroy, Helen or Jules, she asked, "So, who is this T Mercer anyway?"

Rosco shook his head. "Yeah, really. You answer that and we'll all know." With that, Rosco and the others meandered away. Her question was answered more directly when a helpful older woman pointed to a group of people in the far corner. "The tall fellow," she said. "With the floppy hair." She set her eyes on the top of someone's head, a man with a mop of dark brown hair, but couldn't see his face. Meeting him would have to wait for another time. She felt the pressure of unfamiliar surroundings and craved the security of her nest. She made her escape against the tide of new arrivals. She didn't notice Ford and Jarvis watching her from the window.

"We need to talk," Ford said quietly.

Jarvis responded with some sadness in his voice. "Come by tomorrow. I'll pull Larry in and we'll have a go round."

Like a trail horse heading back to the stable, Meg was anxious to see Stoneygate's pillars. A glorious moonrise over the pasture welcomed her home.

Having found the Feed & Seed looking as if time had been arrested within its walls, Meg felt a new kinship with its former inhabitants. Meg pulled out Maggie's Journals and set them all on the coffee table in a stack. "So, let's see if I can find our artist in here. Who the heck is T Mercer?" She put on a pot of water then slipped into her favorite sleeping shirt.

With a cup of tea and intense curiosity, she curled up in bed with the next couple of journals. Leafing through the pages, it didn't take long to find him.

CHAPTER 34

April 6, 1956. Jeff has gone into the hospital again. His gut seems to be a continuing problem and they are going to do exploratory surgery. Lizzie is in good spirits, good health, and the baby's heartbeat is strong.

April 10, 1956. Beau, Sara and I have had to get chest x-rays. With Lizzie pregnant, they said she has to wait until she delivers. They haven't explained why we needed them and all our results are fine. Jeff hasn't had an active TB infection since he left Morganton so it must be something else. They're keeping him for another week.

May 1, 1956. Thomas Baker Mercer born. 9 pounds, 3 ounces, 22 inches long. A healthy, bright eyed bundle of love. Mother and baby are doing well as can be expected for a young mother about to lose her husband. How does one suffer the pain knowing she is birthing a fatherless child? I realize now I know nothing of pain. My heartaches are nothing compared to this.

May 3, 1956. Beau and I are picking up Lizzie and the baby from the hospital today and taking them to Sara's so they can be near Jeff. He can't keep food down and is getting weaker by the day. The pain seems to be getting worse and we fear there is nothing more to do for him but make him as comfortable as we can. The doctor gave us some drops to use sparingly. They help some, but they also make him sleep and he wants to be awake to see his baby boy. I think we're in for a rough few weeks. Thank God we have little Thomas to guide us through this. He's a blessing if ever I saw one.

May 14, 1956. If ever a man wanted to live it is Jeffrey Mercer. With the whole world finally opening up to him, with a son to raise, he is fighting for his life. We opened the windows this morning, in spite of the cool bite to the air, to relieve some of the foul smell of his sick room. Beau hired a nurse to tend to Jeff's needs. Take loved ones off task, to grieve.

May 20, 1956. He cannot eat now at all, and sips only enough water to wet his mouth. The saving grace to our days is holding baby Thomas. I don't know that he has spent an hour out of someone's arms since we brought him home. He is a very good baby of sweet disposition. Sara says he takes after his father.

June 1, 1956. It's all over now. Our Jeffrey is gone. Seems all he needed was for Lizzie to tell him it was alright to leave her and their son, that they'd be safe and secure knowing he would be watching over them from Heaven. And our grieving begins in earnest...

The doctor was called before sunrise and arrived soon after. He found his patient ashen, his skin waxy. He gently folded down the cover and felt Jeff's belly. He listened to the gut with his stethoscope. Through his pain, Jeff tried to smile as he looked to the doctor, then to Lizzie. "He's ready to go," Lizzie said softly.

"Is this so, son?" When Jeff closed his eyes and nodded, the doctor asked if she wanted to leave the room. "Why would I want to do that," she replied in a soothing tone.

"They're using this in Great Britain. It will deal with the pain, but he'll fall asleep," Doc said, assuring himself as much as Sara that they were in agreement. ". . . and he won't rouse again."

"Yes," she said stroking Jeff's forehead. "He'll fall to sleep."

The doctor put the dropper in Jeff's mouth and released a few drops. Jeff closed his eyes and swallowed. He opened his eyes once more to look at his wife and soon drifted off. The doctor left having given instructions to the nurse. Sara, Maggie, Beau and Lizzie sat vigil, watching every fractional rising of his chest. Around noontime, he stirred and arched in pain, but did not fully wake. The nurse administered another dose of drops and he quieted again. She assured them he would not likely stir further. He passed just after sunset.

June 5, 1956. We are all resting. Lizzie has taken Thomas to her parents for the day. And we go about our grieving. The minister at Jeff's service used a psalm I wasn't familiar with but it spoke to me, to the sorry lot of us, like it was written for us. It's a prayer of Moses: "Thou dost sweep men away; they are like a dream, like grass which is renewed in the morning: in the morning it flourishes and is renewed; in the evening it fades and withers. For we are consumed by thy anger; by thy wrath we are overwhelmed. Thou hast set our inequities before thee, our secret sins in the light of thy countenance." At the end he asks God five favors. The second one is a prayer I will pray tonight, and the next and the next. "Make us glad as many days as thou hast afflicted us, and as many years as we have seen evil." Maybe the worst is behind us now, and we can move on through the rest of our days with peace and all good things. Lord knows there have been enough bad things to balance against.

June 19, 1956. Sara had Jarvis Payton put together the papers making Lizzie partner in the Feed & Seed. It would have been Jeff's position, and since Lizzie knows as much about the business as Sara now, it seemed the logical step to take. And the two of them get on together like they were actual mother and daughter. Probably better.

CHAPTER 35

Ford sat in Jarvis's office waiting on Larry, Jarvis's son.

Larry Payton, a pudgy man of fifty, walked in ready for a quick briefing. "No offense, Ford," he said "but you don't really belong in this meeting."

"Ah, come on boy," Jarvis coaxed in his pitiful old man drawl. "He's got his fingers on the pulse of this thing. I brought him into the loop."

Ford chuckled and shook his head. "You really fall for that helpless old man crap, Larry?"

"All my life, man, all my life."

"Tell us where we're at with the Adler mob," Jarvis said.

"I had Doris type up a brief for you," Larry said looking at the chaos that was his father's desk. "No doubt it's in there somewhere."

"How 'bout you just put it in your own words." Jarvis tilted his chin high, looking down his nose at his son in familiar fashion.

"The restraining order is still in place. The Stonemount people can't proposition Ms. Bishop or set foot on the property without her express invitation." Though Larry responded concisely, it was not to the immediate issue, but more to issues unquestioned and previously understood. Jarvis was a man who liked to get to the point of a thing and move on, a man whose impatience generated a good bit of condescension.

"That's nice, son. Good work." Jarvis leaned forward in his chair and folded his arms on his desk. "Now, where are we at with the case?"

Larry explained with a dodging eye to Ford as if to suggest he shouldn't be in the room. Jarvis gave no indication Ford was leaving and simply stared at his son, this time over the top of his reading glasses.

"The descendants of Monty Kenyon's twins are trying to lay claim to the Kenyon estate. They're basing their claim on the accusation that Baker Kenyon coerced Florence Kenyon Adler into relinquishing the property rights of her minor sons in return for his promise not to take them from her. He threatened her. They have a letter Florence wrote a friend describing his threat in detail."

Jarvis scoffed as if to say such things would never hold up in court. "So, you see your job is to break the trust, is that what you're plan is?" Jarvis asked.

"The trust is hardly the issue. I just have to uphold the quitclaim Florence signed. Point of fact," Larry explained, "had the Charleston Kenyon-slash-Adlers raised this matter in '68, when Beau died, they could have taken over the whole place then."

"Do your homework, son. It was Maggie's, by provision, to live on until her demise. The only reason any of this is in contention now is the Goddamned land grab fever around here. Tawny Gale and her boys got digging into old land files, looking for anything they could get their hands on. They found Stoneygate deeded to a trust and went

Kenyon huntin'." Jarvis let out a long sigh and leaned way back in his chair.

"Bottom line?" said Larry, "The only remaining Kenyons are fighting to have the quitclaim deed Florence signed voided on grounds of duress, and reinstate the trust."

Jarvis salved his son's uneasiness. "Why, they can't prove duress based on some letter written years ago by a disgruntled long-dead woman to some nosey so-and-so. It's hearsay at best. Let them fight it. Their rights were signed away free and clear two generations ago. My father drafted that quitclaim deed, witnessed her signing it, and filed it with the county. I don't know what you're so worked up about. Baker could never have gotten custody of those boys, so there was no real threat. What was she thinking? No court in the land would have upheld such a thing, taking children from their mother, especially someone like Baker Kenyon, with a history of lunacy." His eyes went all buggy and he threw up his hands like a crazy person.

To this point, Ford had been silent. "Best case, worst case," he interjected.

Larry hesitated. "Depends on how you look at. The quitclaim deed holds up and Maggie's will is tight. The trust ended with Beau. Meg owns it all outright, to keep or sell, whatever she sees fit to do with it. Worst case, Kenyons get the quitclaim thrown out and they own everything. Either way, there's no guarantee the estate will remain intact."

Ford stood and walked to the window. "Got it," he muttered.

Jarvis sat up straight and stretched. "We're done here."

Larry's eyebrows went all askew at his father's matter of fact I-don't-really-give-a-shit attitude.

"Don't get too worked up about it, boy," Jarvis said.

"This isn't going to be a cake walk, Dad," he muttered as he got up to leave.

"You'll do fine. You worry too much." Larry walked out not knowing if he was being patronized or dismissed.

"So," Jarvis grumbled. "What are you thinking, Ford?"

Ford watched the street below teeming with tourists. "They're on vacation. What's their hurry?"

"Yankee rabble," Jarvis declared. "It's in their genes." He pushed some overstuffed file folders aside, eventually finding a handsome wooden cigar box. He rummaged in it for a fat stogie, dug in his drawer for a clipper and nipped off the end. He methodically stuck it in his mouth, his glossy white dentures holding it firmly in place. "What about the girl?" he said groping around the debris for his lighter.

"I don't know," Ford said. "I can't get a read on her. She's not connecting. Or maybe she is. Can't really tell." He was talking about the property but thinking about himself. Every time he saw Meg, something about her lingered with him for a while. It was more than just having someone on his mind. It was like a presence. If she were any other woman, they'd have had sex already and it would have been long over, at least if history was any kind of predictor. And Meg, as distant as she sometimes was, was breaking his patterns all to hell.

The nuances of Ford's mood hadn't slipped past Jarvis. He'd been observant of an undercurrent since Meg hit town. He opened one drawer after another still looking for his lighter.

"If Larry loses, we know what'll happen," Ford said. "The bulldozers will be there before the ink dries."

"You and I both know it doesn't have to end that way," Jarvis said emphatically.

"I'm not goin' there with you, old man. It's up to you to make sure Larry wins this thing." Ford sighed and returned his glance to the street.

"Now, Ford. This thing is just going to have to play itself out. You worry too much."

"You do remember who you're working for?"

"Of course I do," Jarvis purred.

Ford picked up a gold zippo lighter off the window ledge, snapped it open and lit Jarvis's cigar. "Did you draw up those papers yet?"

Jarvis took a puff. "I'll get right on that."

Ford was about to walk out the door when Jarvis spoke up again. "How you going to know where she rests?"

"I'm working on it."

Meg set out for a walk up Glassy with her journal in hand when she was distracted by something moving along an embankment by the footbridge. She crept closer, then stood still, waiting. Watching. Soon, from a hole under some roots, came the nose of a groundhog, twitching. It backed into the hole and reappeared, twitching, and slipped out entirely, its darkly furred body making its way to the shallow stream where it stopped to nibble on some grass. Meg slowly sat down, took her pen from her pocket, and began drawing. At one point, the groundhog sat on its haunches and she though he smelled or saw her there, but it hadn't. It held a long blade of grass, chomping. By the time it waddled off, she'd made three drawings of it. Having lost interest in a hike, she went back inside, setting her journal next to one of Maggie's, which she picked up and took to the porch.

September 10, 1963. I am so going to enjoy teaching second grade this year. I have Thomas in my class. I am discovering he is an entirely different boy away from home. At home he's quiet, on his own most of the time. Here, he's ebullient. I looked in his desk today and found a collection of paraphernalia - licorice laces tied in a hangman's noose, marbles, a Barbie doll head, a fishing bobber, a swath of cowhide and a rubber band ball. I still can't get used to everyone calling him Ford ...

Meg's mouth fell open as she read it. Ford is Thomas Mercer. How could she have missed it? Why hadn't he told her? Or did he assume she already knew? She thought about the artwork and tried to imagine him in the studio. An artist. He was not at all what she thought he was.

... Mr. Hastings started it. From the time Thomas could talk he was a Ford man. Lord only knows why. He loves his die cast cars and trucks - only Fords. Sara stocks them and the boy used to cry nearly every time someone bought one and took it away. He though they were all his. Used to pull all the Ford ads out of the magazines on Sara's rack. I remember when he was only three and poor Lizzie lost track of him. Then Mr. Hastings shows up with the boy on his shoulders hollering that he was delivering Mr. Ford back home! Seems Thomas saw that brand new 1960 red and white two-tone Ford pick-up truck, just like his toy truck, and he climbed up into the bed of it.

*They were half way to Asheville before Mr.
Hastings saw him in the window. All the way back
to the Feed & Seed he talked about his Ford
collection, that he had a red and white two-tone
car that matched the truck. He was so
disappointed that Mr. Hastings didn't have car at
home to match his truck. Seems like yesterday.
Who knew Mr. Hastings was renaming the boy
for good back then. Mr. Ford.*

Meg suddenly realized Ford's relationship to Maggie was so much more complicated than she imagined. It changed everything, knowing what she knew, and there were so many questions.

Stopping at the post office, she picked up her mail. One letter in particular, forwarded from Chicago, drew her attention and she opened it in the car. Its contents dissolved any interest she had in the rest of the day. She drove straight back to the cottage.

Ford stopped by Stoneygate to clean out the chimney. He knocked on the screen door and hollered inside, but there was no answer. Meg's sketch journal lay on the yellow table. He leafed through it, marveling at the minute detail in some of the drawings contrasted by the bare minimalism of others. A drawing of a dead robin fledgling caught his attention. The eye, still reflective, told him she'd found it soon after death. He wondered how long she'd studied it to get such complete description. He especially liked the line work on one particular page, just a few vague lines. He recognized it as the fox out on the rill bridge, though no one else would probably be able to see it for the vagueness. Ford was familiar with the animal's proclivity for that spot.

A breeze kicked up and blew a piece of paper into the yard from the wicker chair. Retrieving it, he read it.

> Dear Meg, I regret to inform you that Marvin is dead. We had him cremated. I wasn't going to even write you but since you were married to him, I figured you had the right to know. I know he was a troubled boy, but what you did to him was a crime and I will never forgive you. You ruined him and he never did recover. Please do us all the favor of never contacting any of us in the future. Regretfully, Mrs. Adam Stroop

As Ford wondered who Marvin might be, he called out. Again, no response.

On the other side of the property, Meg sat on a log over the big stream, drinking from a bottle of Merlot. The water rustled along below her feet. It was comforting to be in a position where her presence had no impact. The natural world went about its business. Half a dozen different kinds of bees worked the wild flowers on the bank. A squirrel carried a huge green walnut up a tree. A rabbit out in the clearing munched on clover. She did not matter to them and she liked it that way. There was a freedom to stepping into a world that did not exist but for itself.

"So, who's Marvin?" Ford's voice startled her from her thoughts. He stood in the brush of the stream bank.

She took a minute to chain the words together appropriately and then rattled them off. "Marvin was my bi-sexual-deranged-lunatic-ex-husband."

"Oh. So, I guess you're not grieving."

"I'm not grieving."

"How long were you married to him?"

"A couple years."

"Was the bi-sexual thing before, during or after?"

"What?" She'd never spoken about Marvin with anyone except Patrick, the friend renting her condo. So, that she'd said bi-sexual out loud, to Ford, surprised her. "Oh, that. Yeah. Marvin left me for Warren. Warren left Marvin for somebody else." It was only a fraction of the story, and even as the words slipped out, she was aware they were a lie.

Ford watched her feet dangling above the water, her tan skin catching the dappled sunlight. "And the deranged part?" he asked.

She shot him a pained half-smile. "Did I say deranged?" It was a word that could have easily described her as much as Marvin back then. "Hyperbole. "

Ford sat down on a rock, his curiosity brewing. "And?"

"Marvin was a painter on the rise until Warren tired of him and his work fell out of favor. He lost his studio space and came crawling back to me broke and begging for forgiveness."

"You said take a hike."

"Yes."

"And, he didn't listen."

"He didn't listen." She held up the wine bottle.

Ford kicked off his shoes and stepped into the stream, taking the bottle from her.

"Divorced yet at that point?"

"Illinois is not Reno. Takes time."

He turned his back and leaned against the log near her knees. The water pushed cold around his ankles. If he waited long enough, maybe she'd let down her guard and tell him what really happened.

She watched a small eddy in the stream. "I had to get a restraining order against him." She stopped. She'd never told anyone these things. "He kept coming around. Even after I moved. He found me, pounded on my door in the middle of the night. Other stuff." As she said these things, she became aware of something unusual. Normally, like Pavlov's dog, the mere thought of Marvin brought on a panic attack. Not this time.

Ford waited for elaboration. "Other stuff?"

"He stalked me. Sat across the street watching. Followed me. Had him arrested."

"Is that how you ruined him?"

This startled her until she saw the letter in his hand. He gave it to her.

"Ah," she said. "Well, no. They let him out the same day. He stayed away for a while, until after the divorce came through. I was a little frazzled at the time," she said in an attempt to make light of the incident. "I turned into a bit of a recluse and . . ."

"You? A recluse? Imagine that." Ford never cracked a smile, but Meg chuckled.

"That's when I started writing and drawing . . ."

"Keeping away the black dog."

"What?"

"Nothing. Winston Churchill. Painting was a way to clear his mind of the darker, black dog issues at hand. Keep going."

"Well, I had spewed all that negative crap into a bunny named Emerson and put him into a book for kids." She took back the wine bottle. "Is that true about Churchill?"

"Yup. So, what happened next?"

"The first book brought the man back into my life."

"And . . ."

She didn't want to say any more. She didn't want him to see what she was really made of.

"That's not the end of it," Ford insisted.

Meg thought about all the intricate filthy secrets of her life, needing more than anything to wrap it into a tidy little package so he'd let it go and leave her alone.

"His family took him back home to Florida."

Ford leaned against the log for another minute or so processing, waiting. Neither of them spoke. The stream made a slapping sound as it moved over stone and root.

"I'm going to clean your chimney now," he finally said.

"Good."

He stepped up onto the bank, picked up his shoes and started to walk away. "Have you known any normal men?" he asked without looking back.

"Define normal."

Ford understood then that there was much more to this woman than he anticipated, and would tread carefully moving forward.

"Hey, Thomas! Nice show. I like your work a lot."

He turned and looked at her. He knew she had finally figured out who he was. "Thanks," he said. "Stop over any time."

The stream ran crystal clear when it would have been better had it suddenly run thick with sludge. Then, at least, Meg would know her sins had not gone unnoticed, that nature acknowledged the fact she let an off-duty cop beat Marvin to a pulp the last time he violated the restraining order. Still, the water ran clear. There was no punishment but for what she imposed on herself: A life of emotional isolation.

She would not go back to the cottage until she heard Ford's truck drive away.

CHAPTER 36

Late September found Meg standing with Ford in the middle of a huge empty building with a sixteen-foot ceiling. Hanging from huge beams were giant wheels and pulleys some of which still supported wide leather belts. "What was this place?" she asked him.

He said it had been a lot of things. "It was a barrel factory originally, then they made souvenirs here. Became a barrel factory again during the war, and then it was a warehouse." He toured her through it explaining plans to turn it into lofts and offices. "Here," he said pointing to the stairs, "This might interest you."

He led her to the second floor where the light poured in through huge multi-paned windows. "It was built before electrification. They had to work by daylight." Meg was instantly enthralled with the space. He walked her to a corner and stood with his arms outstretched. "Great studio space, don't you think?"

Meg pictured herself camped out with an easel working in the sunshine. "Yeah. Would be nice."

A week later, Ford took her there again. This time, the place was teaming with workers putting in plumbing, wiring, framing in walls, and hanging ductwork. He guided her through the mess upstairs. There was a lot of activity but all of it in the front of the building. Taking her through a door, they left all the commotion behind. He took her again to the corner space. This time, there was a bathroom and utility sink, ceiling lights, outlets and a large storage closet. The walls were roughed in with studs. "What do you think?" he asked her.

"Hell. I'd give my eye teeth for this space if my orthodontist hadn't already pulled 'em."

Ford winced. "That's humor, right? You can work here if you want to. It's O.K. The heat will be hooked up pretty soon. In the meantime, I think the sun will give you enough warmth. You can bring in a space heater if you really need it."

"What's the rent? I mean, nobody's just going to let me squat here." She was nearly drooling with anticipation. The space was perfect. Working at Maggie's suddenly felt claustrophobic.

"Just use it. Can't be rented with all the construction going on. Besides, this will all be studios eventually. Walls should be done by the end of the week. You can bring stuff up any time."

"Are you sure?"

"Yeah. Don't worry. I know the owner."

Another two weeks passed without seeing any sign of Meg again. He thought she'd jump at the chance to use the studio and was disheartened that she hadn't. Each day he checked the space, and each day it was empty.

He hadn't seen the note Meg left on the apartment door at the Feed & Seed. *Gone to get my stuff. Will be great to be in the studio - a space of my OWN! Back in a week or so. - Meg.*

Meg's flight to Chicago was an impulse. The studio represented a space void of Maggie, void of history. It would be her space, her easel, paints, furniture. She couldn't wait to be surrounded by her stuff.

Her brother, Sam, met her at Midway. It was good to see him, for about the first five minutes. He seemed certain she wanted to hear every excruciating detail of his plan for Stoneygate once her year was up. At the house, her mother picked up mid-sentence from her summer advice with the 'must sell' speech. Her father was the only one who didn't want to talk about it. By breakfast the next morning, Meg was ready to get back to North Carolina.

She rented a van and headed to her condo. As she schlepped stuff from her basement storage cage, Patrick appeared and helped her load the van with a roll of canvas, boxes of stretchers, two chairs and several boxes. She told him about her cottage and the mountains and her paths and streams. She surprised herself with the quiet joy it brought, just to describe it all.

"Did you look into the steeple chase thing?" he asked. "Do they still do it down there?"

"Yeah. It's held over in Tryon in the spring. You should come down for it."

"I'll think about it. Oh, almost forgot. I've got something for your studio. It's upstairs."

She headed to the door of her former home wondering how she would feel once inside. Would it bother her? Would she miss seeing Vince lounging on the couch? Would she long to return to familiar surroundings? But, as soon as Patrick opened the door those thoughts disintegrated. "What the hell?" she gasped.

The living room was packed with paintings, boxes, sculptures, and piles and piles of books. "Not what I expected," she said.

"Few things ever are," he responded, heading though a narrow pathway to the kitchen. "Beer?" He disappeared and returned with two micro-brews. Meg cleared off her favorite overstuffed chair.

"Tim wanted the house," he explained. "He's buying me out."

"So sorry. Where's everything else? Your house was an art museum."

"In storage at my mom's place. Out in Dad's old studio."

He rummaged through a pile of stuff in the hallway, pulled a box from the chaos and handed it to Meg. "You always liked this."

"What is it," she asked before opening it.

"The bathroom bell."

"You can't."

"It's yours."

"I am so honored," she said in all sincerity. "So, what about the Thiebaud? I have the perfect place for it."

"Don't get greedy. You know I only have the one."

"Oh, but it's such a lovely one."

Patrick's father spent a year bargaining for the small canvas of a San Francisco streetscape. He'd given it to Patrick when he turned eighteen and it became the beginning of his art collection, which now mingled with some of his father's collection.

"How is it all playing out?" she asked. "Between you and Tim."

"It's basically a divorce without the paperwork. It's such a quiet little death. Quiet life. Quiet death. Fitting, I suppose." He took a long swig of his beer. "I've been replaced."

"Oh, please tell me it isn't one of your students."

Patrick lifted the bottle like a toast. "OK. I won't."

"He'll pay for that in a thousand little ways," Meg said, pawing through a stack of canvases. "You were striking at that age. Especially before you cut all that beautiful blond hair off. But you're fabulous now."

His hand swiped his platinum stubble. "Young is young. Honestly, it's all been more of an inconvenience than heartache. Ten years is enough."

"Speaking of departures, Marvin's dead."

"What? Haven't heard that name in a long time."

Meg pulled a painting out of the pile, one Patrick painted about the time her first book was published. She flushed with embarrassment. "Was just thinking about when you took me out to celebrate Emerson Bunny's launch and I drank too much."

"Carried you up here as I recall."

"That's when I laid the whole Marvin and Warren story on you."

"Jailbird."

"Yeah. Jail."

"Classy broad. Well. Good riddance, as they say." He gulped down the last of his beer. "You want some of this to take back with you? Hometown brew?" He retrieved a six-pack from the floor in the kitchen and set it by the box at the door.

"I want this painting."

"No."

"I'm taking it."

Meg plopped back into her chair. "I should take this to the studio, too."

Patrick leaned on the door. Pensive. "Tim said I didn't make him feel safe. He was afraid I was going to walk out the door any moment. For someone younger. So, he did it first."

"Really. So, aside from the obvious, why do you do it?"

"Do what?"

"What you do. Like Tim. Flings with younger men. I mean you did it to."

"But I keep it simple. Flings. They're alive. They're still genuine. Un compromised. They make me feel alive."

Meg rolled her eyes. "It's still a betrayal to love."

"Love? Tim had a different concept of what that should look like."

"I think most people do."

"Guess I'm not built that way. I teach hoping to find one kid capable of rising above mediocrity. I paint once in a while, hoping I can rise above mediocrity, but the passion's gone. And I'd go home to Tim's nice organized little world where everything was so absolutely, intolerably passive. Living with all that passivity was killing me. Life should never be lived passively."

"Ah. So, you were about to walk out the door anyway when he . .."

"Fuck it. Maybe. I don't know. Megs, take all your shit down to your studio in the mountains and get to work. Open up and do some art. None of that screwed up bunny shit. Paint. Paint!" he shouted. "Splatter some paint on the walls, the ceiling. Get messy!"

"Paint! Paint! Paint! Paint!" they chanted in unison.

"We're artists, damn it!" Meg shouted.

"Yes, we are! Now get out of here." He put the beer on top of her box and handed it to her.

"I'll see you in the spring," she said on her way out the door.

"No promises."

"Can I have my chair?"

"No."

"I'm taking it."

As she was closing the van to leave, he showed up with her big overstuffed chair and together, they crammed it in.

Later that night, her second and last in Chicago, she found her dad alone, watching Letterman. "Can I ask you something," she began carefully. He acted as though he hadn't heard her. "Why do you suppose Maggie did it? Why would she will Stoneygate to me? Not you? You're next in line, not me." She waited and watched. When he finally looked at her with gentle eyes.

"No way of knowing, really," he said. "I suppose she knew I'd never leave here to move there. I don't know, honey. I guess you'll just have to figure that out on your own."

There was no point in delving deeper. He'd said all he was going to say.

CHAPTER 37

Next time Ford went up to Meg's space, he was relieved to find a stack of long flat document drawers, two easels, a drawing table and cabinet. And in the corner sat an overstuffed chair and ottoman with the grungiest slipcover he'd ever seen. Splattered everywhere, ceiling, floor and wall, was a rain of blue paint. "More to come," he whispered with some satisfaction.

When he came back the next afternoon, he found an iron chain stuck through the wall. Hanging from the chain was an oblong piece of wrought iron lacework with a note attached: *Yank my chain.* He did.

From inside came the mellow clang of a bell. Meg immediately opened the door.

"How ya been? Want a cup of coffee?" She rattled on with a nervous energy he hadn't seen in her before. He began investigating the bell.

"Great, isn't it?" she said. "A friend in Chicago gave it to me. His father made it. He was a famous artisan. Patrick Dawson. Worked all over the world."

While Ford wondered about just who that friend was, he was more intrigued with the workings of the bell. An iron panel lay flat to the wall with its edges like delicate torn tissue wafting in a breeze. The support for the bell also looked like a weightless scrap of paper, yet it was all made out of iron. It was like nothing he'd ever seen before.

"Do you mind if I reinstall this for you? It needs a channel through the wall."

"Whatever. Fine. Are you sure I don't need to be paying for this space? Cause I will. It wouldn't be a problem."

"You're fine. Enjoy it."

"You're sure you don't want any coffee?"

"I have to go. I see you found the back entrance and the elevator."

"And the elevator. Really handy."

He turned to leave and hollered on his way down the stairs. "Glad you're back. You might want to cut back on the caffeine."

Ford found an open computer at the library and typed Patrick Dawson into the search engine. "Holy shit", he muttered as he came up with page after page of references on the man. *Architectural Digest, Forbes*, University of Chicago, two biographies, *Chicago Magazine*, IDS Hall of Fame, *Iron News, Chicago Tribune, Sun Times, Industria Italiana Arteferro, Washington Post, New York Times*, and the list continued. He clicked on the link that intrigued him the most: San Francisco Museum of Modern Art, a Patrick Dawson retrospective.

A few links into the site and he was face to face with an eighty-five-year-old Dawson. It was a fine face, deeply lined, with intelligent eyes and an untroubled brow against a snow-white buzz cut. The screen was filled with tiny photos of his work linked to wordy academic descriptions.

He clicked on the slide show and let it run. One after another, images faded in and out. Whole doors and gates and window guards were removed from buildings all over the world for this retrospective. There were lamps and shelf systems and decorative wall displays.

The design elements ranged anywhere from exotic animals and birds to geometric forms. Some shapes were so simple they were pure elegance while others were intricate beyond what he previously thought possible with iron.

Ford selected two photographs for downloading and sent them to the printer up at the main desk. At the end of the bio was a list of articles written on Dawson with links to the archive. He rummaged through them and printed one.

When he went to the desk, Mrs. Martin handed him the printouts. "We have a book on this gentleman, if you'd care to see it." She led him to it and asked if he was thinking of getting into wrought iron. "You know I wouldn't be surprised at all if you're as talented as this fellow." He took the book and papers and headed home.

No longer a captive of Stoneygate, Meg began her next life. Her new routine quickly formulated itself: a leisurely coffee at home, a shower and off to the studio. Creativity swept into her life. New story ideas filled her mind insisting she write them down night or day. Scraps of paper littered the cottage, her car and the studio. She knew the new series would have something to do with the white squirrels of Brevard, but they hadn't yet clarified how they would present themselves. She struggled to manufacture the story line using a carnival backstory with colorful gypsies. She knew she'd have to suffer through the initial surge, putting it all down, sketching frantically until things settled down and the gist of the story revealed itself. It was process. It should have been exciting. But the story so far felt contrived. Pedestrian.

She had only just settled into some sense of productivity when she had to head out on a book tour. She didn't want to leave and was dreading fifteen days on the road, every night in a different bed.

The night before she left, walking out of the studio, she switched off the lights, glanced around, and was drawn back in by the lyrical play of light and shadow. The streetlights were nearly a block down on either side. Their glow created intersecting shafts of half-light that were then dissected by the window's many mullions. She put down her parcel and sat against the wall. Too complicated to draw, she thought. She could never do it justice. Like so many things, seeing, noticing, was enough to make life a little richer. It had begun to drizzle and the cars passing below made a hissing sound on the wet pavement.

Ford drove by the Barrel Factory and looked up to the studio windows hoping to find Meg's light on. Finding it dark, he drove on without thinking to look for her car.

A five-hour layover in Charlotte had Meg darting into town for a quick book signing with a meet-and-greet breakfast. Then she was back on a plane to New York, into a cab, and straight to another signing in Soho. She had plans to meet with her former editor for dinner. A message at the hotel said they wouldn't be able to make it.

When even her old pal Elaine was nowhere to be found, Meg secluded herself in her room and began channel surfing. After a few minutes, she decided she was missing nothing living on Stoneygate without a dish, antennae or cable. She landed on an old movie and turned the sound down low, cracked open a mini bottle of Crown Royal and went out for ice, padding through the hallways in stocking feet and sweats.

Meg had no inclination to go out to any of her favorite haunts. Maybe if it had been summer, she would have, but it was November and the city was cold, unwelcoming. As her mind wandered, it frequently landed on one particular face. She envisioned his white hair brushed back and a glint in his eyes as he looked up from his table saw at the Barrel Factory. Remembering made her happy. Back in the room, she picked up the phone and punched in his number. It rang and rang until she gave up on it. She never got around to giving him the list of cities and numbers where she could be reached. It was a silly thing to carry it around for a week and not hand it to him. It seemed ridiculous sitting there in bed, to be thinking about him so intently. "We aren't *together*. What's the point?" That's when she decided it was good to be away, to clear her mind, and get back to focusing on her tasks.

At some point during the night, an owl woke her and she turned to what should have been the window to look out into the yard, but woke instead to a cramped hotel room. The owl was a dream that even upon waking captured her imagination. She reached down for her laptop, opened it and sat in its glow, waiting for the words. When she started typing, a warmth swept through her bringing with it a comforting sense of belonging. It was the beginning of a new story…

– – – – – – – –

Morning's first light slid quietly through the trees, across the stubbled grasses to a tangle of roots protruding from a steep bank above a shallow stream. A muffled rustling came from a dark hole within the roots. No one was there to notice the groundhog emerge except for the wren, which turned his incessant mating trill into a bitter scolding. The groundhog was no more or less cautious than on any other day, crawling out far enough for his nose to reach clear air, then slightly farther until the sun touched upon him through black walnut branches whose leaves had not yet opened to create their canopy. He squinted as he lifted his head straight up, his muzzle working busily to sense all he could of the world.

Suddenly he heard frantic footfalls approaching fast, snapping twigs and scattering stones as they came. He retracted back into the roots, and listened, heart racing. The disturbance passed quickly overhead. When the swift thumpings faded into the distance, he again emerged into the sunlight. . .

- - - - - - - -

She was six pages in when she stopped for the night. It took some time to fall back to sleep, waiting for the creative surge to wane.

After the signing in Manhattan, she headed out on her road trip, arriving at a New Paltz B&B around four o'clock. She settled into her room, poured herself a tumbler of wine and changed into her sweats. Curious about what she'd written the night before, she opened her laptop and began reading. Spontaneous first drafts often read fine at the time, but looking at it later, lose their luster. This time, this story felt good and she dove back into the writing as if she were mid conversation with an old friend.

- - - - - - - -

His days of late had been hectic. Time after time, he had been quietly resting in the cool darkness of his home beneath the ground when the earth all about him shook with an appalling thunder bringing dirt and pebbles down upon him, sending him fleeing in a panic out this very hole and running for his life to another hole, one he had abandoned a season earlier. The threat came upon him swiftly and was gone just as fast. At this beginning of this particular day, he comprehended only the one task in front of him. It was the same task he had faced and accomplished each of several mornings prior, having discovered the opening to the other end of his home filled with debris that could not be dislodged from inside. Once again, he would need to traverse the stretch of ground between where he was and where he needed to be and work to reopen that entrance. . .

- - - - - - - -

By midnight, she'd written another chapter. She couldn't help but think how her editor would never tolerate such long complicated sentences.

The next afternoon had her on the road again, northeast into Massachusetts. Somewhere on a road in Vermont, the snow began to fall. She wanted to be home. And home was Maggie's cottage. She would not write any more of the story on the trip, being too tired and too dislocated. It had to wait, just as she did, to return to Stoneygate.

After Vermont came Maine, then onto an airplane for points west. The first few days were always the toughest until she got into the rhythm of it. By week's end it would become a thing in motion, powered by its own momentum.

Though she was weary of consoling people over the end of the Emerson series, sales were brisk. She did readings selected from all the books, not just the new one. It was a bit like attending Emerson's funeral. Repeatedly. And in the end, helped to heal the wound of his loss.

Back in North Carolina, Ford worked on a heating duct in Meg's studio. He saw her itinerary on the drawing table. Checking the date, he saw she was in Stowe for the night, Portland, Maine, the next, and would then be flying out to Minneapolis the day after. His first thought was to call her. But she hadn't given him the paper so maybe it was none of his business. He put it back on the table and left. A few minutes later, he returned, folding her itinerary and stuffing it in his jeans pocket.

In an austere hotel room in downtown Denver, Meg undressed and put her clothes in a bag for laundry service. By morning, everything would be clean and pressed, delivered to her room with her morning coffee, juice, fruit, and Danish. But for now, exhausted, she stepped into the steaming shower and drenched her hair, relishing the rivers of hot water pouring over her neck and shoulders.

She was scheduled for a morning signing in Colorado Springs and a dinner signing in Denver. Morning readings were easy. They were mostly mothers keeping track of children. The dinner events were a different story. They were more of an art-league-slash-literary group of adults who expected erudite conversation of Meg. It was a drain trying to be interesting in a group of other people trying to be interesting. Sometimes their efforts were at her expense, proving their knowledge of children's literature far superior to her own. Not a difficult task, she thought. As the water cascaded down her back, she didn't hear the phone ring.

Meg stretched out on the bed with four carefully stacked pillows at her back and one of Maggie's journals. "All right, Maggie. Let's see what the eighties were like for you." Closing her eyes, she held the book in front of her and flipped the pages choosing one at random to begin her night's read. A gift basket sitting in front of the phone obscured the blinking light.

> *May 19, 1989. I can't sleep tonight. Little wonder why and I wonder if Thomas is awake as well. Life is going to be very different from now on. It's just us now. Thomas and me. Not since my Beau passed have I felt so lonely. Sara is gone. It happened suddenly, but how can that be said of a woman pushing ninety? I hoped when Lizzie was ill that the thought of losing her companionship would be more painful than the real thing. I was wrong. . .*

Meg's throat tightened. By skipping journals, she had jumped through time, losing Lizzie without knowing it and now Sara. It was too sad. She skimmed back to find out about Lizzie but whatever happened predated this journal. Her heart went out to Maggie, wanting to reach back in time to comfort her. Then her sympathy fell to Ford. She figured he was thirty-three at that point. Never knew his father. His mother died, and then he lost his grandmother. Maggie was his last connection to his past. Meg suddenly saw him through the dim light of despair.

. . . The anticipation of pain is very real, but its arrival was devastating. Nothing is ever as we envision it I guess. Reality has a way of inventing itself beyond our imagination. I have consciously been aware of Sara these last few years, not for any failing of health, but for the opposite. She thrived. Sara was probably the most vibrant person I have ever known. Even her hair - that spectacular red mane. Funny. It's been gray for years, but still I see it red. The mind is a strange manipulator. Thomas handled everything so beautifully. He called me first so I could have my time with her before the business of death began - before the men came to take her body away, before the minister was called, before the paper was called, before friends begin to pay respects, before, before, before.... I was the second person to know after Thomas. There is an honor about that - being valued enough in someone's life to be among the first to know they've passed. It was odd that he chose to spend the night with her last night. Sara said he had done that more and more over the last few years. Staying in a couple nights a week after they closed the Feed & Seed, cooking her dinner, watching a TV show with her and saying he was too sleepy to drive home - even though it was just across town. She liked having him there that way. Never under foot, just company at the end of a day. I don't know what I expected when he called with the news - how I would find her when I got there. That's not true. I did know what I expected. I couldn't help but think about Beau's heart attack. I don't know how

I got through that day but I did. It took him to his knees right where he stood at the kitchen sink. I remember worrying about his knees taking the blow, that they'd hurt for a while and how would he take his walks. The anguish on his face -- helplessness -- utter surprise. He hollered at me when I rushed to his side. "Get the damn doctor woman!" I made the call and when I returned to the kitchen he was sitting against the cupboard gasping for air. He looked at me with those dear eyes apologizing for being so short with me. He said he loved me -- couldn't believe it happened just like that. Death, all of a sudden, no warning -- uninvited. He tried to stand but -- It broke my heart, every aspect of it. Death was reveling in humbling my humble man and I was so angry. . .

Tears streamed down Meg's face. She never knew Beau except through the journals. Losing him through Maggie's eyes hurt. She wiped her eyes and kept reading.

. . . His was not a good passing. It was unkind in its timing, and cruel in its swiftness. So I was relieved to find Sara so peaceful in her bed. The covers weren't even mussed and Thomas said he hadn't rearranged anything. He let me find his grandmother as he had. It was the perfect death I think. Knowing you had a loved one in the house with you, if such a thought occurs to a person when they die in their sleep. Was she dreaming? Did she know? I will miss her as much as I would miss anyone of my own family. I told Thomas that

*I am his family. He said to me "I know" but I
don't think he does.*

This single act of love and respect, giving Maggie that
time with her friend, made Meg want to call Ford, comfort
him, when she was the one needing comfort.

*June 6, 1989. I still expect to see Sara from day to
day. I am finding that missing her is an altogether
different experience from the others. It is easier
on my spirit - like a gentle breeze that drifts
through my thoughts.*

*June 20, 1989. It isn't really a surprise but
Thomas isn't going to reopen the Feed & Seed. It
hasn't been open since the last time Sara closed
up. He's helped out a few regulars who've
bothered to knock inquiring about something or
other, but that's it. He said he's canceled
outstanding orders and will be returning any new
stock that arrives. What on earth is he going to do
with all that inventory? He said the doors are
closed for good. I worry so about him. He says
he's got an offer on the building he renovated in
old town. I think he should keep it. It's good
income property. He wants that old run down
bakery building. Every penny he's made since his
mother died he turns around and spends. At least
he still has 505 Main. It will always be worth
something.*

The address sounded familiar. It rattled in Meg's brain until she realized it was the art center building, the art film movie house, the offices of Payton and Payton. Assumptions she'd made about Ford began dismantling. Again. He wasn't just an artist, a guy doing odd jobs and yard work to get by. She leafed backwards skimming through pages looking for more references. He bought, renovated and sold half a dozen buildings in old town. He sold his mother's house in town to buy his first building, a "wreck of a place" according to Maggie. He bought the 505 with help form Jarvis and then bought him out. He bought up adjacent buildings one by one until he'd redone nearly the entire block. By the time Meg finished reading, she'd learned Ford almost single handedly built the art district. She lined up the storefronts in her mind and marveled at Ford's hand in it all. The old bakery is the jeweler. The old grocery is the potter's workshop and gallery. One of the buildings is full of weaving looms. Two storefronts are galleries.

In the midst of lauding Ford as the ultimate urban recycler, it dawned on her that he was, underneath it all, a developer, an industrious, ambitious developer with a head for business. Everything she thought she knew began to shift yet again.

It crossed her mind that Stoneygate might be his next project. Everything suddenly became a game to her, wondering who in the hell Ford-Thomas-yard man-artist-bottom-feeding-developer really was.

Taking a bottle of wine from the gift basket, she saw the blinking light on the phone. It was Ford saying he was checking in. Nothing more. "Just checking in." She could have called him back but had no idea what to say, and proceeded to drink most all of the wine, a deep, smooth Malbec.

Meg didn't sleep well that night.

Her turbulent flight into San Francisco matched her mood. The flight gave her time to get used to her new reality. She recalled conversation after conversation with Ford. How many lies had he told her? When he said he'd worked on all those buildings, she assumed he was day labor. He led her to *believe* he was day labor. But they were his buildings. He had manipulated himself into her life for reasons that suddenly might have had nothing to do with her. She thought about the Barrel Factory. "I know the owner pretty well," he'd said. If she wasn't so mad at him, it might have been funny. And, to compound the issue, she wasn't sure why she was mad at him. Was it his fault she presumed as much as she did? Had he really misled her or was that all on her? She began to think he had more connection, more right, to Stoneygate than she did. It all felt too convoluted to sort out.

Eating breakfast at a B&B in Point Reyes, California, the innkeeper's cell phone chimed as she handed Meg her breakfast, then the phone. "He wants to speak with you."

"Yes?" Meg said to the caller.

"I haven't asked you anything yet." It was Ford. The sound of his voice gave her a start. For nearly two weeks she'd wanted nothing more than to talk with him. She missed him. She went to sleep each night thinking about him. She woke up thinking about him. Now he was an unknown with questionable intentions. Even so, something about his voice stirred her.

"You found me," she quipped with little audible emotion.

"I wasn't really looking."

"Ah. How are things there?"

"Fifties. Dreary. Not much sunshine last couple of days."

"Ah. How's my studio?"

"Fine. I fixed the heat vent. You'll be warm in there now."

"Good."

He spoke as he always did, with little inflection, just a soft gentle drawl. She'd never read it as dispassionate before then, but suddenly did.

"Have you heard from Jarvis?" he asked.

"No. Should I have?"

"Nah. Larry got the hearing put off to the spring. He told me to tell you in case we talked."

"O.K."

"You don't want to know any more?"

"What's to know? Everything is so out of my control there's no point."

"What do you mean? Everything."

"Never mind. Anything else on your mind?"

"Nope. Tour going well?"

"Yes. Fine."

"Good."

"Ford?" She had to get it out before she screamed.

"Yeah."

"You own the Barrel Factory, don't you?"

There was a long silence.

"I thought you knew. It was in the will."

"I never read it."

Ford asked her to hold on a minute and he hollered out to someone. "Hey, Jackson! Dump them over there."

"And the 505 is yours too," she said.

"Yeah. So who finally told you?"

"It's in Maggie's journals."

There was another long pause.

"What else is in those journals?" he asked.

She heard an edge in his voice. "You don't know?"

"Never read them."

"I see. Well," she sighed. "I'm going to finish my breakfast and go for a long walk before heading into San Francisco."

"Then to Sacramento and Sonora."

"Yep."

"Be safe. See you when you come home."

"Yeah. One more thing."

"What?"

"What's your next project, Ford?"

He stalled. "Don't know yet. Waiting for something to become available."

"I see. What would that be?"

"Don't worry about it."

"Yeah. You sound like Jarvis." She wanted to test him, to see his reaction to her interest in improving the property. "Before I forget," she said. "I've come up with a garden plan for the old foundation of the main house. It would make a fine kitchen garden. I have it all mapped out."

"Hm. Well, then, see you next week."

He clipped off the line and Meg handed the phone back to the inn-keeper who by then was eating her own breakfast. "He has a nice voice," she said, peering over her coffee cup.

Ford snapped his cell phone closed and threw it in the truck. He was at Stoneygate watching two men stack fieldstones within the old foundation while another dug out all the perennials and set them aside. The original walls were nearly repaired to a uniform height of fifteen inches.

Like a floor plan the walls delineated the perimeter of five areas, the largest one in the center. Stone pillars on either side of openings created the impression of doorways. He walked over and spoke with the stonemason. "I've got the compost and soil coming in day after tomorrow. That going to work for you?"

The mason tapped a stone in place with the butt of his trowel and stood up. "That will be just fine." The kitchen garden was almost done.

A storm in Atlanta delayed the flight out of Dallas. Meg sat for two hours biding her time waiting for the boarding call. Another half an hour and she'd miss the last flight to Asheville. Forty-five minutes later, they began boarding. She spent the night in a Hyatt in Atlanta courtesy of the airlines.

Ford checked the flight status. When it was clear Meg wouldn't make it back that night, he went to the cottage and packed up the dinner he'd left for her and carted it home.

Driving toward Stoneygate, Meg felt comforted by rhododendron, mountain laurel and pines along the road. She paused on the bridge at the entrance and rolled down her window. The stream ran high. The cold water somehow crackled louder than normal against the rocks as it passed beneath. Pulling forward, clearing the rise, she stopped again. Before her, across the yard at the corner of the garden, stood a beautiful new building. She drove on slowly as if any other approach would scare it away.

It was a stunning garden shed built halfway with cordwood and mortar, shingled the rest of the way with cedar, and roofed in corrugated metal. The porch was just as she had imagined it with double Dutch doors and windows hinged on their sides. As she pulled closer, she saw the barn style door on the end. Around back she could hardly believe her eyes. Cobbled together from old windows, was an attached greenhouse.

She didn't even notice the foundation garden until she walked out of the greenhouse and saw it there, across the drive. Passing thru its entry posts, running her hands along beautifully crafted stone walls, she grabbed a handful of the rich loamy soil and smelled it, the sweet pungent aroma filling her mind and seducing her spirit. She didn't know what to make of it. Not knowing Ford's intent dampened her spirit. He could have built it for himself.

When Ford drove in that evening, Meg wanted to welcome him with open arms, cook for him, tell him how wonderful the shed was, and the rock walls, and laugh with him and get close to him. But, instead, she withheld. She stood on the porch, arms across her chest, constantly convincing herself she couldn't trust him.

When Ford set out to see her that evening, he had more on his mind than explaining the venting and drainage functions of the shed and greenhouse. He'd entertained thoughts of a pleasant evening together. She would tell him about her trip, he'd fill her in on what he'd been doing, and then, maybe - but, he knew better. He needed to keep his distance, though it was getting more difficult all the time. It was tough to stay away from her. But those feelings came into question when he arrived to find an ice queen on the porch.

"C'mon. I'll show you how the greenhouse works." It was all he could say.

She walked out to the shed, not to him, without speaking. He didn't bother to explain anything about it. It would be months before it would be of any use and her reaction, so unenthusiastic, pissed him off.

"The property needed it," was all she said.

She had to stay low key. It was a defense. By the time the shed would be of any use, the property could well belong to the Adlers, or Ford, because whatever the verdict on the trust, she was certain she'd be pressured to sell. What she felt for him and what she thought about him were diametrically opposed. The voice of reason won out. She barely cracked a smile.

"Should have done it a long time ago," he said, not knowing what to make of her attitude. He built it all with a kind of blind faith that it would help bind her to the place, and maybe to him. But something changed over the course of her book tour. Maybe being away felt good. Maybe she decided she didn't want to move to the Carolinas. He knew that come next May, when the courts upheld the will, she could sell out to the developers in a heartbeat. Her indifferent attitude convinced him of it. He got back in his truck, stuck the wine under the seat, and drove away. The brown paper sack on the floor next to him began to rustle. A crab claw poked through a small tear. "Looks like I'm cooking y'all at home tonight," he mumbled.

CHAPTER 38

Thanksgiving. Meg was too sick of traveling to fly to Chicago and spent the weekend alone. There was one point when she almost called Ford, but decided to keep clear. It was the safer choice. Whenever she saw him, she was drawn to him and risked her defenses caving in. She still didn't trust him. Moreover, she didn't trust herself.

It was a dreary, half-light, jacket-weather day. She wandered through what was left of the vegetable garden and pulled a baby carrot from September's second planting. Brushing it off, she bit into the sweet fingerling. She pulled a few more, dug some sweet potatoes, pulled a couple onions she'd left behind, broke off some kale, picked some parsley and headed back indoors to cook them. It was raining when she ate her dinner.

Ford spent Thanksgiving with Jarvis and his family. He'd almost called Meg, but decided to give her some space. He wasn't in the mood to suffer whatever mood she was in. He stopped by her place a few days later to check the boiler, mostly to check up on her, but she wasn't home. What he found in the cellar brought a smile to his face. All the garden tools - rakes, shovels, trowels and such - had shiny red handles. She'd sanded them down and painted them. She'd worked on the rusty metal parts as well and left them oiled. This, he thought, was a very good sign.

A few days into December, he landed in her studio unannounced. He found her, wine glass in hand, staring at a blank canvas. She glanced up and saw him in her doorway. He had that look about him that said he didn't have a care in the world and he knew exactly who he was and what he was doing.

Her grin was the open invitation he'd hoped for.

"Got another glass around here?" he asked. She reached over to a table, nearly falling off her stool, and grabbed a coffee cup. "This will do, I think." Ford took the cup, looked into the bottom, blew out some debris and poured wine into it.

"I noticed the big pulleys are gone, from out in the warehouse," Meg said with a hint of approval. "And the leather straps. You must be working."

"Yeah, well, they're in storage at the moment. Not sure what I'll make of them yet. Need to live with them a while longer."

Meg chuckled. "Like me and this canvas." They clinked glass to coffee cup and Ford took up residence in the big chair.

There was an awkward few moments of silence before she spoke. "How is it you never married?" She had not meant to ask it. The words spilled out like wine from a tipped glass. She wasn't even aware it was on her mind.

Ford looked at her with a gentle expression as though her question had not disturbed him when in fact it had. He was tired of the question so often asked by close friends and the most casual acquaintance. Younger women trying to mask their flagrant curiosity by pretending to be impartial confidants would ask it with sincere little smiles. They didn't know he was raised by three women thereby knowing their kind better than they knew themselves.

He understood the depth of a woman's endurance and resilience, and that she didn't need a man for anything. She might want one for company, but she didn't need one, not if she was worth anything to him. He had little tolerance for any person who would hide her capabilities under a veil of southern charm. His married friends would ask him the question, both the women and the men, both the divorced and the intolerably coupled. It always confounded him that they could expose their marriages to him with all their wounds and insults and indifferences and then ask why he hadn't been interested in the institution. To them, he always threw off a jovial quip about being too indecisive to ever choose just one woman. Then he would remind them he got all the best out of marriage just hanging around them - a good meal now and then and someone to throw him a birthday party. And now Meg was asking him in this quiet corner of her studio with a glass of wine balanced delicately in her hand and the evening sun shooting shards of light through the golden liquid. He looked at her and thought for the first time he might actually answer the question honestly.

"What would be the point actually?" he began. "Of marriage. It didn't do you any favors." He winced when he saw her eyes tighten to slivers. He hadn't meant to upset her. "Look. My father died just after I was born. I never knew my grandfather. He died when my father was a boy. So, how would I honestly know what a marriage is? Is it inviting some person into your home to juggle schedules and needs and accommodations? I wouldn't know how to do that. I see friends give up what they want to do for the sake of the spouse. Sometimes it works, most times I think it breeds resentment. They may bury it, but it's there. And women always have this idea that there can't be anything if there isn't eventually a wedding. Do they really think of the after part? Of the getting along all the time?"

He leaned forward resting his elbows on his knees. "I've been allowed such freedoms and indulgences from the day I was born, no one could put up with me. And I'm not interested in compromise." He thought about the women he'd sleep with from time to time. Eventually they'd move on because he wouldn't move forward. "So, Miss Meg, I suppose there it is, exactly how it is, that I never married." He fell back into the chair grinning.

She let his words settle into the room. "I think you're one of the lucky ones," she said. "You aren't haunted by the perfect little life your family envisioned for you. Marriage. Kids. Putting everyone else first. It's like being brainwashed. Even in my best years, I am afraid I'm wasting my youth by myself. I suppose that's why I put up with Vince for so long. Because if I think clearly about it, I knew it wasn't going anywhere but it was going to be his doing, not mine. Does that make any sense?"

"Nope. Not a lick. Who's Vince?"

"Oh. Well, I left him back in Chicago. A lingering error that righted itself. Over. History." She took the last swallow from her glass and Ford poured more into it.

"The BMW."

Meg cocked her head, peering at Ford. "Yes. He drives a BMW." She took a sip of wine, then a gulp. "What I'm trying to say is that you live the way most of us would really rather live. I'm stuck with this stupid ass concept that I won't appear normal until I'm coupled up. I have fantasies about being a mom, but I can't see how the rest of it fits together. You're right about the sacrifices and I think people just irrationally believe they'll be up to it. Lots of people do it and survive. And then there's that love issue."

"The love issue?"

"Yeah. You know . . ." she said real slow, ". . .all those hormones and pheromones blinding you to logic. That's what does it. You get this overwhelming sense of being able to overcome any and all obstacles." She leaned forward holding tight to eye contact. "My shrink calls it temporary insanity."

Ford laughed and refilled his mug. "I hear that," he said. "Absolute insanity. But, fortunately," he took a drink, "some people come to their senses before it's too late."

"Exactly. Before everything gets cor-rup-ted."

"And I thought I was a cynic."

"Corrupted with contempt," she continued. "I believe intimacy breeds contempt." It was another comment that shouldn't have made it through the filter between her brain and her mouth, but wine blew right through. The rest of it just slipped out, delivered through a grimace poorly disguised as a grin. "In the beginning, you get the best of each other. Smiles and kindnesses and accommodations. Eventually, once you're committed to a long haul together, that changes. Slowly, everyone else gets the good stuff - the jovial mood, the polite considerations, the simple courtesies. And that's all wrong because your lover should be the one person on the planet who you're the nicest to. It just hasn't been my experience to work out that way."

"Of course not. Because it isn't real. That's part of the problem. Women expect too much. The being congenial all the time is the public face. When a person gets into his own space, he doesn't want to have to behave any one way or another. If he doesn't want to talk, fine. If he wants to swear or complain or laugh or shout, fine. If he wants to fuck or fish, it shouldn't matter." Meg's eyes widened. She'd never heard him swear. "Nice is contrived," he lectured. "It isn't real. You can't expect it. And you can't expect yourself to live up to a standard like that. You'll fail."

Meg let out a long resolute sigh. "Well, there it is then." All his words disintegrated except *You'll fail. You'll fail. You'll fail.* Her stomach twitched.

Ford thought he'd made a good point and didn't realize the impact of his last words. Later on, he wouldn't even remember saying them. The visit hadn't gone as he'd hoped. He tried to shake off the disappointment and drank the last swallow in the cup. "O.K." he said. His voice was quieter, low and intimate. Meg could have listened to it all night, no matter what the words. She didn't expect what came next. "On my way, then."

He rose out of the chair and put the cup on the table. Avoiding eye contact, he glanced about the studio. He pointed to a canvas Meg had started two weeks earlier and not worked on since. "No closer to a show, then?"

She could only agree with the obvious. "No closer to a show. I'll get there. Just takes time to let it arrive."

"What? More paint?" he asked automatically.

"Inspiration," she replied. "That other temporary insanity. When it arrives, you just get out of the way and let it take over."

Ford heard the words and stopped at the door. *Get out of the way and let it take over.* He took two steps back to Meg until they were standing face to face. He wanted to kiss her and if she had looked up to meet his eyes for even an instant, it might have happened. It would have been very natural. He could have leaned in only a few inches and his lips would touch hers. But she didn't look up, and the wanting was a temporary insanity he couldn't allow. He pulled his eyes from her face to the easel. "Go on. Get back to work."

Meg wanted to kiss him. She only had to lean in ever so slightly and it would have been inevitable. But, her walls were too strong and her head overruled her heart. Ford took a quick step back and walked out. Meg stepped into the hallway and watched until he disappeared down the stairs. "See ya, Thomas." He was half way down when her words caught up to him. No one but total strangers, his mother, grandmother and Maggie ever called him that. Something about hearing it from Meg felt warm and good. He liked it.

He returned to his routine visits to the studio and Stoneygate, checking on the boiler as well as Meg. Their conversations were brief, but cordial. She seemed to be working again. It gave him hope.

CHAPTER 39

Meg's winter evening routine developed not long after cold set in. Before going to bed, she prepped the coffee pot and brought kindling and wood in from the porch to be at the ready in the morning. Ford had stacked wood to the porch and she liked stowing in it the rack inside, feeding the fire, judging what size log would keep the heat steady. Waking during the night, she'd hear the hissing and clanking of the radiators take over for the dying fire.

Upon rising, she'd turned on the burner under the coffee and build a fresh fire. Often, there were embers left from the night before. Every third day, she let the fire go cold to clean out the ash. She liked the fresh empty firebox. It was orderly, as was her wood stack in the house and on the porch. When her kindling ran low, she went looking for a hatchet in the cellar and set about splitting some of the smaller pieces of firewood and found herself to be quite good at it. She liked having chores.

Her efforts did not go unnoticed by Ford. He was impressed that she took to the lifestyle so naturally. He hadn't expected it.

On a cold mid-December night, Meg snuggled in bed, skimming through a couple of Maggie's journals. The radiators hissed and clanked as the antique boiler circulated steam. Having spent the whole day and much of the evening in the studio, she was too tired to bother with a fire. The radiators did a fine job on their own and she had plenty of oil in the tank.

Maggie's journal entries after Beau died in the sixties were vague. It was almost as if she had grown bored with journaling and was keeping it up as a chore, not a pleasure. It occurred to Meg it should have been the opposite. With no one left to share her life, wouldn't she put more of her thoughts on paper? Perhaps, she surmised, in losing Beau, she also lost an aspect of herself, the zeal or joy or whatever it is that inspires a person to live to their fullest capacity. Reading them had become equally a chore, leaving Meg to trudge through a good ten year's worth.

> *March 14, 1978. Lizzie came through surgery in good shape. The doctor says she should be able to make it to Thomas's graduation. That gives her two months to get back in shape. She has been so brave through it all, insisting life is worth a breast or two if that's what it takes to keep living it.*

> *March 16, 1978. Ford called. He's bringing home a girl. They'll be here this weekend.*

> *March 18, 1978. We brought Lizzie to the Feed & Seed to recuperate. She's very sore and is worried about not being able to lift with her right arm, or help out with the workload. Sara keeps telling her not to worry, that she can handle*

things. She finally hired a man to work part time. But I know they both worry separately about the store. After all, Sara will be seventy-six this year.

March 21, 1978. I expected I'd be writing all about Ford's girl today but nothing much to say. She never showed. He came to visit, but she couldn't make it. Apparently we won't meet her until graduation. Turns out she's not just any girl. She's THE girl. Seems a bit sudden to me. He says he's going to marry her. He's already asked and she said yes. Our Ford had quite a glow about him so she must be something special. He is growing into such a man all of a sudden. Maybe we just didn't want to see before, but listening to him talk about marriage, and a new job, and buying a house, it all makes him seem so grown up. And Columbia isn't so far away I guess. Sara is disappointed they won't be living here. I don't think it ever crossed our minds he'd move away. He could hardly refuse the job offer her father laid at his feet. Still, I'll believe it when I see it.

March 26, 1978. Ford came home again this weekend. Alone again. I think seeing his mother so weak last weekend got to him. She's much stronger this week and will only get more so, but something tells me he had to see for himself.

May 19, 1978. Sara, Lizzie and I are off to Columbia for graduation. A Bachelor of Science degree in Industrial Design. Beau would be so proud. Lord knows what he'll do with it, but there it is. He has it. And we'll finally get to meet his girl. Alison. I can't seem to make it stick in my head. Maybe I need to write it a hundred times. Well, I suppose I'll get used to it soon enough. Next weekend we'll have Ford's party here. This weekend is Alison's party down in South Carolina. Don't know if Lizzie's really up for it, but we'll see. We can always excuse ourselves early and come back home.

Memorial Day - I knew the instant I met her that it wasn't going to work out. There will be no calling you Ford while I'm around. She giggled when she said it - I suppose she thinks she's cute - but she wasn't kidding. And her face when he brought her home to our little Feed & Seed - watching that poor girl watch him dote on his mother. I'll give her credit. At least she was honest with him. They didn't know we three were listening through the floorboards. After seeing the kind of money she comes from last weekend it was no surprise she was disappointed here. Makes me wonder what he told her about the place to make her think it was anything more than it is. I know that feeling. Beau had all kinds of ideas blooming in my mind about this place before I got here. I expected heaven on earth and found old and overgrown. I see the beauty now, but it was a jolt in the beginning. It was fine with Alison when she thought she was getting him out of here and into her daddy's firm, but when he said he wanted to settle here in Laurel County - that was the end of it. Poor Lizzie thinks it's all her fault because of the cancer. That's ridiculous. I think that was just the impetus he needed to see things straight, make him think he might want to stay a little closer. He isn't cut out for all that fancy living down in Columbia, working normal hours in some corporation. He's a free spirit and I'll admit he's spoiled to the core but I don't believe we did him any real harm. And he's better off without that girl. Alison needs to stick with her own kind. I'm sure her daddy will have her married off in no time flat. In the meantime, Thomas will go back to being our Ford and he is just going to have to find his way again. He'll be fine. Better to know the truth now than after the wedding.

Meg dialed Ford's number and listened to it ring and ring. She wanted to tell him she knew about Alison, to come clean that she'd been snooping through his life again. "The number you are calling is temporarily out of service. Please try again later." She smiled. Yet again, Maggie speaks. "Things always happen for a reason." Alison was ancient history. If he'd wanted to talk about her, he would have.

She pulled out her laptop and re-read the story she started on the book tour. What had begun as a wave of inspiration stalled. Having tried several times to continue working on it, it never felt true. She couldn't find the rhythm. The story always felt just out of reach. She closed it down for the night, stacked the journals on the nightstand and turned off the lamp. Moonlight flooded the bedroom like an invitation. Pulling on her jacket and gloves, Meg ventured out into the crisp night air.

Standing just steps from the porch, she sensed the same magic in the moment she used to feel as a child. Peering out to the bridge, just on the edge of the wooded pasture, she saw a shadow, as if a child knelt there. Meg strained to see better but somehow looking right at it was impossible and she tried to look just off to the side of it because sometimes that's the only way to really see a thing at night. She walked forward slowly, feeling curious and a little thrilled. As she approached, a cloud drifted over the moon and the shadow vanished, but the image of the child lingered in her imagination.

When she was young, Meg would go wandering about Stoneygate at night when everyone was asleep. She would sit on the bridge, legs dangling, hoping to see the fox go by, or a raccoon. Meg ventured out to that spot on the bridge, sat down and listened to the cold night woods. Then came a rustling as a breeze stirred the bushes and sticks snapped not far away. It was a raccoon meandering along the stream bank. It walked within six feet of her and never seemed to notice she was there. In those few moments, she was eight years old again. The next day, she began to write a new story.

- - - - - - - -

Lilly was eight and a half when her mother got sick. It was springtime, her mother's favorite season because she was a gardener and an artist and loved being outdoors. Spring, she said, brought the promise of summer and flowers and all things fresh and new. Some days Lilly's mother would sit on the ground in the garden, hidden by peonies, just watching things grow. "Bathing in the promise", she'd say. . .

- - - - - - - -

Over the next couple of weeks, the story spilled out of her, chapter after chapter, drawn from imagination, observations, and the sketches in her journal. A story within a story, it chronicled two young girls on parallel journeys. The writing felt true and honest and at last Meg felt the synchronicity she'd been missing.

CHAPTER 40

Christmas day began as a cold clear day. Meg's only plan was dinner with the Paytons. She had made her pies the night before and gone to an eleven o'clock church service at All Souls Episcopal in Asheville. She wasn't a church-goer, but Jarvis told her their choir and little orchestra did a fine job with the holiday music. "I'm too damn old to stay up that late," he told her. "But I'm sure you'll enjoy it." She was all the more surprised to run into him and his wife there, along with their son, Larry, his wife and three teenagers. It was a moving service that left her with a Christmas comfort she'd lost somewhere.

She lay in bed Christmas morning enjoying the sunlight, wishing for a nice hot cup of coffee to arrive bedside on a silver platter. Accepting reality, she crawled out and went to the kitchen, going about her morning ritual. She was putting fresh wood atop the remaining embers when the phone rang.

"Merry Christmas, dear. How are you?"

"Hi Mom. Merry Christmas to you, too."

Their conversation held nothing new. Meg defended her choice to stay in North Carolina instead of going home. Her mother said she was greatly missed. They reviewed the day's menu and the weather. Her father hollered merry

Christmas from across the room. With little left to say, they finally hung up agreeing to speak again at New Year's.

Meg contemplated the plight of empty nest mothers. They toil all those years manufacturing warm holiday memories for their children, who for the most part take it all for granted. Then the kids leave and the mother is left with no one to amuse except the indifferent father. Poor Daddy, she thought.

She threw her winter jacket over her flannel nightshirt and stepped out to grab more wood. "Nice outfit! Merry Christmas!" came a loud voice from the gardens. She looked up, startled to find Ford at the old foundation.

"Back at ya, Ford! What are you up to? Want some breakfast? It's gunna be good!"

"Sure. I'll be there in a bit."

The day suddenly had a completeness about it. Meg threw on some thick black leggings and a bright red hoody and went about the task of preparing eggs benedict. It was a tradition she began for herself a decade earlier, a little gift she gave herself.

She cut leftover baked potatoes into chunks and added sweet onion, a bit of red pepper and rosemary. While it was browning, she made the hollandaise from scratch and set it aside. She threw together some oranges, bananas, grapes and a handful of frozen strawberries from last season's garden. She prepped the English muffins for toasting and put the Canadian bacon on to brown before heading out back to the storm cellar.

Ford arrived in time to lift the heavy door for her and latch it to the post. "What's your jam of choice this Christmas day?" She asked. "We have Blueberry, peach, strawberry, grape conserve or gooseberry."

"And cherry," he said. "You decide. I'll take some more wood in."

Meg stood in the cool stone-walled basement admiring her larder. She picked out a red jar and a green one to match the spirit of the day. "Cherry jam and pepper jelly?" she hollered up through the floorboards.

"Pepper jelly?" Ford hollered back. "Jarvis loves that stuff. You give that to him today, why don't you." Then he went into the bathroom to wash up. Meg's robe hung next to the sink, its cuffs blackened with soot from tending the stove. Something about its condition, without pretense or apology, made him feel comfortable, safe, though safe from what, who could tell? When he emerged, he found Meg at the stove putting the eggs on to poach.

"What are you doing out there?" she asked, watching him pour a steaming cup of coffee.

"After breakfast. I'll need some help."

Their movements setting the table, pouring juice, refilling coffee cups, and filling plates seemed choreographed. For the smallness of the space, they maneuvered seamlessly.

"I was going to invite you for this," she lied. "I just thought your friends would probably have you occupied." She hadn't asked him because she knew exactly what he'd always done on Christmas morning. It was all in the journals. It had long been the tradition that Maggie made the breakfast for Beau, Sara, Lizzie and Thomas. The main meal of the day was at Lizzie's in town, then in later years moved to Sara's at the Feed & Seed after Lizzie passed. Meg struggled with the decision for two weeks to ask him or not ask him out to breakfast. Afraid she might step on his traditions, she decided not to mention it. "And, ya know, it's Christmas and people usually have their own thing to do."

"Naw," he sighed. "Christmas is for families." He'd thought about staying home, wondering if being at Maggie's would make him sad. There was a lot about Maggie he missed and sometimes the melancholy would blindside him. But, when he woke up that morning he figured he was being asinine and just headed out to Stoneygate like he had every Christmas morning for his entire life.

"Families, yeah. In all the years my family gathered as adults, I can't think of one instance when anyone brought a friend along." Suddenly she wondered who she might have slighted in that practice. "Would you like your Christmas present now or later?" Meg asked with a sly glance. Until that minute she didn't know if she would actually give it to him.

"Now," he said like a little kid.

A large flat package leaned against the end table upon which sat a diminutive pine sapling trying hard to pass as a Christmas tree. Its only decoration was a lackluster string of cranberries and popcorn. She brought the package to Ford. "If you don't like it, I'll paint you another."

Removing the wrapping carefully he discovered a painting of three chairs on the porch of the Feed & Seed. "I saw them the first time I went up there," she explained to him. "They fascinated me. I had to paint them."

"I've seen this in the studio. I was going to ask you if I could have it. Buy it. Something."

She was comforted by his response. Giving away artwork can backfire when the recipient doesn't really like it but feels compelled to keep it not realizing the artist would rather have it back than have it stuck in a closet somewhere.

By the time they finished eating, the day had warmed to nearly fifty. Ford helped with the dishes and then directed her outside to the foundation garden. "Feeling strong?" he asked.

Leaning against the stone pillars of the main opening to the foundation garden, was a wrought iron gate. It was elegantly simple with the silhouette of a frolicking fox poised on the top bar. Meg helped him lift it onto the hinge pins. It fit perfectly. Ford gave it a push and watched it swing with ease. "Well, there it is then. Done."

"It's beautiful." Meg looked out beyond the foundation garden, out to the pasture, around to the cottage, past the garden shed and down the drive until she'd done a complete three-sixty. She wanted to confess to him. She wanted to say she'd been holding back. "I decided before I arrived not to get too attached," She finally admitted. There followed a silence filled only with the sound of a squirrel digging around in the leaf litter. "If I were to lose it all now …"

"Hey," Ford said casually. "Don't worry about it. Too nice a day to worry. And it's Christmas. How about a hike up Glassy? We're not due at Paytons until five."

"O.K. but I'm still going to worry."

"That would be your waste of energy. Not mine." He looked around trying to muster some nerve. "I have a better idea. What if we go hang the painting?"

"At your place."

"Yeah."

Meg had often imagined Ford in the apartment over the studio at the Feed & Seed. It seemed to fit him, living among the elements of his art, not giving in to the plusher aspects of home. It gave him a simplicity she respected.

Leaving Stoneygate, he turned right out of the drive, but on the way out of town, he passed the Feed & Seed.

"I thought we were going to your place," she said.

"We are." He hesitated for a moment, puzzled at her confusion. When it hit him, he laughed out loud.

"What?" she demanded.

"Nothing," he said with a grin, shaking his head.

They headed out on the road to Brevard. He cut off onto a road into new territory, up a grade into deep woods. They turned off onto a two track and went in even deeper. Meg's curiosity was about to get the better of her but she kept quiet. Ford finally broke the silence.

"You didn't really think I lived at the Feed & Seed did you?"

"Well, yeah."

Just then he pulled around a bend into a clearing. It opened into a ten-acre meadow rising to meet a forest. Before them was the house she'd seen months earlier from the edge of her Pisgah property. Meg was stunned. "This is yours? You live here?"

"Well, yeah."

"Is there anything else you want to tell me? Am I missing anything else?"

He opened the truck door for her. "Go on in and warm up. I've got to check on something." She stepped slowly onto the porch, taking it all in. When she opened the front door, she found herself in a large open space and all she could do was gasp.

Unlike any house Meg had ever seen, there wasn't a scrap of sheetrock anywhere. The walls were plank wood, smooth and richly grained. The house was built within a structure of huge square-cut posts and beams all cut to fit like a massive puzzle. On one end of the long rectangle was an open loft walled off below by more plank wood, two handmade doors and a huge field stone wall and a fireplace where a generous bed of coals still glowed. The other end held the kitchen.

Light spilled in through a bank of dormers in the ceiling between rafters exposed to the ridgeline. The open floor plan included a sitting area and a small office space with a computer and oak file cabinets. There were windows all along the back, facing woods. She wandered over to the kitchen. It was a cross between William Sonoma and a tool shop. The best cookware she could ever dream of hung from a hand-crafted rack made from copper piping. He had a brass and bronze espresso machine, granite counter tops, two ovens and a microwave convection oven. His fridge was massive with a subzero freezer. There were delights everywhere she looked. The drawer pulls were gears and machine parts. Coat racks and doorknobs were branches and antlers. At the other end of the house, bookcases nearly enclosed a corner by the stone fireplace. The house was spotless.

When Ford returned, he called out. "I want you to meet Laurel! She lives here with me." Meg felt her knees give way a bit, her mind wildly trying to place a woman in his life, a woman she'd never heard of. At that moment she understood her own feelings were much more than she was admitting. She attempted to muster enough composure to be friendly and nonchalant to this woman she envied so entirely. Just then, a gawky yellow Labrador puppy sniffed her out and peed by her shoe.

Ford stepped over with a towel and dabbed up the puddle. "Laurel, we've talked about working on this, remember."

Meg's relief erupted in laughter. She picked up the puppy, its warm fat belly cradled in her arms, its eager tongue licking her cheek.

"This is the old stable, isn't it?" Meg asked quietly. "I recognize it now. From photos."

Ford was lost for a response, thrown off that she would know so much. Reminiscent of their initial attempts at conversation, he offered a simple dead-ended "Yeah." He stoked the fire, then busied himself in the kitchen. He told her to go warm up by the fire.

Meg settled onto the floor against the couch with ten pounds of puppy. Behind her she heard frothing and hissing. "That thing works?"

"Of course it does. Cinnamon or cocoa sprinkles?"

"Cocoa. Absolutely cocoa."

"A little sugar?"

"Two spoons."

"Natural or fake?"

"Natural. And how about a chewy. She thinks my hand is a teething bone." When he brought her a frothy cappuccino he found her sitting against the couch with a lap full of sleepy puppy. He put a hard brown triangle of translucent pig's ear on the floor next to her. Laurel tipped her head just enough to sniff it then pawed it a bit and slowly, with as little effort as possible, crawled off Meg's lap and flopped down beside her, licking the hide a couple times before falling asleep on top of it.

Ford put another log on the fire and a few smaller pieces into a potbelly stove across the room, an ancient relic surrounded by seven rickety wooden chairs.

"That isn't," Meg asked, amazed, "from the Feed & Seed."

He settled back down next to her, slurping his coffee. "You know too much."

"Your house is," Meg hesitated, "eclectic. Very *Ford*."

The fire set to a gentle blaze.

"What's the worst case scenario? With Stoneygate," she quietly asked.

"It's Christmas. You really don't want to let this go today, do ya?"

She'd momentarily forgotten it was Christmas. And it struck her as a nice thing. No hype. In fact, if this was all there was to it, a nice breakfast, a simple gift exchange, and a nice visit with a puppy, she wouldn't mind at all. "You wouldn't know it was Christmas from this place."

"There's my ornament. And my stocking." He pointed out a purple bauble hanging from the mantle and an old decorated felt stocking with Thomas stitched on it hanging from the fire poker stand. "You'll get all the Christmas you want over at Payton's this afternoon. She goes all out and you won't have to eat for a week after." He sipped his coffee. "By then it will be time for New Year's and she'll do it again."

The puppy stirred and Meg stroked its soft fur. It stretched out as far as it could then retracted like a rubber band back into limpness. "So, what do you think? About the property."

It would have been as natural as breathing to slide in next to Meg, pull her in close, kiss her. He shook off the thought. He had to keep his distance and that was getting more difficult to do. He reached over her to pet Laurel, his arm against Meg's leg.

In his touch Meg felt a warmth overtake her, softening her hard corners.

"What makes you think I know any more about it than you do?" he asked.

Meg rolled her eyes. "Because you do."

"Not really."

She asked what he thought their chances were of winning the case.

"Don't worry about it."

"There you go again. Don't worry about it. It's all I think about any more."

"Like I said. It's your waste of energy. Not mine."

"What if I can't afford it? I mean, what if I never come up with another book?"

Get off your ass and get back to work. Ford did not say it out loud.

"What would you do if you got your hands on it, Ford? She wouldn't have given you first right of refusal if you couldn't afford it. For all I know, you have big plans for the place."

He didn't answer.

"Well?" she insisted.

"I'm not who you think I am," he said quietly without looking at her.

Ford took a long bitter sip of coffee and wondered what the hell had happened. He picked up Laurel and carried her outside. "It's almost time to head over to Payton's," he said from the doorway, but Meg was already across the room putting her cup in the dishwasher. She couldn't look at him and he didn't particularly want to look at her.

CHAPTER 41

Mid-January brought six inches of snow to Western North Carolina. Meg awoke to it and giggled. She dug out her boots and coat and wrapped a bright pink scarf laced with shimmery threads around her neck. It was a Christmas gift from her mother who'd attached a smiley face note: *In case you ever get tired of wearing black.*

She headed out into the woods, straying from the paths, wandering, taking in the smell of snow and pine. When hunger got the better of her, she went back home to make a batch of pancakes. When she took her coat off, she realized the scarf had fallen off somewhere.

The rest of January passed much the same as December had. Meg spent most days at the studio having planned to work on the new book. But with Ford's continued renovations in the building, the constant cacophony of construction noise was not conducive to structured thought. Meg began painting portraits of workmen who then sent their wives and girlfriends to her. The paintings were not flattering. They were expressionistic renderings of light and shape and mood, mostly her mood. No one ever bought the paintings. They just got pinned up around the room, a growing collection of faces watching her every move, standing testament to the fact she'd not yet begun to illustrate a book with too many words.

One night late January, Ford came to Meg's for dinner. She cooked comfort food. Meatloaf, green beans and twice-baked potatoes with cheese on top. Afterward, he stretched out on the couch with one of Beau's old hunting magazines. Laurel curled up at his feet. Meg sat on the floor mindlessly leafing through seed catalogs. The fire burned brightly, radiating a steady, even warmth.

There was a comfort in acting like an old married couple, as if too entrenched in habit to be aroused by infatuation or lust, too weary of each other, too familiar, too lazy to touch. Any stirring just under her skin, any vibration along the surface of muscle, was easily quelled by the brain's transactional machinations. Too many daunting questions. Too much at risk. Why then, she wondered, did they spend so much time together? And what was he thinking in his solitude not three feet from her, close, but cordoned off as surely as she was?

Suddenly unsettled with the silence, Meg rose to retrieve a journal. "I have to read you something." He all but ignored her when she returned with two journals and began leafing through one for a particular passage.

"Here," she said.

> *Jan. 25, 1960. They've arrived again. The highlight of my winter. The seed catalogs. For all the industry of the summer and our time outdoors, this time in winter to rest and restore ourselves brings great satisfaction to me. As I am preoccupied with my catalogs and dreams of next summer's abundance of vegetables and flowers, I am also aware of the ease of this household. Beau*

lays on his couch, his nose in a book, deep in his study of Teddy Roosevelt, his favorite topic of late. And here I sit on the floor, half a dozen catalogs strewn about, and a note pad scribbled with ideas.

Ford's response was unexpectedly curt. The room, the evening, suddenly felt staged. "What else does she say in those books?"

"Probably more than you wish she did," Meg joked. "For instance, I know she paid for your college education. Do you want to know about the first time they called you Ford?"

"Not really," he said, putting down his magazine. He watched her open the other journal to a page marked with a scrap of paper.

"It took a while for the name to stick," she said. "Hm. This isn't it but it's cute."

His discomfort grew.

May Day, 1961. Thomas is four years old today. We're having a little party for him at his mother's house. Beau and I have a little cowboy outfit for him with a leather holster, two six shooters, a vest, a red flannel hat and the cutest cowboy boots I've ever seen!

"I remember that cowboy stuff," he said without any particular joy. "I think I slept in it."

"There's more. . ." She flipped a few more pages, scanning, flipped again, oblivious to Ford's growing irritation. "It was about you ripping all the Ford ads out of magazines." Unable to find the passage, she snapped it closed and let go with an unrelated nugget of information. "Maggie thought you were crazy when you started buying buildings and renovating them."

Ford stood. "She always was a worrier," he said. "Lots to do tomorrow. Better hit it." He and the dog were out the door in a matter of seconds. He stopped on the porch, clearly ticked off. "There's a lot that isn't in those books," he sniped.

Only then did Meg realize she'd overstepped some invisible boundary. She watched him leave. The room felt sorely empty without him and the puppy.

Ignoring the fact he was uncomfortable with her nosing around in his life, she picked up another journal and settled into the couch. Closing her eyes, she leafed through the pages randomly finding the night's read. "Your choice tonight, Maggie," she said aloud.

Feb 2, 1969. I wait on the coming of spring. The incremental additional sunshine in the morning will be a clue, but almost too gradual to take stock in. The first time that sun warms the air over 50, we begin to believe winter is almost done with us. The real jolt to the system is the bird song. The robin we've seen all winter in the yard starts to sound off. Then the cardinals begin, and a bluebird calls out on the fly, and our favorite sound of all, the meadowlark. Sound is the element that stirs hope into anticipation. But, as I write this, I must realize there is no 'we' anymore. Only 'me'. I need the birds and the garden. Nothing generates expectation and anticipation like it, especially in a life otherwise void of it. It is a positive endeavor, a productive use of time. Everyone can see the value in it, or at least appreciate it either for its beauty or bounty. Something is always growing, budding, blooming, ripening, right down to the end of the season. I find myself anticipating the anticipation. And, that is all I anticipate. I have somehow avoided the emotion, still. The sentries at my heart tell me not to take it all seriously, that this separation is temporary. Beau is simply away for a while and will return. He was taken away so fast, like an amputation. I still feel him. Something, someday, probably soon, will make it all perfectly clear. The gate will open and my heart will spill out, like floodwaters. And I will have the hard choices to make: Do I dwell on what was, or look ahead and build my new life without him. This will be a long process, one I fear I've yet to begin.

Meg read it again, deciding that repression ran deep in her gene pool. She hadn't yet experienced a love like Maggie's and felt her life lacking. She understood well the concept of sentries at the gate. It was easier to blame them than to take responsibility for never having loved so deeply.

Beau was only fifty-six when he died. The morning he passed, Sara was Maggie's second call, the doctor being the first. Sara arrived, jumped out of the car before Lizzie had even stopped. She ran to the cottage porch, stopped at the door, and quietly walked through. "I'm in here, in the kitchen," came Maggie's voice. "The doctor's on the way," she said. Beau was laying on the floor, his face wet with sweat.

"I always did like you in red wool," Sara said softly as she knelt down next to her dearest friend.

"Thomas is going to be a little disappointed," Beau sputtered. "I don't think we'll be hunting today." Maggie softly shushed him. Her hands were shaking awfully. Sara took them firmly in her own and tried to transfer some of her fortitude. Lizzie stood in the middle of the living room, tears streaming down her face. Maggie went to her, giving Sara a moment alone with Beau.

"You're left with it now," he whispered, barely able to find the breath. "With what we did."

"I'm left with what?" she whispered. "With love and a family and my life?"

"You know what I mean," he said with a frightened expression.

"Yes," she said stroking his chest trying to sooth him. "There is no darkness left in the thing, Beau. Thomas is the light of it. I've let it go."

A quiet smile came over him and suddenly he seemed to be without pain. "It was Mandy," he sighed with the joy of revelation. "Why didn't I see it before? Oh, Sara, there was no devil .... it was Mandy…" His words were so weak Sara could barely make them out.

"Get my Maggie," he said.

Sara motioned to Lizzie who in turn whispered to Maggie. Sara took one last look at her old friend and touched Maggie on the arm as they changed places. Maggie lay down on the floor next to her husband and wrapped her arm over his chest. The last thing he heard was her gentle voice saying she loved him.

The doctor arrived soon after. Beau arrived a few minutes after that, ready to hunt, not grieve.

CHAPTER 42

It was late afternoon, toward the end of January, when Ford came by the cottage on the flimsy excuse of checking the boiler. He knew it was fine, in fact it was probably the most well-built and reliable piece of equipment he'd ever seen. Designed to last decades, this one had worked perfectly for over seventy years, thanks to meticulous maintenance by Baker, then Beau, and now him. It was a thing of beauty in his eyes.

Having an early fascination for all things mechanical, Ford used to beg Beau to let him help tend to the boiler. Being a man of painstaking thoroughness, Beau explained every step of the process to the boy, how to clean and polish the heavy doors and casing, how to empty and flush the pipe and tank every season. Ford wanted to take over the task after Beau passed away. Because he was only ten, Maggie had a boiler installer from town do it. In the spring, Ford insisted he be allowed to flush the system and blow the lines for summer. The professional oversaw the process and said he couldn't have done it better himself. Ford replaced the regulator back in '85. He found one, brand new in its box, on a shelf in the Feed & Seed.

As to why he'd shown up in Meg's cellar this particular day was a puzzle even to him. Maybe it was a bit of free-floating melancholy, or something altogether different. Whatever the case, he was just driving out that way and turned in the drive, for no clear reason. Hence, the invention of one. Laurel sniffed in the corners and he tapped the pressure gauge. A knocking on the floorboards above them made Laurel bark and run to Ford's feet, letting out a little growl.

"Would you eat some pancakes?" came Meg's muffled voice. He thought for a moment about the peculiar timing for pancakes, in the middle of a winter's day.

"Checking on the boiler."

"OK. Do you want some pancakes?"

"Sure. Be right up."

On his way in, he grabbed an armload of wood only to find her log rack inside carefully stacked full. He wrestled with the idea of putting it back outside. "It could probably use another log right now," Meg said, poking her head around the corner. "Just put the rest of it on the floor over there. Cup of tea?" Laurel bounded to her and slid on the floor, thumping into the doorframe.

"Got a beer?" With some poking and shifting, he managed to get a smaller split of hickory into the firebox and put the others on the floor, careful not to get bark bits on the rug. "It's good to keep the boiler on a good simmer so it can keep the radiators from getting cold," he said loud enough for her to hear in the kitchen, not realizing she was right behind him with a cold beer in hand.

"And was it on a good simmer?" she asked.

"Yes. It was good."

"It runs most every day while I'm in town working. And I hear the radiator pop and creak at night."

He took off his jacket, hung it on the coat tree, then took the bottle of beer.

"Come on in the kitchen," she said.

Ford watched as Meg poured a cup of milk into a measuring cup. She poured in a little vinegar and stirred it. She pulled down a wide-mouth jar from the shelf, opened its wire bail latch, and spooned a bit of flour into Maggie's old tin measuring cup. She replaced that jar and took down another, until she had taken flour from five jars. He was intrigued that she wasn't exactly measure anything. It reminded him of Maggie. When the cup was full, she dumped it into a crockery bowl, the one Maggie always used for mixing batters.

"What is all that?" he asked.

"Flour, corn, buckwheat, oat and brown rice."

Using a regular teaspoon, she dug some baking powder out of a can, a bit of baking soda from a box, and some sugar from a bowl. She sprinkled in some salt and whisked the dry stuff together.

"Nice old jars," he said. "Where'd you get them?"

"Where do ya think?" she said grinning over her shoulder. "I stopped over one day, you weren't around, and, well, everything else in this place came from the Feed & Seed, so, I sort of went shopping."

"I see," he said, with quiet delight.

She cracked an egg into the thickening milk, added a random pouring of olive oil and blended it by spinning the whisk between her palms. Then, she poured it into the dry ingredients and whisked it all with great urgency.

"I can't tell if I'm watching art or science," he said, finishing his beer.

"A little of both, probably."

When she ladled the batter to the hot griddle, it was thick and bubbly. As the first ones cooked, she put a bowl of yogurt, another of blueberries, and jar of blackstrap molasses on the table. "I have maple syrup and butter, if you prefer. This is a little healthier, that's all."

She placed a pancake on his plate and applied a dollop of yogurt. "I sweeten it just a bit," she said. "With honey." Then, she scooped a generous helping of warm, dark blue berries into the white of the yogurt, and drizzled molasses all over it, crisscrossing the plate with little squiggles.

Meg ate hers standing at the stove cooking the last of the batter. They talked about the two new artists moving into the Barrel Factory studios. It wasn't a discussion of anything significant, just vague references to the individuals and the nature of their work.

When he was finished eating, he took his plate to the sink.

"Heading out?" Meg said rinsing the batter bowl.

This surprised him. He did indeed want to 'head out' as she put it. Her saying so pleased him in a way he couldn't quite grasp. It freed him of obligation to linger. Driving away, he felt content. Whatever restlessness had drawn him to the cottage had been relieved.

CHAPTER 43

Meg and Ford spent the remainder of the winter drifting toward each other and apart. He had a habit of stopping out to Stoneygate unannounced to check on things. Was the wood stove working well? Did the oil tank need filling? Were the pipes handling the cold? Was the water pump running hot? Was the pressure tank going to last another season? Was Meg keeping enough heat on during the day when she was gone? There was always a reason. It was never just a social call. Yet, he always managed to stop by when she was most likely to be home. She generally left the studio between two and three.

He liked that she often dropped what she was doing and insisted on feeding him, much the way Maggie had. Her favorite seemed to be muffins. No recipe. Just thrown together like the pancakes. She made him corn muffins with butter and syrup, blueberry with cinnamon sugar, and plain ones filled with pecans and brown sugar. He didn't stop in after dark unless she asked him to, and she rarely did. Daylight visits kept intentions less obscure.

Meg enjoyed his visits. There were no empty moments to fill with meaningless conversation. There was purpose in their activities. His was whatever he came to do. Hers was baking. The in between moments belonged to

Laurel, who was all legs and paws. Her efforts to stay upright on the fly were pure entertainment. Because their visits, however enjoyable, were brief, Meg spent many hours on her own.

The story of the groundhog and the little girl was almost done, but there was more to it that had yet to reveal itself. Its ending lingered somewhere on the edge of her consciousness, just beyond reach.

Meg had been resistant to read Maggie's last journal. Like finishing a book, it would bring a finality to that chapter of her life, and ending to Maggie. There weren't many entries that last year.

October 12, 1999 - 22 years I had him. 34 now since he's been gone. All feels like a blip. So far away now I can't see it clearly. Like he's standing in the meadow, sun on him, way out there. The more I try to see him, run to him, the further away he is. Sometimes, my heart breaks fresh. At least, alone, I can grieve in peace. No one to attempt to soothe, ask me to explain. I am still with him, alone out here. Still hoping he's not gone, just on the porch whittling something. So strange to be the only one left. Like I missed the bus they were all on. I can't go to the Feed & Seed. Not the way it is. Shuttered. Dusty. Time stopped like maybe it forgot me. It needs Sara back. And Lizzie. Where is Thomas if not running the aisles with Beau at the turn? Laughter. I miss laughter. I don't mean to be so mopey but some days it just catches me up and I miss my life. My sisters when we were young. Mother and Father. He was so protective of me. Funny thing is, this sadness is comforting.

Like being wrapped in all their love but I can't touch them. They are all here, watching me, waiting on me and I want so much to be with them. This life is thinning with so little left to anticipate. Nothing to look forward to. So I look back and my heart nearly bursts for all the love I knew. Thomas will be here soon. He's taking me for a drive. No telling where we'll end up or how long we'll be gone. He is all I have left. I'd be lost without him.

Meg put the journal on the nightstand. A floorboard creaked across the room. Another in the living room. A gust of wind rattled a window in the kitchen. "You're right. They're all here. Even you." She went back to the early journals, landing on 1947 when her dad would have been ten or eleven.

July 16 1947 - Beau's making sandwiches. Somebody's getting a hike tomorrow.

July 17 - Poor Virginia. Beside herself. Beau disappeared with Jack today. I don't think she realizes how resilient a ten-year-old is. Still weren't home when they got back from Boone and it was nearly dark when Beau and Jack sauntered home across the pasture. I thought she was going to have a fit when she demanded to know where Jack was all day. – None of your business, woman – That's what Jack told his mother! – None of your business, woman. – Larry laughed but I think Virginia would like to ring Beau's neck. I wish Jack could spend the summer with us. I think Beau would like it.

Meg called her dad asking where he went on his walks with Beau.

Jack laughed and spoke sternly. "None of your business, woman."

Meg laughed. "You went up Glassy, didn't you?"

"Not tellin'."

"C'mon."

"Sometimes it was Glassy. Other times we'd just head off into the woods on a ramble."

"What about your brothers? Did he take them?"

"Took Dennis once, for an hour maybe. Allen never. Didn't particularly care for nature. A lot like your brother Tim."

"Did he ever take Sam or Tim?"

"No, no. They were too little. You weren't even a year old when he died."

"What was he like? Beau."

"Quiet. A little sullen. So. Ford keeping an eye on things for you?"

"What?"

He was quiet. After a heavy sigh he said Maggie wrote him a letter, too. "She and your grandmother hatched this plan for you a few years back. Asked me to keep my mouth shut about it."

"So, every time I asked you about the will, this place, you lied?"

"I did not. I just didn't think I had anything to add to the dialogue."

"I see. Aunt Maggie and Grandma Virginia."

"Never could argue with either one of them. How are you doing down there?"

"OK. It's a different life here."

"Yeah, but one I think you might be suited to."

Meg sighed.

"I'll tell your mother you called."

"Oh, let's not."

"As you wish."

Meg was quiet for a moment. "I wish I could talk to Grandma. Both of them. I miss them. This losing people is hard."

"Yes. It is. Very hard."

"Bye, Dad."

Meg hung up and scrounged for journal entries for 1968. A photo fell to the floor from one of them. It was a photo of Beau holding a baby. Written on the back: *July 30, 1968 Beau and baby Margaret.* Meg longed to have known Beau.

Meg hit Maggie's bookshelf and read everything she could find on starting plants from seed. She read about greenhouse temperature, sunlight, and moisture levels. She read about soil mixes and amendments and organic fertilizers and root stimulators. She placed orders for seed and supplies in January for February delivery. When they arrived it was all she could do to not start planting. Every warm day tried to lure her to put seeds to dirt in the new greenhouse. She resisted.

Ford stopped out the first day of March to find Meg busy in the greenhouse. There were seed trays everywhere in neat rows with packets and notes taped to sticks. It surprised him that seeing her, so engrossed in the task, would make him so happy. As Laurel sniffed about, he gave the building a once-over, checking vent hinges and rearranging the water hose. They both found satisfaction in their activities.

When their chores were accomplished, the three headed out into the woods for a hike. Laurel bounded through the woods, in and out of streams, exploring every smell. She disappeared over a rise and started a frantic barking. Ford called out but the barking continued. When they found her, she was barking at Meg's pink scarf hanging from a branch, dangling in the breeze.

"Laurel, you're my hero!" In collecting it, something broke free in her mind and the rest of the book came rushing at her. She spent the next few days writing it all down. They were some of the best days she'd had in years. So long as she was in the thick of writing, she could keep the black dog away: the fear of losing Stoneygate.

Meg sat in Jarvis's office, waiting. The room looked as old as Jarvis himself, full of books and files and loose stacks of papers. She imagined he'd kept papers back to his first case sixty years earlier. His desk had three distinct, though sloppy, piles of folders, each one more dog-eared than the next. The tabs were layered thick with label upon label. The original recycler, she thought.

"It's a mess, isn't it?" came a voice from behind her. Jarvis ambled in and took up residence behind his desk. "Drives my wife crazy. She cleaned it once. Fifty years ago. Not allowed in after that. Did you know Ford remodeled the whole building without ever touching my office? He did. Said he couldn't do it, but he did. So, what's on your mind?"

"You asked me here, Mr. Payton." She was smiling, but a little annoyed.

"Jarvis, damn it. You've eaten at my table. It's Jarvis," he scolded.

"I think it's seeing you in your element," she said, smiling.

"Yes," he sighed. "I suppose so. Well, it's been a year, hasn't it."

"Yes. It's been a year."

"And, I suppose you're wondering when the place is going to be yours now that you've fulfilled your end of the bargain."

"Well, yes."

"Can't help you. Still up to the courts."

"I don't understand. What's taking so long?"

"Well," Jarvis drawled, "these things can get a might drawn out. I've tried to get it on the docket for months." He lied. "Just keeps getting pushed aside." Thanks to his efforts. "I wouldn't worry about it. It will get straightened out."

"When? I'd like to get some normalcy in my life, to know what my next move is."

"And, just what is your next move, if you don't mind my asking."

"Please just get the court date, will you? I need to get this thing resolved. I need to get my life resolved."

With that, Jarvis started to stand up, his signal the meeting was over, but sat back down and waved her off instead. She walked out knowing no more than when she walked in.

"That's a real nice parcel of woods up in the Pisgah. Ever thought about building up there?" His words hit her sideways in the hallway. She spoke the first thought that came to mind. "Why would I want to do that?

CHAPTER 44

Jarvis arrived at his office late the next morning. A man rose from a chair as he entered.

"I hope you don't mind," the man said. "Your secretary moved some things so I could sit." He extended his hand to shake. "Rudy Adler."

Jarvis took his hand graciously saying it was most unusual to be meeting with the opposition. Jarvis moved a stack of books off another chair in front of his desk and sat facing Rudy, taking measure of him. Looked a bit worn for sixty. Khaki pants. Scuffed loafers. White oxford shirt frayed at the collar. "Rudyard Kenyon Adler," Jarvis said, the syllables rolling out with precise enunciation. "There's a lot of Kenyon in that name."

Rudy shook his head in exasperation. "Grandmother Florence's doing. She had a list of Kenyon names. Made us all vow to keep using them. Kenyon by blood, she'd say, *but those Carolina Kenyons stole your fortune. Robbed you of your ancestral lands.* I've heard it all my life." He held up his hands. "Kenyons even barred us from ever setting foot in North Carolina."

Jarvis laughed at the absurdity. "Armed guards at every entry."

"Kenyons. Kenyons. Kenyons," Rudy said. "That name is the reason for every goddamned failure in this family. And I can tell you there's a lot of failure in this family. And I can tell you that name is the root of all of it! Automatic redemption for every mistake if you invoke the Kenyon name.

"My first cousins, Marie Louise and Monty? She married a gold digger who grew up hearing all the stories how Adlers had an estate up north in the Carolinas. Just waiting on the Kenyons there to die off. Remy Coates thought he married up when he got Marie Louise. Quite the surprise when he had to actually work for a living. Hand to mouth. Her brother Monty didn't even make it to fifty. Alcoholic. Their boys? Monty and Kenyon? The craziest of the bunch. Believe every word of the myth. Grandmother Florence's words lived on. *You just wait. One day we'll come into it. We'll be so rich.* How does a man motivate to make something of himself when he's raised thinking he doesn't have to?"

"Holy God!" Jarvis said. "You all have a most peculiar way of naming folks after a family you supposedly revile. Every generation, right down to your grandson. Naming him Kenyon? And your daughter? Another Marie Louise, this time with Kenyon Adler Richelieu tacked on. That's a lot of name to carry around."

"Not my idea. My wife's. She bought into all that Kenyon BS. Might be why she married me. Probably why she divorced me. Tired of waiting. At least they shortened it all for my grandson. Kenyon Richelieu."

"Progress," Jarvis said with a slight grin.

"I think it might have all finally settled out, you know, reality, some kind of realization that none of it was ever going to happen, but then the Stonemount people showed up. They hit every one of us. Like locusts. Reignited the greed. Said they could make us all rich. Offered a shit load of money if we let them go after the estate. I swear it's like everybody in my family is holding a megabucks lottery ticket waiting on the last number! Tried giving me a new car. A new car! Just to get me onboard. I don't know who the hell they are, but they put me on edge."

A pause in the conversation let the room settle a bit. Jarvis took a long look at Rudy, a man weighed down by history. "Rudy, why are you here today? How can I help?"

Rudy's eyes grew wide, pleading with Jarvis. "Put an end to it. That's what I want. I want it all to end. Once and for all!"

Jarvis leaned back, hands collected in his lap, quizzical look on his face. "And, how do you see that happening?"

"Make damn sure that girl from Chicago keeps it. For good! Forever! You did it last time it was challenged. Back when the last of them died. You made it stand then. His wife kept Stoneygate."

"When Beau died. Back in '68. I didn't know anyone was paying attention."

"Oh, they were. Believe me. Hell, one of my cousins tried to get us all to reimburse him for what he paid a lawyer just to look into it."

"I do recall someone calling on a rather regular basis about it," Jarvis said, looking to the ceiling and shrugging his shoulders.

Rudy shook his head, grinning. "He got charged for every one of those calls till he couldn't afford to go any further." He leaned forward. "Now there's Stonemount money behind it. You stopped it then. All I'm saying, is do it again."

"It's not that simple, Mr. Adler. Those were different circumstances."

"Mr. Payton. If it comes to a Kenyon? I'm it! I'm the oldest. I'm the poor bastard who has to take it over. I don't want it!" Rudy ejected from his chair. "I don't want any part of it! Not the money. Not the responsibility of ripping some pristine land to shreds. None of it! It's not ours. Never was. It's torn my family apart for years and it needs to stop. Once and for all. I don't care how you do it. Just kill it."

CHAPTER 45

In early April, Patrick arrived in North Carolina to visit Meg. He met up with her and Ford at the Tryon steeplechase. It wasn't until she saw them side-by-side that she realized how much they looked alike, both in their forties, tall, well-proportioned, both with white hair, though Patrick's was close-cropped.

Ford asked Patrick if he was named after the man who made the iron bell in Meg's studio.

"My father."

"I looked him up," Ford said. "Hell of a master. Did you get any of those genes?"

"I paint and sculpt. Mostly I teach." Patrick craned his neck to find the racetrack. "This is not what I expected," he grumbled as they made their way into the thick of the crowd. "According to my father, the steeple chase was an elegant event. And the place, well, I suppose nothing could live up to my father's idealized memories. Maybe that's why he never came back. It could never live up to what he'd made of it."

"What did you expect exactly?" Meg asked.

"Well, not a municipal horse park in the middle of town. I was told it was held at some big estate. Huge stable, beautiful house, beautiful pool, beautiful people, beautiful mountain views, never-ending forests."

"You're talking about old Stoneygate," Ford said.

"He never mentioned that name. Stoneygate. Is it close by?"

"You have to get Meg to take you out there."

"She knows where it is?"

"Of course," Meg laughed. "It's where I live. Stoneygate. I told you, didn't I? Maybe not. I just thought it sounded sort of elitist to say I was moving to an estate. With a name. Ya know?"

Jarvis joined a herd of spectators making their way across the road, maneuvering through a steady stream of cars crawling by on their way to the west parking lot. The road had recently received a topping of asphalt, something the city manager said would cut down on dust and make maintenance more manageable. Jarvis liked the road the way it used to be, a nearly impassable washboard of gravel and dirt. The better the road, the more outsiders on it. He wasn't fond of outsiders.

Jarvis raised his head high, thrusting his cane out boldly in front of him. His stringy white hair, his most unruly aspect, flowed back off his face, and sometimes fell over his left eye as he walked. His face was deeply creviced, his skin like oiled leather. The baby blue suit, familiar to anyone who frequented the courthouse, was neat and sharp. Tiny red horses galloped across a field of pale yellow on his tie, too wide for the times and a little askew. He made his way through the throng, across the grass field toward his favorite spot on the fence at the third jump. Muttering not altogether quietly, he suffered the fashion-challenged sea of shorts, jeans and T-shirts. "Doesn't anybody dress for anything these days? What a bunch of reprobates. This mess gets messier every year." He began shouting, drawing the gaze of those around him. "It's about time someone just shoot this fiasco and let it die!"

Relieved to finally see Ford up ahead, Jarvis strode up to him, smacked him square on the back, and let out a boisterous greeting. "Finally got a haircut, did ya? Went a bit too far maybe?" The man turned. It was not Ford, yet was still inexplicably familiar. Jarvis struggled to place the face, suffering the unsettling sensation of time stumbling to a standstill then sling-shotting him back to another era. Memories of his youth swept over him, blowing away the years like heavy dust. He knew this man standing before him, but from a time so far gone it was impossible. The moment passed and time regained its footing. Jarvis was aware he must have appeared dazed yet continued to study the stranger.

When Ford turned, Jarvis stood aghast, taken by the similarities. "Well, I'll be damned," he finally said, though still not able to attach a name to the face.

"What are you doing out here in this crowd, old man?" Ford asked. "You must be, what, about a hundred or something?"

"I am not a day over ninety-one and I will ask you to mind your manners, you young shit." He noticed Meg standing nearby and greeted her with a gentle kiss to her cheek. "It is fine to see you here, my dear. If you have any imagination at all you will be able to divine from this disaster what a regal experience this horse race used to be. And I trust you will not hold it against any of us what we have allowed it to become!" With no particular interest in a response, he turned again to the stranger. "Who's your friend here?"

Meg obediently provided the introduction. "Jarvis Payton, this is Patrick Dawson. Patrick is renting my condo in Chicago . . ." Jarvis only half listened. The name Patrick Dawson rattled like a key in an old lock until the tumblers fell into place.

"Chicago?" he sighed.

"Yes, sir," responded Patrick.

"And, how is it Miss Bishop, that you know this gentleman?"

"From the Chicago Art Institute. He teaches there. He . . ."

"Well, now, isn't this peculiar," Jarvis interrupted. "Patrick Dawson. Son, I knew your granddaddy, Patrick Dawson."

"I believe you're thinking about my father. My grandfather was Derrick."

Jarvis replied slowly with a gracious smile. "Really, Patrick is your daddy. Well, marvelous, just marvelous. You look just like him. Spitting image." Something about his voice carried a sadness. "You know, I haven't seen your father since we were young men. If I had to put a year on it, I'd say it hasn't been since the last chase at Stoneygate. That would make it around the mid-to-late twenties. He probably wasn't much more than twenty or so. What do you think? Is my memory serving me well?"

"Watch out for this one. His mind is a steel trap," Ford said.

"If memory serves," Jarvis continued, "he announced his engagement to some shipping heiress and that's the last we ever heard of him. That must be your mother, I suspect."

"Well, first off, as my father would quickly point out, he did not do any proposing or announcing. It was arranged for him by my grandfather and announced for him by my grandmother. My father had nothing to do with it. And, no, that woman would not be my mother"

"Yes, yes, as I think about it, that would have been impossible anyhow, now wouldn't it. I mean, unless there was some miracle of science, seeing as how she would've had to have given birth well after she went through the change. You'll have to tell us all about it, on the way over there to that fence." He pointed to a mass of humanity beginning to congeal. With outstretched cane Jarvis prodded his way through, clearing the way with a smack to random shins. Appearing somewhat daft, he'd apologize with a beguiling smile and lazy drawl. He was not averse to taking advantage of his age.

Meg and Patrick followed in his wake, both reveling in the serendipity of the moment. Ford hung back a bit, watching their interactions, watching Patrick wrap his arm around her, watching her lean into him.

Claiming their space on the fence, Jarvis pointed to a boxwood thicket with a water hazard in the middle of the wide grassy track. "This is the third jump of eight," he explained. He reached out for Ford's arm and gripped it tightly for support, yet looked directly at Patrick as he reminisced. "I remember your father as a gentle spirit, a good soul. Never did much see him fitting into the father's steel business. Cut of different cloth, those two."

"As it turned out, he left steel for iron. Wrought iron," explained Patrick.

"Quite a renowned craftsman," Ford added.

"Wait a minute," Meg said. "No offense Jarvis, but a contemporary of yours is his father? Get out!"

"Contemporary, hell! He was five years older!" Jarvis quipped, flailing his arm to punctuate his point.

"OK," Patrick said with a grin. "You have to be a true romantic to appreciate this story. And you have to understand also that my father was well into his seventies before he told me about it. Told anybody for that matter."

Suddenly, like a flood pushing downstream, cheers grew from up the fence line to where they stood. "They're coming! They're coming!"

Jarvis took Meg by the elbow and pointed to the woodlot across from them. "Look just beyond and you'll see them. Like ghosts." Meg squinted, trying to focus past the foliage to the horses. "I see them," she sighed. Jarvis didn't take his eyes off the animals, all running full throttle. Soon they were coming around the far turn into clear view. Muffled hooves pounding the hard grass track could barely be heard for the crowd.

There was no hesitation in their strides as they jumped the second fence. When they approached on the straightaway, there were a dozen or so horses charging to the third jump right in front of Meg. She was inexorably swept up in the raw power of the animals. Their muscles flexing, pushing, pounding. Their nostrils flared wide, snorts emanating with every breath.

The first two made the jump clean, their riders in full control. The third horse hesitated, lost momentum and cleared the bush but hit the water, lost footing and went down. The crowd cried out in a chorus of fear and exhilaration. The rider hung on and with wild panic in his eyes coaxed the animal quickly to its feet and out of the way as the next riders came in a tight pack and took the jump together. One of them seemed to go through the shrubbery as much as over it leaving the horse stumbling to regain footing on the other side. The next one refused the jump in spite of aggressive whipping. It screamed in protest as he was yanked about, run back up field, yanked about again and driven back again to the wall only to refuse again. The next trio had to dodge him, making their jump all the more spectacular for the awkwardness. The last horse pounded down the straight but refused at the last instant, propelling its rider deep into the greenery. He slowly emerged and straightened up carefully. The other rider, having given up the jump, dismounted and collected both horses. Together they walked them into the woods.

Meg found herself out of breath, her heart pounding. Ford was nonchalant, commenting only that it wasn't as bad as other years. "Not as bad?" asked Meg.

"Yeah. Some years riders break bones on this jump."

"Oh, plenty of time for that," asserted Jarvis. "Four more races to go today."

The crowd settled down and thinned out.

"Patrick," Jarvis commanded as if on cross-examination. "Tell us your story. You were in the middle of a good story. You have my full attention. Your father was engaged by proxy and weaseled out of it . . . and . . ."

Patrick took a deep breath and told the tale as if it was the stuff of legends. "The last time my father was down here, it was for a steeple chase. He promised the love of his life that he would return for her in spite of his engagement, in spite of his family. He would return." Jarvis hung on every word spilling so effortlessly from the man's mouth. Like bad whiskey, the words burned going down. He propped his cane in front of him, and leaned hard against it trying to control his shaking hands. His glance shifted to Ford on occasion, who by all outward appearances wasn't listening.

"He promised this girl he'd break free," Patrick said, "and marry her. But both families up north were committed to the Stanton marriage so he did everything he could to get his fiancé to call it off. He broke dates with her, showed up plastered, even made sure he was seen out with other women. None of it worked. Just when he thought she'd break, the invitations were in the mail. That was in November. The wedding was to be in March."

"But he didn't go through with it, did he?" asked Meg.

"No. He had a talk with old man Stanton, his would-be father-in-law, over the holidays and that was that."

"What did he say?" asked Meg.

"He announced he wasn't going into the family business and wouldn't be able to support his daughter in the style she expected. Stanton broke it off. It pissed Grandfather off pretty good. My father walked away and never looked back. He was about to come down here but he got the letter saying she'd died. His love, down here. She died."

A wicked ache took hold of Jarvis's heart and he felt his knees go unsteady. His anguish brewed with the sickening realization of time lost and whole lives lived in error. He rested his mind on images of the last chase at Stoneygate. It was the last time he'd seen Patrick. The last time they were all happy and innocent.

Patrick continued. "He couldn't take losing her and sort of checked out for a couple of decades. Buried himself in his work. She was his life's regret."

"Mine, too," Jarvis whispered, though no one heard him.

"You know, that man was fifty before he married my mother."

"What was her name? The love of his life," asked Meg.

Patrick shook his head with a disappointed sigh. "He never told us."

Jarvis mumbled indecipherably, "Our girl."

A woman of about thirty popped up to the group. "So, what did you think Megs? Good fun, eh?"

"Hey, Mandy," Patrick said. "Mr. Payton, this is my sister. Amanda."

"Mandy," she said.

Jarvis fought for composure. "So pleased to meet you, Miss Mandy," he said with uncharacteristic sweetness. "Meg, I think you should take these fine people back to your house. This is a zoo and I'm weary of it. I, of course, will be joining you."

"Absolutely," Meg agreed.

"You all go ahead," Jarvis directed. "I will make it in my own time. Ford will assist me. Go on now." He shooed them with his cane and hung back. Ford stepped over to his side. He said nothing as Jarvis stared off into the distance, looking through people as if they weren't there. A crowd began gathering again, flowing past the two men like a river around a boulder.

Jarvis lifted his chin and squared his shoulders but his face held an aspect of grief. His next words were barely audible. "He never knew."

The crowd thinned around them, gathering again at the fence behind them.

Ford was pensive. "What do I do with this, old man?"

Jarvis seemed to wobble a bit and Ford reached for his arm.

"Just leave me alone, goddamnit. If I want your assistance, I'll ask for it. Go away." Jarvis smacked him with his cane. Ford didn't budge. Jarvis looked up.

"Thomas," His eyes welled. "Walk an old man to his car. I'm feeling a bit afflicted."

The two men sauntered down the road, their silence in contrast to the frenzied crowd cheering another raft of horses pounding down the course.

Opening his car door, Jarvis asked if Ford was going to Meg's.

"I don't know."

"Yeah, I know that tone. I'll make your apologies."

"I don't care what you tell them."

CHAPTER 46

Patrick, Mandy and Jarvis gathered in Meg's living room while she busied herself in the kitchen preparing appetizers.

"Your father and I were quite good friends when we were children," Jarvis began as the two Dawsons perused the photos on the bookshelves. "Quite good friends. Guess you could say we all sort of grew up together, one steeple chase at a time. It was Beau Kenyon, the deceased owner of this cottage, your father, and myself, though I was much younger. The Dawsons used to stay right here at Stoneygate. In the big house. Of course it was very grand then. So, tell me, how is your father?" When Patrick said he had passed away a few years earlier, another layer of sadness settled over Jarvis. "Yes," he muttered. "Well, that's a shame. Healthy to the end, was he?"

"He was," Patrick said.

"He went quick," Mandy said. "It was a shock to us all. I just assumed he'd live forever."

Patrick found a photo of interest. "That's my father. Right there." Jarvis poked a finger at the picture to point out himself as a young man. "That is indeed your father," he said. "With that makeshift fiancée, and Beau, and Beau's sister, yours truly and a couple others who didn't matter much then but are making a nuisance of themselves now. Be that as it may. That was taken the year before the last steeple chase here."

A photo in the bedroom lured Mandy's attention. "Oh, my goodness. Patrick, you have to see this." She took the ornate silver frame from the shelf and carried it to the living room. "We have a copy of this in a bunch of old family photos, but no one could identify her."

Jarvis muttered quietly to his dead friend Maggie. "There is some kind of mystery at work here, my friend. And I see your hand in it."

"Who is she?" asked Mandy, handing him the photo.

Jarvis explained with fond recollection. "That, my girl, is Amanda."

Mandy got a shiver. "That's my name."

"Yes," Jarvis sighed. "That would make sense."

Meg called them to the porch where she poured a crisp Pinot Grigio and served little toasted bread rounds with fresh pesto, soft mozzarella, and tomato. Sunshine warmed the air as a gentle breeze rustled through treetops. "What have I missed? Fill me in."

Mandy sat in the swing, Patrick on the steps and Meg the rocker. Jarvis nestled into the big wicker chair, holding Amanda's picture. He spoke slowly, as if his words traveled from some great distance.

"Truth be known, we were all surprised when your father's engagement was announced. My dear mother was mortified to have the announcement made at her luncheon. It was not done with her permission and the incident cemented in her mind forever the brash, uncultured nature of all northerners." The fact that he was surrounded by Yankees made no impression on him. He took a glass of wine from Meg, put it on the table, and continued slow and steady. "Yes, no one was more surprised than Beau and I. Except maybe Amanda. She wasn't much the same that summer." Jarvis paused, then added "Her light went out." He handed the photo back to Mandy. "Of course, that's all hindsight. We were boys. What the hell did we know. Nothing." He looked off to the woods imagining the four of them young again, innocent. "That's what we knew. Nothing."

Mandy pulled her necklace out from under her blouse and unhooked the chain. "Would you look at this?" she said quietly. She held her St. Francis pendant next to the pendant around Amanda's neck. They were the same.

"Little A, big K, little M," she said.

"What?" Meg asked.

"AKM. I always wondered what it meant. The letters inscribed on the back of my St. Francis medal. My dad gave it to me when I turned eighteen."

"AKM. They're initials, girl. Let me see that."

She handed it to him.

"Amanda Marie Kenyon." Jarvis held it in the palm of his hand. "The last letter was always in the middle. In case you're confused," he added looking over his glasses at the girl.

"How could that be? Why would Daddy have her necklace?"

"Amanda's father gave it to her when she was about ten. He called her his patron saint of strays because she took in every stray animal in the county. Baby birds, raccoons, rabbits, mangy dogs, even an injured fox one winter. She told us she lost this medal. And I think maybe that was a lie."

"She was Daddy's love, wasn't she?" Mandy asked, a tear welling.

"Would appear so," Jarvis sighed.

Mandy got very quiet and searched the old man's face for permission to ask how Amanda died. Her question was met with a scowl and Jarvis spoke aloud a truth he'd wanted to speak for too many years.

"She went away to school that next fall. Or, at least that's what we were all told. Even her own brother was spoon-fed the lie. None of us knew she was pregnant."

Patrick leaned quickly forward. "Pregnant?"

"In those days," Jarvis continued, "girls were sent away to have their little bastards in secret so no one was the wiser." His bitterness boiled up. "She died giving birth. February 1928. No family with her. Alone. She was only seventeen." He clenched his lips to fight back the anguish. "She had a son."

Meg was stunned. Jarvis snapped at her. "You read a little further in those journals, you're bound to come across something about it. You just keep reading!"

"Oh, my god," Mandy cried. "It had to be Daddy's. Don't you think?"

"If it were anyone else, she'd have spoken up." Jarvis was getting riled. "Of course it was your father's!"

"So, Dad had a son and never knew it?" Patrick said, growing angry. "All those years heartsick and he could have been raising his boy? How could anybody deny a man that right?"

"We have to try to understand, son," Jarvis urged, his patience wearing thin. "None of us knew. We all thought your father was getting married. Amanda was sent away. End of story. Perhaps if she'd told somebody who the father was, but she didn't. My god, boy. It was years before any of us even knew she'd had a child." He stopped talking, already too worked up and a might short on air.

"So, we have a half-brother," said Patrick, refreshed by curiosity. "Where is he? We need to meet him."

"I'm afraid that's impossible," sighed Jarvis. He gave back the St. Francis medal and pulled himself slowly to his feet with the help of his cane. "Well, now, this has all been a lot for an old fart like me to take in a day."

"Wait a minute," interjected Patrick. "That's it? You won't tell us anymore?"

"There's no more to tell, boy. His son is dead and gone and that's the end of it."

"But," Patrick wouldn't let it go.

"I have big doings in court this week and need my rest," Jarvis said, taking the porch steps carefully. "Has Meg told y'all that the Kenyon clan is fighting to take Stoneygate from her." He glanced back at them. "They're contesting the will."

Meg rolled her eyes and stood up to walk him to his car. "They're contesting the will, the deed, and, well hell, they're contesting me."

"I'm fine on my own," he muttered. "You just stay with your guests. I imagine you must be hungry to be with your own kind."

"What kind would that be?" asked Meg.

He took a couple steps and turned. "Yankees." He walked a bit further and added, "Oh, Ford said he had something to do so I wouldn't expect him if I were you."

CHAPTER 47

In May of 1927, young Patrick Dawson strode the Stoneygate paddock calling for Amanda. It was late afternoon and the building was quiet except for a thoroughbred mare pawing the floor of her stall. Everyone was out inspecting the steeplechase course. Women were off visiting at the various luncheons being held about town. It was the day before the main events. "Amanda" he called out again, peering into the stall. "I know you're in here somewhere."

Amanda sat motionless in a dark corner of the hayloft where she had been hiding since returning from lunch at the Payton's. Through tear filled eyes, she'd watched him walk across the yard. She heard him calling just below her.

She woke that morning full of hope and anticipation. She was irrepressibly in love with Patrick, someone she'd known all her life. Yet over sixteen years they'd only spent a matter of weeks together. He was from Chicago and came to North Carolina for the annual chase, and sometimes in the late fall for hunting. That was all they had, maybe two weeks every year. Amanda built her entire existence around those few days in May when Patrick would visit and they would play in the stream, read books in the pasture, and take long hikes up Glassy.

Yet this year, that would change. This was to be the year Patrick would notice how much she'd grown, that she was a woman, that he loved her, and would ask her to marry him. Instead, she was hiding in the hayloft, crying, contemplating the rest of her life without him.

A northern ingénue had spoiled everything. Rachel Stanton had arrived that morning with Patrick's parents. She was a nerved-up creature, thin lipped, with tight eyes. Her shapeless body flattered the new straight sheath dresses. She carried herself with the casual arrogance of the filthy rich. Amanda knew all about that sort having had years of experience hosting them for the chase. While she herself was born into money, it seemed to her that southern wealth was inherently more gracious than northern wealth. The yanks, whether from Washington D.C., upstate New York, Boston or Chicago, always seemed to flaunt it, like some unstated competition. She took an instant dislike to the young woman from Chicago who so flamboyantly displayed her father's affluence. Dislike soon grew to passionate loathing, when, as lunch was served at the Payton's, Patrick's mother stood up in front of all the guests, called her son and Rachel to her side, cupped their hands together and announced the two of them were to be married. Amanda was ambushed by the news and quietly excused herself from the table, found her way back home and retreated to her hayloft to grieve in private.

"I knew I'd find you. I always do." There he was, standing in front of her, the man she loved and suddenly hated. She quickly wiped her face and summoned false fortitude.

"She acts like you're her prize bull!"

"Who, my mother or Rachel?" He sat down next to her and pushed a lock of auburn hair out of her face.

"Patrick you should have told me. You really should have." She straightened the fabric of her skirt. "Do you realize I'm supposed to share my room with her tonight?"

He hesitated for a moment. "I suppose I was being selfish. I came down a few days early to tell you. But, well, it was so good to see you, being together, I didn't want to spoil it. And then, I guess I'm a coward. Part of me thought I could actually stop this thing, the engagement, get them to forget about it."

"What's so hard about it? You take it back. You just say 'I don't love you and I'm not getting married', unless of course you do love her."

"Oh, Mandy please."

Her heart nearly broke. He was the only one who called her that.

"Love has nothing to do with this mess. It's all been arranged. My life is arranged. I had nothing to do with it. It's more of a merger than a marriage."

"Then stand up to them. This is your life they're playing with."

"Life up there is so much more complicated than it is here."

"I don't accept that. Seems to me you can make it anything you want."

"You are so naïve."

"I am not! I know that you are smart and strong and can do whatever you put your mind to."

"You know people have a lot of misconceptions about gentile southern women."

"I'm no southern belle. And you know that."

"Know that? I love that. I have loved you for as long as I can remember. And I don't know how I'm going to extricate myself from these wedding plans, but I will." He put his hands on her shoulders and looked her straight in the eyes. "I will get out of this mess, and I will be back for you. I'll move down here if that's what you want. I have one more year at school and I'll be . . ." Before he could finish his sentence, she kissed him. It was their first kiss, eagerly anticipated yet arriving by surprise. Patrick pushed her away. Her eyes were large and dark and desperate. He gave in to the moment and gently kissed her again. Their warm lips met in some ritual more natural than anything either of them could fight.

Her emotions led the way as she pulled herself tight to his body, wrapping her arms around him, feeling his back muscles flex under her fingertips. Their kiss was eagerly followed by another and another as his hands took command of her body. One slid across her ribs, around and up to cradle the back of her head, while the other slid down to the hollow of her back pulling her closer. She responded to his touch in ways she'd never dreamt of. What she had always feared would be difficult, was suddenly the most natural thing in life. She felt her entire being spring to life as she discovered the nature of passion.

They made tender love up in the hayloft that afternoon. It was her first time and he carefully guided her through it. It was a quick encounter, intense and passionate. Afterward, she rested in his arms feeling his heart pound in his chest as he dozed off.

When Patrick woke up, Amanda was already up and dressed. Late afternoon sun spilled thru the open loft door illuminating her white cotton dress, turning her auburn hair into a golden halo. He would idealize that image of her, standing there in the hay, young, glowing, vibrant. That image would come to be the instrument of torture and comfort over the years. He blinked, and she stepped out of the light and was gone. The riders were coming back in.

He pulled on his pants and brushed himself off. Bracing himself on a post timber, he watched Amanda walk away toward the house. His fingers felt something on the wood. He smiled knowing exactly what it was. They were initials he'd carved there when he was just a kid. "Hey, Dawson," hollered an approaching rider. "Throw us down some of that good Carolina alfalfa, will you?" He obliged them, but not until Amanda was completely out of his sight.

Lifting a fork full of hay, a flash of gold caught his eye. He looked carefully and found Amanda's St. Francis medal. The chain had broken. He put it in his pocket, planning to give it back to her later.

Later never came. Amanda overheard Patrick and his father that night talking about the engagement. *You stick close to me, son, and I'll get you through this. So, I can count on you?* Amanda waited for Patrick to tell him no, that he wouldn't marry the Stanton girl, but Patrick said yes. *Yes, you can count on me*, and in that admission, lie that it was, Amanda's heart broke. The next day she stayed well out of sight, hidden in the old treehouse, an act of self-preservation her heart demanded.

CHAPTER 48

Meg lay in bed thinking about Patrick's father and Amanda Kenyon, wondering about their child, how he died and when. It was all too tragic. She wondered why there was no mention of him in Maggie's journals. Did she even know? Did any of them know?

Outside, the wind came in freight train waves through the woods. Thunder rumbled off the mountains in the distance. Another gust swept over the pasture buffeting the house. Meg tried sleeping but the story she'd been trying to finish wouldn't let her.

- - - - - - - -

Allamanda's ferocious shrieking carried out through the windows, surging through damp woods, slithering into the stream. Her anger was swept into the river where it traveled many miles. Everywhere the eerie sound passed, frightened animals cried out and ran away. Birds took flight in vast murmurations. Allamanda's rage traveled all the next day, turning blue waters gray ...

- - - - - - - -

It was just a story, coming out as it wished. Meg hadn't considered it was dismal until she read it aloud. She spent the next week unraveling the flurry of ideas, trying to weave them together into something logical when logic had nothing to do with it. It was a story of a young girl fighting all odds to set her world right, to find her footing and find joy again. She thought she had it figured out, but the last part, the part she thought she had nailed down, would not come to resolution.

Ford headed to Stoneygate with every intention of telling Meg the truth. But when he got there, she was preoccupied. The writing was not going well. She berated him for not showing up when Patrick and Mandy were there. She rattled on about Amanda Kenyon and Patrick's father being lovers and every word she used, sounding like gossip, made him withdraw a little more.

Meg thought Ford would be interested in all of it, the star-crossed lovers, the lost son, Patrick's sadness over never knowing his half-brother. She couldn't figure out why he just stood there, silent, letting her go on and on until, finally, she gave up. "I can see you don't really care about this," she said. "I should get back to work. This book isn't going to write itself."

"No," he said. "I guess it won't. What's it about, this new book."

"It's a chapter book for young readers."

"No illustration."

"No."

"Ever done one of those before?"

"Nope. No earthly idea what I'm doing."

He knew in that moment what would have to happen. She left him no option. Without another word, he walked out the door in a manner unusual for him. He always had an air of indifference about him, as if nothing really touched him, but this departure was different. He seemed defiant. "I'm taking a walk."

"I'll come with you."

"No." It was abrupt but honest. She shut the door behind him and went back to work.

Ford took the better part of the afternoon wandering the property to find his peace with things. As the sun slipped behind Glassy, he looked into the cottage to see Meg typing away. He would normally have stopped in to say he was heading out, but chose not to.

Two nights before the hearing, Jarvis sat in his office alone, in the dark. He pulled the chain on his desk lamp and lifted an old manila envelope out of his desk drawer. There was a soft knocking from the other side of the room. A familiar figure stood in the doorway.

A woman in her fifties stood there, smiling. "You summoned me?" she asked.

Jarvis waved her in, poured her a shot of bourbon from a fine crystal decanter and withdrew the contents of the envelope.

"This is highly irregular, you know," she told him.

"Highly irregular circumstances," he said, laying each piece out, one by one in a line in front of her. She took a sip, smiled deeply, and studied the papers. When she had a firm grasp on what he'd showed her, she picked up a photograph of two women on a couch. "Oh my," she sighed.

CHAPTER 49

In November of 1927, a photographer stood in the parlor of Hawthorn House, his camera boxes at his feet. He was a stout man in his late forties with a full beard wearing a suit that may have fit him a few pounds earlier, but not anymore. The tall starched collar had nearly rubbed a raw spot on his neck.

Through the closed door to the office, he heard the argument between three women. The argument, it seemed, was about him. Being the mild-mannered man he was, this made him very uneasy. Three pregnant girls on the couch staring at him did not help his predicament, yet his photographer's eye had him staring right back. Two sat like bookends, one leaning to the left and slouching with legs outstretched, the other draped over the heavily padded fiddle neck arm to the right. The third lay sprawled between them. If it weren't for their rounded middles, accentuated by half unbuttoned cardigans sweaters, they could have been any three teenage girls lounging about in their winter wool dresses and thick cotton leggings. They each held a book, though only one of them seemed to be reading.

As the argument continued behind him, he contemplated photographing the girls. He would rearrange them only slightly to take better advantage of the light from the side window, and he would have to do something about the backlight, possibly pull the curtain over slightly. It would be a photograph for his private collection, as the connotation of immorality would scarcely agree with the public's delicate sensibilities. And then there was his wife who would complain about the waste of good paper and chemicals on a photograph he could not sell. Times were tight, she would remind him. And, being a man who did not enjoy quarrels, he would obey her wishes, taking his creative photographs only in his mind's eye, cataloging each one throughout the day, imagining the opening of his one man show in a salon in New York.

Two distinct voices on the other side of the door continued arguing.

"I know it's not done. I don't care if it is improper."

"This is highly unusual. We've stepped over the line already farther than I care to."

"This woman will be the only mother your child will ever know. Why, she doesn't even have to tell the child it's adopted."

"But it will come up. It may eventually be obvious. And this would answer at least one question. What did my mother look like?"

"It is a connection, the only connection, between me and my child. If I am to give it up, I have to at least know it will know some small bit of me in years to come."

"The child could use it to track you down in the future. Causing you undesirable discomfort."

"Undesirable discomfort! How dare you infer such a thing. Do you, madam, not think this whole predicament to be an undesirable discomfort?"

Another voice entered the fray. "If this child that I take to raise as my own learns I am not its real mother, and then desires to find the real one, it must be because I have failed him in some way and then what course could he take but to seek out the true mother lost to him?"

"The files are sealed. He would have no way to learn any such truth."

"Are we breaking any law by having our photograph taken?"

"Well, no, there are no laws."

"Then, madam, I beseech you to allow this kind gentleman into the drawing room with his equipment so that he may take our photograph together."

The door opened startling the photographer.

"Very well," the woman said. "But you must understand, it is not with the blessing of this establishment and we highly object."

"We are merely two friends having our portrait taken. Nothing more," said Sara as she took Amanda's hand leading her out of the office.

"Right," said Amanda defiantly, "two friends. Almost three." She laid her hand gently on her very rounded belly and smiled sadly.

The photographer prepared the room for the shot asking Sara and Amanda to make themselves comfortable on the divan in the bay window. As he unpacked his big box camera, attaching it to the tripod, he studied their faces, angles, edges, shadows. Light spilled in from the window highlighting the slope of their necks. Light such as that was rare and he was anxious not to lose it. Without a word, he directed the ladies to shift ever so slightly their positions, using his hands like wands to show how he wanted them to turn one way or another.

Sara was somewhat rigid and self aware until the photographer gave her a reassuring smile and touched her knee with his fingertips. "Breathe," he said softly. She took a deep breath and felt her muscles release. "I'm so glad we're doing this," she said.

"It does feels right, doesn't it," Amanda said as the photographer gently adjusted the tilt of her head. She found his concentration fascinating. She had had many portraits taken at Stoneygate, but none by someone who seemed to have such a passion for it.

"Amanda, I make no judgment on you," Sara whispered as the photographer held up the palms of his hands before them. He seemed to pat the air, fixing his frame.

"Now, hold that for me ladies while I ready the camera." He quickly went to his camera and buried his head under a black cloth.

Holding very still, Sara continued. "I only want you to know that your child will be loved and cared for with everything I have to give. He has a right to know how beautiful his mother is. After all, he, or she, will eventually want to know why I have such wild red hair and they don't!" They both laughed in a way that suggested they were old friends talking of far lighter topics.

"Sara," asked Amanda with some hesitation. "Would it be possible, if it's a boy, to give him my grandfather's name? Maybe just his middle name? It's Parson."

"Of course I will. I'll just say my father was a preacher. Lord only knows he was far from it."

The photographer emerged from under the cloth and chided them for moving. They straightened up, and stiffened up, at which point he coaxed them back into position. "Just breathe, ladies. This will be a beautiful picture," and he went back under his cloak.

Quite careful not to move, Amanda beseeched Sara. "You won't show him, or her, until they grow, and maybe only if they ask?"

Sara reached over and took Amanda's hand. "The time will bring itself, if ever. Don't worry."

The photographer quickly emerged from the cloth with a smile of intense anticipation. The lines created by their joined hands and the light upon them was splendid and he didn't want to miss it. He took the rubber bulb in his hand and squeezed, releasing the shutter. Certain of the exposure, he thanked the ladies and began packing up.

There were two prints made from the negative. One went to Sara, and one the photographer kept for himself. In years to come, it would be one of his favorite photographs and one he would reflect on with bittersweet pride for having taken it.

The conversation that day between Sara and Amanda was only their second ever, and would be their last.

It took nearly a decade for the photograph to find its way home.

CHAPTER 50

The day Errol Mercer was buried in 1934, Sara was left on her own to raise Jeffrey. Although they were both safer without Errol's abuse, he had left her nothing. Though she owned the house, she never wanted to set foot in it again. She wanted no money from it. It was of Errol. Tainted. Feeling destitute, she saw only one option. Since the day she saw Amanda's picture in Baker's house, she knew the truth. She knew Jeffrey was a Kenyon.

If she showed Baker the photograph of her and Amanda, he would have to acknowledge Jeffrey's birthright. It was what the child deserved. She knew it could mean giving him up to Baker. Still, it had to be done. She had been churning it over in her mind since the night she and Beau stood together in the rain, since the night Errol flew off the road out of their lives. If there were any other way, she couldn't fathom it.

Standing graveside with young Jeffrey at her side, she cried. They weren't the tears of a grieving widow, they were the tears of a mother about to give up her son. The preacher had no more than said his last word when Merle Payton came up behind her.

"Mrs. Mercer," he said quietly, "we all feel your loss."

"You have no idea, sir," she responded without looking at him.

Baker asked if she wouldn't mind going out to the cottage for a bite. "You don't need to go home right now," he told her. "Spend some time with friends. How does that sound?"

Sara agreed. He had presented the perfect opportunity to do what needed to be done. She felt her purse, assuring herself the photograph was still inside. If she had to wait for another occasion, her nerve might fade. She reached for Jeffrey's hand but he wasn't there. Her heart broke to realize what life could be like without him, how empty it would be if his hand were no longer reaching for hers. A frantic scan of the area found him laughing with Beau. She realized in that instant she could not do it. One way or another, she would find a way to get by. The photograph would have to be destroyed.

Riding with Baker and Beau out to Stoneygate, Sara and Jeffrey sat quietly in the back. "Take that suit coat off, boy," Beau teased. "You'd think you'd been to a funeral or something." Jeffrey quickly obliged and began to relax.

As the foursome finished supper, Merle Payton arrived. "Could anyone use a bit of dessert?" he called out stepping onto the porch. Baker invited him in. Merle took one look at the boy and handed him a cookie.

"My boy, you look like you're about to go half crazy. Why don't you take off those fine suit trousers and get out of here. Go play." Jeffrey looked to his mother.

"In my underwear?" he asked.

"You can go out there as God created you if you want," Sara said. "He's the only one who'll see you." It took him seconds to pull off his shoes, socks, trousers and shirt and he was out the door in his underpants. He turned just before jumping off the porch. "I forgot something!" He charged back in to grab a handful of cookies. In an instant he was gone leaving the adults to their private agendas.

Baker told Beau to sit down. "This concerns you, too, son." Merle and Baker exchanged glances and Merle handed Sara a piece of paper. She looked at it, read it, and tears filled her eyes as an uneasy smile came to her face. It was Jeffrey's birth certificate with Amanda Kenyon listed as birth mother. "How long have you known?" she asked trying not to give in to the tears.

"That isn't important," Baker said.

"Yes," she sighed, "I suppose you're right. I have something for you as well," and she pulled the photograph from her bag. "It was taken a few weeks before, uh," she wanted to say before Amanda died, but the words stuck in her throat. ". . . before Jeffrey was born." The photograph was passed from Merle to Baker to Beau. It affected all of them as if Amanda had just that day been taken from them. Baker got up and walked out. Beau just leaned back on the sofa and wiped his cheeks dry as the pieces of history tumbled into place.

That day at Hawthorn House he'd seen the girls crying and suddenly realized they were not plump, but pregnant. He should have put it together from the beginning, but he hadn't. He tried to remember the hallway, and what was behind the door that closed as he passed. He recalled a man in a white coat, a woman standing at a table in front of them. It hadn't even crossed his mind that Amanda died giving birth or that there was a baby. Then he thought about the train ride and holding that screaming infant until it fell asleep, with no idea he was holding his nephew. When he recognized the thin thread of events that led him to take up with Errol, and that if he hadn't, they'd have likely lost

Jeffrey forever, it was nearly more than he could bear. He couldn't help but see Amanda's hand in all of it and the tears poured down his face.

Sara tried to be stoic. "I suppose Mr. Kenyon will be wanting to take my boy to raise," she said to Merle. Merle looked at her in shock.

"Why, good God no, woman. Why would he want to do a thing like that? You are the boy's mother. He's made arrangements, yes. But, the boy is not a thing to be claimed like some cow." He moved closer to Sara and took her hands from her lap and held them. Tears ran down her face as her body bounced with soft sobs.

"Baker?" Merle hollered. "Get back in here. We have some business to tend to." Beau went out to find Jeffrey, hoping in doing so, maybe he'd find his sister again.

Sara was given the deed to the Laurel County Feed & Seed that afternoon. All present were in agreement that exposing Jeffrey's parentage would serve no purpose. Sara was relieved to have her secret revealed, and Baker was comforted to have some closure to his grief. The photograph was put in an envelope with Jeffrey Parson Mercer's birth certificate and placed in a lock box at the bank.

Beau helped Sara turn the upstairs of the Feed & Seed into a comfortable apartment. As a housewarming present, Beau and Baker built the veranda across the entire back of the building. Sara and Jeffrey moved in, abandoning entirely the house in Saluda.

Beau asked his father how long he'd known about Jeffrey.

"Do you remember the night I asked you to tell me how you met Sara and Errol a few years ago," said Baker.

"Yes. Of course. I said I met them on a train."

"That was when I knew."

The morning after that conversation, with hope hanging on hope, Baker had taken the daybreak train to Raleigh. Late afternoon found him at Hawthorn House sitting across the desk from Mrs. Nash.

"Mr. Kenyon," Mrs. Nash admonished, "No one ever said the child died."

"You implied as much. You said he was gone. You made arrangements."

"Yes, sir. Gone. To a family. The adoption was all arranged. The parents were at hand. They took him home."

"I called later, and was told of the burial."

"I don't know who you spoke to, or what was said. There was no burial that day, Mr. Kenyon, or any other day that winter. Your daughter's baby was a healthy boy."

What's in a word, he thought: Gone. So overcome with grief for Amanda, he never thought to attach any other meaning than death to it. If only this woman in front of him knew what her ill-chosen word had cost. But Baker needed to control these thoughts to get what he'd come for. "I need to know where he is."

"That is quite impossible."

"I see." Baker pulled a thick envelope of cash from his coat pocket. "I have only one question."

Mrs. Nash looked at the envelope as if it were a hunting knife pointed at her. "I can't sir. We'll lose our license."

He handed her the envelope and told her to open it. As she did so, he could see her resolve melt away. He showed her a photograph of Sara and Jeffrey. "Is this the woman who took the baby?" he asked.

"Mr. Kenyon. Please."

"Is that the woman?"

Mrs. Nash opened the desk drawer, put the envelope in and pushed it shut. "Yes."

Baker rose without speaking and left. Until that day he had moved through his life with purpose but no meaning. This woman behind the desk had just given him his life back. He'd have paid anything for it.

CHAPTER 51

The day before court, Jarvis drove out to Stoneygate hoping Meg was not home. She wasn't. He spent the better part of the morning wandering the woods at Stoneygate, as he had as a child, wondering how and when he'd gotten so old. He tortured himself with images of what could have been had Amanda lived through childbirth, had she confessed about Patrick. She and Patrick would have raised their son on Stoneygate, and Suzanna and Baker would have grown old together. Jeffrey would never have gone to prison, never contracted TB. He found a boulder wrapped in tree roots, pondering if the stone was being pulled into the depths, or had been drawn up from them. Either way, it was trapped.

He was not the only one seeking some form of solace from Stoneygate. Late that night, Ford parked off the edge of the wooded pasture. His feet planted in the soft earth, he seemed to be lost to the generations, finally feeling the bond he'd been searching for since he opened the lock box a year earlier. Meeting Patrick seemed to have been the lynch pin he needed. He was not the son of a criminal. He was of better stock. Creative stock. Kenyon stock. Dawson stock. He imagined himself in the center of a circle, surrounded by

Baker, Beau, Maggie, Jeffrey, Sara and Lizzie. Standing on either side of him were his grandparents Amanda and Patrick. They were all smiling, hearts full, the circle complete. He was all of them and himself at the same time. Bathed in the strength of long held secrets, he felt a welcoming rush of warmth radiate through his body. The legacy he was once willing to deny was now his to protect. All his actions over the year to reach out to Meg, to help her connect, suddenly seemed little more than errors in judgment. He now knew the legacy left to him to protect. He'd been a child whose father should not have died as he had, whose life should have been so very different. Resentments swelled within him and there was nothing to do but seek resolution.

Meg didn't have the stomach to be in the courtroom, yet, mustering the courage, she forced herself to go. Her life was in the hands of a judge and she resented the hell out of it.

Judge Nancy Strong entered the courtroom carrying a thick file of papers. She sat down. She took a long draw of water. She pulled out the photograph Jarvis had given her a few nights before and laid it prominently on the desk, apart from the other papers. In the courtroom in front of her sat Larry Payton alone at one table. At the opposing table, Rudyard Kenyon Adler, grandson of Montgomery Kenyon, sat with a three-person legal team representing Monty's descendants. Kenyon Coates, Monty Kenyon Adler, Marie Louise Kenyon Adler Richelieu and her son Kenyon Richelieu sat anxiously behind them chattering among themselves with terse little quips, like mice arguing over a scrap of cheese. Behind them sat Tawny Gale and three men in suits, the developers of Stonemount.

"Here's how this is going to go," said the judge. "I could sit here all day and listen to you all present the information that I have right here in front of me. But honestly, I've had some really smart people piece this thing together for me. And this case is complicated enough without having to listen to your spin jobs. So, I'm going to spell it out as I see it. Anything you think is incorrect, factually," she insisted, "feel free to object."

"Your Honor, this is highly irregular," said an Adler attorney.

"I agree, sir, but I remind you this is not a trial. There are no witnesses. I am charged with determination of ownership. And I have all the information required to do that."

"I object, your Honor," he said.

"So noted."

There was an uneasiness in the courtroom, a sort of general twitching that soon settled down. The judge sifted through papers, settled on one and began speaking.

"Parson Kenyon, the Trustor, set up the Kenyon family trust in 1915 assigning his son Baker as the Successor Trustee and naming his sons Baker, Matthew, Thomas . . ." She leafed through the papers, muttering to herself. "Wasn't there another son in here somewhere? Ah, yes. Your Montgomery," she said, looking to all the eager Adlers. "OK. So the four sons are named primary beneficiaries and any offspring are secondary beneficiaries." She paused for a moment, seeming to be lost in something she was reading. "Montgomery died the day before the trust was set up. Interesting."

"I object," interrupted one of the Adler attorneys. "His death has no relevance."

"Really? I guess I just found it interesting considering timing is so important in this sort of thing," the judge said without looking up. "He died not knowing he was going to be a father. Sad for him." She glanced up and smiled. The attorney sat down.

"Continuing on, a family trust cannot go on in perpetuity. It is a finite thing. It may be considered in effect for up to twenty-one years after the death of the last identifiable individual living at the time the interest was created. Enter Montgomery's twins. So long as they were conceived prior to Parson setting up the trust, which it appears they were, they are considered identifiable individuals living at the time the trust was created. Even though their father was not. You see now why I found it so interesting?" She looked over her glasses to the Adler team. "Details are pertinent. Since the last of the twins," she shuffled papers again, "just a moment. It's tough keeping all these names straight here. Uh, here he is. The last of Montgomery's twins, Paul Kenyon Adler, died in 1988. Twelve years ago. Therefore the Kenyon family trust is still in effect."

The Adlers were ebullient and began to hug each other. Rudy hung his head.

Meg sat in the back row of the courtroom suffering a slight wave of nausea. She felt a ripping as if some part of her soul was being torn away. She thought she had prepared for the worst. She hadn't.

Larry Payton objected. "Your honor, taking into account the quitclaim deed signed by Monty's widow, Florence Adler, the trust retired in 1987, twenty-one years after the death of Beau Kenyon, leaving Margaret Kenyon's will ..."

Judge Strong interrupted him. "Now let's all calm down here," the judge continued. "We'll get to all that. Back to the trust, if I may." She looked to Larry. "That's OK with you? If I continue on my path here?" Larry sat down. "Thank you. As I was saying, this is where it gets sticky. The trust is explicit in how the property should be managed in simple, though somewhat vague, terms. *Preserve and protect for future generations the heart of Stoneygate, described in detail in this abstract . . .*" She held up the abstract papers then laid them back to her desk. ". . . including some fifty acres which looks to be smack in the middle of the present Stoneygate parcel. It allows for the acquisition, sale and otherwise sound management of all additional acreage held in the trust as is in the best interest of the family for future generations. What comes next goes to intent."

"Your honor, I object," hollered another Adler attorney. "Intent has nothing…"

"Denied," she interrupted. "Sit." He sat. "Now, the trustee is bound by law to follow the exact instructions given by the trust. The trustee is bound by a fiduciary duty to handle the property exactly as the trust directs." The judge spoke slowly, exaggerating her enunciation. "Baker Kenyon, finding himself compromised by the loss of his wife and daughter, and suddenly presented with the twin sons of his deceased brother, relinquished his trustee duties in 1928. In this act, he behaved *in the interest of the trust* believing he was no longer capable of sound judgment. Then, acting on behalf of her twin sons, Florence Blackburn Kenyon Adler gave her husband, Jason Adler, authority to act in their interest as custodian of the lands. Honestly, folks, what he did, the havoc he wreaked on that property, was criminal."

"Your honor, I object," hollered a Adler attorney.

"Yes," she replied. "I'm sure you do. So do I. Look at this mess." She pointed to a foot-high stack of papers, all shapes and sizes. "This is the rats nest of title transfers, mortgages, short sales, liens, losses, lumber rights sold and held. I doubt even you've walked through all this mess. My point here," she glared at the Adlers, "is that he did not act in the *spirit of the trust*. He did not exercise *sound management* of the acreage held in the trust for the best interest of the family for future generations. He stripped it . . ."

One of the Adler attorneys sighed heavily, pushed his chair back and stood up. "Your honor," he groaned. "This has no bearing on the matter at hand. Baker Kenyon used extortion to cheat those boys out of their rightful inheritance."

The judge shot a scowl to him. "Sit down. I'm not done," she directed. He sat. "You did not pay attention to my statement. The havoc he wreaked on that property was *criminal*. He stripped it to line his own pockets. You know those really smart people I said I had looking at this file? They can't find the money. Whatever Adler sold, that money never found its way into the trust. He stole it. He eventually lost it, but before that, he stole it."

The Adler table, all four of them, sat mouths agape. Rudy had the makings of a smile brewing. Kenyon, Monty, and Marie Louise reached for each other's hands. The Stonemount people sat stone-faced.

"The decision before this court," she said, "is whether anyone living today has a claim to the Kenyon family trust. It could just as easily be a matter of finding the person liable for those missing funds." She looked hard to the Adler table. "You see where I could go with this, don't you? But as it is, this court is asked to make a judgment on a collection of quitclaim deeds signed by Florence Blackburn Kenyon Adler on behalf of Montgomery and Paul Kenyon Adler, Montgomery Kenyon's twin sons, as well as a document signed in 1929 removing them as beneficiaries of the Kenyon Trust. The plaintiff has proposed the documents were signed under duress and therefore null and void. I have some difficulty with this one. In signing multiple quit claim deeds as well as a document absolving her sons of all rights into perpetuity . . ." She stopped and looked directly to Rudy Adler. "You really want me to believe she didn't know what she was doing?"

"Your honor," Rudy said. "I have no opinion whatsoever in the matter. Please. Continue."

"In signing those papers, Flo was also released from the sizable debt associated with the property. Not to mention liability for the missing funds. I believe it was in her every interest to distance herself and her children from such encumbrances. The only duress I see is with respect to a woman whose husband had just committed suicide after having wiped out *her entire personal fortune*, leaving her to raise two sons on her own with a mountain of debt down in Charleston, having nothing whatsoever to do with the Kenyon estate."

The Adler clan began to droop.

"Further, even after negating the twins' right to the trust, Baker Kenyon could surely have held Flo liable for the money her husband stole. He could have filed criminal charges against her. So, to my mind, the likelihood that the quitclaim deed was acquired through extortion, by threatening a custody battle over her sons, gives me pause. I don't buy it. It is the ruling of this court to uphold her decision to relinquish all rights related to her sons, Montgomery and Paul Kenyon Adler."

"No!" came a communal outburst from the Adlers.

The Stonemount men walked out, leaving Tawny on her own.

Meg felt a rush. Stoneygate was hers.

The judge banged her gavel hard to settle the courtroom. "It is my ruling, however, that the Kenyon family trust still stands."

Meg gasped.

Larry rose to object.

The judge told him to sit down.

"It would appear," said the judge, "Beau Kenyon, Baker's son, was the last legal heir. When he passed in 1968, the trust should have ended with him, leaving him every right to will the property to his wife Margaret Kenyon's to do with as she pleased."

Meg grinned.

"However . . ."

Meg felt her throat tighten.

"I have here a birth certificate," said the judge, "and adoption papers for one Jeffrey Parson Mercer, son born out of wedlock to Amanda Marie Kenyon, daughter of Baker Kenyon, sister to Beau Kenyon. I also have here a birth certificate for Thomas Baker Mercer, son of Jeffrey Parson Mercer . . ." The judge paused and looked up with a grin. "Beginning to see a pattern here, with all those Kenyon family names? In case you aren't following, that makes Thomas Mercer Beau's great nephew and next of kin. In keeping with the spirit of the Trust, I declare him the sole heir to the Kenyon Trust. I am sorry, Ms. Bishop. I suggest you work it out with Ford."

The Adlers started yelling at each other. Tawny Gale yelled at the attorneys. Meg almost threw up.

"Furthermore," shouted the judge pounding her gavel again. "Furthermore, Stonemount LLC is hereby ordered to cease and desist all business and restrain from attempts to coerce, or by any means, legal or otherwise, acquire said land until, and if, such time arises as Mr. Mercer decides to entertain any reasonable offers." She looked out into the courtroom landing her scowl on Tawny Gale. "Ms. Gale, I presume you'll be returning a good many deposits. Checks in the mail by end of the day tomorrow. This court is adjourned." The judge left her courtroom in turmoil.

Meg walked out in a daze, unable to process any of it. She saw Jarvis and nearly accosted him. "How long has Ford - Thomas - known Stoneygate was actually his?" she demanded. The resentment in her tone didn't register with Jarvis and he responded politely.

"Oh, he's known since before you arrived, I suspect."

Meg felt the familiar stabbing pain in her chest, turned and walked slowly to the doors. In her mind she was running for all she was worth, but in reality, she seemed utterly composed. She did not see Ford standing in the side hall as she left the building.

Jarvis went to Ford. "Well, it's done," Jarvis sighed.

Ford leaned against the wall, staring at the ceiling. "Not that I give a shit," he said, "but the Kenyon name could have done without a couple of bastards. I liked who I was. Who my father was. All of it. I liked being a Mercer. Who the hell am I now?"

"You're a Dawson."

"No, I'm a bastard Kenyon."

"First of all, you young shit, Maggie left us no option. Your great-grandfather left us no option."

The words great-grandfather, reinforcing the blood tie to Stoneygate, hit like lightning through Ford's psyche. Since first learning the truth, he'd hovered above the reality of it all, only recently allowing himself to settle into his Kenyon legacy. "I know. I know. I just should have been straight with her."

"This isn't on you. Whether you wanted that land or not, it's yours."

CHAPTER 52

Meg rummaged through drawers yanking out everything and throwing it to the bed. Losing Stoneygate cut to the bone. The lies fed to her so deliberately since the day she arrived raced through her head shattering everything good in their path. She could sense the pain to come, igniting her instinct to run. Everything she had was strewn about the living room when Ford appeared at the screen door.

"What are you doing?" he asked.

Hearing his voice, she followed her first impulse. She shouted. "Come to lay claim then? Fine! I'll be out within the hour!" She stepped to the bedroom doorway and looked at him through the screen expecting to see something different, maybe sinister, or snide, but he hadn't changed. "It's been a nice vacation," she said. "And now it's over." She disappeared and returned with an armload of bedding. "So have you all had a good laugh on my account this year?" She still had not invited him in. "And you can buy that Pisgah acreage in your back yard at a thousand an acre. That shouldn't be too rich for your blood."

"A thousand an acre?" he said without any indication of interest. "I can't put my hands on that kind of money."

Meg cut him a doubtful glance and picked up a stack of books and threw them to the floor. "These were Maggie's. I'm taking them!"

He asked her to stop what she was doing and let him come in.

"Come in. Stay out," she blurted. "No matter to me. It's not my house, now is it?"

Ford opened the screen door. "You have to stop this. Please." With every chair piled full of stuff he told her to go out on the porch.

She stepped out, side stepping him significantly enough to avoid the slightest contact.

"I wish you'd try to understand," he said. "This isn't how it was supposed to end up."

"Really?" Meg sniped. "Seemed pretty air tight from my perspective. I tried to prepare to lose it if I had to, but, to you? Like this? And you knew all along? I trusted you!"

"It was Jarvis's job to see this place stayed in the family. He was just doing his job."

"And aren't you proud of him." Meg took a deep breath. "Look, I get it. It's yours. But why put me through hell all year? I don't understand."

Watching the panic behind her eyes, his first impulse was to comfort her but he knew there was nothing he could say that wouldn't make it worse. He'd gone to the cottage to convince her to stay, to tell her the truth. He hoped she'd realize he never intended to hurt her, but in her current state, he opted to disengage. His silence brought fresh tears to her eyes and she quickly wiped them away. "I'm out," she sighed. "I've had a hell of a year here. And now I'm out. You all let me feel like I belonged here. And I gotta tell ya, this place grows on a person." She stopped in such a way that it seemed her entire being hit pause. Her breathing slowed, her shoulders surrendered their clench. "Just leave," she whispered. "Please, just leave."

He turned to go, even made it off the porch steps, but something made him stop. "So, you think this has been easy on me?" he said to her. "I've watched you for an entire year muddle through all your personal bullshit."

Meg's eyes widened. He'd never been so abrupt.

Everything he'd held back, everything he'd wanted to say all year rose to the surface and he had no inclination to withhold any of it. "I've watched you go through one made up crisis after another. Your book contract is cancelled. So what? Write something else. Your pseudo boyfriend went back to his wife. You didn't lose anything because you hadn't invested anything. Then you find out your whacked out ex-husband died and you go into some tailspin over that. You expose just enough to make me think you're reaching out, then you pull back. You've moped around here, hiding out, waiting, dodging, hell, I don't know what the hell you've been doing here. Maggie asked me to help you feel welcome, to help you learn how to take care of Stoneygate. I tried. But she had no earthly idea who you really are." He started to shout. "I tried to help you but you don't want to be helped. You like playing the injured recluse. Do you have any idea how hard it was for me? Here you were, having this place handed to you, and not even sure you wanted it. You have no idea how many times I just wanted to tell you to go the hell back to Chicago."

Ford quieted, but his words still had a bite. "I thought maybe you were coming around, that it was growing on you. I thought you were starting to build a life, with the studio, maybe even with me – oh now there's a shocker isn't it? I thought you were actually starting to think about me as more than some handy man."

"A life with you? Seriously?" she retaliated. "Mr. Come-and-go-as-I-please?"

"All I've been to you," he said, raising his voice again, "is some convenience you can take or leave. How in the hell did it take you so long to figure out I was Thomas Mercer not just some guy named after a truck? Did you ever ask? Did you ever even attempt to know who I am? Hell no. Heaven help you if you get too close to anyone. You know, I had papers drawn up way back in the beginning – when this whole thing started. A quit claim deed." He pulled the papers from his pocket and waved them at her, looking for some kind of recognition but found only despondency. "Look at you," he said. "So occupied with what this all means to you. Have you even thought to ask what it means to me? All my life I knew who I was until Maggie died and I found out I didn't know shit. Have you given one thought about how that affects me? To find out Beau's sister was my grandmother and no one told me? That I was related to him? A Kenyon? And every time I came out here to walk the place, or visit the cottage, to try to connect with memories of them, you were always here, acting like I came to see you." Twelve months of frustration poured out and it felt too good to stop. "You act like everything is always about you. You're so wrapped up in your life you don't see anybody else, what they want, how they feel, what kind of pain they carry around. You're not the only one to feel alone in this world. We all feel that way."

Ford had never shouted at a woman before, much less gotten so angry.

"I don't need to take this," Meg snapped and charged back inside. "I don't want to listen to any more lies."

Ford followed her in, and stood in the doorway, watching her reach for a stack of clothes and throw them in a box. "Lies," he said shaking his head. "OK. You want some truth? Do you want to know what the plan was? Maggie leaving Stoneygate to you was all about the money." He stopped himself for an instant, fighting the landslide, but it overpowered him. His next words came out slowly, like a confession. "You were chosen because you were the only one not likely to sell it off. More finely put, the only one who could afford to keep it." He waited for his words to register. "You lost this all on your own my friend." His voice was quiet, lending a cruel severity to what came next. "I fought Jarvis, but I gotta tell you, I'm glad he's the stubborn-ass lawyer he is. Because you've learned nothing here. I kept believing you'd buck up, come around. But you're still cold and injured and not one bit interested in moving forward. So, you pack up. You leave. Leave Stoneygate and this town and your studio, and me. And do us all a favor. Don't look back. Because if you do, you'll realize you love this place and you love me and that's going to be too much for you. You just might break. And I'm not interested in picking up any more pieces of Meg Bishop."

Meg stood frozen, her defenses failing, her fortress crumbling. She watched him walk out the door, off the porch and across the yard. He was already pulling away when her warrior within sprang forth, and she bolted after him, stood in the middle of the yard, fists clenched, body shaking, her energy reverberating through the woods, through branches. "Where do you get off saying I never thought about anybody but myself? You, my friend, are not the most open book I've ever come across. You may think a lot of stuff in that head of yours but none of it – I mean NONE of it – makes it out of your mouth. You try having a conversation with yourself some time. I DARE you! You could have told me right away you were an artist, that you didn't live at the Feed & Seed, that you owned the building where my studio was, that the house in the Pisgah was yours, but NO! You had to keep all your little secrets. Because everything you did was a lie! And you wonder why I stay alone? Why I won't let my guard down? But you're wrong about something. This land healed me. I am different now. I'm stronger. But I'm leaving. Because I know now I don't belong here. I never did."

She read Ford's silence as an affirmation. She turned and walked back into the cottage, slamming the door. It was over. All of it. The year of discovering her true self and discarding the crap was over. The year of traipsing around Stoneygate, watching the groundhogs and fox and cows and woodpeckers and owls was over. A year of feeling so connected to the natural world that she finally found her way out of her personal hell was over. The year that led her to believe she could love again, was over.

Ford drove away.

Anyone not as stubborn, not as afraid, not as preservationist would have recognized the anger between them was just two hearts fighting their way out of exile. Every harsh yet painfully accurate word they spoke was a twisted declaration of love. But the force was too overwhelming and they were swept away by the only feeling they recognized – pain. They weren't ready.

They left each other. Alone.

Meg sat in the kitchen, looking at all of Maggie's things trying to put the day in some sort of perspective. She had to go back to Chicago, to sort out the lies from the truth, reality from fantasy. She spent the rest of the day packing her car.

Later that evening Jarvis returned to the cottage to find Meg on the porch swing, wine glass in hand. "Permission to come aboard?" he said in a half-hearted effort at levity.

She'd calmed down by then, suffering the exhaustion that follows emotional upheaval, having moved from rage to resignation.

"The thought of leaving this place pulling you down, is it?" he asked. "I've got some hard truth for you if you're ready to listen."

She looked at him thinking nothing he could say could make it worse.

"I think I've had about as much hard truth as I can take."

"You were part of an evil plot," he said.

"So I've heard," she said. "The only one who could afford to keep Stoneygate."

He hadn't expected she would know. "Did he tell you the taxes alone on all this land are close to ten grand a year? You were the only one Maggie knew who could afford them, much less maybe be willing to pay them. It was a calculated risk, my dear. May I sit?"

She nodded and he settled into the wicker chair.

Meg gulped her wine and poured some more. "What about Ford? Ten grand a year isn't that much."

"Oh, my dear sweet girl. I've told you. He doesn't have two dimes to rub together. He lives off the rent of the 505 and that isn't much. Everything else goes to upkeep and taxes on his other properties. The arts district is not exactly an income generator."

"What about the barrel factory? He owns …"

Jarvis cut her off. "Maggie gave him the building. It was falling down. Hell, the building inspector told him to tear it down. He mortgaged it to renovate it. It has to start bringing in some money soon or he's in trouble. Never did a loan before. Not his style." He sighed heavily. "So, you see, dear. He may be land wealthy, but he has no money. We thought we were getting a successful author who would settle into the loving embrace of our mountains and save Stoneygate. Instead, well, we got you."

"I resent that!"

"Really? You made it clear from the beginning you didn't want to be here. Then you lost your book contract, and got all emotional and isolationist on us."

Meg sat with her mouth hanging open but nothing he said was incorrect. He and Ford had pretty much nailed it.

"Everything was hanging on you," he said. "I knew the trust was solid. Ford kept believing you'd eventually commit to Stoneygate's preservation. He wanted to let you keep it. But he couldn't convince me. Were his reasons selfish? Yes ma'am, to a degree."

"You mean he wanted me to foot the bill."

"Yes. I suppose that's exactly what we all wanted. You've put him in a very difficult position."

"And what's that?"

"Between a rock and a hard place. He has to sell something else to maintain this. Probably his house in the Pisgah. Nothing else he owns will bring enough money for any long-term security."

"But Maggie left money for the taxes."

"Only for two years."

"He can't sell his house," she argued. "It's so beautiful. It's the old stable for Pete's sake."

"He can and he will." He watched her expression carefully to see how far he could go. When she looked sufficiently humbled, he went in for the kill. "Everything he did this year, helping you settle in, inviting you to his opening, building that damned green house, and that studio. It was all to get you back on your feet so you'd write another book. Your success was paramount to our success. No one won if you couldn't afford Stoneygate either. You'd end up selling and Ford could never afford to buy it. There'd be a golf course here by the end of next year, or the next, depending on how fast you let it go. So, when you didn't come around, it was up to me. I had to make sure you didn't get to keep it. I upheld the trust. I exposed the Kenyon secret. I turned Thomas's life upside down. Because of you, my dear." He stood to leave, exhausted from the day's events. On his way down the steps, he stopped and put his hand on the porch swing. "He did everything he could to make you fall in love with this place, to get you back to work. I've never seen anything like it from him before. You can't blame the boy for being disappointed."

"What will happen now?"

"We'll figure it out. One way or another." He looked down and saw the Quit Claim Deed laying in the dirt. He picked it up.

"I wouldn't have let him do it," Meg said. "Not knowing what I know. This is his legacy."

"Good girl."

"What should I do?" she asked quietly.

"Time to think for yourself, young lady. But, given all that's occurred, maybe you should just go back to your people in Chicago. He's used to women leaving him by now." He started to walk away. "But the ones he loved didn't leave by choice." He turned back to her. "They died."

Meg could say nothing. She watched Jarvis drive off. She berated herself as selfish and foolish and oblivious. She couldn't tell how much of what Ford had done was just to save the land and how much was motivated by something else. She couldn't be sure any of it had been honest. Then a single clarity drifted in and she saw it all for what it was. He'd never kissed her. If he had, she'd have seen right through his deceit and he knew it. So there it was. It was never love. It was manipulation.

The barred owl hooted from a high branch above her. It took to the air, swooping down and out over the wooded pasture. Its departure left her empty, and in that void her first thought was to call Ford, an impulse she would have to overcome.

Meg went inside, and froze in place. It was her last night. There would be no more. Over recent months she had come to reject any notion of ever leaving. It would all work out. This was home. But it had fallen apart. All of it slipped away. In her mind she was touching every row of books, sweeping her fingertips across the couch, the chairs, the table and windowsill. Yet she had not moved. This, she thought, is what it will be like now. Imagining these things.

She wondered how long Maggie had known that Ford was a Kenyon. One particular journal entry came to mind, from 1968, written after Beau died. Finding it, she read it again with deeper understanding. She wrote a note on a scrap of paper and bookmarked the page.

She dropped the journal at Ford's studio on her way out of town the next morning. Her studio would get packed up another time. She needed to leave, to get as far away as possible as quickly as possible.

It was late afternoon when Ford stopped at the studio. He'd spent the day at the Barrel Factory demolishing a brick wall. It felt good. He wouldn't have noticed the plastic bag hanging off the fence if Laurel hadn't barked at it. In it, he found the journal and Meg's note tucked to a specific page.

Thomas, I understand now - Meg.
The journal read:

> *To know something so important and have to stay
> silent, give it no acknowledgement, is harder than
> anything I've ever done . . . I suppose I'll get
> used to it, but every conversation feels like some
> little lie hides behind my words . . . Unspoken
> thoughts are a heavy load. . . . As much as it
> pains me, I will oblige him with my silence.*

Ford put Laurel back in the truck and went home to pack up some dog food and clothes. He was going north. To retrieve Meg. He pulled into his drive to find her sitting on his doorstep. She'd turned around at Knoxville.

The instant she stood up, Ford rushed her and kissed her. She kissed him back. All the pent-up emotions found their release. His arms held tight, her hands clenched his shirt. Entwined, they stumbled into the house, getting as far as the couch, falling into it. He pulled his shirt over his head. She raked her hands over his chest. He pulled off her dress and he undid her bra with one swift move. In an instant, they were naked, writhing, kissing in a fervor, rolling off onto the floor and in what seemed like a only a moment he took her and it was over. Breathless, they broke out laughing, Laurel whining at the door.

Waking the next morning in Ford's bed under the beams of what had been the old hayloft, Meg noticed an abundance of initials carved in the wood. One set stood out to her, a pair of initials Ford had never noticed. PD&AK. It had been there all along. All anyone had to do was look. Patrick Dawson and Amanda Kenyon.

"What's done is done," Ford said. "Only one thing left to do." He pulled a penknife from the bedside table and carved TD&MB. Though raised as Mercer, he chose to take his place as a Dawson. Thus began their life together.

CHAPTER 53

A year later, on one particularly exceptional spring afternoon, Ford picked Meg up from a local book signing. Her new young reader chapter book, *Lilly, Hero & The Garnet Ring,* had just been released. She climbed in and they headed down the old road to Saluda.

Her morning sickness had been miserable for weeks but she woke that day feeling almost normal again, at least until they rounded one hairpin turn too many and she became queasy. Ford pulled off onto the shoulder. Bending over a blooming patch of myrtle to throw up, Meg heard rushing water in the ravine below her. As she looked over the edge, she saw shimmering. She wiped her mouth and headed downward, at which point Ford made her wait so he could go down in front of her.

On the floor of the ravine blanketed with trillium and ferns, they came upon a small pool, deep and clear. It seemed a giant boulder had fallen there, split in two, and dammed the stream. How long it had been there was anyone's guess. Water cackled between the two halves, spilling from the pool down to the stream, meandering on its way through the forest.

There was such stillness in the woods. A squirrel traversed high branches. A distant bird trill brought a responding trill from overhead. Meg kicked off her sandals, sat down on a rock, and dipped a toe in. It was cold, refreshing. Dangling both feet, she leaned against the smooth rock face.

Ford watched her, thinking she looked like some sort of mystical wood nymph. He picked some mountain laurel clusters and tossed them into the pool. Meg laughed and put a hand to her barely bulging belly.

"My god, Thomas" she sighed. "This is a little slice of heaven." Ford smiled knowing how content she had to be to call him by his given name. She didn't do it often and it always took his breath. He sat opposite her, against the other boulder, wondering how it was he'd come to find himself so happy. They would never make it to Saluda that day, choosing instead to linger there.

Neither of them noticed that a few yards away, nestled in a thicket, lay the rusted skeleton of Errol Mercer's 1933 Chevrolet.

- The End -